LOVE'S SILVER BULLET

Published by Julie Lessman, LLC
Copyright © 2020 by Julie Lessman

ASIN: B071K6ZQJH

Cover Design and Interior Format

© THE KILLION GROUP INC.

LOVE'S SILVER BULLET

Silver Lining Ranch Series ∞Book Two

JULIE LESSMAN

ACCLAIM FOR JULIE LESSMAN

"I have loved Julie Lessman's writing for years, but I can't believe how great she writes cowboys. I love westerns and reading Julie's version is pure fun." —**Mary Connealy, award-winning author of** *Brides of Hope Mountain Series*

"JULIE LESSMAN + WESTERN ROMANCE = GOLD RUSH! You heard it here, folks. I think Julie Lessman was created to write westerns." —**Reading is my SuperPower Blog**

"*Whoa, Whoa, Whoa!* If you think sparks were flying between characters in Julie Lessman's Daughters of Boston novels, then you have GOT to get a load of her new Silver Lining Ranch" novels." —**My Favorite Pastime Blog**

"*A Wing and a Prayer* isn't just a great novel, it's an epic story that follows star-crossed lovers through the dangerous times of World War II. From WASP training in Texas to Europe's front lines, I guarantee you'll be smitten with both the characters and the story. You'll learn history, you'll cry, you'll shout, your heart will pound at the danger and then swell at the romance. But most of all, you'll come away with a huge sigh of satisfaction and a smile on your face. Don't miss this one!" —**MaryLu Tyndall, award-winning author of** *Legacy of the King's Pirates*

A Wing and a Prayer is set against a thrilling stretch of time. Women in new roles. Wartime. Heroes and heroines in a terrible battle for freedom. In that exciting era come two characters at odds with each other. The very real things keeping them apart battling with an attraction so powerful it can't be resisted, though they certainly try. A fun, fast, exciting addition to the O'Connor saga. —**Mary Connealy, award-winning author of** *Brides of Hope Mountain Series*

"In *Isle of Hope* Lessman tells a poignant tale of first loves reunited and families reconciled. Both emotionally captivating and spiritually challenging, this sweet southern love story deals with issues of forgiveness and restoration. Fans of Lessman will be absolutely delighted with this riveting tale!" —**Denise Hunter, bestselling author of** *Falling Like Snowflakes*

"In *Isle of Hope*, award-winning author Julie Lessman weaves a story of how past choices collide with future consequences. Lessman's novel has it all: lush details, dynamic characters, and a storyline that keeps you turning the pages. The characters Lessman created in *Isle of Hope* confront their (in)ability to forgive – and as you fall in love with these characters, be prepared to question your beliefs about forgiveness." —**Beth K. Vogt, author of** *Crazy Little Thing Called Love*, **and a 2015 RITA® Finalist and a 2015 and 2014 Carol Award finalist**

"Fans of Julie Lessman's historical romances will love this modern day love story! *Isle of Hope* is a heartwarming and inspirational novel about forgiveness sought and restoration found. I'm enamored with the large and wonderful O'Bryen family and I thoroughly enjoyed the romances Julie skillfully crafted for both Jack O'Bryen and his mom Tess. A delight!" —**Becky Wade, award-winning author of** *My Stubborn Heart* **and The Porter Family series including** *A Love Like Ours*

"Truly masterful plot twists ..." —*Romantic Times Book Reviews*

"Readers who like heartwarming novels, such as those written by Debbie Macomber, are sure to enjoy this book."
—*Booklist Online*

"Julie is one of the best there is today at writing intensely passionate romance novels. Her ability to thread romance and longing, deception and forgiveness, and lots of humor are unparalleled by anyone else in the Christian market today."
—**Rachel McRae of LifeWay Stores**

"Julie Lessman's prose and character development is masterful." —*Church Libraries Magazine*

"With memorable characters and an effervescent plot that's as buoyant as it is entertaining, *Dare to Love Again* is Julie Lessman at her zestful best." —**Tamera Alexander, bestselling author of *A Lasting Impression* and *To Whisper Her Name***

"In a powerful and skillfully written novel, Lessman exposes raw human emotions, proving once again that it's through our greatest pain that God can lead us to our true heart, revealed and restored. Thoroughly enthralling!" —**Maggie Brendan, author of the Heart of the West and The Blue Willow Brides series**

"Julie Lessman brings all her passion for romance rooted in her passion for God to *A Heart Revealed*. Emma Malloy is her finest heroine yet. These characters, with their own personal struggles and the ignited flame of an impossible love, fill the pages of this powerful, passionate, fast-paced romance." —**Mary Connealy, bestselling author of the Lassoed in Texas, Montana Marriages, Trouble in Texas, and Wild at Heart series**

"What an interesting mix of characters. Rather than a single boy-meets-girl romance, Julie Lessman's latest novel takes readers on an emotional roller coaster with several couples—some married, some yearning to be married—as they seek to embrace love, honor the Lord, and uncover a dark truth that's been hidden for a decade. Readers who long for passion in their love stories will find it in abundance here!" —**Liz Curtis Higgs, bestselling author of Thorn in My Heart**

"Readers will not be able to part with these characters come 'The End." —**Laura Frantz, award-winning author of** *Love's Reckoning*

"With an artist's brushstroke, Julie Lessman creates another masterpiece filled with family and love and passion. *Love at Any Cost* will not only soothe your soul, but it will make you laugh, stir your heart, and release a sigh of satisfaction when you turn the last page." —**MaryLu Tyndall, bestselling author of** *Veil of Pearls*

Cast of Characters in Love's Silver Lining

The Heroine:
Sheridan Marie Donovan: Eighteen-year-old sister of Blaze, Dash, and Shaylee Donovan, niece of Finn & Libby McShane, and a Vassar student.

The Secondary Heroine:
Liberty "Libby" Margaret O'Shea: Ex-Vassar teacher, suffragette, wife of Mayor Finn McShane and aunt to Sheridan, Blaze, Dash, and Shaylee, daughter of Maeve and Aiden O'Shea, and heroine from series prequel novel, *For Love of Liberty*.

The Hero:
Jake (Sully) Sullivan: Blaze Donovan's best friend, close friend of the Donovan family, and assistant manager of Silver Lining Ranch.

The Secondary Hero:
Griffin Alexander "Finn" McShane: Mayor of Virginia City and owner of the Silver Lining Ranch and Silver Mine, husband of Libby McShane, uncle to Sheridan, Blaze, Shaylee, and Dash Donovan, and hero from series prequel novel, *For Love of Liberty*.

The Rest of the Cast:
Margaret Rose "Maggie" Mullaney: Suffragette and goddaughter of Libby O'Shea McShane, married to Blaze Donovan, sister-in-law to Sheridan, heroine from book 1, *Love's Silver Lining*.

Brendan Zachery "Blaze" Donovan: Best friend of the hero, Jake Sullivan, nephew of Finn McShane, older brother to Dash, Sheridan, and Shaylee, husband to Maggie Mullaney Donovan, foreman of Silver Lining Ranch, hero from book 1, *Love's Silver Lining.*

Dashiell "Dash" Donovan: Brother to Blaze, Sheridan, and Shaylee, nephew of Finn & Libby McShane.

Shaylee Ann Donovan: Youngest sister of Blaze, Dash, and Sheridan, tomboy niece of Finn & Libby McShane.

Mrs. Poppy: A Pastor's widow and mentor to Finn and Libby McShane.

Maeve and Aiden O'Shea: Libby McShane's parents.

Gertie: The O'Shea's cook and maid.

Angus: Finn's and the Donovan family's cowhand cook.

Aunt Marie: Sheridan's great aunt and Libby's aunt in Poughkeepsie, New York.

Kathy Jean Rightler and Sophia Lopez: Childhood friends of heroine, Sheridan Donovan.

Megan Joy Burdzy: Daughter of a merchant in town who's sweet on Jake.

Grace and Gray Carmody: College friends of heroine, Sheridan Donovan.

Clay Morgan: Nephew of Buffalo Bill Cody who is sweet on Sheridan.

Mrs. Genevieve Carmody: Grandmother of Grace and Gray Carmody.

Lady Friends of Aunt Marie: Mrs. Rhiannon Feuerstein, Mrs. Carrie Booth Schmidt, Mrs. Sherida Stewart, and Mrs. Monika Cotrill.

Professor Stephanie Cassandra McCall: Teacher of heroine, Sheridan Donovan, at Vassar.

Sister "Fred" Frederica: Head Administrator of St. Mary Louise Hospital and St. Mary Louise Orphanage.

Miss Mary Cramer: Administrator of St. Mary Louise Orphanage.

DEDICATION

To my precious prayer partners & dear friends,
Karen Chancellor, Pat Stiehr, Joy Bollinger,
Sandie Hea, & Susan Keeton —
Thank you for praying me through this entire plot.
Between you and the Holy Spirit,
We got 'er done!

As far as the east is from the west,
so far hath he removed our transgressions from us.
—Psalm 103:12

PROLOGUE

Virginia City, Nevada, 1872

"WE ARE GATHERED HERE IN this barn today to unite this man and this '*woman*' ..." Voice cracking, Blaze Donovan appeared ready to bust with laughter, mouth pinched and cheeks puffed with restraint while he held the family Bible.

Twelve-year-old Jake Sullivan peered up at his idiot best friend through slitted eyes, not appreciating the smirk on Blaze's face one little bit. Scowling, Jake nervously shifted from one boot to the other while he stood next to Blaze's four-year-old sister Sheridan, a tow-headed mite that barely came to his knees.

A snort escaped Blaze's nose as he continued. "... in the bonds of holy matrimony." Officiating in an empty stall of the Silver Lining Ranch before an audience of dolls propped against logs, Sheridan's turtle, a bored donkey, and his younger brother, Dash, Blaze elevated his chin, his pious stance meant to restrain the mockery in his eyes.

It didn't work.

"Do you Jacob Michael Sullivan take Sheridan Marie Donovan to be your lawfully wedded wife, to have and to hold, from this day forward, for better or worse, richer or poorer, in sickness and in health, and through games of jacks, hopscotch, and pretend wedding or school, till death do you part?"

Jake singed Blaze with a look that could have set the Bible aflame. "I *do*," he said in a terse tone meant to relay his intent for eventual payback.

Blaze's ridicule relaxed into affection as he turned to his little sister. Sheridan looked adorable in a pink frilly pinafore dress complete with a makeshift veil her Uncle Finn had fashioned out of wire and tulle fabric from Mort's Mercantile. "And you, Sheridan Marie Donovan, do you take Jacob Michael Sullivan to be your lawfully wedded husband, to have and to hold, from this day forward, for better or worse, richer or poorer, in sickness and in health, despite smelling like a cow at the end of the day, stinky socks, and lemon drops and peppermints purchased at Burdzy's Emporium to hide the stench of onions he eats raw, till death do you part?"

Death do you part. Jake's mouth compressed. *Which for the pastor, could be sooner than he thinks.*

Giggling, Sheridan peered up with the face of an angel, blue eyes brimming with so much adoration, that Jake's scowl automatically softened into a smile.

"Ahem." Slapping the Bible closed, Blaze laid it on the half wall of the stall behind him before turning back with an evil gleam in his eyes. "Then by the authority vested in me by the horses and cows in this here barn, I now pronounce you husband and wife." He grinned as he cocked a hip to the wood with a loose fold of arms. "You may now kiss the bride," he said with an equally diabolical laugh that matched that of his little brother, Dash, the two of them breaking into raucous laughter like a pack of drunken hyenas.

In stark contrast, the congregation remained somber, not unlike Jake at the moment, who hurled a dirty look at his best friend before he bent on one knee to press a kiss to Sheridan's riot of blonde curls.

"No, Jakie," she whispered in that little-girl voice that always disarmed him, the tiny crimp above her button nose like a sock in the gut. "You have to kiss me like a man kisses a woman," she said, dropping her loose bouquet of wildflowers to plant two pudgy hands on either side of his face. "Like this." She proceeded to pucker rose-petal lips against his, as soft as a butterfly wing.

Blaze bounced off the walls with laughter as Dash literally rolled in the hay, legs dancing in the air with glee while tears spilled from their eyes, both of their faces as red as a baboon's butt.

Ignoring them, Jake cradled a calloused hand against Sheridan's silky cheek, thinking she was the sweetest and prettiest little thing he had ever seen.

At least since Josie.

The memory stabbed hard, ruining the precious moment he'd just been given.

"Jakie?" Her soft-spoken scold was accompanied by a serious lift of miniature flaxen brows that were barely there. "You forgot to put the ring on my finger."

Despite the annoyance of donning his Sunday best in the middle of the week and the mockery of his two best friends, Jake felt a smile tug as her tiny fingers dug into the pocket of his suit for the clover ring he'd made. He didn't know how she did it, but somehow that sweet, innocent voice always managed a tone of authority that made Jake feel like he was the four-year-old instead of her.

But then she *was* the wedding expert after all, weekly weddings the favorite game she loved to play with her big brothers. *And* the game required of them before their Uncle Finn would allow fishing at Silver Lake *without* their little sister.

Dash lumbered up from the hay, rubbing the tears from his eyes. "By jingo, I just love weddings, don't you, Blaze?"

"Sure do, Dash, and it couldn't happen to a nicer guy than old Sully."

Jake speared them with a lidded look. "Knock it off, you two, or you'll be playing the groom next time."

Chuckling, Blaze backed up with palms in the air. "No sirree, Jacob Michael, that wouldn't be fittin', us blood-related to the bride and all. Plus, you're the only one she ever wants as a groom, and you know it."

A silent sigh leaked from Jake's lips. Yeah, he knew it. Little Sheridan Donovan had followed him around like a lost calf since the day Finn had taken him in, a situation he both bucked and embraced. Bucked because Blaze and Dash ribbed him incessantly, and embraced because Sher symbolized everything he'd lost and never thought he'd have again.

An orphan with a family who died, Jake had finally come *home* at the Silver Lining Ranch, forever grateful to Finn McShane, the man who had not only given him a home, but a job, a family, and two best friends.

Or used to be.

Thumbs hooked in the pockets of his blue jeans, Blaze rolled back on his heels with a broad grin. "So, Dash and I just want to offer our congratulations, Sul, and wish you and the little missus the best of luck."

"Oh, no—it broke!" Jake froze at the sound of Sheridan's stricken whisper as the wilted clover ring dangled from her tiny hand, torn in two.

His heart cramped when a pool of tears wobbled on the tips of her tiny lashes, and frantic to stop their flow, he lunged for a pink daisy wildflower from the bouquet she'd dropped at his feet. "Look, Half-Pint, I can make you a new one that's even prettier," he said, scooping up the daisy with the strongest stem. "See?"

She watched as he wound it round and round until he could tie it off at the end, finally producing a perfect little ring with a pink daisy on top. Heart pounding, he held it against her ruffled pink dress and pinafore. "And it even matches your dress."

"B-But it'll j-just die l-like the other one."

Jake gulped at the fresh tears brimming in her eyes. "Sure, sweetheart," he said in a rush, desperate to bring a smile back to her face, "but that's okay because I can make you a real one out of silver from your uncle's silver mine. Would you like that?"

Her lips trembled into a beautiful smile that made him feel like he'd just beat the pants off Blaze in a shootin' contest. "Oh, Jakie, yes!" She held out a tiny hand, and he carefully pushed the daisy ring on, amazed at how perfectly it fit.

"It's beee-uuu-tiful!" she said in a near squeal, tiny arms hugging him the best that she could.

"Okay, wedding's over, Sullivan, so buck up." Blaze tucked the Bible under his arm as he moved toward the door, his and Dash's hilarity apparently appeased for the moment. "Those fish won't catch themselves."

"Yeah, Jakie," Dash said, tossing a grin over his shoulder as he followed his brother, "after all, you still have to change so you can catch some fish for your bride."

"Can I go, Jake, please, please?" Sheridan bounced up and down, the makeshift veil flopping in the air along with his heart.

"Uh-oh," Blaze said to Dash, grimacing as he backed out of the stall. "Definitely our cue to make tracks." He blew a kiss to his sister. "Sher, you make a beautiful bride, darlin', although I can't say too much for the groom"—he winked at Jake—"'cause I think you could have done better."

"Jakie, *please?*" Sheridan kept hopping, hands in prayer mode while that adorable jut of her lower lip reeled him in faster than a blue gill on a cricket dipped in bacon grease.

Jake pinched the bridge of his nose, thinking this shouldn't be that difficult for a twelve-year-old pretend groom. But blue blazes, it was hard to say no to this little gal!

Expelling a heavy sigh, he gently gripped her arms, reverting to big-brother mode. "Now, Half-Pint, you know the rules, sweetheart. Your brothers and I play wedding with you, and you let us go fishing without a fuss, right?"

She gave a jerky little nod while two fat tears made an encore. "But it c-could be our h-honeymoon ..." she said with a little heave that all but broke his heart.

Honeymoon? Jake blinked. She was barely four years old, for crying out loud. Where the devil did she get these things anyway, in a house of bachelors, no less?

Shaking the absurdity of her statement off, Jake homed in on those soggy blue eyes once more. "Silver Lake is no place for a little girl, Sher, and you know it. Weeds and snakes and chiggers and heaven knows what else." He gave the lace on her frilly puff sleeve a gentle tug. "Besides, you've got your best dress on."

"I can change ..." she whispered.

"Sully, you coming or not?!" Blaze's impatience echoed from the entrance of the barn, ringing in Jake's ears. "So, help me—we'll start the blasted tournament without you ..."

"Coming!" he shouted with a lift of his head before carefully brushing Sheridan's long silky curls over her shoulder. "Look, Sher, how 'bout I ask Angus to makes us wedding cake for dessert after dinner, and I'll even help you cut it. Would you like that?"

She sniffed and nodded. "And will you sit by me too?" She sounded so frail and sad that Jake all but melted into the hay.

"You bet, and I'll even eat any vegetable on your plate you don't want"—he leaned close to whisper, as if it were their secret—"without your uncle being any wiser, okay?"

"Okay," she said in voice as small as she, allowing him to brush away her tears with his thumb. A tiny smile peeked through her pout like the sun through a thunderhead, brightening his day. "Cross your heart and hope to die?" she whispered with a blink of blue eyes that captured his heart all over again.

"Jaaaaaake!!" Blaze's screech could have splintered the walls.

He slapped a hand to his heart, face solemn as he repeated their own personal oath he'd taught her one day. "Cross my heart and hope to die." Giving her a squeeze, he stood to his feet. "Gotta go, sweet stuff, but I'll see you at dinner, all right?"

"Okay," she said softly, the sadness in her eyes twisting his heart. "But I wish I could marry you for real someday."

He winced, praying for the day she'd finally grow up and fall in love, setting him free to be the big brother he longed to be. "I do, too, darlin'," he said softly, squatting once more to press a gentle kiss to her forehead. "But you have to remember, Sher, I'm like a big brother, so this is only make-believe. Which means no amount of wishing can ever make it true, okay?"

He waited for the shaky nod that never came, finally pulling her into a hug. Propping his chin on top of her silky head, he wandered into a dead stare. Because he had no doubt whatsoever that when it came to him and wishes of marriage …

He was plumb out of luck.

CHAPTER ONE

Virginia City, Nevada, June 1886

"COME ON, SULLY, YOU PROMISED." Blaze Donovan snatched a piece of hay up from the barn floor and stuck it in his mouth. He cocked a hip to the wooden wall of the horse stall, hay twirling in his mouth while the smell of fresh manure permeated the air.

Twenty-seven-year-old Jake "Sully" Sullivan wasn't sure if he should blame his horse for stinking up the barn or the best friend who was trying to unload a pile of dung onto his day.

Make that former best friend, Jake thought as he peered up at Blaze through narrowed eyes, hefting his saddle over his horse, Midnight, with a scowl. Mouth in a mulish press, he cinched up the straps and jerked them good and tight. *Just* like he wished he could do to his so-called best friend at the moment, who seemed hellbent on pushing Jake into precarious situations with Sheridan, Blaze's little sister.

And Jake's for the last fourteen years.

"No, *you* promised, Donovan," Jake snapped, tired of these pesky feelings that had suddenly sprung up toward the little girl who used to follow him and her brothers around from the age of four.

He stifled a grunt. "Little girl"? *If only!* Because at eighteen years of age, Sheridan was anything but. Jake secured his saddle with a final yank, scorching Blaze with a heated glare. "And all because *you're* too dad-burned weak-kneed to say no to your little sister."

Blaze had the gall to grin while he massaged his left

shoulder with a fake grimace. "I know. Just like *you're* too 'weak-kneed' to say no to me since I saved your sorry butt from falling off that cliff, wrenching my shoulder in the process."

Jake cut loose with a groan as he pinched the bridge of his nose, figuring he'd long since paid his debt to Blaze Donovan for saving his life when they were kids. "Blue blazes, Donovan, how long you plan to milk that cow, anyway?"

"For as long as I can, my friend." Blaze slapped Jake on the back before he moseyed over to lean against the railing of Midnight's stall, arms in a casual fold while he propped a dusty boot to the lowest slat. "Because all Sheridan asked for as a graduation gift was for somebody to teach her how to shoot, and we all know you're the best shot on this ranch, my friend, *and* in the state, for that matter. So naturally Uncle Finn and I thought it should be you."

Naturally. A second groan slipped through Jake's clamped lips as he dropped his forehead against Midnight's saddle. *Uncle Finn.* Otherwise known as Mayor Griffin McShane. Otherwise known as the man who rescued Jake from the Virginia City orphanage, when he took him in as a "cowhand in training," something he often did for homeless boys.

His employer.

His second father.

And the one man other than Blaze he'd do anything for.

Blaze cleared his throat. "And, of course, Sheridan thought you'd be perfect too," he said, humor lacing his tone.

Oh, I just bet she did! Jake banged his head against the saddle over and over while Blaze's laughter ricocheted off the barn walls, both of them fully aware that Sheridan had had a ferocious crush on Jake since he'd arrived at the Silver Lining Ranch. Which was just fine and dandy when she wore pinafores and bows at age four and overalls and dirt through age ten.

But the moment she turned eleven, it seemed all she wanted to do was pretty up again in dresses and bows, which wouldn't have mattered a whit if those dad-gum dresses hadn't started sprouting curves at age sixteen. And now that she was an eighteen-year-old woman heading off to college in three months? Sweet mercy, Jake couldn't wait for her to go!

Because the truth was that over the last two years, Sheridan Marie Donovan had begun filling out those gingham dresses and blue jeans a *little* too well to suit, unleashing wayward thoughts in Jake's brain that no adopted big brother should have.

Blaze always thought Jake tried to dodge Sheridan's flirtations because he saw her as a "little sister" annoyance, always tagging on his heels. And he'd be partially right. She *was* an annoyance.

Almond-shaped eyes, as clear and turquoise as a glacier stream.

Long flaxen curls, as shiny as corn silk halfway to harvest.

And a petite body with more deadly curves than a sky-high mountain road.

Huffing out a heavy sigh, Jake stood up tall to face his best friend with a plea he'd given more than once over the last year. "Come on, Blaze—have a heart. I'm not comfortable around Sher since she's all grown up and you know it, especially since she's made it perfectly clear that she likes me as more than a big brother. So why can't one of the other hands just teach her? Clint is almost as good as I am with a gun, and Charlie is right behind, so why not one of them?"

"You know why, Sully." Blaze's eyes crinkled in sympathy like always when Jake tried to dodge close interaction with his sister. "Neither Uncle Finn nor I are comfortable with any of the hands being around Sher but you, because you know how moony that girl is about romance. Blue blazes, she may be the smartest girl in the county when it comes to schoolin', but she doesn't own a lick of common sense when it comes to the real world, especially men. So, you're the only one we trust since you're immune to her."

Yeah, immune. Like a bee to honey.

"Which is why you're so perfect," he continued in that quiet, arm-twisting tone, "because it's *you* she wants to teach her. Heck, Sul, she's practically your little sister, so you're the big brother who can protect her by teaching her to shoot the derringer Uncle Finn bought her for Christmas."

Jake stifled a grunt. *Yeah, but who's going to protect me?*

"Face it," Blaze said, "none of us are comfortable with Sher traipsing across the country on her own to attend college, especially since she'll be taking trains back and forth for holidays. So, we all want to make sure she can shoot since we won't be around, and we both know Uncle Finn has been too busy with town business to do it."

He held up his right hand, which was swathed in a bulky plaster of Paris cast on his wrist, thumb, and palm. "And I'm as riled as a rhino with rabies that I hurt my shooting hand busting that bronc last week, so I can't teach her, and Dash?"—Blaze wrinkled his nose at mention of Sheridan's other older brother, who spent most of his time managing the Ponderosa Saloon—"well, let's just say his talents lie in other areas, so that just leaves you." Blaze pushed off from the stall to approach Jake with hands deep in his pockets and that hang-dog look that said he understood completely.

Only he didn't. Because if he did, he sure in the devil wouldn't be asking Jake to do this. "Rule number one," Finn McShane had told the cowhands when Sheridan turned sixteen, "is no one—and I mean *no one*—is to even look cross-eyed at my niece on this ranch no matter how much she flirts or bats her eyes, understood? Because if you do, you'll be drawing a paycheck somewhere else with your butt branded by a flaming footprint."

Jake swallowed hard. Oh, yeah, he understood, better than any cowhand on this ranch.

"The only exception I'll allow," Finn had continued, staring every single one of the cowhands down with his needle-thin gaze, "is maybe a dance or two at the annual rodeo." His look

of warning was tempered by the barest crook of a smile that
in no way offered any leeway, "because I sure in the devil
don't want that girl to think she's flat-out ugly."

All the cowhands had laughed except Jake, who sure didn't
think it was funny. Not when Sheridan dogged his every step,
fluttering those lashes so hard it gave him a stiff neck. And
not when Finn had forced every man on his ranch to take an
oath of honor to "defend, protect, and *ignore*" his eldest niece
who seemed hellbent on finding romance. He swallowed
hard.

With me.

Which didn't matter when she wore pigtails and mud pies.

"Jake," Finn had said later, taking him aside after last
year's rodeo dance when the newest cowhand, Murrell, had
approached Sheridan several times, "I'm counting on you to
be a big brother to Sheridan when Blaze, Dash, and I aren't
around. I like Murrell well enough, and I didn't mind him
asking Sher for a dance or two because that's what the rodeo
hoedown is for—an annual event for town folk to mingle."

Finn's gaze suddenly wandered into a distant stare over
Jake's shoulder, trailing off like his voice into what Jake
sensed was a painful regret buried deep in his soul. "But I
don't want my niece ending up like her mother—so in love
with the idea of love, she marries the wrong man, and so
blasted young, she has two babies before she's a full-grown
woman."

A sad smile shadowed the lips of this man Jake so admired
while Finn's memories seemed to take him faraway.
"Sheridan reminds me so much of my sister Peg—good girls
both, but heads in the clouds about romance, thinking it's the
key to happiness."

The smile slowly faded, his eyes still in a glazed stare. "But
for Peg, it was the key to destroying her life, her desire for
love so overpowering that she"—his Adam's apple hitched
hard in his throat—"succumbed, bringing shame to herself
and my family." His mouth tamped tight, so imperceptibly

that Jake might have imagined it. "*And* to her oldest son, who was born illegitimate until my brother-in-law finally married Peg when Blaze was almost a year."

Jake gulped, not exactly sure what to say. "I'm sorry, sir—I had no idea."

"I don't wonder," Finn said in a monotone, still lost in his thoughts. "Blaze was so ashamed when he found out—from kids calling him a bastard, no less—that he tried to bury it deep, not telling anyone. I'll wager even Maggie doesn't know."

Finn's gaze suddenly snapped back to Jake, the resolve in his eyes as hard as the steel in his tone. "I'm telling you this for a reason, son, because you've always been like a brother to Blaze and a son to me, and never one to judge."

"No, sir." Jake barely breathed, stock still as he stared wide-eyed at Finn.

"I'm telling you because I want you to understand just why Blaze and I, in particular, are so overprotective of Sheridan." One edge of his lip kicked up. "Or maybe obsessive might be a better word, to the point of infringing upon her freedom, as she would say, and she's right. At least when it comes to men."

Finn gouged the bridge of his nose, lids closed. "But the truth is, she's so much like my sister that I … I …"—he opened his eyes, and Jake was shocked to see a sorrowful sheen glazing their depths—"I'm afraid to see her in a relationship before she's able to handle it. She's … she's"—his throat ducked once again as a seed of a smile broke through, his affection for his niece as potent as his need to protect—"so blasted passionate and trusting and beautiful that I … I just want to keep her safe, you know?"

"Yes, sir," Jake whispered in a hoarse voice, understanding Finn's and Blaze's overly restrictive guardianship better than he ever had before.

A long, wavering sigh slipped from Finn's lips before he pinned Jake with a pointed stare that burned as intensely as his voice. "But … the biggest reason I hover over that girl is a promise I made my sister before she died. On her deathbed, Peg made me swear that I'd watch Sheridan and Shaylee like a hawk, seeing to it they both got an education instead of marrying in their teens like her, and that's a promise I intend to keep, *even* if it kills me."

Jake swallowed hard. *Or me.*

Finn tunneled a hand through his hair at the back of his head. "Which will be no easy task, mind you, especially with Sheridan. Heaven knows she's always been over the top when it comes to romance and marriage, obsessed with doll weddings from the age of four. My saving grace, of course, is that her second favorite game was playing teacher."

His lips quirked in a fond smile as he wandered off again, clearly indicating his affection for his oldest niece. "I swear if that girl wasn't marrying off her dolls"—his gaze flicked to Jake—"or you," he said with a grin before veering off once more, "she was teaching them to read and write." A chuckle slipped from his lips. "I suppose I should be grateful she wasn't teaching them to cook or she might have burned the place down."

Jake grinned along with him, remembering all the times Sher would pester Blaze and Dash to play wedding or school. His grin took a wry twist at the memory of the Donovan brothers ribbing him to no end when Jake was always chosen to be her groom or star student.

"Nope," Finn resumed with a firm dip of his chin, "her mother wanted Sheridan to have the opportunity to get an education before settling down and so do I, which means I don't want to smell even a whiff of romance around that girl for a long time to come. Because I have no doubt whatsoever that if Sheridan fell in love, I'd never be able to keep my promise to my sister because I wouldn't put it past her to elope."

A scowl suddenly tainted his lips. "I practically had to hogtie her at the age of sixteen to get her even thinking about college at all. Argued with me for months on end that she had no intention of doing anything but getting married, period." He grunted. "Over my dead body."

He'd hooked Jake's shoulder then with a firm clasp of his arm. "She's always liked and respected you, Jake, mooning over you from the get-go, so in a way, you have more influence than Blaze, Dash, or me. That's why I'm relying on you, son, to help us keep her path clear till then."

"Yes, sir," Jake had said with a quick bob of his throat, forever grateful that the man who had saved his life could trust him with something as precious as family. "I give you my solemn word, sir, I'll ward off any and all signs of romance till your niece comes home from college with a degree in her hand."

"Thank you, Jake—that means the world to me and greatly puts my heart at ease." He reached to shake Jake's hand.

Yeah? Jake swallowed a gulp as he shook it. *And mine in panic mode ...*

"Outside of Blaze and Dash, there's no one I trust more to be a big brother to Sher, so don't let me down, you hear?"

"No, sir."

"Oh, and just one more thing." He'd glanced around the barn as if he expected Sheridan to jump out of the hay at any moment, the smile in his eyes dimming to dead serious. "You can never, *ever* let her know about our agreement till she graduates college because she's already miffed that Blaze, Dash, and I guard her like a pack of coyotes over a nest of rabbits. She expects us to be vigilant, of course, but not so much you, son, which means she won't be as careful around you. So, if she does try to go astray, more than likely, you'll probably be the first to know."

"Yes, sir."

"Good man," he said with a firm slap on Jake's back, tossing a grin over his shoulder on his way to the door. "Then this'll be our secret, Jake, all right?"

"Yes, sir. Jake's eyelids sank with a heavy sigh at the

memory of that conversation with Finn he wished he'd never had. He suddenly jumped when Blaze cuffed him on the shoulder, jolting him back to the present where his best friend had just hog-tied him to temptation. "Thanks, buddy. We owe you for putting our minds at ease, knowing Sher is in good hands with a man we can trust."

A man we can trust.

Stomach in knots, Jake watched as Blaze walked out of the barn, burden free while his best friend carried the weight of the world on his shoulders.

Now if I can just trust myself ...

CHAPTER TWO

"**SO** ... WHAT DO YOU think, chica?" Carefully adjusting the gauzy peasant-style blouse slightly off Sheridan's shoulders along with her chemise, her friend Sophia Lopez stepped aside with a gleam of pride twinkling in her black eyes. "Es bueno, no?"

Sheridan blinked in front of her wardrobe mirror, cheeks warm over the hint of cleavage she saw at the scoop neck of a blouse that was as thin as the camisole beneath. Swallowing hard, she studied Sophia's handiwork with a wary chew of her lip, wondering if this was going too far.

Sophia's embroidered blouse certainly emphasized Sheridan's full breasts far more than any calico dress, proving she was definitely a woman. And her long blonde hair caught in a leather tie at the back of her head did, indeed, expose more of Sheridan's neck and shoulders, which Sophia's older sister Lolita insisted would be a good thing. More heat stormed Sheridan's cheeks. "Uh, I'm ... not ... completely sure about this, Soph ..."

"Ay-ay-ay!" Throwing her hands in the air, Sophia stood back with a firm fold of her arms, tapping a toe in impatience. "You look ... how do you say, 'voluptuosa,' chica, which Lolita said is a must to convince that thick-headed man you are no longer a little bebe. Think about it, Sher. Other than the rodeo dance last year, this will be the closest you get to that Irish mula of yours, so you have to make the most of it, si?"

"He's *not* my 'Irish mula,'" Sheridan whispered, fully aware that Sophia was right, which prompted an immediate square of her shoulders. *At least ... not yet.*

"Lolita said he *could* be your Irish mula, you know," Sophia said with a sympathetic slope of brows. She leaned in close, as if afraid anyone other than she, Sher, and their other best friend Kathy Jean Rightler might hear in spite of Sheridan's locked bedroom door. *"If* you got close enough to steal a kiss …"

"Sophia Adriana Lopez!" Sheridan gaped in shock, the idea of kissing Jake first completely unnerving her. "B-But … but … I don't know the first thing about kissing a boy!"

"No worries, chica." Smile gentle, Sophia squeezed Sheridan's hand. "Lolita said she would teach you with some of her most successful tips before she leaves for work."

Sheridan's cheeks burned crimson, and Kathy Jean's weren't far behind, the mere mention of Lolita's "tips"—the most popular dance-hall girl at the Ponderosa Saloon— scorching both Sheridan's mind and her body.

"For the love of all that's decent, Sophia Lopez," Kathy Jean said with a wide span of brown eyes, "that's a little extreme, isn't it?" Her usually shy smile was suddenly lost in a drop of her jaw. Definitely the prim-and-proper one of the three friends, Kathy Jean was what Sophia's older sister Lolita affectionately dubbed a "fuddy-duddy" or "goody-goody." Which, if Lolita had her way, is something her younger sister Sophia would definitely not be.

Sophia offered a sympathetic shrug. "Only if she wants to get her cowboy's attention because it does not look to me like she has it so far." With raven-black hair to match her almond-shaped eyes, Sophia had a modestly endowed figure that someday would, no doubt, compare to that of her voluptuous older sister. But Sophia was, thank goodness, far more studious and less provocative than Lolita, who was notorious for being an insatiable flirt. *Which* is why Sophia had asked for her sister's advice in helping Sheridan win Jake's heart.

But peeking at herself in the mirror with a hard swallow, Sheridan wasn't so sure Lolita's advice was the route she should take.

Sophia homed in on Sheridan's obvious reluctance with a serious blink of black eyes in the mirror. "And who knows, chica? *This* could be your last chance."

My last chance. Sheridan chewed a piece of skin from the edge of her lip, pretty sure Sophia was right. She had only a few months left to make Jake fall in love with her before Aunt Libby and Maggie whisked her off to college, and she sure wasn't making great strides so far. Today was her third lesson with Jake on how to shoot a gun, and the man had *yet* to get within two feet of her.

Lesson number one had been on gun safety and terminology on the front porch—*in front* of her entire family!

Lesson number two had been on types of guns and how to clean and load them in the barn—*in front* of her brother Blaze and a number of the other cowhands.

And lesson number three? A shy smile tickled her lips. Actual stance and shooting at Silver Lake tomorrow, a mile or so down the road, where all the cowhands took gun practice.

"After lunch tomorrow," Jake had said in that deadly serious tone he used with Sheridan ever since Blaze had strong-armed him into teaching her to shoot, "I'll set up your shooting range at Silver Lake. Then you, Blaze, and Maggie will mosey on over at 1:30 p.m. or so for target practice, got it?"

Oh, she "got" it all right. After all, one wasn't valedictorian of her class for nothing, no matter how inept her brothers and uncle thought her to be when it came to boys. The truth was that Jacob Michael Sullivan wanted *nothing* to do with being alone with her, which is why he insisted Blaze and Maggie join them at the lake for Sheridan's first official shooting lesson after church.

A smile twitched as she peeked at herself in the mirror once again, teeth grating her lower lip while she imagined the look on his face when he realized Maggie and Blaze most definitely wouldn't be coming …

"Maggie, *please?*" Sheridan had begged her sister-in-law

a few days ago, pleading her case to the woman who had become both a friend and big sister since she'd married her brother Blaze three months ago. "It's bad enough Uncle Finn is forcing me to go to Vassar against my will in the fall, leaving you and my family, but to leave Jake, too? Without *ever* getting the chance to be alone with him just *once*, so I can tell him how I really feel and hopefully convince him to see me as a woman?"

Maggie had studied her with a tender smile laced with sympathy as she gently brushed Sheridan's hair over her shoulder. "I just don't want you to get hurt if he turns you away, Sher, you know?"

"I'm *already* 'hurt,' Maggie," she'd said quietly, staving off the quiver of her lip. "I've loved Jake Sullivan all of my life, and deep down, I just know he's the one for me."

"But how can you know that for sure? You're so young—"

Sheridan's chin had nudged up. "Old enough to go off to college across the country on my own, Maggie," she'd said with a hard duck of her throat, tears stinging that Jake might never accept that she was the woman he was meant to love. "*And* old enough to ache inside at never getting the chance to prove we were meant to be."

A soft sigh of surrender had parted from Maggie's lips as she gathered Sheridan into a tight hug. "All right, Sher. I don't know how I'll do it, but somehow I'll find a way to extend my surprise picnic lunch after church."

Sheridan had giggled as she squeezed Maggie back. "You're a newlywed, Margaret Rose Donovan, so I have every confidence you can divert my brother's attention."

"Sheridan Marie!" Maggie had pulled away with an open-mouthed smile, a hint of rose blooming in her cheeks. "With wayward thoughts like that, young lady, I have a good mind to spare Jake your shameful shenanigans. And I would," she'd said with a playful wag of her finger, the squirm of her smile belying her scold, "if I didn't think you two were perfect for each other in the first place."

A wispy sigh floated from Sheridan's lips as her thoughts returned to the "voluptuosa" girl in the mirror. *Now, if I can just get Jake to think the same* ... Battling a shiver, Sheridan spun around to pose for Kathy Jean, who sat cross-legged on Sheridan's bed, biting her nails. "So, what do *you* think, Kathy Jean?" she asked, hands propped on the hips of her leather-fringed riding skirt. "You don't think it's"—she gave in to a gulp—"too much ... do you?"

"Uh ..." Kathy Jean spit out a sliver of thumbnail. "More like too *little*, Sher, if you ask me." She scanned both Sheridan's bare shoulders and the tightly gathered bodice of Sophia's scoop-necked embroidered blouse, which clearly accentuated Sheridan's assets.

"Bah! I think you look beautiful, chica." Sophia plopped down on the bed next to Kathy Jean, bouncing their prim-and-proper friend. Tossing her thick, black braid over her shoulder, she readjusted her own peasant blouse which, Sheridan noted with a nervous nibble of her lip, appeared considerably looser on her than it was on Sheridan. "This is what Lolita wears to work, and Mama and I wear, too, when we work in the garden, with far more ease of movement than any silly, old dress." She assessed Sheridan through a squint. "But Lolita says to make sure you tug it down *down* for shooting practice, si?"

A blush dusted Sheridan's cheeks as she assessed herself in the mirror, wondering if she was going a wee bit too far. She wished she didn't have to resort to such blatant female tactics, but she'd tried for two solid years to get Jake Sullivan to see her as a woman without an iota of success. So, what choice did she have? Resigned, she huffed out a gust of air. "Well, it's certainly far more comfortable, I'll give it that."

"Si," Sophia said with a nod, "and *far* more 'seductor' too, which Lolita says will light a fire to scorch away any 'intento fraternal.' And trust me, chica, with a mula like Jake, she says only a kiss can do that."

"*You*, I trust," Sheridan whispered, turning once again to

stare at herself with a gulp. "Lolita, not so much." Cheeks warm, she blinked at the girl in the mirror, pretty sure that at this point, she was willing to try almost anything to get Jake's attention. Expelling a heavy sigh, she made up her mind right then and there that for all of her wild ways, Lolita was right. She needed to light a fire under Jake Sullivan to scorch any 'brotherly intent.' And by gum, she would, even if it took a kiss to do it!

Making a quick sign of the cross, she couldn't help but inch the neckline of her blouse up along with the sleeves on her shoulders, hoping that when she lit that blasted fire …

It wouldn't be her who got burned.

CHAPTER THREE

WHERE THE DEVIL ARE BLAZE and Maggie? Gouging a hand through his hair, Jake paced back and forth in front of the shooting gallery he'd built long ago to train the greenhorn cowhands on the Silver Lining Ranch. Blaze was the foreman of the ranch and Jake only his assistant manager, no question. But when it came to training tenderfoots how to defend themselves and their herds on the range, everyone knew that Jake was the man in charge. Which is why Finn had allowed him to build a top-notch shooting range on the edge of Silver Lake, one of Jake's favorite places.

Or used to be.

Fingers twitchy, he strode toward the wagon opposite the handmade targets and tin cans he'd carefully spaced on a homemade stand of varying levels. Opening his gun box, he jerked out the rifle he'd selected for Sheridan to shoot and made sure the bore was even and smooth, even though he already knew it was because he'd cleaned it himself last night.

The edge of his lip kicked up. Not to mention inspected the blasted thing at least three times while he waited here like a sittin' duck. He slammed the barrel closed and laid the rifle down, his stomach in knots as he scanned across the field toward the road. *Where in tarnation are Blaze and Maggie?!*

Because there was no way he should be doing this alone. He grunted as he took to pacing again. Blame it all—there was no way he should be doing it *at all!* As assistant ranch manager, it was his job to make sure the cowhands of Silver Lining Ranch were the best in the state because a man had to learn how to defend himself, his herd, and those he loved.

Jake's jaw tensed. A lesson he'd definitely learned the hard way. His gaze flicked back to the road, narrowing along with the clamp of his mouth.

Not teach somebody's little sister how to shoot.

Dash it all, *his* little sister, if truth be told, no matter how much his pulse denied it whenever she came around, a situation he tried to avoid like the devil. Because that was the only way he could keep his promise to Finn.

"I don't want to smell even a whiff of romance around that girl for a long time to come ... so promise you'll help us keep her path clear until then."

And he'd done it—*over and over* since then. Putting the fear of God into poor Murrell if he so much as glanced at Sheridan after last year's rodeo dance. Or threatening the job of any cowhand who even thought about winking Sher's way. God help him, he'd even gone as far as the evil eye and "friendly" chats at church with any boy who smiled in her direction, all the time repenting for the way his own blood heated anytime she was near.

But the hardest thing of all had been keeping his distance when the blasted woman—no, make that *little girl*, because he *refused* to see her as a woman—buzzed around, always flirting and teasing with that lovesick look in her eyes. Which meant he had to work all the harder to hide the same look in his own, making good and sure nobody *ever* suspected that he felt the same exact way.

Not Finn, not his best friend or his brother, not Finn's wife Libby, Blaze's wife Maggie, or anyone else in Virginia City. *Especially* one Sheridan Marie Donovan, the little-girl pest who'd turned into a big one almost overnight.

Jake mauled his face with his hands. *Only three months to go!* Then the temptation would be gone off to college, at least till Christmas.

His head jerked up at the sound of hoofbeats, and a slow reedy breath seeped through his lips. "It's about blasted time, Donovan," he muttered. But the moment the rider cleared the trees, a low groan cleared his lips as well when the wrong Donovan appeared, galloping across the field with flaxen hair streaming behind, blowing in the wind.

Noooooooo! Snatching his pocket watch from inside his vest, he groaned again, painfully aware *she* was early and Blaze was late.

"Hi, Jake," she said with a bright smile as she trotted up to where he stood with mouth agape, eyes pert near bulging at the get-up that she wore. With practiced ease, she dismounted her tan and white paint, Honey—short for "Honeymoon," she'd once told him with a flutter of lashes at the age of fourteen—landing with a little hop. The jump flared her fringed leather skirt up enough to give him a glimpse of skin above her dainty leather boots. "I'm ready."

Yeah? Well, he sure wasn't. His mouth was so dry, he couldn't even gulp, Adam's apple frozen at the sight of creamy bare shoulders and a neckline that taunted his eyes. He hadn't seen that much of Sheridan's skin since the age of four when she swam in her knickers in the very lake behind her. "Where's Maggie?" he croaked, voice cracking with the effort.

"Oh, she decided to pack a picnic lunch for her and Blaze to celebrate their three-month anniversary after church." She tipped her head in a shy smile, that thick, silken clasp of hair swaying with the motion. "It's a surprise."

No joke.

"Then, when the devil are they coming?" he snapped in a tone far more like Blaze on a bad day, thinking he had a "surprise" for his best friend, too, if he didn't get here soon.

Like my fist.

She gave a little shrug of her shoulders. *Her blatantly bare shoulders.* "She didn't say," she said with a shy smile that suddenly took on a twinkle all its own, "but I got the distinct impression it might be awhile, so we should probably get started."

A groan trapped in his throat as he surveyed her shoulderless shirt—if you could even call it a shirt. "What the devil are you wearing?" he rasped, voice still reduced to prepuberty. "That's hardly proper attire for learning to shoot."

She glanced down at the fringed skirt and cowhide boots before she looked up with a blink of blue eyes. "It's what I always wear for outdoor activities."

"No, *that*," he said in a voice dangerously akin to a growl, flinging a hand in the direction of her indecent blouse, wondering if this dad-burned crabby mood Blaze had thrust him into would ever leave. *Yeah, in three months or so.* He huffed out a cranky sigh, figuring he'd issued more of those in the last month than he'd had in the last ten years. "For Pete's sake, Sheridan, may as well wear a blasted chemise."

Color bloomed in her cheeks as she lifted her chin. "My friend Sophia lent it to me—for ease of movement."

"I'll bet," he muttered, striding over to jerk the rifle from the box with a noisy gust of air, pretty sure sweet Sophia Lopez was unduly influenced by her older sister Lolita. One of the prettiest—and flirtiest—women in town, Lolita had quite an effect on the male element of Virginia City.

Jake's mouth compressed. Not unlike the effect Sheridan's get-up had on *him*. "Well, let's get this over with then," he said in a near snarl, wondering how one mite of a woman— blast it all, *little girl!*—could transform a happy-go-lucky, easy-going guy like him into Blaze Donovan. Ignoring her, he marched over to the line he'd marked with a large rock, his back to her while he waited for her to join him.

And waited.

And waited.

"Do you want me to teach you how to shoot or not?" he said, tossing an unhappy look over his shoulder that instantly halted the breath in his lungs.

"If you don't want to do this, Jake, just say so," she whispered, that lush lower lip trembling as tears did the same in her eyes.

God help me, I don't want to do this!

But he couldn't tell her that, not with his ribs caving in over the pain swimming in the eyes of the woman he loved. No, *girl*, by thunder! Dropping his head in his hand, he expelled a repentant sigh, slowly turning to extend the rifle. "Sorry, Half-Pint," he said, side-stepping her comment to avoid telling a lie, "but it's Blaze I'm cranky with, not you, so forgive me for snapping like I did."

"O… k-kay." It was that same quivering, little-girl voice she'd always used as a mite, when Dash, Blaze, and he left her behind, always halting him dead in his tracks till he went back to soothe. Swooping her up, he'd always mount her on his shoulders, battling her brothers into letting her tag along.

Only, sweet mother of pearl, he didn't want her tagging along *now*.

"Let's get started, Annie Oakley, all right?" He schooled his voice toward gentle as he waved her over, making up his mind right then and there to make the best of a bad situation. He steeled his jaw. Because he could always duke it out with Blaze later.

And God knows he *would*.

Gaze downcast, she slowly moved to where he stood, which gave his eyes the opportunity to swallow her whole. Sweet mother of mercy, but she was a beauty! Every bit of eighteen in that gossamer blouse and then some, her petite five-foot-two height allowing him a bird's-eye-view into a deep crevice at her neckline that said she was every bit a woman.

A woman he could *not* have.

Ever.

"Okay, Half-Pint, let's get you into position," he said in a taut voice, waving her toward the starting-line rock. Tugging her forward, he worked hard to ignore the fact that the blouse she wore appeared to be sliding down her shoulders. "When it comes to shooting, you can lay down, sit, kneel, or stand, but for our purposes today," he said, retrieving his rifle from the wagon, "we're going to stand. If you're right-handed like you and me, your firing hand will be your right hand, so you want to square your shoulders up with the target and feet like so."

He demonstrated with his boots a shoulder-width apart and right foot staggered about six inches behind. Tucking the rifle butt against his shoulder, he took aim, cheek resting against the stock before he turned to hand the rifle over. "Okay, your turn, Half-Pint."

Nibbling at the edge of her smile, she gave him a shy peek as she took it, straddling her legs a bit too far while she brought the gun to her shoulder. "Like this?"

"No, ma'am, like this." He took the gun back with a patient smile and demonstrated the stance once again before returning her rifle, which—*once again*—she got wrong. He bit back a groan on her third try because it was pretty clear she'd need hands-on instruction, *which* wouldn't be easy for a man determined to remain "hands off."

Moving behind her, he squatted and pointed to where her right boot should be, about six inches back. When she barely moved, his impatience—*or* his frustration with Blaze, more likely—took over as he slid her foot in position himself with a silent sigh. And, *apparently*, a little too much force.

"Whoa, steady there!" He shot up to brace her waist when she wobbled as much as his heart, appearing ready to tip over. "Sorry about that, Sher, but stance is important, sweetheart, so let's get this right."

He froze. *Sweetheart?* Blue blazes—had he really said that??

She peeked over her shoulder—her soft and creamy *bare* shoulder—and his mouth instantly went dry. "That's what I'm trying to do, Jake," she whispered, voice husky as she nervously licked her lips—her pink and plump *wet* lips— "trying to get it right."

Against his will, his gaze lingered on her mouth, causing what felt like a passel of fire ants tracking up the back of his neck when he realized his hands still circled her waist.

"Ahem." With a gruff clear of his throat, he quickly adjusted her position before jerking away, fingers on fire as if he'd been burned. And, oh sweet mother of mercy, he would be if Blaze didn't get here soon …

Slashing quivering fingers through his hair, he shot a troubled glance at the road, hoping and praying Sheridan's brother would somehow magically appear. Because as sure as the fire licking Jake's collar, if he didn't …

Jake wouldn't be the only one going down in flames.

CHAPTER FOUR

"JAKE?" IT WAS EVERYTHING SHERIDAN could do to keep her grin in check, the fluster in his manner as obvious as the flush bleeding up his neck. Which could only mean one thing: Jake Sullivan, the man of her dreams, was as nervous around her as she was around him!

The grin squirmed on her lips, just aching to cut free, but she knew she couldn't let it because this was *too* important. *He* was too important for her to mess up the only chance she'd ever had to be alone with the man that she loved.

And love him she did, without one iota of doubt. From that maddening slow and easy manner to that ready smile that lit her up like a Christmas tree inside and out. *Or used to.* Her smile faded a hair at the thought that he didn't seem to smile at her quite like before, with that adorable big-brother tease and swagger that was suddenly nowhere in sight.

She scrutinized his profile as he stared toward the road, his pale-blue gaze so fixed in a trance, it was as if he were willing Blaze to appear out of thin air.

He plowed through his thick black hair with mammoth hands embedded with square nails that were always clean, causing it to fall in disarray over a forehead wrinkled with worry and slick with sweat. His deeply bronzed skin—compliments of his Black Irish heritage—now bore a trace of ruddiness at his cheekbones, offset by an early shadow of dark beard that bristled a perfectly sculpted square jaw.

His Adam's apple ducking for the umpteenth time, it lured her gaze down past beautifully broad shoulders to a perfectly sculpted chest that sported a hint of dark hair peeking out from an open collar. At six-foot-three, he literally towered

over her, but then he'd always had from little on, and not just
in height either. He was kind and funny and smart—and loyal
to both her brothers and uncle to a fault.

But the moment he'd sided with her over her brothers at
the age of four, he had become *her* hero, *her* defender, *her*
forever cowboy with whom she longed to ride off into a
blazing sunset. Her mouth crooked. Sweet choir of angels,
she just hoped she was still young enough to enjoy it if and
when it ever *did* happen! Because Jacob Michael Sullivan
was perfect for her in every single way except one.

He didn't know it.

But he would after today, Sheridan vowed. Because she
intended to tell him.

Point blank if need be.

Or point kiss.

Her jaw lifted in battle despite the sudden heat in her
cheeks. Whatever it took. "Jake?" Resolve fairly gilded her
tone as she tapped on his shoulder.

"What?" He spun around to face her as if he'd forgotten
she was even there.

Not a good sign.

Or … maybe it *was* …

She tipped her head to study him—his body unnaturally
still like a buck in the sight of a hunter, olive skin suddenly as
pale as the circled whites of his eyes. Jake Sullivan was one
of the bravest men she knew, but for some reason, right now
she could almost *smell* his fear.

Suddenly his usual intoxicating scent of leather and cedar
soap with a hint of peppermint and lemon—from his addiction
to lemon drops and peppermints purchased at Burdzy's
Emporium—was tinged with a trace of manly sweat, telling
Sheridan the brave and wonderful cowboy before her was as
anxious as he looked.

And then in one wild clip of her heart, she suddenly caught
her breath, eyes blinking wide in instant awareness, hardly
able to believe she hadn't seen it before. All the avoidance.

All the "Half-Pint" smirks. All the ribbing he dished out about her being a little girl. Her lips slowly curled in a truly sweet smile.

And *all* because he really didn't *see* her as a little girl like he always let on.

Do you, Jake? She peered up with a smile brighter than the sun, her newfound confidence completely reversing their roles in her mind. All at once, she was the adult instead of the little girl he always claimed her to be and he the nervous little boy, despite the fact he was almost eight years her senior.

Patting his arm, she soothed him with a parental tone. "You know, Jake, the sooner we continue, the sooner we'll be done, and then you can get on with your day, all right?" Utilizing her most studious voice, she attempted to get back into position. "So, is this right?"

"Nope." He expelled what sounded like a long, arduous sigh before he roughly circled her waist again to jerk her into position none too gently, actually grabbing her knee back to force her foot into the proper position. "Stay there," he ordered in a clipped tone that almost made her grin outright. Jake was generally a good-natured man who was never surly or cross unless you forced him to something he didn't want to do.

Like the time Blaze made him muck all the stalls after he lost a bet. Great balls of fire, he'd slammed things around in the barn so hard, a litter of kittens had flown out in a ruckus of howls, hisses, and shrieks while Blaze and Dash laughed till they cried.

Mumbling under his breath, he snatched his own rifle from the wagon and stomped back over to where she stood totally still, not moving a muscle.

Except for the twitch of her mouth.

All but ignoring her, he matched her stance and positioned his own rifle. "Okay, you place the rifle butt firmly in the pocket of your firing shoulder like this," he said, tucking it against the V of his arm. "Not the fleshy part of your armpit beneath it, mind you, or on your collarbone, but firmly in the pocket against your shoulder to absorb the recoil."

"Pocket," she repeated, trying to follow suit, although not really sure if she did.

Not sparing a glance or a smile, he continued on in that nasty tone that said he'd rather be mucking a stall. "Next, you steady the handgrip with your non-firing hand midway down the tube," he said with a firm grip of the barrel, "resting the stock in the "V" created by your thumb and forefingers. This will help give you control over the muzzle when aiming, which you want because precision is key."

"Okay ..." She tried to emulate him, watching closely as he brought the rifle to his head and pressed his cheek against the butt of the gun.

"Keep your elbows down and in, relax your neck, and then let your cheek fall naturally to the stock, which will help your eye align to the sight. Your trigger finger should be straight—don't curl it around the trigger until you're ready to fire, got it?"

No. "Yes, I think so," she whispered, desperately trying to hold onto the gun along with her temper as she tried to match his grip and his aim. "How's this?"

His long, noisy sigh made her wince. Stomping over to the wagon, he dropped his rifle into the bed and stalked back to stand behind her, mumbling under his breath before he blasted out another exhale of frustration so loud, it ruffled both her hair and her ire.

She spun around. "Oh, for crying out loud in a bucket, Sullivan. If you don't want to teach me, just say so."

"All right, Donovan, I will!" He parked blunt hands on his hips, leaning in to stare her down with eyes as hard as a jagged piece of ice-blue agate. "I flat-out don't want to teach you, so there! No pretty, dad-burned too delicate little girl has any blasted business learning to shoot a gun. But for some inane reason, I'm the poor idiot that's been tapped to teach you."

She blinked. *Pretty?*

She frowned. *Too delicate??*

She scowled. *Little girl?!*

She stepped in and slapped her hands to her hips, her glare matching his to a scowl. "Well, you sure got the 'idiot' part right, Jake Sullivan, and while we're at it, you can add 'blind' and 'bullheaded' to the list, too, because if you think I'm still a little girl, you need to see Doc Wilson about some specs."

Her stomach did a funny flip when his gaze flicked to the cleft between her breasts for a split second before jerking back up with a firm clamp of his jaw. The blood gorging his cheeks suddenly went head-to-head with the heat in her own.

She slashed her jaw up, the "idiot" so ridiculously tall, she was getting a pain in the neck to match the one in her posterior. "So, you going to teach me to shoot or not, Sullivan? Or will I have to tell Uncle Finn you flat-out refused because, blue thunder, the man's hardly done *anything* for you at all."

The blue eyes thinned along with his mouth. "I'll do it, dag-nabit, but I sure in the devil don't have to like it."

Wanna bet? Sheridan whirled back around to get into position, making up her mind right then and there that she would take Sophia's and Lolita's advice and steal a kiss if she could. Because it was crystal clear from his reaction to her "get-up" and his surly mood that Mr. Sullivan *did* see her as a woman and was just flat-out afraid of it. Jaw tight, she lifted her gun to aim in the sloppiest manner she could, completely ignoring all the specifics he'd given her earlier. "How's this?" she asked sweetly, her smile as tight as her grip on the gun.

"Pitiful." He snatched the rifle from her so fast, she cried out when the trigger nicked the tip of her finger, which she'd purposely curled rather than keeping straight like he'd instructed.

Tears pooled as quickly as the blood on her finger.

The whites of his eyes expanded in shock while he practically hurled the gun down, quickly laying it aside to gently take Sheridan's hand. "Oh, Sher, please forgive me—I never meant to hurt you like that, sweetheart."

No, just in a million other ways ... She sniffed, somewhat mollified by his second use of "sweetheart."

He fished a handkerchief from his pocket and carefully blotted her finger, peering up with a truly repentant look. "I'm so sorry, Sher, for this and for acting like a complete jackass. Will you forgive me—*please*? I'll make it up to you, I promise."

She gave a wobbly nod. *If you make it up to me.*

He assessed the cut, eyes in a squint as he dabbed more blood away. He glanced up. "Does it still hurt?"

More than you will ever know ... She nodded again, the tender look he gave her causing her heart to ache more than her silly finger.

Still holding her hand, he promptly bent to one knee. "Doc Wilson told me once that spit not only can heal a wound, but it can help the pain, too," he muttered before halting the air in her throat when he gently took her finger into his mouth without a second thought, gently sucking on the wound.

Mouth gaping, her lids were dry sockets of shock, a tossup over which was warmer—his mouth wrapped around her finger, or the swirling effect deep down in her belly. "There you go," he said, giving it one final caress with his lips that all but weakened the tendons at the back of her knees. "How does it feel now?"

Her breathing shallowed considerably. *You don't want to know, Jake, trust me.*

"Better?" he asked again, thick black brows lifted in hope.

She offered a nod as dizzy as the heat whirling in her tummy.

"Good!" He rose to his feet and pulled her into a gentle hug. "Gosh, I'm so sorry, Sher, and you have my word I'll be on my best behavior from now on if you want to continue."

She managed a small smile. *Only if you're not on your best behavior.*

He pulled away, hands braced to her arms as he cocked a brow in question. "Does your finger hurt too much to try again?"

"No." She peeked up with a shy nibble of her lip. "If you don't mind helping position my stance and grip again, that is."

"Sure," he said, not a trace of surly in his tone, his eagerness to make it all up to her almost making her smile. He stood behind to reposition her stance, then handed her the rifle, his body so close, she could feel the heat. When she lifted the gun, he adjusted her grip from behind, arms encircling while he tucked the butt into her pocket on one side and carefully straightened her trigger finger on the other. "Almost perfect," he said, his words warm against the side of her head as he adjusted her left-handed grip on the barrel. "Now tuck your cheek against the stock and relax your body."

Relax? When Jake Sullivan was so close she could feel his every breath?

"Come on, Sher, you can do it," he said, the warmth of his palm against the small of her back almost singeing her skin. "Just relax your body and assume a calm breathing rhythm."

Easy for you to say, she muttered in her mind, then suddenly noticed his breathing sounded as ragged as hers.

Mmm ... maybe not.

"How's this?" she whispered, loathe to even move a hair lest Jake back away.

"Perfect. Now close your eyes, relax, and memorize the feel of your stance and grip. Get comfortable with it, because comfort enhances confidence, and confidence enhances skill."

Comfortable? With the heat of his body setting fire to hers?

"You just need to relax your left hand on the barrel a bit more"—he reached around to help her loosen both her grip on the barrel and her finger trigger on the other side. "So, how's that feel?" he asked.

Oh, sweet chorus of angels—like heaven! "Uh ... good."

A nervous laugh tripped from her lips. "How does it look to you?" she asked, turning to see his expression. Only when she did, his face was so close, all she could see were *those lips* mere inches away. Those full, sensuous lips that she'd dreamed of over and over ... always caressing hers.

Her pulse took off while her breathing accelerated, and looking up, she saw the flare of surprise in pale blue eyes that suddenly darkened to deep-blue. His half-lidded gaze dropped to her mouth, and in one wild, thundering beat of her heart, she knew he was feeling the same thing too. "Oh, Jake," she whispered, "I'm crazy about—"

His body jerked as if he'd been shot while panic expanded the whites of his eyes. Throat bobbing twice, he stumbled back with a hard shake of his head. "This lesson is over, Half-Pint," he whispered, voice raw with denial, "and I'm taking off right now."

Which he did. Arms flailing in the air, he fell backwards with a hard grunt.

Right over that blessed rock.

CHAPTER FIVE

SWEET MOTHER OF MERCY—WHO HIT me over the head? Jake had no bloomin' idea how long he'd conked out, but he knew that he had because his memory was as fuzzy as his brain while he lay flat on his back with eyes shut. There was an ache all over his body that matched the one in his chest as he lay inert, struggling to remember ...

"Jake, please wake up!"

He felt the soft press of a hand to his cheek and froze, nothing moving but his wayward pulse, begging for mercy.

God help him, he knew that voice, and it didn't bode well for his state of mind.

Or his body.

"Jake, *please*—look at me!" A flurry of activity flickered the sun beyond his closed lids, and the last thing he wanted to do was open them again. To see once more the blue of those eyes that had rounded in shock, as surprised as he when she'd unexpectedly turned, her lips aligned mere inches from his own. A moment in time when paralysis had claimed them both, separated only by rasps of ragged air and a craving so potent, he'd felt the fire clear to his toes.

So help him, for one thundering heartbeat, all he could think about was tasting those luscious lips, caressing them, fondling them, coaxing them with his mouth to places he had no right to go.

"Jake!" Gentle fingers stroked his jaw, luring a groan up his throat that he quickly squelched because it had nothing to do with the pain in his body, only his heart. The *same* shameful pain that plagued his dreams for the last two years, now slipping out in a moment of stun, exposing a weakness he hoped and prayed she hadn't seen in his eyes.

Attraction.

Longing.

Love forbidden ... and desire denied.

"Promise you'll help us keep her path clear until then."

Another groan almost sandpapered his throat, but he quickly cut it off.

"Heck, Sul, she's practically your little sister, so you're the big brother who can protect her from herself."

Heaven help him, he was trying, but the Almighty sure wasn't making it easy ...

"Jake, open your eyes, please!" More fabric rustling and the deadly scent of lavender shivered him as much as her gentle shake on his arm. His eyelids almost jerked open at the sudden catch of her breath when her hand gently touched the back of his head.

"Oh, no—you're bleeding!" she rasped, and the panic in her voice unleashed an onslaught of guilt. Fortunately, it *also* unleashed an idea to save him from a shooting lesson he did *not* want to continue. He held his breath. Maybe—just maybe— if she thought he was knocked unconscious, she would go for help ...

Wouldn't she?

He barely breathed as he lay perfectly still, pretty sure this was his best option. Because the last thing he wanted was to return to a lesson where he was besotted with creamy bare shoulders, bewitched by a deadly neckline, or betrayed by a look of longing—in both his eyes *and* hers.

"Jake, wake up!" She rattled him but good this time, and a part of him felt almost guilty at the terror that laced her tone, but it was for her own good, he told himself. It took everything in him to battle a gulp. *And mine.*

"Oh ... J-Jake!" Tears wobbled her voice as she threw herself across his chest to hug his neck, her weeping wracking his soul as much as his body. "Don't die, please!"

But sweet mother of mercy, he just might because the

moment her body landed on top of his, he'd stopped breathing altogether. So much heat scorched through him, it was a wonder she didn't go up in smoke. He couldn't see because his eyelids were pasted to his eyeballs, but he sure in the devil could feel, giving his mind's eye a vision he'd seen more than once in his dreams.

The press of her body against his, the scent of lavender surrounding him like the silk of her hair, which now splayed haphazardly across his mouth. Tears dampened his neck as she wept, her heaves nearly twitching his arms with the impulse to hold her, comfort her.

Sheridan! Go-get-help, he mentally commanded, desperate to get her off of his chest, away from his arms, miles from his lips. But she just continued to cry, drenching his neck with her tears while her sorrow drenched his conscience with guilt. She moved a hair, and his body went to stone at the touch of something warm and soft on his neck, the caress of her lips kindling a fire deep down inside. *No! Please, God, make her go ...*

"J-Jake, I'm so -s-orry ..." she whispered, her voice nasal with grief as she hugged him close once again while her hair tickled his nose. "I'm going to go get help now, so don't move ..."

Move? Well, he sure didn't want to, but God help him, a tingling sensation began to burn inside his nostrils, mounting every time Sheridan's hair grazed the tip of his nose ... until *... until ...*

Nooooo!! But it was no use. Against his will, his body drew in a sharp breath that tightened the muscles in his chest, eyes squeezing shut while he ...

"Ah-choo!"

Sheridan froze, body jolted from the force of Jake's sneeze. "Jake?" She shot up, fingers trembling as she gripped his shirt, lips parted in hope while she scanned his face for some sign of recovery. "Jake—wake up—*please!*" she begged, but his eyes remained closed as his breathing suspended. She saw a faint twitch in his eyelid, and in one erratic beat of her heart, it all came back, something Maggie had once told her.

As a nurse at St. Mary Louise Hospital in Virginia City, Maggie had cared for an adorable little boy named Wally who was recovering from a particularly nasty case of influenza. All the staff loved him, of course, but the little stinker *hated* taking his medicine. So every time the nurses tried, little Wally Wilder would pretend to be asleep.

"Let him sleep," the doctor ordered, "because he needs that more than anything, then treat him when he's awake."

So, every time Maggie arrived to give his medicine, of course Wally was sleeping. *Until* one day he sneezed. "People don't sneeze when they're sleeping, unconscious, or in a coma," Maggie explained, so she promptly tiptoed over and tickled Wally into a fit of giggles that won her his heart, a game they continued until the day his parents took him home.

Sheridan's eyes narrowed as she studied Jake with more precision—his even breathing, his face an unmovable mask save the almost imperceptible flicker of his lids, body stone-cold still and silent ...

Except for that sneeze.

A slow smile slid across her lips as she hiked a teasing brow. *Ah-ha! Playing games, are we now, Mr. Sullivan? Well, I've got a few games to play too ...*

Smiling, she leaned in to breathe warm in his ear, her words laden with concern. "Now, don't you worry, Jake—I'll be right back with help." She pressed a soft kiss to his cheek and couldn't help a grin when that formidable jaw tightened hard as rock.

Pretending to rise, she sat up to admire him because heaven knows she may never get this close again. Ridiculously long lashes as thick as his ebony hair rested on high cheekbones in a hard-sculpted face that had always melted her with a smile. Until today.

No, today, Jake Sullivan had shown her a side of his personality she'd never seen before.

Hard. Determined. Dangerous.

Scared.

With a shy grin tugging at her mouth, she grated her teeth against her lower lip while she studied olive skin bronzed by the sun and peppered with a shadow of dark bristle. She supposed she could tickle him like Maggie had with that little boy, but that would only make him laugh.

Her chin nudged up in a show of resolve despite the nervous lump in her throat. And she didn't want him to laugh. She swallowed hard as she stroked his sandpaper jaw with trembling fingers. No, she wanted him to groan in surrender when her lips finally caressed his …

"And trust me, chica, with a mula like Jake, only a kiss can do that."

"But … but … what if I d-do it wrong?" Sheridan had said when Lolita had instructed her on various kissing tips, any boldness she might have had as damp as the palms of her hands. "I've never even been alone with a man, much less kiss one."

Lolita had rolled her eyes. "Bah! Those brothers of yours are handsome, si, but they stick to you like a Puttington agent deeped in tar."

"Pinkerton," Sheridan had corrected with a smile, pretty much in agreement with Lolita's assessment. Between Uncle Finn, Blaze, Dash, *and* Jake, Sheridan had never even been alone to *flirt* with a boy or man *properly*—not on the ranch, not at the annual rodeo dances, not in town, not even at church. A wispy sigh breezed from her lips. *So, how on earth am I going to kiss Jake?*

"But … but … what if he hates it?" she'd asked with a bite of her thumbnail, a sliver of nail flying through the air.

A low throaty laugh had bubbled from Lolita's lips as she winked. "A man would have to hit his head on a rock, chica, out cold to hate a kiss from you in this." She'd tugged

Sheridan's blouse a tad lower on her shoulders.

Close. But a rock *was* involved ...

Sheridan blinked, her focus returning to the comatose man lying beside her.

If, that is, Jake really *was* out cold.

Only one way to find out. And like Sophia said, this *could* be her last chance.

"Jake," she whispered, voice as quivery as her stomach, "before I go, there's something I need to tell you while you're unconscious because I don't know if I'd have the courage to say it when you're awake ... but I love you *so* very much, and to prove it ..." Fortifying with a deep ingest of air, she expelled it again in one long, trembling exhale before lowering to carefully brush her lips against his. She forced herself to ignore the sudden jolt of his body—*and hers*—to focus on giving his lower lip a gentle scrape with her teeth just like Lolita had instructed.

"As easy as breathing," her friend had said, and oh, sweet mother of mercy, it was! And ragged breathing at that! Heart pumping, she lost herself in the wonder of Jake, the delicious taste of mint and man muddling her mind while she suckled his lower lip, body tingling so much, she felt like she was floating on air. Which she pretty much was when ...

Whoooooosh!

"What in Sam Hill do you think you're doing?" he croaked, tumbling her on her back so fast she caught her breath with a grunt, blue fire shooting from his gaze while he pinned her to the ground. "Are you *crazy?*" His shout echoed across the lake, the whites of his eyes as wild as his hair, which dangled precariously over his forehead and hers.

"As a matter of fact, I ... *am* crazy, Jake ..." Her voice trembled as much as her insides, and she didn't miss the tremble of his own arms as he hovered over her, biceps bulging with the strain of his weight. "Over you." A knot ducked in her throat. "And I think you're crazy for me too."

Hissing what might have been a swear word, he gave her

a little shake. "Your head is full of pipedreams, little girl, so you need to get rid of any cock-eyed notions that you and I will *ever* get together, Sher, you hear me? Because I am *not* attracted to you that way, Half-Pint, and you need to face that." Still hovering over her, he shook his head with a scowl, every word out of his mouth pooling more tears in her eyes. "For pity's sake, Sheridan, I'm a man almost eight years older than you, so I only see you as a little sister!"

Liar! Sheridan wanted to smack him, but his hands still shackled her arms, anchoring her to the ground.

He softened his tone, the tears trailing her cheeks obviously having an effect. Gently wiping the wetness from her face, he started to rise. "I'm sorry to be so blunt, Half-Pint, but—"

Arms suddenly free, she lunged for his neck, determined to show Jake Sullivan once and for all that he was lying through his teeth. He *was* attracted to her and she knew it! If not from the near-silent moan that had leaked out when she'd kissed him, then surely from his glazed look when their eyes met during the lesson. *Now*, she just had to prove it to *him* …

Catching him off-guard, she hurtled all of her weight against him, toppling him on his back with a grunt of shock. Flopping down, she kissed him with everything she had, pulse pounding as she waited for him to push her away.

Only he didn't.

With a pained groan that literally melted in her mouth, he rolled her over so quickly, she had time for only one quivering breath … before he descended with a kiss that stole it all over again.

CHAPTER SIX

JUST ONE TASTE, PLEASE ... that's all I want ...
That had been the lone thought that betrayed him, along with his body, when Sheridan Marie Donovan's lips met his for the second time in mere minutes, sealing his fate. When she'd first brushed her mouth to his, he'd been stunned to stone, which was good because he needed to remain still to keep the illusion alive that he was "out cold." Even *if* he was "on fire" instead.

Okay, fine, he was man enough to handle the innocent brush of her lips for a second or two before she left to go get help, because really, it was so soft and sweet, it could have been a kiss on the cheek. But then she'd turned up the heat to scalding with a tug of his lower lip, actually taking it into her mouth.

Definitely no kiss on the cheek!

That was the moment he discovered he was a bit *more* than man enough to respond like any red-blooded American male would. Especially one who craved the very woman—*no, dad-burn-it, little girl!*—who delivered the kiss that singed not only his body, but all good intentions as well.

Sweet, soul-saving mercy! If one could even call it a kiss at all! Jake's body had melted into a puddle, no desire to do anything but yank the woman—*little girl, dad-gummit!*—closer to respond in kind. *Blue smoke of Hades, where in the devil did she learn to kiss like that?* She hadn't been out of his or her brothers' sight since she turned sixteen, when Finn had laid down the law. Only it hadn't been the law laying down when she'd kissed him, it'd been *him*, flat on his back before he'd finally come to his senses—and his consciousness—

enough to push her away and rail on her but good.

"Are you *crazy?*" he'd shouted after he disarmed her with a quick roll, pinning her to the ground to keep her from doing anything like that ever again.

"I ... *am* crazy, Jake ..." she'd said in that quivery, little-girl voice that had always wrapped him around her little finger. "And I think you're crazy for me too."

Oh, he was crazy, all right. Crazy enough to lie to the blasted woman—*dash it all, little girl!*—telling her he wasn't attracted to her when he knew darn good and well that he was. But he'd never been a good liar because he was too partial to the truth, and yet he didn't want her—*or* anyone in Nevada—to know his true feelings.

Yeah, good job with that, knothead! He was surprised his blasted nose hadn't grown like that Pinocchio character in the fairytale story his mother used to read to him, letting Sheridan know the minute he'd lied.

Only it wouldn't be the nose that labeled him a liar, but this blasted kiss he craved to lay on her right now, taking over from where she'd begun after flipping him—and his heart—flat for a second time. Forbidden fruit that was busting his hard-practiced restraint like a bronc out of stall, kicking and stomping all the way.

Well, that was *exactly* what he'd intended to do right now, he thought as he hovered over her wild-eyed, his biceps as strained as his self-control—first "kick" himself, then "stomp" this deadly attraction to dust before it could go any further.

Right after I finish this kiss ... Dropping down, he'd had no power over the groan that escaped as he lost himself in the stuff of his dreams, deeper and deeper ...

God, please *give me strength—my heart can't take this ...*

"I knew it!" Shoving him back, Sheridan sat up, rudely interrupting the kiss that had pert near brought him to his knees in his mind, ready to propose. "You *are* attracted to me, Jake Sullivan, and I defy you to deny it!" She thumped a fist on his chest and slapped her arms into a tight fold, that cute little chin nudging up while those lips—now swollen to a glossy pink—clamped tight, slamming the gates to heaven tighter than if he'd been the devil himself.

He silently winced. Which wasn't far off given his abominable lack of control.

"I'm not going to deny anything, Half-Pint," he said with a heavy sigh as he slowly lumbered up, desperate to restore his dignity, his promise to Finn …

His blood pressure to normal.

Slapping the dust from his denim work pants, he extended a hand to help Sheridan up, the aches in his body near as bad as the one in his chest. He let her hand go the moment she was stable on her feet, which was saying a whole heck of a lot more than his heart. "But I'm not going to admit it either, Sher, because you're a sister to me, so this can't ever happen again."

She stomped her foot, reminding him a lot of that adorable little girl who'd demanded he marry her for her eighth birthday. "I am *not* your sister, Jake Sullivan, and you don't *have* to admit it because your kiss did it for you and *then* some."

Heat blazed up the back of his neck like a dad-gum prairie fire, all the way to the tips of his ears, torching his temper. "Yeah, well that tends to happen when a girl looks and acts more like a painted gal at The Silver Pistol than the proper daughter of the mayor."

Her catch of breath was so harsh, it almost echoed over the lake, telling him he'd taken it a step too far. Water instantly welled in those blue eyes while the rose in her cheeks bled into her face, a poor complement to the whisker burn that now pinked her jaw. But when her lower lip began to tremble and a single tear slithered down, he knew he was a goner.

Crack!

Especially when she hauled off and slapped him clean across the chops. Eyes glazing over, he wobbled like a tree about to topple.

"Don't you dare compare me to those women at The Silver Pistol, Jake Donovan," she said through a choked heave while more of those blasted tears rolled down her cheeks, quivering as much as that pert little chin.

"Aw, Sher ..." Huffing out a sorrowful sigh, he bundled her close in a protective hug, heartsick over causing her any pain at all, even if it was the only way to nip this infatuation in the bud. "I'm sorry for hurting you like that, Half-Pint, but the truth is if you go around kissing men like that, you're in for a whole passel of heartbreak, and I sure hate to see that, darlin'."

"But I d-don't go around k-kissing men like that," she said with a sniff, her tone nasal from congestion, "only you because you're my first kiss ever ..."

Well, thank God for that anyway! He fished a handkerchief from his pocket and handed it to her with a tender smile. "Well, as much as I appreciate that honor, darlin', this can't happen again."

"But why? You liked it, I know you did." She peeked up with red-rimmed eyes, wearing the same woe-begone look as when she'd skinned her knee at the age of six and asked him to kiss it.

Only the kind of kisses she was looking for now were way too dangerous to consider.

He cuffed the back of his neck with a gruff clear of his throat, desperate to remain calm and rational. After all, he was the adult here. His conscience squirmed. *Although, you couldn't have guessed that from a few moments earlier.* "Well, because I'm almost eight years older than you for one thing, Half-Pint, and you're too young to fall in love."

"Ha! Tell that to my heart," she said with a wobble in her voice, punctuating it with a loud blow of her nose that coaxed a smile to his lips.

Yeah, and while you're at it, my body as well, he thought with a sprint of his pulse, his smile fading considerably when he realized how serious this was.

"Aunt Libby told me her father is almost eleven years older than her mother, and even Blaze is way older than Maggie."

He steeled both his resolve and his jaw. "For crying out loud, Half-Pint, you're like a little sister to me, so it's just not right."

She arched a beautiful blonde brow. "But that's just it, Jake—I'm *not* your sister. That may be what your brain is saying, but your body said a whole 'nother thing, because that was *no* little-sister kiss, and you know it. So, you're going to have to give me a better reason than that."

"I give you my solemn word, sir, I'll ward off any and all signs of romance till your niece comes home from college with a degree in her hand."

Jake stalled, the tic in his jaw keeping time with the thud of his heart, wishing more than anything he could just tell Sheridan the truth—that her uncle made him promise to keep all men away.

Including me.

"Oh, and just one more thing," Finn's words came back to haunt, *"You can never let her know about our agreement till she graduates college, Jake, because she's already miffed that Blaze, Dash, and I guard her like a pack of coyotes over a nest of rabbits. She expects us to be vigilant, of course, but not so much you, son, which means she won't be as careful around you. So, if she does try to go astray, more than likely, you'll be the first to know."*

Jake gulped. *No kidding.* He quickly averted his gaze from Sheridan's needle-thin stare, making him feel like one of those blasted coyotes.

"Well?" She tapped her toe, chin high and brows raised, looking so much like the schoolmarm she aspired to be, he had to squelch a smile. He buried a grunt. Not all that hard when his gaze dropped to the bare shoulders and deep V of that dad-burned blouse, which was *anything* but schoolmarm.

"Well ..." Head down, he ruffled the back of his hair,

straining his brain to come up with something—*anything*—that would satisfy Sheridan enough to keep her away.

Or someone? A silent sigh of relief slowly eased through his lips when pretty Megan Joy Burdzy came to mind. Daughter of the owner of Burdzy's Emporium, Megan Joy always waited on him at her father's mercantile whenever Jake purchased his weekly supply of lemon drops and peppermints.

With her flirtatious manner and extra lemon drops and peppermints she always slipped in his bags, it was no secret she'd like to step out with him. And heck, Jake had even toyed with the idea himself. After all, he liked Megan Joy a lot. She was smart and lively and a real lady who sure was easy on the eyes, so maybe now was the perfect time to explore a new relationship.

Besides, with Finn and Blaze newly married, Sheridan off limits, Shaylee in bed by nine, and Dash managing the Ponderosa Saloon most nights till he could afford to buy it, Jake had been downright lonely. Sure, the other ranch hands always wanted him to join in playing poker or drinking in town, but he'd learned a long time ago that those were two vices that only got a man in trouble.

Peering up beneath half-lidded lashes, he offered Sheridan his well-practiced big-brother smile, fine-tuned over the last two years to keep her at bay.

Yeah, sure worked today ...

He cleared his throat, plunging his hands deep in his pockets. "Uh, I haven't told this to anybody yet, Sher"—he swallowed hard. *Especially* Megan Joy—"but I've been kinda … sorta … seeing Megan Joy Burdzy …" He let that trail off, thinking it wasn't exactly a lie because he *was* seeing her after all—weekly to buy his lemon drops and peppermints.

"Megan Joy?" She said the name so soft and pitiful, he wanted to scoop her up and make it all better like kissing all those skinned knees and elbows.

Only he couldn't. Not this time.

"Do you"—that bare creamy throat bobbed several times, drawing his attention to porcelain shoulders and deadly décolletage no little girl should have—"like her?"

He nodded with a little too much force. "Oh, yeah, sure, she's a fine girl—*woman*," he quickly amended, grateful Megan Joy was at least older than Sheridan at the ripe, old age of twenty-two.

"Then why," she whispered, catching that lush lower lip in her teeth so shyly he couldn't look away, hypnotized by the fact that his mouth had just done the same mere moments before, "did you kiss me?"

"W-What?" Her question broke the trance of his wayward thoughts, causing him to blink in confusion as he forced his gaze up to her eyes.

"I *said*"—her shyness disappeared faster than the blink of a doe in the sight of a hunter—"if you're seeing Megan Joy, *why* did you kiss *me*?" She slapped those beautiful bare arms into a tight fold that only lowered the neckline of that blasted blouse, tripping his temper all the more.

His jaw dropped. "Might I remind you, *little girl*," he said, emphasizing the one phrase she hated as he aimed a stiff finger, "that *you* kissed me!"

She stepped into his space, fists parked on her hips while she stared up with fire in her eyes. "Yes, I did, because you're too bloomin' blind to see we were meant for each other, Jake Sullivan, so I had to do something to open up your eyes. But we both know a lot more than your eyes opened up, mister, because you devoured me like a bag of lemon drops."

Heat blasted his face like a red barn afire, and all Jake wanted to do was to end this right here and now. Jaw stiff, he took a step back, his tone as cool as the sweat on his neck in a sudden gust of breeze. "Yes, I did, Sheridan, and you have my heartfelt apologies because I was wrong."

"Jake, no—"

He held up a steeled palm. "Not only was it a betrayal of your uncle and brothers, but it was a betrayal of both you and my core values because this"—he waved a hand between them—"is neither something I want nor will ever allow."

"Oh, Jake ..."

As hard as it was, he ignored the sheen of saltwater that pooled in her eyes, determined to make up for his abysmal lack of restraint just moments before. Picking up the rifles, he placed them in the box at the back of the wagon as she watched with a stricken look. "I don't plan to mention this to anyone, Sheridan, and I'm asking you to do the same." He turned, voice solemn as he faced her with a stoic look. "And I think it's best if we just end these lessons altogether—"

"Noooo!" Her voice cracked as she ran to his side, gripping his arms with trembling fingers. "Jake, I love you. Don't leave me, please! You're breaking my heart ..."

He paused to tenderly brush a stray hair from her eyes, ribcage constricting as he traced a finger down the face he saw every night in his dreams. "No, darlin'," he whispered, "I'm trying to save it." And gently loosing her hold from his arms, he turned to mount the wagon, her frail sobs shattering his heart as he turned the rig toward home.

The sun still shone in the sky as he wheeled away, but for him, the day had turned black as night because in one violent beat of his heart, everything had changed. He'd had no choice but to turn her away, hurting both himself and someone for whom he cared a great deal, but it was the only thing he could do. His shoulders slumped, heavy with the weight of what he had done, ushering into the reality of day the demons he'd once only wrestled in his dreams.

The shame of forbidden desire.

The guilt of a promise betrayed.

And the pain of a friendship that could no longer be.

CHAPTER SEVEN

"**S**HER?" MAGGIE KNOCKED ON THE door of her sister-in-law's bedroom, concerned that according to Libby, Sheridan had come home from her lesson with Jake early and gone straight to bed with a headache. Which was so odd because she had been in great spirits at church just a few hours ago, so very excited about her third lesson with Jake. She knocked again, unable to keep the concern from her voice. "Sheridan, honey—are you okay?"

"Oh, Maggie ..." The muffled cry on the other side of the door twisted Maggie's heart, and turning the knob, she peeked in. Her stomach bottomed out when she saw Sheridan curled in a ball on her bed, a shaft of sunlight illuminating her tear-stained face.

"Goodness, Sheridan—what happened?" Maggie closed the door behind her before she hurried over to sit down beside her, leaning to gently brush Sheridan's hair from her face.

"H-He ... h-he ... hates me ..." Her voice trailed off into a sob.

"What?" Maggie stroked her head. "Oh, honey, no—Jake loves you!"

"No, h-he d-doesn't." Her voice wobbled as much as her head as she shook it back and forth. "He ... he s-said mean things to me, comparing me to a p-painted gal at The Silver P-Pistol."

"What?" Maggie sat straight up. "Why on earth would he—" She stopped, suddenly noticing Sheridan's off-the-shoulder blouse. Expelling a quiet sigh, she tugged the sleeves higher up on Sheridan's shoulders. "Oh, sweetheart—did you wear this blouse to your lesson?"

Sheridan lumbered up with a nod. "Sophia said it would get his attention, and it did, Maggie. His eyes about bugged out of his head when he saw me, and then he got all flustered and crabby. He was snapping at me left and right, finally admitting he didn't want to teach me. Said I have no business learning to shoot."

"No!" Maggie gaped, hardly able to believe someone as sweet and even-tempered as Jake Sullivan would ever act like that with the little sister he all but adored. "That doesn't sound like Jake."

"No, I know," Sheridan said with a sad sniff. She held up a finger, which was black and blue with a good-sized scratch. "And then he snatched the gun out of my hand so fast, he cut my finger."

Maggie gasped, reaching to take Sheridan's hand. "Oh, Sher, no! Why on earth would he do that?"

"Because he's attracted to me, Maggie, but he won't admit it."

"What??" Maggie blinked, well aware of Sheridan's crush on Jake, but also pretty sure Jake had never reciprocated, which worried Maggie for her sister-in-law, given Sheridan's strong feelings. "How do you know?"

Swiping at her eyes, Sheridan lumbered up to lock the door before slogging back to the bed and plopping down in an unhappy heap. "I'll tell you, Maggie, but you have to promise not to breathe a word of what I say to anyone, not even Blaze because you know how he and Jake are thick as thieves."

"Unfortunately, yes." Maggie's mouth swerved off-center. "Thieves notorious for stealing girls' hearts," she muttered, so grateful that that part of Blaze's life—as Virginia City's most determined bachelor—was over and done. She raised her palm. "You have my solemn promise, Sheridan—not a word."

"Thank you." Sheridan expelled a long, quivering sigh. "I know Jake's attracted to me because of the way he acted when he saw me in this blouse," she said with a limp flip of the floppy sleeve. "That's not like him, just like you said, and it suddenly hit me that maybe he was nervous and angry around me because he *was* attracted to me and didn't want to be."

A slow, fragile breath parted from Maggie's lips as she laid a hand on Sheridan's arm, desperate to prevent her sweet sister-in-law from getting her hopes up too high. "Sher, you don't know that, sweetheart."

"No, but I do *know* what I saw in his eyes, Maggie, when he was helping me with my aim. I suddenly turned to smile at him, and his face was so close to mine"—a shiver rattled her body—"I swear I could feel his breath on my skin." She stared, her eyes blue orbs of sadness as she gave Maggie a forlorn look, chin perched on top of her knees. "I saw desire, Maggie, clear as day, and when his gaze dropped to my lips, I knew he felt it, too, because he jerked back so hard, he fell over a rock."

"What?!" Maggie was starting to feel like she needed to expand her vocabulary. "Oh my goodness, did he get hurt?"

"No, but I sure thought so, because he was passed out cold, flat on his back. But then he sneezed." Her chest rose and fell in a wispy sigh. "And I suddenly remembered what you told me about little Wally Wilder. You know—how it's impossible to sneeze while you're asleep or unconscious, so I decided he was pretending." A fresh sheen of saltwater glazed in her eyes. "And all because he didn't want to admit he was attracted to me."

Maggie's look was tender as she squeezed Sheridan's knee. "Sher, nothing would make me happier than knowing that Jake felt about you the way you feel about him. But honey, I don't think his fluster and crabbiness and a certain look in his eyes exactly qualifies as attrac—"

"No, but his kiss sure did," she whispered, her chin rising a hair while a hint of color tinged her cheeks.

"What??!!" Maggie was goggle-eyed by now, pretty sure that repetitive and monosyllabic responses now qualified

her as an idiot. "Jake *kissed* you??"

She gave a little nod, teeth tugging at the edge of a shy smile. "And then some, Maggie, and it was wonderful," she said with a pretty blush, eyes aglow with wonder. "I knew kisses meant lip to lip, but merciful heavens, Jake's involved a *whole* lot more than that."

Maggie blinked, not sure who was blushing more—her or Sheridan. *Sweet cherubs of chastity!* She swallowed hard, Jake kissing Sheridan putting a whole new spin on the wagon wheel. "How on earth did it happen?" she said with a croak.

"Well ..." Sheridan began picking at her nails, avoiding Maggie's gaze. "Like I said, I remembered about sneezing not being possible while someone was unconscious, so I decided to ... um ... test it."

"Test it?" Maggie could only gawk, grateful she was at least up to two-word responses.

A lump ducked in Sheridan's throat as she dislodged a sliver of nail. "I ... uh ... well ... kissed *him*."

Eyes saucer wide, Maggie clamped a hand over her mouth rather than revert to another monosyllable.

Sheridan peeked up. "I know it sounds bad, Maggie, but I needed to find out if he was truly unconscious or"—she gave a little shrug—"just uninterested."

"And ...???" *Oh, goody—she was back to one word.*

"*And* ... he popped up like a Mexican jumping bean, flipping me on my back so fast, I stopped breathing while he straddled me with a glare."

Sweet heavenly hosts! Maggie made a quick sign of the cross, pretty much speechless at this point.

Sheridan's gaze wandered out the window into a distant stare while a sigh gusted from her lips, laden with melancholy. "Told me flat out he wasn't attracted to me that way and I should get those pipedreams out of my head because it was never going to happen."

"Oh, Sher ..." Maggie reached to give her a hug, her heart breaking for this girl who was as dear as a sister.

"So, I lunged for his neck and toppled him over like he did me"—nibbling the edge of her thumbnail, she barely looked up, as if hiding beneath a thick curtain of lashes—"right before I flopped down and kissed the daylights out of him."

Sweet mother of Job! Maggie could only blink, fingers suddenly itching for a rosary.

"I know I shouldn't have done something so brazen," Sheridan said in a rush, "but I had to prove him wrong, Maggie, didn't I?"

"Uh ..."

"And I did, too, because the man turned the tables to kiss me like he was struggling to breathe and I was his only chance for air."

"Sweet mother of mercy—I need to lie down." Near dizzy from the telling, Maggie bumped Sheridan's shoulder for her to move over, lying down flat while she stared saucer-eyed at the ceiling.

"So, you see, Maggie? He *is* attracted to me, but he's just too stupid or too stubborn to admit it."

"My vote would be stubborn," Maggie said with a hand to her chest to steady her breathing, truly caught off-guard that Jake was drawn—*that* way—to the girl he'd always considered a little sister.

"So, what do I do?" Sheridan's voice was a lovesick moan, cramping Maggie's heart. "He told me flat out it could never happen again, then stomped off, saying the shooting lessons were over for good. Even though I told him I love him, and I know he loves me, too. But I want him to love me as a woman, not as a little sister because dog-gone-it, Maggie, I *am* a woman nearly nineteen!"

Maggie slid her a sideways look while a smile tugged at her lips. "Eighteen and a half, sweetheart, but you do have a point." Her smile faded into a squint. "Did you ask him why?"

A rare grunt slipped from Sheridan's lips. "Of course I did, straight to his teeth, but he started babbling on about how he was almost eight years older than me and I was too young to fall in love. When I argued that Aunt Libby's father is almost eleven years older than her mother, and that Blaze is a lot older than you, he refused to hear it. Said I was like a sister to him, and it wasn't right."

"Did you remind him that you're *not* his sister?" Maggie's lips twitched with a smile.

"Repeatedly, pointing out quite emphatically that his kiss agreed with *my* opinion on the subject and not his."

"Whoops." Maggie winked. "Bet he didn't like that."

"Of course not. He was too busy bucking all reasonable rationale like a rabid mule against the side of a barn." She huffed out a noisy sigh while she crossed her arms over her knees. "Until he came up with the lowest, sneakiest excuse yet."

Maggie glanced over, face in a scrunch. "And what was that?"

Sheridan's blue gaze narrowed like a sliver of sky between strands of cirrus clouds. "That he was seeing Megan Joy Burdzy."

"What??" Maggie sat up, face screwed in a frown. "Since when? Because if that were true, it would be common knowledge."

"Claims he hasn't told anybody yet."

"Ha! He wouldn't have to, because Megan Joy would shout it from the top of the flagpole in the town square," Maggie said, knowing full well Megan Joy had been crazy for Jake for a while now. Her head tilted, lips easing into a coy smile. "Unless, of course, it wasn't true, and he was just trying to put you off."

"Exactly." Sheridan plopped back against the headboard with a low groan. "Which only frustrates me all the more because knowing Jake and his aversion to lying, he'll probably march right down to Burdzy's and make all of Megan Joy's dreams come true." Moisture brimmed in her eyes as she clunked her head against the headboard, lashes spiking with tears while her voice trailed off. "Instead of mine ..."

Maggie studied her sister-in-law, eyes soft with sympathy as a seed of an idea germinated in her brain, thinking she probably shouldn't get involved at all. But how could she watch Sher suffer in total misery knowing that Jake might very well follow through with Megan Joy? Exhaling loudly, she threw caution to the wind, coaxing Sheridan's chin up with a mischievous wink. "And then again, sweetheart ... maybe not."

CHAPTER EIGHT

SHERIDAN GLANCED AT MAGGIE WITH a definite flicker of hope in her eyes. "What do you mean?" she whispered.

"Well ..." Maggie adjusted her skirt to sit Indian-style, conspiracy thick in her tone. "I can't guarantee it will work, of course, but it sure did with Blaze ..."

A delighted gasp popped from Sheridan's mouth as her lips curved in a little-girl smile. "Oh, tell me, please!" she begged, voice breathy with anticipation.

"As you know, Blaze and I were good friends first—"

"Yes, I know"—Sheridan's smile dimmed—"like Jake and I used to be before I grew up."

"And will be again if my plan works, sweetie, so take heart."

Sheridan's lips took a slant. "Believe me, I'm trying to 'take heart,' Maggie—Jake's!"

Maggie grinned. "Well, then, this may help. I don't think anyone knew this at the time, but both Blaze and I struggled with our attraction to each other from the very beginning. But your brother made it abundantly clear he was *not* interested in a romantic relationship with a 'so-called good girl,' who would just 'harp on him about God and church the rest of his days.'"

Sheridan smiled, her eyes aglow with gratitude. "I know, and we are all forever indebted to you, Maggie."

"You're welcome, but I owe a great debt to all of you as well for becoming the close-knit family I never had. Anyway," she said with a quick brush of moisture from her eyes, "Blaze and I agreed to be no more than good friends"—she wiggled her brows—"*until* you bamboozled me into going to the annual rodeo dance with Clint Keller, which lit a fire under Blaze when Clint made a pass."

Sheridan giggled. "You're welcome."

Maggie grinned. "Well, *that* was the night Blaze's jealousy turned our relationship on its ear, coercing him into courting me good and proper."

A wispy sigh floated from Sheridan's lips as her gaze lapsed into a lovesick stare. "Ah, yes, I remember how romantic it was when you first told us." Her gaze flicked back to Maggie with a scrunch of her nose. "Until my mule of a brother had to go and ruin it."

Maggie's nose immediately wrinkled as well, that rough patch in her and Blaze's relationship not a happy memory. "Yes, well, the point I'm trying to make is, maybe if you suddenly focused on someone else other than Jake—"

"Ha! Don't you think I've tried over the last two years? But between Uncle Finn, my brothers, and Jake, I've never been able to be *alone* with another fellow to even get to know them, much less make Jake jealous." Her head flopped back down on her knees, face sagging. "And most of the boys at church and in town avoid me like the plague because of it, and the cowhands?" She grunted. "They steer clear like I have hoof and mouth disease, *probably* because Uncle Finn threatened them with their lives."

"Mmm ... that *is* a problem." Elbow propped on her leg, Maggie gave it some thought, wishing there could be more of a balance in Sheridan's life. Somewhere between being constantly thrown at suitors for profitable marital alliances like her stepfather had done to Maggie, and being locked away in a tower like Rapunzel by brothers and an uncle who just wanted to protect.

And there was no talking to Blaze, Dash, or Finn about giving Sheridan more freedom because Maggie had already done that a number of times at Sheridan's request, all to no avail. The McShane and Donovan men were a stubborn lot, she'd quickly learned, especially when it came to family.

But at least Sheridan would have more freedom when she left for Vassar in September, Maggie mused, although she knew that even there, her uncle and brothers had their means of keeping tabs on her, unbeknownst to Sheridan.

Despite Finn's reluctance to send Sheridan so far away to college, Libby had been relentless in convincing him to send their niece to her alma mater. Not only had she promised careful supervision by Libby's Aunt Marie and butler, but via her former teacher friends at Vassar as well, where Libby had taught for over seventeen years.

She'd even talked Finn and Blaze into allowing Libby and Maggie to accompany Sheridan to New York to get her settled in at Libby's Aunt Marie's home for the first week. But Maggie knew Finn also had his own eyes and ears in New York to keep watch over his niece because Blaze had told her so. From the Dean of Vassar, to an old friend from Finn's days at Central Pacific Railroad, Maggie had no doubt Sheridan's uncle had his means of keeping her on a short rein.

Maggie peeked up at her sister-in-law, whose usual sunny smile was nowhere to be found. She wrestled back and forth, wondering if tight supervision—and more time to grow up— wouldn't be the best thing for Sheridan after all, a sweet young woman yearning to experience love to the full, especially given her sheltered upbringing. At almost nineteen—Maggie smiled—or eighteen and a half—her sister-in-law was bursting with hunger and passion for life, not the safest of mindsets when coupled with a flirty innocence and naivete.

From little on, Sheridan had always been overtly affectionate according to Blaze, which was fine, he said, when she was a little girl with whom they could indulge in tickle fests or sit on their laps and smother them with kisses. But when she started blossoming into a woman, it put all the men in the family on guard, afraid her flirtatious nature—no matter how innocent—would get her in trouble where men were concerned.

Maggie sighed, her glum mood suddenly in tandem with Sheridan's. "I don't know, sweetheart—maybe waiting till you're a little older is the best path to take after all, like your Uncle Finn wants you to do. You'll be almost twenty-one by the time you graduate with your teaching degree, which is certainly old enough to finally catch Jake's eye if he's the one for you." She gave Sheridan's leg a gentle pat. "What do you say we pray about it, Sher?"

Sheridan groaned, butting her head back against the headboard with a look of anguish. "That's just it, Maggie, I *have* prayed about it—over and over—my entire life because Uncle Finn has always drilled it into our heads that prayer should be the first thing we do, not the last. Which I've always done, especially over the last two years, and I truly believe in my heart Jake is the one God has for me."

Maggie's smile was tender. "Then, if that's true, sweetheart, Jake will still be here when you graduate, hopefully ready to fall in love with you as the woman God has had for him all along."

"Not if he falls in love with Megan Joy Burdzy or some other woman first! Don't you see, Maggie?"—her eyes pleaded with Maggie to understand—"I *have* to follow my heart!"

"And I couldn't agree more," Maggie said softly, giving Sheridan's hand a gentle squeeze. "We *do* have to follow our hearts, sweetheart …always!" She paused, gaze potent as it locked on her sister-in-law's. "*As long* as our hearts are aligned with God's, Sheridan. Because therein is the safest place to be …"

A sudden sheen glimmered in Sheridan's eyes before she looked away, chin quivering. "I know, Maggie, and that's what I want, too, truly. But I can't go to New York without knowing if this attraction between Jake and me could grow into something more." She offered a wobbly smile. "You already know how much I don't want to leave home—you, my family, Jake—to go away to college. But it will be all the more unbearable knowing I could lose him while I'm gone, Maggie, and I can't risk that."

She reached to squeeze Maggie's hand in return. "I only have three months left to make Jake fall in love with me or even just admit that he could and would be willing to wait. Honestly, Maggie, if that happened, I could wait the entire two years without a peep, perfectly content to get that teaching degree that Uncle Finn so wants me to have."

Maggie smiled. "Deep down, you want that degree too, Sheridan Donovan, so don't try and deny it."

"Yes … yes, I do," she said with a dip of her head, nodding her frail assent, "but *only* if I knew that Jake would be waiting for me when I got back because even deeper down, Maggie, I want *him*."

Maggie's bodice expanded with a heavy sigh, the idea of Sheridan getting hurt over Jake instilling a dull pain in her heart. Skimming her sister-in-law's face with a light caress, she fairly ached over that very prospect, which given Jake's response so far, seemed inevitable. "You know, Sheridan," she said softly, "you can't force a man's heart."

The seeds of a smile sprouted on Sheridan's lips. "Why not?" She pressed her palm over Maggie's hand, which now cradled Sheridan's jaw, her voice husky with tease. "You did, Maggie."

Maggie blinked several times, realizing that Sheridan was right. *Why not, indeed?* After all, hadn't Maggie forced Blaze's heart before they'd gotten engaged? All the time they'd been courting, he'd kept pushing her further and further for romantic favors while all the while pushing the prospect of marriage further and further away. It hadn't been till she forced his heart—and his hand—by ending the courtship that Blaze not only eventually proposed, but discovered his newfound faith in God.

A mischievous gleam replaced the sheen of tears in Sheridan's eyes. "So, if *you* could force Blaze's heart to both turn to God *and* propose, why can't *I* force Jake's heart to admit he loves me?"

Maggie scrunched her nose. "I don't know, Sher—maybe 'force' isn't the right word ..."

"Then, how about 'enlighten'?" Sheridan said with a bright smile. "After all, that's what God does for us when we ask Him for wisdom, right? So, actually, it's almost spiritual!"

Maggie chuckled as she pinched Sheridan's knee. "I suppose that depends on your methods, Miss Donovan." She arched a brow. "For instance, I doubt the Almighty would look favorably on plopping on top of Jake to kiss him senseless!" Heat scorched Maggie's cheeks the moment the words were out of her mouth, matching no doubt, the pretty shade of pink creeping up Sheridan's face. She slapped a hand to her lips. "Sweet mother of mercy—I can't believe I said that!"

"Me, either," Sheridan said with a quick fan of her hand, giggles bubbling forth. "Because now I'll be thinking about it!"

"Me, too, with Blaze." Maggie delivered a smug smile. "Only *I* get to do something about it."

Responding with a playful tease, Sheridan stuck out her tongue. "Rub it in, Mrs. Donovan, why don't you? But don't forget—someday I'll be able to do something about it too."

Maggie stayed her with a tender touch of her arm, sympathy soft in her tone. "Only if Jake's the right one for you sweetheart, which he may not be, so if I'm going to help you, you have to promise me one thing."

The smile faded on Sheridan's face, her voice as fragile as Maggie's. "What's that, Maggie?"

A quiet sigh parted from Maggie's lips, languishing in the air as she took Sheridan's hand in her own. "It may not happen this summer, Sher, despite all of our efforts, if it's not God's timing and Jake refuses to comply. And if that's the case"—she paused to give her sister-in-law's hand a gentle squeeze—"I need you to promise you'll let it go for the rest of this year until Christmas at least, and try to enjoy your new life at school with all the new people you're going to meet."

Sheridan bowed her head as if Maggie's words had just sucked the wind out of her hope. Maggie ducked to peek up with a shadow of a smile skimming her lips. "Many of whom, I might add," she said with a touch of tease, "will be very eligible and very attractive young men smitten by a certain Virginia City girl, I promise." She reached to cradle a hand to Sheridan's jaw, praying her sister-in-law would find God's choice for her instead of her own. "So, promise me, Sheridan, that if this summer doesn't go the way you hope, you'll lay it aside for the rest of this year to enjoy your time away at school. *And* to pray for God's perfect timing *and* beau, all right?"

Sheridan's shoulders rose and fell with a heavy sigh as she cupped her hand over Maggie's, a semblance of a smile flickering at the corners of her mouth. "All right, Maggie, you have my word. If nothing happens with Jake this summer, I promise to try my best to let it go and enjoy school." A hint of mischief twinkled in her eyes. "Until Christmas."

"And …?" Maggie arched a brow.

Teasing with an exaggerated sigh, Sheridan rolled her eyes. "And I promise to pray for God's perfect timing *and* beau, all right?" Folding her hands in prayer in a dramatic pose, she cast a hopeful gaze toward the ceiling. "But if it's all the same to you, God"—she paused to give Maggie a sassy wink—"could you please make sure it's Jake?"

CHAPTER NINE

"*WHAT??!!*" BLAZE SPUN AROUND, A branding iron dangling in his left hand as he gaped at Jake while they finished up the last few cows on the south 40. He stepped in close, shoulders as stiff as his jaw while his eyes fired up, hotter than the red-hot poker in his hand. *Which* he now held out like a threat. "So, help me, Sullivan, if you kissed her …"

Jake took a healthy step back, heat singeing the tips of his ears, a condition he wished he could blame on the hot Nevada sun after a full day of branding cattle. "Keep your voice down, Donovan," he hissed, casting a nervous glance around to make sure the rest of the hands had moved on to the next pasture. As much as Jake hadn't wanted to tell Blaze what happened between him and Sheridan, he knew he had to—for his sake as well as hers.

Heaven knows Blaze hadn't taken any of the hints Jake had tossed around today about turning Sheridan's shooting lessons over to somebody else, bucking him at every turn with one excuse or another. So, being a stickler for honesty, in the end, Jake figured the truth—or at least some of it— would be the best deterrent to keep Sheridan at a distance.

Wasn't truth always the best option? Jake swallowed hard. Yeah, *except* with Sheridan.

But partial truth or not, that didn't mean Blaze wouldn't chew him up and spit him out when he found out.

"Then what the devil did you mean by, 'things got pretty heated in more ways than one'?" Blaze shouted, waving that dad-gum poker like he wanted to brand Jake instead of the silly cow. "Did you kiss her or not?"

Jake's Adam's apple ducked while he searched for the right response. The *one* that would keep a Bar SLR brand off his butt.

"So, help me, Sullivan—spit it out," Blaze snapped with another wave of the firebrand. "Did you or didn't you?"

Well, technically, she kissed me first ... His nose twitched, as if getting ready to grow, warring with the truth in his mind because it *had* been her kiss that started it all, right? He cleared his throat. "Uh, I'd say it was the other way around, old buddy," Jake said with as much confidence as he could muster given the branding iron in Blaze's hand, completely sidestepping his involvement in the kiss—and the temptation to lie—altogether. He sucked in a fortifying breath, releasing it again in a slow, steady stream while he perched hands to his hips. "Which is why you need to find somebody else to teach her to shoot."

"Hot hogs in Hades, how the devil did this happen?" Blaze stormed over to the fire pit and hurled the brand back in, flames licking the steel like fire licked the inside of Jake's collar.

Jake casually scratched the back of his neck, nothing casual about the vice banding his chest. "Well, first she showed up in this ... this"—he waved a hand in front of his shoulder and chest—"downright obscene get-up, some Mexican-looking blouse hanging clear off her shoulders and pretty darn low at the neckline to boot."

A rare curse shot from Blaze's mouth as he started to pace, gouging shaky fingers through his hair.

"I don't mind sayin' I was pretty hot under the collar when I saw that," Jake said, "but she claimed it was for 'ease of movement.'"

"Yeah, I'll just bet." Blaze kicked at a clump of dirt.

"That's exactly what I said, and I wasn't a bit nice about it either, I can tell you that. Sniped at her left and right until she turned on the tears, and then all I wanted to do was get through that dad-burned lesson as quick as possible, hoping and praying you'd show up soon."

Blaze sent a rock flying with his boot, mumbling what sounded like an apology under his breath.

"I tried to show her stance and aim by demonstrating with my own gun, but I'll tell you, Blaze, she was downright awful, and the last thing I wanted to do was get close enough to show her how. But I felt so bad after jerking the gun away, nicking her finger in the process, that I went ahead and positioned her, arms around her to show her how."

Blaze halted mid-pace, thunderous brows digging low. "Is that when she kissed you?"

Jake shook his head, fighting back a warm shiver at the memory. "No, but when she turned to smile at me over that bare shoulder of hers, I swear our lips were so close, I panicked when I saw that lovesick look in her eyes. You know, the one she always gets when I come around?"

Blaze resumed pacing. "Yeah, I know," he mumbled. "So, what happened next?"

"I fell real hard"—Jake dipped his head, leveling a smirk in a sad attempt at humor—"*not* over your sister, mind you— but over a small boulder I used as a marker, landing me flat on my backside."

Blaze obviously didn't see the humor given the nasty scowl on his face.

Jake cleared his throat. "The next thing I know, she's flopped over my chest, wailing up a storm because she thought I was dead, and don't think I didn't wish I was for a moment or two."

Blaze spun to face him, sparks popping from the fire that matched the ones in his eyes. "Was that when she kissed you?"

"Well, yeah, sort of, but—"

"Sort of?" A swear word sizzled the air along with an explosion of sparks when Blaze kicked a rock in the fire. "Tarnation, Sul, why the devil didn't you just push her away?"

"I did!" Jake defended staunchly, the sunburn bleeding up

his neck not helping one iota. It was his turn to kick a rock, sailing it into the side of a cow chewing its cud, its hide a whole lot tougher than Jake's at the moment. The cow tossed a lazy glance his way before lumbering off. Kinda like Jake wanted to do. Actually jealous of the stupid cow, Jake cuffed the back of his neck. "Sort of."

"Sort-of?" Blaze said it dangerously slow, kind of like his approach before he confronted Jake nose to nose. *"Sort of?? What the devil does that mean?"* His voice ratcheted up several octaves as the words spit in Jake's face. *Literally.*

"It means I played possum, dad-burn-it," he spit right back, wondering why in tarnation *he* was getting raked over the coals when this was all Blaze's fault in the first place. The very thought triggered his temper, prompting him to jab a hard finger into Blaze's chest. "Because the last thing I wanted to do, you pea-brained brick-head, was give your sister another blasted chance to taunt me with goo-goo eyes and bare shoulders. I wanted the lesson over! Done! Finito! You got that, Donovan? And yelling sure didn't work 'cause that just turned on the waterworks, making me feel like cow dirt, especially after I hurt her blasted finger." He delivered a final stab for good measure. "So, forgive me if I erred in thinking being unconscious was the quickest way to end the dad-gum debacle that *you* foisted on me in the first place."

Blaze hurled Jake's finger away, his tone considerably calmer. "Go on ..." he muttered, obviously chastened by his best friend's acute frustration, giving rise to a temper he seldom saw.

"And it worked, dad-burn-it, drenching me with tears while she promised to go for help." Jake mauled his face with his hands. "Until I sneezed." Huffing out a weary breath, he dropped his hands to his sides before slowly burying them in his pockets. "She must have figured out I was pulling the wool over her eyes because the next thing I know"—he gulped, not really wanting to divulge the extent of Sheridan's kiss, but figuring her brother had a right to know his little sister was in way over her head. *And his!*—"she kissed me like she pilfered a tip sheet from the Ponderosa."

Ooomph! Blaze's punch caught him off-guard, even using his weaker left hand. Jake stumbled back, rubbing the side of his jaw while his best friend brandished a finger in his face, grinding out his words. "Do *not* ever mention my sister in the same sentence with the Ponderosa—do-you-understand?"

Jake nodded, expelling a noisy sigh. "I didn't want to, Blaze—God's truth—but the kiss your little sister gave me about curled my toes, so somebody's giving her tips because she said she's never been kissed before, which frankly, I found pretty hard to believe."

Blaze's eyes narrowed to slits of blue glass, his tone deadly slow. "Are you saying … you *liked* it?"

The air in Jake's lungs stilled along with his body, his brain straining to figure out which answer he should give. A 'yes' would convince Blaze he was the wrong man for the job of watching over his sister, which is exactly what Jake wanted. But a 'no' would shackle him forever as a guardian to a woman who curled his toes, not to mention being a bald-faced lie, which Jake didn't cotton to.

So, he opted for the safest response, if not the most honest—sidestepping as usual with an insulted clench of fists and stage-perfect drop of his jaw. "For all that's good and decent, Donovan," he shouted, sweat trickling down the back of his neck, "Sheridan is like a sister to me, so how in the devil can you ask that?"

Some of the heat faded from Blaze's eyes as he tunneled unsteady fingers through his hair. "Sorry, Jake. Stupid question. You're the only man alive we trust around Sheridan, so the very thought just curdled my stomach, that's all.

Tell me about it. "I know, me too, but I love her like a sister just like you and Dash, so I'd be lying if I didn't say I was worried because she's too blasted young and innocent to be acting like that. And since I'm the one she's been hankering for since the age of four, that makes *me* the one she's most vulnerable around."

He hesitated, sinking his hands back in his pockets as he pierced his best friend with a pleading gaze. "So, I hope you understand … that I should definitely keep my distance, right? Which also means I shouldn't be the one to teach her to shoot."

A gust of noisy air blasted from Blaze's lips, his scowl confirmation that this was not welcome news. "Yeah, I understand, but I'm not sure Uncle Finn will."

"If he asks, just tell him I tried, but we were like two stallions in a stall, bucking left and right, and you and I agreed it would be best for you to teach her."

Face in a scrunch, Blaze rubbed his forehead with the cast. "All right, but he's not going to like it, I can tell you that. He wants Sher trained and trained well, not only on that derringer, but on a rifle and pistol too, and doc said six to eight weeks for this blasted cast to come off. Which doesn't leave me much time before she leaves for New York, not to mention Sher's as antsy as a nest of fire ants at a picnic, just chomping to learn how to shoot."

Jake's chest expanded and contracted in a truly grateful sigh. "Thank you. And needless to say, I'm asking you not to divulge any details from this … this incident … to another living soul for Sheridan's sake as well as mine. Not Finn, not Dash, and definitely not Maggie." He paused. "Can I have your word on that?"

Blaze peered up with a troubled gaze. "Yes, you have my word. But you'll still keep an eye on Sheridan from afar, right?"

A silent breath of relief quietly filtered through Jake's lips. "You bet—always, my friend." He slapped Blaze on the back, the knots in his stomach slowly unraveling as their friendship finally returned to solid ground. "After all, she's my little sister too." He swallowed a gulp.

Whether she—or I—like it or not.

CHAPTER TEN

"**M**ERCIFUL HEAVENS, HOW I LOVE Buffalo Bill's Wild West show!" Near breathless, Sheridan waited alongside Maggie for the opening parade with a palm pressed to her heart. She swore her pulse was galloping faster than the graceful horses would be during the show, soon to start in this massive dirt arena surrounded by tent canopies for the audience on the outskirts of town.

From historical reenactments, displays of showmanship, sharp-shooting, hunts, racing, and rodeo style events, Buffalo Bill's Wild West show guaranteed three hours of sheer fun and entertainment for thousands of people all over the U.S. And *today*—goosebumps instantly pebbled Sheridan's skin, body buzzing from the thrill of it all—*she* and her family were among the truly fortunate people to attend the very first show in Virginia City!

Growing up on the Silver Lining Ranch with an uncle, two brothers, a tomboy sister, and too many rugged cowboys to count, Sheridan's stomach fairly skittered with anticipation over the rodeo events to come. Bronc busting, bull riding, bareback riding, and barrel racing—it didn't matter as long as it involved riding hard and fast, two things she dearly loved.

She expelled a wishful sigh. Even though her Uncle Finn never allowed her or her fourteen-year-old sister Shaylee to get even close to doing any of those things, Sheridan always pretended she could whenever she rode her mare, Honey, because thrilling rides were one of the things she loved most in the world.

A smile tipped her lips. *After Jake, of course.*

Hands clasped to her mouth, she chewed on a thumbnail,

hardly able to wait for the show to begin. She slid Maggie a sideways grin. "Sweet heavenly days, I swear I haven't been this excited since Uncle Finn bought me my derringer for Christmas last year!"

"Oh, sure you have," Maggie said with a lazy grin. She bumped Sheridan's shoulder with her own as she snuck a peek past Finn and Libby chatting with Libby's parents in the middle of the first row reserved for the mayor and guests. Both her and Sheridan's gazes homed in on Jake, who—of course!—hunkered down in the very last seat at the very end of the row, laughing with Blaze and several other cowhands loitering in the aisle.

As far away as he could possibly get, Sheridan noted with a dull ache, face flaming at Maggie's insinuation. Jake hadn't spoken to her—not once—since the kiss disaster two weeks ago, and watching him laugh with their cook Angus and then Gert, the cook for Aunt Libby's parents, only caused her smile to wither along with her good mood.

"Hey ... I was just teasing," Maggie said softly, looking over to make sure Blaze was still jawing with Jake and the other cowhands. "I didn't mean to wipe the smile off your face, Sher." She slipped an arm to Sheridan's waist to give her a squeeze. "Look at it this way, honey. Jake is going to an awful lot of trouble to avoid you, so you must have affected him as much as he did you, right?" She tossed a quick glance several rows back to where Megan Joy Burdzy sat with her family, gaze glued to the back of Jake's head. "And he didn't ask Megan Joy to come to the show with him, so that's a good sign too, yes?"

"*Yet,*" Sheridan said with a mournful sigh. "I told you he hates me. He hasn't come within twenty feet of me since then. All of a sudden he's taking all his meals in the chow hall instead of eating supper with us like usual, claiming he's got so many new cowhands to train, he needs all the time with them he can get." Moisture burned at the back of her lids as she offered Maggie a pitiful look. "He's never done that before, Maggie, and you know it."

"Aw, honey." Maggie massaged Sheridan's back with a tender smile, the consummate big sister Sheridan had always wanted. At five years older than Sheridan, Maggie was young enough to understand the heartbreak she felt inside, but old enough to keep her from making a complete fool of herself crying and mooning over Jake. "Give it time, Sher. Once he sees you chatting and flirting with other boys like we talked about you doing, he'll start to wake up."

Sheridan laid her head on Maggie's shoulder, her lower lip jutting into a pout. "But that's just it, Maggie—I don't *have* time on my side. I leave for college in two and a half months, and between Jake and Dash hovering like thunderclouds everywhere I go, I don't have a lot of chances to chat and flirt with other boys. If anything, my brothers seem to be more protective than ever." She slid a narrow gaze Jake's way, biting hard on her lower lip. "Almost as if he told them what happened even though he said he wouldn't."

Maggie bent forward to meet Sheridan's gaze. "But I *saw* you with Owen Miller before church on Sunday, talking and laughing up a storm, Sher, and he seemed quite taken with you, so maybe—"

"'*Before church*' being the operative phrase." Sheridan sent Blaze a scowl while he still hob-nobbed with the men. "Blaze showed up and shooed me inside just as Owen asked if he could call on me, promising to wait for me after the service so we could set a date. But when I looked for him after church, he was nowhere to be found, so I suspect Blaze threatened him like he usually does with any boy that glances my way."

"*What?* Well, that's just not right." Maggie joined Sheridan in scowling at her husband. "I knew your brothers were protective, but I had no idea they threatened boys to stay away."

Sheridan gave a limp nod, gaze lapsing into a melancholy stare. "Ever since I turned sixteen. I actually thought I was ugly until I overheard two of the hands talking about how pretty I was. They'd said what a shame it was they couldn't even risk looking my way or the Boss'd fire 'em."

Maggie's eyes spanned wide. "I knew your Uncle Finn has been feeling downright nervous with you going away to college, but I had no idea he was involved in threatening boys to stay away too!"

Sheridan's shoulders rose and fell in a quiet breath of surrender. "Are you kidding? He's as bad as Blaze and Dash, so I wouldn't be surprised if it was his idea in the first place. When it comes to me and boys, they're like the Three Musketeers, pledged to ruin my life. 'One for all, and all for one,' only *I'm* the 'one' on the outside, hindered at every turn." She sent another lingering glance Jake's way. "The only male they let come around is Jake, and now I can't even be around him."

Maggie gently tucked a stray curl behind Sheridan's ear. "Well, I suppose you could look at it like they love you enough to protect you, but it still isn't right, robbing you of the freedom to be a normal young woman."

"I think their plan is to love me right into a convent, which is a real shame," Sheridan muttered sadly, a shiver tiptoeing down her spine over the awful black habits Sister Frederica and the rest of the nuns wore at St. Mary Louise Hospital. She offered Maggie a woe-begone look. "I look awful in black."

Maggie bumped her shoulder again. "You are *not* going to be a nun, young lady, so get that idea out of your head right now. Not only are you too pretty to dress in black day in and day out, but frankly, you've never struck me as the overly religious type." Maggie's brows tipped in apology. "I hope that doesn't offend you."

"No, it's true." Sheridan expelled a weary sigh. "Uncle Finn has preached and preached to us as long as I can remember"— she paused, eyes in a squint—"or maybe it was just to Shaylee and me since we were the girls in the family—but at any rate, I may have never bucked him because deep down I always wanted to be 'the good niece.' But, I'm ashamed to admit, I really didn't like hearing him talk about God."

She wrinkled her nose. "Maybe because I remember my mama yelling and nagging at my daddy all the time, in between reading her Bible. Which made the whole God thing not set real well with me, I guess. I suppose that's why I've steered clear of the Bible over the years." Her shoulders lifted in an awkward shrug. "Which is probably why my faith isn't as strong as it should be, you know?"

"Yes, I know." Maggie's smile skewed off-center. "How *well* I know because my stepfather was an associate judge on the New York Court of Appeals, so he was considered a pillar of both the community *and* the church. Problem is"— Maggie's smile went flat—"inside he was full of dead men's bones."

Sheridan blinked, brows in a scrunch. "Huh?"

"It's something from the Bible that Jesus said in Matthew 23:17—'Woe to you, scribes and Pharisees, hypocrites, for ye are like whited sepulchers, which appear beautiful outwardly, but within are full of dead men's bones and all uncleanness.' Which means," Maggie said, understanding warm in her eyes, "not everyone who professes a belief in God acts like it, Sher, so you can't blame God or the Bible for that. I learned that from my mother, who was one of the finest human beings I've ever known and a true woman of God."

A sheen of moisture glimmered in Maggie's eyes as her gaze trailed into a melancholy stare. "If it wasn't for her example, I would have never known that God is a loving Father who only wants to bless us with good." She refocused on Sheridan with a misty smile that reminded Sher of just how lucky they were to have Maggie in their family. "And if it wasn't for God, I wouldn't know all the peace and joy I've experienced since I came to Virginia City. So you see, Sheridan, I owe my mother—and God—my life in so many more ways than one."

She gave a nod over her shoulder to where Blaze was still

gabbing. "Beginning with that big, overprotective lug of a brother of yours"—she turned to give Sheridan a hug—"all the way down to the dearest, sweetest sister I ever imagined I could have."

"Oh, Maggie!" With a matching glaze of tears, Sheridan squeezed her sister-in-law with all her might. "Then I owe your mother and God, too, because you have brought me so much happiness—not only to my brother, but to me and my family as well."

"And *that*, my dear sister-in-law," Maggie said with a weepy giggle, "is the ripple effect of faith." She pulled back to cradle Sheridan's face with the palm of her hand, eyes tender. "Loving God helps us to love others, and loving others helps us to love God. Because when we see the changes for good He brings into people's lives through us—through our love, our prayers, our faith—it fills our hearts with so much joy, so much peace, that we love Him all the more."

Something fluttered in Sheridan's heart at the sound of Maggie's words, and she decided right then and there that she wanted what Maggie had too. "Oh, Maggie, I have so much to learn from you and so little time!"

"Everything you need to know, Sher, is in that Bible I saw on the shelf in your closet, sweetheart." Smile slanting toward dry, she nipped at Sheridan's waist with her fingers as she angled a brow. "You know, the one covered with a layer of dust?"

Sheridan chewed on the edge of her smile while a blush warmed her cheeks. "Uncle Finn gave that to me on my tenth birthday, and I'm ashamed to say I haven't opened it since, but I will now, I promise."

"Good girl." Maggie swallowed her in another fond embrace. "Because as human beings, professed Christians don't always live up to the ideals of Jesus because we are fallible"—a twinkle lit in her eyes—"but the Word of God is *not*. So, if you want to truly know how to be a Christian, it's best to learn at the feet of the Master through *His* Word, not actions of professed Christians, which don't always line up with the Bible."

She gave Sheridan's hand a gentle squeeze. "All I know, Sher, is that based on that very Bible, God loves you more than you can ever imagine and desperately wants to give you good things."

A smile tugged at Sheridan's lips as she snuck a look Jake's way. "I'll tell you what, Maggie—if one of those 'good things' is that bull-headed cowboy sitting at the end of our row—that sure would go a long way in shoring up my faith."

Maggie patted Sheridan's arm with a firm jut of her chin. "Then, we'll just have to pray about it—*again*. Not only that God provides the perfect young man to put a burr in Jake's saddle, but this time we'll pray that if Jake is the one God has in store for you, it will happen before you go off to college, all right?"

"Ooooo, I like the sound of that," Sheridan said, rubbing her hands together.

"But if it doesn't"—Maggie paused with a pointed look, fingers gently caressing Sheridan's arm—"you'll go off to school with your head and hopes high, knowing that God is in control of your future, and all you have to do is seek Him through his Word and pray." Maggie delivered a sassy wink. "Then just open your ears and listen."

"O … kay." Sheridan gulped, some of her euphoria leaking out. *No Jake?*

Maggie homed in with a duck of her head, her gentle gaze piercing Sheridan's heart clear through. "Because whether your future is with Jake, someone else, or with some other wonderful plan God has in store, you need to know one thing for dead sure, Sheridan Marie."

"What?" Sheridan said in a wide-eyed whisper, barely breathing lest she miss what Maggie would say.

Her sister-in-law drew back with a look of supreme confidence, her rock-solid assurance evident in the firm heft of her chin, which slowly softened into a truly affectionate smile. She wiggled her brows. "You're in for one heck of a ride."

CHAPTER ELEVEN

*P*OW! POW! POW!
Jake's gaze quickly shifted from Blaze onto the field, where an old coot of a villain with a handlebar moustache and dressed in black was shooting up a storm while he ran after a clown in stilts. Laughter echoed throughout the tents around the arena in what Jake suspected was a warm-up act, a sure sign the show would be starting soon.

"Won't be long now," Blaze said with an evil grin, nudging Jake's leg with his boot, "till we see what real marksmanship is, eh fellas?"

The group of cowhands laughed, each and every one aware that their foreman was ribbing his assistant foreman who always beat him and every other cowboy in the Nevada state shooting competition year after year.

"And real bronc busting, too, eh Boss?" More chuckles rose over Clint Keller's jibe, the cowhand who'd beaten Blaze in last year's statewide rodeo bronc-busting contest, seldom letting anyone forget he'd been the one to end Blaze's winning streak.

"Excuse us."

Jake glanced over his shoulder to where Maggie and Sheridan waited for Angus and Gert and him to rise from their seats so they could pass.

"Where you ladies going?" Blaze said with a furrow above his nose. "The show's about to start any minute."

Maggie arched a brow. "*Not* that it's any of your business, *husband*," she said with a teasing smirk, drawing laughter and catcalls from the cowhands, "but Sheridan and I need to use the necessary before the show starts."

Jake rose to let the ladies scoot by, heat sparking through every limb when Sheridan's calicoed derriere brushed past his body.

"Sorry, Jake," she said in a husky whisper that joined forces with the confounded spark that scorched through his body, upping his blood pressure by several degrees. His lips compressed in a tight smile.

Not as sorry as I am.

Blaze groaned. "For crying out loud, Maggie—why didn't you ladies attend to that earlier, instead of waiting until the show is ready to start?"

Sheridan lifted on tiptoe to pinch Blaze's cheek as she passed by. "Goodness, big brother, you should know better than anybody that Maggie is brilliant, opting to avoid long lines by skipping out now, when everybody else is rushing back to their seats."

Shoving his Stetson up, Blaze cut loose with another groan. "Dad-burn-it, Maggie, now I'll have to escort you—"

Maggie spun around, a sharp brow jagging high. "I beg your pardon, *Brendan Zachary*." Amused jeers and chuckles rose among the cowhands as they shuffled back to their seats, Maggie's schoolmarm use of Blaze's given name a gentle mix of both threat and reprimand. "But I assure you, *husband*, that your eighteen-year-old sister and I are perfectly capable of escorting ourselves to and from the necessary. So, I suggest you head back to your seat, darling, before the show begins." She reached up to brush a conciliatory kiss to his lips. "We'll be right back."

Lips pursed, Blaze shifted his gaze to Sheridan and back, settling into a mulish press as he issued a warning with a stern point of his finger. "So help me, Maggie Donovan, if you aren't back in ten minutes, I'm sending in the cavalry."

"Yes, sir," she said with a snappy salute, tucking her arm through Sheridan's to lead her away as she blew him a kiss over her shoulder.

Blaze gusted out a noisy sigh. "Women!" he muttered as he

watched them navigate the incoming crowd like two trouts on a leisurely paddle upstream. His smile took a hard slant as he looked down at Jake. "Remind me again, old buddy, just why I'm married and you're not?"

Jake slid him an easy grin. "Because I'm smart and you're not?" he quipped, not believing it for one solitary moment because Maggie was a true blessing in Blaze's life, and everyone knew it. He rose to allow Blaze to pass on his way back to his seat, slapping his best friend on the back. "And because you couldn't help but fall in love with one of the most amazing women either of us have ever seen?"

A sheepish grin glided Blaze's lips as he gave Jake a wicked wink. "Yesirree. And the perks aren't bad either, if you know what I mean."

Unfortunately, Jake thought with a grim smile, refusing to dignify Blaze's taunt with a comment. He had enough trouble keeping his mind off the perks of loving a woman.

None of which he had a right to, deep feelings for Sheridan or no. He grunted. *Yeah, tell that to my dreams ...*

Applause delivered him from his wayward thoughts as the sold-out audience shot to their feet to cheer the start of the parade.

Ten minutes later, a spitball bounced off Jake's nose, and he didn't have to guess who shot it. He knew Blaze had been timing the girls' absence as closely as Jake, so jaw tight, he turned to acknowledge his friend's signal. Blaze motioned toward the back of the tent.

Affording his best friend a curt nod, Jake rose to head toward the row of outhouses lining the far end of the field. With a tug of his Stetson to shield his eyes, he made his way to the tree line, where a scattering of folks milled about in front of skillfully constructed privies the show obviously put up and tore down in each city. He scanned to find the girls, and when he saw them making their way back to the arena, his pulse picked up pace along with his gait.

Who the devil are they talking to anyway? Barely stopping, he kicked at a cactus in his way, sights set on a tall, fancy-dressed cowboy talking to Maggie and Sher, aiming to send him on his way. Fingers trigger twitchy, he squinted hard, wondering who in the Sam Hill this unwelcome intruder was. He offered a tight smile and a nod to the butcher and his wife in passing, obviously on their way back from the latrine.

He frowned when he heard Sheridan's laughter, peeved that Maggie and she appeared to be smiling up at the dandy like he was Buffalo Bill himself. Only this stranger was cleanshaven and well-dressed, leather booths shined up so bloomin' well, they practically gleamed along with the gold studs on his hat, glinting in the sun. Well, whoever this snake of a rustler was, Jake intended to make darn sure he moved on to rustle somebody else's girls, because these two ladies were spoken for.

One by his best friend in marriage.

His scowl deepened. And the other by a man in his dreams.

CHAPTER TWELVE

"**S**O, YOU REALLY AND TRULY work for Buffalo Bill?" Sheridan asked, certain she had stars in her eyes as she peeked up at the handsome cowboy, hand shielding her face to block out the glare while she silently swooned. Without question, Mr. Clay Morgan was one of the most exciting men she'd ever met, and the fact he was a sharpshooter trainer for Buffalo Bill was just diamond-studded silver spurs on full-grain leather boots.

"Yes, ma'am, I do," he said with a tip of his black Stetson with gold studs on the band, the twinkle in brown eyes the color of melted milk chocolate—her favorite!—pert near melting *her*.

"If you don't mind my asking, Mr. Morgan," Maggie said evenly, head tilted in curiosity, "if you work for Buffalo Bill, then why are you out here instead of performing in the arena?"

"I don't mind you asking at all, Miss—?"

"Donovan. *Mrs.* Donovan." Maggie's smile was patiently calm, unlike Sheridan's which was impatiently giddy as Mr. Morgan extended a courteous smile, his perfectly white teeth a striking complement to ebony hair and a well-chiseled jaw.

"Well, you see, Mrs. Donovan and Miss ...?" He turned to Sheridan with a faint lift of thick, dark brows, and she could have sworn those brown eyes deepened to dark chocolate— her new favorite—as they settled on her with a slow and easy smile.

"D-Donovan," she managed with only a gulp, mouth as dry as the desert floor while she scuffed her lip with her teeth, "*Miss* Donovan."

"*Miss* Donovan." His voice was slow and deliberate with a tinge of husky as he emphasized her single status like she had, the low timbre of his voice doing funny things to her stomach. "I am Bill's road manager, scout, and trainer, which means I'm not usually in the show unless I'm filling in for one of the Rough Riders."

Sheridan's mouth parted in awe.

He smiled, fixed on her face. "I actually oversee the staff for all planning, setup, and teardown for the Wild West show, traveling ahead to procure licenses, rental of ten to fifteen acres required for the show lot, the purchase of supplies like flour, meat, coffee, and other necessities, as well as setting up all publicity and advertisement. Everything from long-term scheduling to arranging for final cleanup before we move on to the next city."

Dipping his head, he casually scratched the back of his neatly trimmed dark-brown hair with a sheepish smile, the bulge of a powerful arm more than evident beneath his white shirt with a black vest. "Of course, once the show is up and running, my main job is to fill in if needed and audition marksmen for the various acts in Bill's show." He slowly tore his gaze away to flash a smile Maggie's direction before refocusing on Sheridan. "A job I take most seriously since Bill Cody is my uncle."

Sheridan's jaw dropped a full inch, gob-smacked not only by this man's remarkable physique, but his connection to the legendary William "Buffalo Bill" Cody and one of the most popular touring shows in the country.

"Goodness—that's quite a resume!" Maggie said with an impressed lift of brows, her smile as bright as the sun. She hesitated for the briefest of moments. "Do you mind if I ask how old you are, Mr. Morgan?"

"Not at all, ma'am. I'm twenty-eight and have worked for Uncle Bill for over six years now, ever since I graduated from college. Three years during his Scouts of the Plains show and the last three years in his Wild West show." A hint of ruddiness crept up his neck, the first dent Sheridan noticed in his otherwise confident demeanor. "Even though Bill is my uncle, I like to think I've worked my way up in the organization, ma'am, becoming an integral part of one of the finest shows in the world."

"I certainly concur with that, Mr. Morgan, so I applaud you on your obvious ambition and success. And auditioning and training as well? Mmm ... sounds like you may be around a while, sir."

"Yes, ma'am," he said with another slight tip of his hat to Maggie. "A solid month, as a matter of fact. Virginia City is centrally located between Nevada, California, Oregon, Idaho, Utah, and Arizona, so Bill chose it as our show hub." His gaze shifted to Sheridan with a secret smile. "And I don't mind saying, ladies, that right about now, I'm pretty happy about that."

Heat swamped Sheridan's face, making her wish she had more experience flirting with men, but then Uncle Finn and her brothers had certainly taken care of that. And heaven knows that although she'd tried and tried to practice on Jake, the bull-headed man never reciprocated!

"You know, ma'am," Clay continued, thumbs hitched idly into the belt of a black tooled leather holster, complete with a custom-designed ivory-gripped Colt revolver, "fond as I am of Bill and the crew, I sure would appreciate some company occasionally for a fine dinner at the hotel or a show at your famous opera house here in Virginia City."

He removed his hat and paused while he fingered the rim, eyes locked on Sheridan with a hopeful look that fluttered her stomach. "I was raised as the only boy in a family of eight girls, so I'd be lying if I didn't say I miss gentler company from time to time, because it gets a mite lonely traveling with nothing but a troupe of swearin', swillin' Rough Riders."

"But there *are* women in the show too, right?" Sheridan finally managed, her voice more than a bit breathy. "I read the Wild West show features cowgirls and female sharpshooters as well, not to mention Annie Oakley, of course—my absolute idol!"

Clay grinned, rotating his Stetson in his hands. "Yes, ma'am, there are a few gals in the show, but they tend to step out with their husbands who are also in the show, you know, which makes it pretty lonely for a single man not prone to alcohol or cards."

He rubbed the back of his neck with a quick flash of teeth. "And as good of friends as we all are, I have no doubt Frank Butler would have my hide if I even thought about stepping out with Annie since she is, after all, his wife." He offered a teasing grimace. "Nor am I inclined to cozy up to a woman who can shoot the edge of a playing card at thirty paces, snuff out a candle with a bullet, or shoot a lit cigarette from her husband's lips."

"Oh my goodness!" Sheridan gaped in awe, hand to her mouth.

Maggie chuckled. "Then it would seem that you are a very wise man, Mr. Morgan."

He slid Maggie a wink. "Maybe, Mrs. Donovan, but 'wise' sure isn't the cure for 'lonely,' ma'am." He refocused his attention on Sheridan once again. "Unless, of course, this pretty young lady right here agrees to have dinner with me"—his gaze flicked back to Maggie—"chaperoned by you and your husband, of course, if you'd be gracious enough to accept."

Sheridan caught her breath.

Maggie smiled. "As grateful as I am for the invite, Mr. Morgan, I'm afraid my husband wouldn't feel the same way." Her nose scrunched in sympathy as she offered Sheridan a commiserative smile before addressing Clay once more. "You see, when it comes to his sister, I'm afraid he's rather overprotective ..."

A groan lodged in Sheridan's throat.

Clay raised his hand as if in an oath. "You and your husband have my word, Mrs. Donovan, that my intentions are purely honorable because I assure you my mama would tan my hide if they weren't."

A smile squirmed at the edge of Maggie's lips. "That may be, sir, but … your mama isn't here, and my husband is."

Head bowed, he smiled. "No, that's true, ma'am. My mama isn't here"—the sparkle in his eyes reappeared as he glanced up—"but her brother—my Uncle Bill—is, and he tends to keep my mother well-informed on her son's behavior, I assure you. Not to mention I'm pretty sure I could coax Annie and Frank to chaperone."

What?! Sheridan tried to catch her breath again, but couldn't—her tongue and throat were completely paralyzed along with the breath in her lungs. *Dinner with Annie Oakley and Frank Butler??*

Maggie appeared as stunned as Sheridan, eyes wide in surprise.

"Ma'am," Clay continued, gaze locked with Maggie's, "I'm on the road a lot for limited periods in most towns, so I don't make a habit of stepping out with ladies under those circumstances. But we're here to stay for a while, and to be honest"—his smile softened as he turned back to Sheridan—"the moment I saw you and your sister-in-law exit the ticket gate a few moments ago, I'm not sure if I can explain why, but I just felt compelled to get to know you better. That is"—he dipped his head in polite request, gaze glued to Sheridan's face—"if your sister-in-law is so inclined—"

"Yes!" The high-pitched consent popped out of Sheridan's mouth before she could stop it, her smile shy as her teeth tugged at her lower lip. Reveling in the obvious interest in the man's perusal, Sheridan felt her confidence surge, stunned at how pretty he made her feel—a totally new experience, empowering her for the first time in her life. She squared her shoulders with a smile. "But I'm afraid you'll have to ask my uncle in person, Mr. Morgan, if that's agreeable to you?"

He grinned. "Oh, yes, ma'am. Just name the time and place."

Sheridan grabbed Maggie's hand, searching her sister-in-law's face in a silent plea. "What do you think, Maggie, if Mr. Morgan showed up on Sunday to ask Uncle Finn's permission during our horseshoe tournament and barbecue?"

"Uh ... I don't know, Sheridan—"

Sheridan's chin nudged up. "Mr. Morgan is a guest in our town, Maggie, so what's the harm in inviting him to my graduation barbecue, where Uncle Finn can meet him before he makes his decision? I mean the worst that can happen is Uncle Finn says no, and Mr. Morgan gets a free meal, right?"

Clay Morgan seemed to watch the interchange closely, stance shifting from one foot to the other.

"Well, I suppose it couldn't hurt"—Maggie's gaze suddenly flicked past Sheridan with a hesitant purse of lips—"and then again, it just might ..."

Sheridan glanced over her shoulder to see Jake barreling toward them, still halfway across the field. Returning her attention to Clay, she delivered a polite smile while she nodded toward Jake in the distance. "It looks like they've sent a posse out after us, Mr. Morgan, so we need to take our leave before he arrives. But if you can come to The Silver Lining Ranch on Sunday at about 3:00 PM, we'll take it from there, although I can't promise anything."

"Understood, Miss Donovan, but I'll be there, ma'am, on time, guaranteed." He tipped his hat before tugging it back on, tossing a glance at Jake before he headed in the direction of the privy. "Enjoy the show, ladies."

"Oh, wait!" Sheridan shouted, and he turned. "How are you at horseshoes?"

A slow grin eased across his lips. "My daddy is a blacksmith, Miss Donovan, so what do you think?" With another lift of his hat, he grinned and disappeared into the crowd making their way to the latrines.

Sheridan grinned at Maggie. "If that man doesn't light a fire under Jake Sullivan, I don't know what will."

Maggie nodded toward Jake, who was now close enough

for them to see the scowl on his face. "I think it already has, sweetheart," she said as she hooked her arm through Sheridan's, ushering her forward to meet the raging bull head on. "Because if I'm not mistaken"—she winked—"that sure looks like smoke coming out of his ears."

CHAPTER THIRTEEN

"" **J** UST WHO IN THE SAM Hill were you talking to?"
Jake snapped when he finally reached the girls en
route back to the arena, as miffed at Maggie for allowing
the cowboy dandy to fawn over Sheridan as he was with the
blasted cowboy.

"Excuse me, Jake," Sheridan said in a sweet voice as she
moved around his straddled stance with a hike of her chin,
"but that's none of your business."

"The devil, it isn't." Shooting Maggie a glare, he spun
around to catch up with Sheridan, halting her with a firm
clasp of her arm. "It took you two so dog-gone long, your
brother sent me out to make sure you weren't kidnapped."

"Nope, all safe and sound," Maggie said with a bright
smile, hooking Sheridan's elbow in one fluid movement as
she breezed by Jake, the two of them arm and arm on their
way back to the arena.

"You didn't answer my question," Jake said, falling into
step with the girls, his voice more of a growl than a query.
"Who the devil were you talking to?"

"That's because you didn't ask in a civilized manner,
Jake Sullivan," Sheridan said with a pert lift of her chin, her
manner far more serene than Jake's. She nodded to several
people she knew who were heading to the privy. "Haven't
you ever heard the expression, 'catch more flies with honey
than vinegar?'"

Jake's jaw began to grind as he slowly counted to ten to
restrain a curt response. He had no doubt his scowl rivaled that
of Sitting Bull's in war paint, whose posters were plastered
across the wooden wall that cordoned off the entrance area

from the arena tents. Yep, no question his near-nonexistent temper had been steeped in vinegar rather than honey these last few weeks.

Since that dad-burned kiss.

Filling his lungs with air, he slowly expelled it again in one long, wavering breath. "All right, Sheridan, Maggie—may I ask, then, who you were talking to back there?"

"Why, certainly," Sheridan said with a sweet smile. "That was the manager for the Wild West Show."

"Then what the devil is he doing out here instead of the arena?" he sniped, wishing Blaze had handled this himself instead of asking Jake. He didn't like being grumpy. And lately, interacting with Sheridan *always* made him grumpy.

Sheridan halted with an arch of a brow, lips clamped tightly to deny a response.

Hands moored loose on his thighs, he huffed out a noisy sigh, gaze fused to the tips of his boots. "Sorry for the grouchy tone, ladies, but it's never safe hobnobbing with strangers, especially dandies from a road show, so we're just concerned for your safety."

"And we appreciate that, Jake," Maggie said with a patient smile, reaching out to lay a gentle hand on his arm. "We actually asked him the same thing as to why he wasn't inside the arena. It seems that although he does occasionally fill in for one of the Rough Riders when they're sick, his main duties relate to overseeing all planning, setup, and teardown for the Wild West show. So, he's a very busy man. And guess what?" She wiggled her brows. "He's Buffalo Bill's nephew to boot."

Some of Jake's frustration leaked out, quickly replaced by a swell of gratitude that not only would the dandy probably be too busy to be a problem, but probably too cocky as well, anxious to ply his celebrity status on the next pretty gal he saw. Jake's jaw steeled as he ushered the ladies through the stanchions at the front entrance.

Which would *not* be Sheridan Donovan if Jake had anything

to say about it.

And he did.

Whoops and hollers and gunshots peppered the air, signaling the main show had finally begun, and Jake expelled a giant sigh of relief as he and the ladies displayed their tickets for re-entrance. Road shows usually blew in and blew out like the wind, which was a darn good thing because those dandies were notorious for womanizing, hog-tying women's hearts from town to town as often as they did steers.

Guiding the ladies to their seats, Jake felt his blood pressure returning to normal once again. "Well, next time, ladies, I'd appreciate you asking Blaze, Dash, or me to escort you, because with so many strangers in town, you can never trust men you don't know."

"And sometimes, not even those you do," Sheridan said in a sweet tone over her shoulder, her insinuation blasting his face with fire.

Lips pinched, he worked hard to keep the grumpy Jake at bay, unwilling to give the little brat the dignity of a response. Oh, she could trust him all right.

To keep her sassy self out of trouble by putting as much distance as humanly possible between her and any want-to-be suitors that might look her way. Taking his seat at the end of the row, resolve hardened his bones as he focused on the show.

And I'm right at the top of the list.

CHAPTER FOURTEEN

"SO, WHAT DO YOU THINK, Maggie?" Sheridan whispered, stomach skittering with anticipation like the corn pones Angus was frying in bacon drippings for Sheridan's graduation barbecue. The heavenly smell floated in the air along with the scent of Aunt Libby's roses while the two women descended the steps of the two-story log ranch house they all called home.

Tucked at the base of the Sierra Nevada mountains, Uncle Finn's ranch house provided a majestic backdrop for miles of wood-slatted fence and meadows dotted with cattle, horses, and pines. Working her lower lip, Sheridan slid a sideways peek at her sister-in-law, so very grateful for their close friendship. "You think he'll come?"

"Ha! Is the sky blue?" Maggie gave Sheridan a playful pinch, her hazel eyes gleaming more than the shiny gold horseshoes Blaze was pitching in a practice round with Shaylee. Not only to give his baby sister tips on how to throw before the game started, but to practice himself as well in tossing with a cast on his wrist and palm. He'd gifted the horseshoes to Uncle Finn one Christmas, using nuggets of gold and silver he'd gleaned from her uncle's mine to gold- and silver-plate a full set for Finn's favorite game.

Sheridan grinned, gaze drinking in the sapphire sky kissed by occasional puffs of clouds. "It is, indeed, and I'm hoping and praying it stays that way till *long* after Mr. Morgan arrives." She snuck a peek over her shoulder to where Uncle Finn, Libby and her parents all chatted in rocking chairs on the wrap-around porch. "Do you think Jake will even care?"

A low chuckle rolled from Maggie's lips as she nodded

to Dash and Jake. The two of them were sprawled in log-hewn lawn chairs beneath a wispy copse of quaking aspen, the trees' delicate, heart-shaped leaves fluttering in a rare summer breeze. "Is Jake's mood black?"

Sheridan sighed as she glanced Jake's way, a rare scowl on his face while he and Dash watched Blaze finish up with Shaylee before the horseshoe tournament could begin. *Darker than a black angus bull seeing red.*

She knew he didn't want to be here because she'd overheard him arguing with Blaze in the barn a few days back, claiming he had too much training to do.

"Hang it all, Sully, it's Sunday, and you need a blasted day off!" Blaze had been all but shouting as Sheridan approached the barn, so she'd quickly hid outside the door to avoid interrupting. "Besides, this is a family tournament, dog-gone-it, and you're family whether you want to be or not. And if I can play with a pound of plaster of Paris on my dad-gum hand, you sure in the devil can, Sheridan or no. Besides, Shaylee needs a partner and you're it, my friend. You're one of the best at horseshoes, and poor Shaylee is one of the worst, so she needs you, Sul."

"I suppose I should be grateful you're making me partner with Shaylee instead of Sheridan," he'd all but growled, his voice tinged with a frustrated edge that pierced Sheridan straight through.

"Yes, you should be, because I've honored both your request to take your suppers with the hands for a season and to find someone else to teach Sheridan to shoot, opting to do it myself once my hand heals."

Sheridan's lids had weighted closed, not really believing Jake had meant what he'd said about ending their lessons.

"You're my best friend, Jake," Blaze had continued, a note of desperation lacing his words, "and an important part of this family, so I refuse to let"—his voice hesitated as if he were trying to find the right word—"this … this *thing* between you and Sher destroy what we have."

This thing. Moisture had stung the back of Sheridan's lids. An inconvenience. A regret. A denial of all that was meant to be.

A loud and cumbersome sigh drifted out the barn door, and Sheridan had no doubt it had come from Jake. "All right, Blaze," Jake finally said, his consent quiet, but his unwillingness loud and clear. "You win."

And I lost. Swiping the wetness from her eyes, Sheridan had quickly made her way back to the house, heart cramping in her chest.

"Sher? Are you all right?" Maggie's question jolted her back from her unwelcome reverie, melancholy stealing her good mood as her gaze shifted from the unhappy look on Jake's face to the look of concern on Maggie's.

"Yes, I'm fine," she said with a square of her shoulders, chin rising in challenge, "at least a whole lot better than Jake will be after Mr. Morgan arrives." A smile wrapped around her sigh. "*If* Mr. Morgan arrives."

"Oh, he'll be here," Maggie said with the utmost confidence, peeking down at the watch pinned to her bodice before she gave Sheridan a squeeze. "Any minute now, as a matter of fact. And if Jake cares at all—which based on what you told me, sure seems like he does—I'd say Mr. Clay Morgan should sufficiently rattle Jake's spurs whether your uncle says yes or not." Maggie's smile took a slant as she huffed out a heavy sigh. "Which is probably as likely as snow in July."

Or Jake talking to me, Sheridan mused, thinking snow in July would be a whole lot warmer than Jake had been to her of late. Her thoughts drifted to Clay Morgan, and some of the sting of Jake's rejection eased somewhat because after all, Clay was a mighty attractive man …

Dash stretched in the chair with an exaggerated yawn. "You two done practicing yet? I'd like to be young enough to still hurl a horseshoe."

"Just trying to give Shay a little practice since she's so new at this, not to mention myself," Blaze said. He held up the bulky cast on his wrist and palm, so thick, it looked like a boxing glove. He shot Jake a wink. "After all, she's gotta carry Jake."

Dash chuckled as he and Jake lumbered up from their chairs. "Just like Sher's gotta carry me on our team, right, Sher?" He ambled over to hook Shaylee's arm, tugging her toward the farthest horseshoe pit. "Come on, kiddo. One team member on each side, so I'm keepin' my eye on you."

"Hey, how 'bout we do men on one side and women on the other?" Jake said in a rush, all but vaulting from the chair to drag Dash to the closest pit with him, neatly avoiding being at the same pit as Sheridan. "It'll be fairer that way—men tossing against men and the girls tossing against girls."

Sheridan halted on her way to Jake's sand pit, hands perched on the hips of her lace-collared blue Sunday dress. "Actually, I think you're just afraid to throw against me, Jake Sullivan, because you know I'll win."

Picking up the horseshoes, Jake handed two off to Dash as he singed Sheridan with a half-lidded look, lips ground into a tight smile. "Actually I'm sparing your feelings, Half-Pint, because I already know you won't."

"Whooooo-ee, sounds like we have ourselves a do-or-die competition." Dash chuckled as he ambled over to his and Jake's sandpit.

"You have no idea," Sheridan muttered, looping an arm over Shaylee's shoulder as they headed for the far sandpit, leaning to whisper in her sister's ear. "Come on, Shay, let's make monkeys out of them, all right?"

"Ground rules," Uncle Finn called from the front porch. "Shaylee automatically starts with five points because she's new at this game. Winning team plays Maggie & Blaze and then Libby and me for the final prize."

Groans rose from the two teams because everyone knew when it came to horseshoes, Uncle Finn usually walked away with the win, especially since he'd been working with Aunt Libby on her game as well. A slow smile eased across his lips as he leaned back to prop his long legs on the railing, boots crossed at the ankles. "Top prize is dinner at the Gold Hill Hotel for the family"—the smile bloomed into a wide grin—"paid for by both losing teams."

More groans rose as Dash threw his hands up the air. "Well, there goes my paycheck—"

"Followed by," Finn continued with a wink, "Miss Lillie Langtry at Piper Opera House on me, front row seats. And since you boys all have jobs and Sher and Shay don't, I'll be gracious enough to pony up for the girls' part of the bill."

"Crawling cactus, Uncle Finn," Shaylee shouted with several jubilant hops, "that's just like Christmas!" Her pigtails did a little bounce on the shoulders of her standard overalls, which she immediately changed back into after church.

"Yeah, and just as expensive." Blaze turned to Maggie with a tense threading his tone. "Now would be a good time to employ some of those prayers you're always prayin', darlin, or that house we're hopin' to build is gonna take a whole lot longer."

"Oh, I'm praying, all right," Maggie said with a chuckle, catching Sheridan's eye to give her a wink. "But since this is Sher's graduation barbecue, I'm afraid all my prayers are busy elsewhere, darling."

"Who the devil is that?" Jake muttered, the sound of hoofbeats drawing his and everyone else's attention to the log-and-stone entrance for the Silver Lining Ranch. A lone horseman galloped through, leaving a cloud of dust in his wake as he slowed to leisurely trot up the winding drive toward the house.

"You expecting anyone, Uncle Finn?" Blaze rose from his chair with a curious squint.

"Nope." Dropping his legs to the ground, Finn stood from his own chair to scrutinize the stranger whose features were just now coming into view. "But that animal he's riding is a mighty fine piece of horseflesh, I can tell you that."

And man flesh, too! Sheridan glanced down at the watch

pinned to her blue fitted bodice—the one that matched her eyes—before shooting Maggie a tiny smile that just ached to break into a grin. *Three o'clock sharp—right on time.*

Finn slowly descended the front steps, hand to his eyes to try and make out who it was. "Never seen him or his horse before, so anybody else know who he is?"

Opting to remain silent along with Maggie, Sheridan adjusted her skirt with sweaty hands, smoothing it out as the rider tipped his hat, slowing his approach with a polite smile. *Yes, he's the answer to my prayers.* Her gaze flicked to where Jake stood with a menacing scowl, hands planted defiantly on his hips, and she couldn't stem a satisfied smile.

At least one of them ...

CHAPTER FIFTEEN

SOMETHING ABOUT THIS GUY SEEMED familiar, but for the life of him, Jake couldn't figure out what. Had he seen him at church this morning? Or at the Ponderosa Saloon where Dash worked? He had played several games of pool with Blaze and Dash there a few nights ago before Dash clocked in for his shift, and the place had been busting at the seams with patrons. Could have been one of them. Or even at Buffalo Bill's Wild West show because there had been hundreds of new faces from all over Nevada and the surrounding states.

Jake's gaze thinned as the stranger dismounted, the fancy gold studs on the band of his black Stetson marking him as a dandy to Jake's way of thinking.

"Mayor McShane?" The cowboy removed his hat as he approached the front porch, homing in on Finn who stood at the base of the stairs, one boot resting on the first step.

Finn nodded. "That would be me, son, and you are?"

"Clay Morgan, sir," the cowboy said with arm extended, shaking Finn's hand with more enthusiasm than Jake liked. "I have the privilege of being the road manager, scout, and trainer for Buffalo Bill's Wild West Show, and I'm here to extend an invitation to dinner on behalf of my uncle and me next Sunday night, which is the show's day off."

"Well, that's mighty nice of you and your uncle, son, but if you don't mind my asking, what might his name be?"

A hint of ruddy color crept up the back of the cowboy's clean-shaven neck as he fiddled with the hat. "My apologies, Mayor, for not properly introducing my uncle—Buffalo Bill Cody."

Gasps popped from both Libby and her mother on the porch as the cowboy continued. "My uncle and I would like to express our gratitude to you for opening up your fine city to our traveling show, providing us with the finest central hub in six states."

Shoulders squaring, the dandy gave a polite nod. "So, I've been dispatched to personally issue an invitation for you and your family to dine with my uncle and me as well as Annie Oakley and her husband, Frank Butler, in my uncle's personal dining tent."

This time Sheridan and Maggie gasped along with the other ladies, drawing Jake's gaze their way for a brief moment before it returned to the cowboy. Sunlight glinted off the gold studs in the man's hat as he absently fiddled with it, jogging Jake's memory with a jolt. His fist automatically curled around the horseshoe, tempted to throw it at the back of the dandy's head. His jaw ground tight.

The same dandy who'd been fawning over Sher and Maggie at the show.

"Well, son, I'd say that's an invitation I'm mighty honored to accept. I met your uncle briefly at the show, but I'm looking forward to getting to know him better. He's a fine showman. And if I'm not mistaken, Mr. Morgan, you were the one who arranged everything with my right-hand assistant, Mrs. Caldwell, correct?"

"Yes, sir, I was, and I was delighted to meet Mrs. Caldwell upon our arrival, when I believe you were out of town for the week."

Finn nodded. "Ah, yes, that happens a lot, I'm afraid." He motioned a hand toward Libby and her parents. "Allow me to introduce my family—my wife, Libby, and her parents, Mr. and Mrs. Aiden and Maeve O'Shea."

The dandy gave a half bow, acknowledging both Libby's and the O'Sheas' greetings. "It's a pleasure to meet you as well, Mrs. McShane, and Mr. and Mrs. O'Shea—please note that the invitation for dinner extends to you as well."

"Why, thank you, Mr. Morgan," Maeve said, beaming more than the blasted sun.

"Yes, sirree, son," Aiden boomed, obviously delighted given the broad smile on his face, "Maeve and I would be honored."

Finn tossed a glance over the dandy's head toward the rest of the family. "Over there by the horseshoe pits is my nephew Blaze Donovan and his wife, Maggie, along with my other nephew Dash and my nieces Sheridan and Shaylee. And last but not least, our assistant foreman who is like a nephew himself, Jake Sullivan."

"Pleased to meet you all," the dandy said with another brief bow acknowledging each of their greetings with a polite smile, finally settling on Sheridan with a smile that warmed way too much for Jake's comfort. "I look forward to getting to know each and every one of you, especially since we'll be in Virginia City for a solid month."

A silent groan rattled in Jake's chest.

Finn offered the dandy a friendly slap on the shoulder. "Tell me, Mr. Morgan—do you happen to play horseshoes?"

Jake blinked with a drop of his jaw, hardly able to believe Finn was considering inviting the dandy to stay.

"What the devil is Uncle Finn doing?" Blaze said, tone harsh as he came up behind Jake, the furrow in his brow matching Jake's to a groove. "Can't he see how that guy is ogling Sheridan?"

"Apparently not," Jake muttered, "since he can't see the drool on his face like we can."

The flash of the dandy's teeth was pert near more blinding than the glare of his dad-burned gold studs on that blasted hat. "As a matter of fact I do, sir, why?"

Finn nodded toward the lawn where Sheridan and Maggie stood frozen like statues in that confounded game they used to play on this very lawn. "We have a horseshoe tournament starting, son, and I'm pretty sure my wife would be most grateful if you'd be her proxy on my team, followed, of course, by the best barbecue this side of the Rockies right after, so are you game?"

The gleam of the polecat's grin—if possible—shone brighter than the golden horseshoes glinting in the sun. "Why, I do believe that would make my evening, sir, so thank you!"

Another groan rammed the back of Jake's teeth as he bent close to Blaze with a gritted smile. "And he sure in the devil doesn't know that's the same tomcat I saw sniffing around Sheridan and Maggie outside the arena the other day."

"What?" Blaze gaped at Jake, the sharp hiss of his voice earning a curious look from Sheridan. "We need to tell Uncle Finn—"

"Too late," Jake muttered as they both watched Finn usher the dandy up to the porch to join the others.

Libby shot up so fast, her chair bucked like a mule as she hurried to pour the dandy some lemonade while Jake and Blaze just stared, their scowls way more sour than the drink in her hand. "Here you go, Mr. Morgan," she said with a wide smile, "and please make yourself comfortable while we wait to see who wins the challenge against my husband and you, of course, since I gladly abdicate my turn."

"Well, ma'am, only if you're sure—"

"She's sure," Sheridan and Maggie called in unison, both obviously delighted to have the varmint join the family game. "Please?"

"They're right, Mr. Morgan," Finn said with a chuckle, looping an arm to Libby's waist. "I'm afraid I wore Libby's wrist out practicing with her this week for this family tournament, so I'm quite certain she'd be happy to sit this one out to nurse a sore wrist, forever grateful."

"Yes, thank you, Mr. Morgan," Libby said with a pretty grin, obviously as enamored with the dandy as Maeve, Maggie, and Sheridan appeared to be.

"Well, all right ladies." The dandy gave a brief bow first to Libby, and then to Sheridan and Maggie. "But only if you call me Clay."

"Yeah, and I'd like to bury him in clay," Jake mumbled, mouth clamped tight as they watched the ladies smile and swoon.

"This isn't good," Blaze said under his breath. "He's only been here all of five minutes, and already he's weaseled his way in with all the ladies."

"I know." Shaking his head, Jake bent to snatch up his two horseshoes, glancing over at sweet Shaylee to see if she was gawking along with the rest of the females. His scowl softened when he noted she didn't seem as impressed in the least, opting instead to practice with two horseshoes instead. Jake grunted.

Good. At least one of the females still had some sense.

CHAPTER SIXTEEN

"**U**H ... WHAT ON EARTH just happened?" Sheridan could only gape with a whisper of shock, jaw dangling along with Maggie's as they watched Uncle Finn lead Clay up to the porch for lemonade.

"It would appear, Sheridan Marie," Maggie said with a bump of her hip against Sheridan's, "that Mr. Clay Morgan is not only gorgeous, but quite clever as well."

Sheridan turned to Maggie with an open-mouthed smile, totally caught off-guard that it could be this easy. She stifled a giggle with a hand to her mouth, careful to cover the grin inching ear to ear. "Brilliant might be a better word, Mags, because sweet mother of Job, would you take a look at the scowl on our boys' faces!"

Maggie shot a glance over her shoulder and chuckled before tweaking the back of Sheridan's neck. "I'd say that's a definite answer to our first prayer about 'the perfect young man to put a burr in Jake's saddle,' Sher, so let's just see if we can make short work of the second one, all right?" Giving Sheridan a quick hug, Maggie made a beeline for her husband.

Sheridan sighed, the memory of Maggie's prayer warming her as much as the Nevada sun. *"If Jake is the one God has in store for you, it will happen before you go off to college."*

"Oh, Lord, I hope so!" Sheridan said under her breath, tempering her grin as she snuck a peek Jake's way, his grumpy mood obviously still intact given the hard clamp of his jaw.

"Hey, sis, ready to kick some backside?" Dash ambled over to loop an arm around Sheridan's shoulder, "because I'm counting on all that practicing of yours to snag us the win."

She grinned, so very grateful she'd taken to perfecting her game with lots of practice ever since she won against Jake last year, forcing him to take her to the rodeo dance. "Count on it, Dash, at least with Jake and Shaylee, but I'm not too sure about Clay Morgan," she said with a quick glance at the front porch, thrilled to see him laughing and chatting with Uncle Finn.

"Well, since Jake's as good as you, he's our real threat at the moment, Sher, so let's just focus on him for now, okay?" He gave her a side hug.

Sheridan grinned. *Believe me, I'm trying!*

Dash cut loose with a piercing whistle. "Okay, everybody, let's get this buggy in motion, shall we?" Grinning, he loped over to the sand pit where Shaylee was practicing, leaving Jake to pair up with Sheridan at the other pit since one team member had to be on each side.

"Hey, Dash, we're pairing the girls on one side and the men on the other, remember?" Jake waved Dash over to his pit, hurting Sheridan's feelings that he wasn't even willing to stand next to her in a game of horseshoes. "And Shay can have the first throw."

"I couldn't agree more." Flipping her hair over her shoulder, Sheridan hurried over to Shaylee and Dash's pit with her nose in the air, more anxious than ever to rub Mr. Clay Morgan into Jake Sullivan's face.

"Holy thunder, what is Jake's problem today anyway?" Dash said, shaking his head as Sheridan took his place next to Shaylee. "He's in the surliest mood I've ever seen."

Yes, and it's about to get worse. "Hate to say it, Shay, but your partner is a crab." Smiling, Sheridan gave a tug of her sister's braid.

"I know," Shaylee said with a pinch of concern, "just imagine how he'll be if we lose ..."

Oh, I am. Sheridan's smile broke into a grin.

And the grin only grew bigger and bigger as Dash and

Sheridan made easy work, first of Jake and Shaylee despite the 5-point handicap, then Maggie and Blaze, finally bringing Clay Morgan to the pit to stand next to Sheridan.

"Congratulations on the wins," Clay said as he approached Sheridan with a lazy smile that all but melted the tendons at the back of her knees. She thought she just might need a handicap advantage, too, just to stay on her feet.

She forced a confident smile. "Thank you, but I think the win goes to you, Mr. Morgan, since you just accomplished something no man has ever been able to do."

"And what's that, Miss Donovan?" he said as he slowly rolled the sleeves of his shirt, black eyes twinkling more than the flash of white teeth.

Her smile tipped off-center as she jerked her chin toward Uncle Finn and Dash at the other pit, where they waited for her first toss while the rest of the family looked on from the porch. "My uncle hasn't allowed any man outside my family to even talk to me, much less wrangle an invitation to a family tournament and dinner, so congratulations."

He grinned. "Well, I suppose that should give you some idea of just how badly I wanted to see you again, Miss Donovan."

She swallowed hard. "Call me Sheridan, please," she whispered, quickly turning away lest he spy the blush in her cheeks. Sucking in a deep breath, she forced herself to focus on the far pit, not sure if all the practice in the world could have prepared her to play a calm and steady game with Clay Morgan by her side.

"All right, Sheridan ... as long as you call me Clay."

His husky tone did nothing for her concentration as she tried to center her thoughts on the far sandpit. She squinted hard to fixate on the stake, biting back a groan when the raspy tenor of his voice caused her arms to go as limp as her legs. *Focus, Sheridan!* Blocking him out, she tossed her first horseshoe, and immediately the loud ping of steel against stake stabilized her once again.

"Go, Sheridan!" Maggie called from the porch, and Sheridan felt her confidence resurge as she snagged a second ringer.

"Mmm ... looks like I have my work cut out for me," Clay said as he bypassed Sheridan to throw his own horseshoes.

No more than me, she thought with a quiet sigh, glancing toward the front porch. Jake stood, hip butted to a post and arms crossed, his face mostly hidden by the shade of his hat except for the sullen bent of his lips.

Sheridan's stomach did a dizzy cartwheel. *The same lips that devoured mine.*

Ping!

Her gaze jerked back to the game when Clay interrupted her wool-gathering with a ringer, cancelling hers out. Dash's groans merged with Uncle Finn's cheers, exacerbated by Jake's and Blaze's whoops and whistles. Lips compressed, Sheridan made up her mind right then and there not to let anything interfere with winning.

Not even the man she was trying to win.

Clay turned and winked as he stepped back with a knowing smile, allowing her the space to throw. Gaze homing in on the stake on the other side, she closed her mind off from anything but winning because she knew when it came to men, she *also* had her work cut out for her. Her jaw locked in resolve as she sailed the shoe in the air.

Both the one beside her.

And the one scowling up on the porch.

CHAPTER SEVENTEEN

"I HAVE TO SAY, MAYOR FINN," Clay Morgan said with a pat of his stomach, "if that was my last meal, I could die a happy man."

Yeah, me too. Blaze upended his sarsaparilla, wishing this *was* the dandy's last meal, at least with Blaze's family. He clunked his glass back down, not a bit happy that his favorite meal—Angus's barbecued ribs and Gert's special mayonnaise potato salad—had been tainted by the presence of Clay Morgan.

Not to mention the absence of his best friend, who'd begged off on the barbecue for other plans in town. He ripped two ribs apart with more force than necessary. *Blast it all, Jake, I could have used some support here!* Because now the dandy was making headway with Finn and everyone else, apparently, fawning over the blowhard.

Blaze's brows dug low. But Finn didn't know that ol' Clay had more than likely set his sights on Sheridan if Jake's assessment of the situation was correct. And Jake was seldom wrong when it came to gut feelings, which was one of the reasons Finn trusted him enough to make him second in command at the Silver Lining Ranch. *And* the biggest reason Blaze trusted him enough to be his best friend.

"Maggie and Sheridan were laughing it up with some fancy cowboy by the latrines," Jake had told him privately after the Wild West show, "and although I was a fair distance away, they appeared to be enamored by the dandy before I was able to rein them back in."

The dandy. Ah, yes, the same one that was charming the socks off his family right now. Blaze's eyes narrowed as he listened to Clay regale the table with various adventures on the road, pretty sure if Finn knew what Blaze knew, Mr. Clay Morgan would be long gone without a lick of Angus's famous smoky sauce.

"So, you're a sharpshooter as well as managing the show?" Sheridan asked after Angus's peach cobbler had been served and scarfed down along with Gert's homemade ice cream. Her blue eyes were wide with wonder as she stared at the dandy like he'd just descended from heaven.

Black eyes Blaze didn't trust for a minute settled on his sister with a twinkle that came off part sheepish, part smug. "Well, I'm no Annie Oakley or Frank Butler, ma'am, but as the only boy out of eight girls, Uncle Bill made good and sure I knew how to both ride and shoot when I was knee-high to a pony."

He winked as he casually rose from his seat at the head of the table. "In fact," he said, flinging a coin out into the yard and drawing his gun so fast, Blaze barely saw it before the coin shattered mid-air, "part of my job for Uncle Bill is training new hires on how to fine-tune their shooting skills."

His grin was downright cocky as he sat back down, the ladies clapping so wildly, Blaze had to fight off a roll of his eyes. *Confound it, Jake, why aren't you here to shut this show-off up?*

"So ..." the dandy continued, "I suppose I know how to shoot well enough with most every kind of weapon there is. Had to," he said with a wink that flat-out got on Blaze's nerves, "Uncle Bill insists everyone on the show know how to shoot and ride fairly fancy, male and female."

"Holy frog spit," Shaylee shouted, eyes bugged as wide as the gape of her mouth. "How old do you have to be to be in the show?"

"Way older than you, young lady," Finn interjected with the barest trace of a smile, "and for the umpteenth time, there is nothing holy about frog spit, Shaylee Ann."

Sheridan's head swiveled toward Uncle Finn, her

expression of surprise making her look far more like the little sister he wanted to protect rather than an eighteen-year-old woman heading off to college by herself. "But, Uncle Finn, Annie Oakley was only fifteen when she won that shooting match against Frank E. Butler," she defended, "and Lillian Smith joined Buffalo Bill's Wild West show as a trick shooter at age fifteen too. Isn't that right, Clay?"

Clay cuffed the back of his neck, obviously uncomfortable to be dragged into a disagreement between Finn and his nieces. "Well, yesssss, I suppose that is true, Sheridan, but Annie didn't actually join Buffalo Bill's show till the age of twenty-four along with her sharpshooter husband, Frank. Not to mention she'd been shooting and trapping since the age of eight to support her siblings and widowed mother while her sisters played with dolls."

"I hate dolls," Shaylee announced with a scrunch of her nose, shoveling in the last of her peach cobbler as if to rid the sour taste of dolls from her mouth. Blaze couldn't help but smile over his little tomboy sister, far more interested in critters than dolls from little on, including her pet tarantula, Annabelle.

"And as far as Lillian goes," Clay continued, offering both Sheridan and Shaylee a sympathetic smile, "she began shooting at the age of seven and was already competing by the age of ten, so she was pretty good by the time Uncle Bill hired her."

"Shaylee and I might have been good, too, if Uncle Finn had taught us to shoot in the first place," Sheridan said with a mock pout, the tease in her tone unable to mask his sister's dream to be a sharpshooter since she first read about Annie Oakley at the age of twelve. "It's not fair."

"Eighteen years old is soon enough for a young lady to learn how to shoot," Finn said, taking a sip of his coffee.

"But you bought both Blaze and Dash rifles and taught them to shoot when they were only ten and eight," Sheridan countered.

"Who told you that?" Finn set his coffee cup down, eyes in a squint.

"Dash did," Shaylee volunteered as she licked first her spoon and then her plate, which Aunt Libby promptly removed from her hand with a parental smile.

"Well, that should be your first clue it wasn't true," Blaze said with an evil grin, finger-shooting a watermelon seed into Dash's hair. "The only thing Dash ever learned how to shoot off was his mouth."

Chuckles rounded the table while Finn addressed Sheridan with a patient smile. "Your brothers are men, sweetheart. Men have to learn to hunt and protect their families. Besides, shooting comes more naturally to men."

"Unless you're Dash," Blaze quipped, earning more laughter.

Aunt Libby grunted. "I'd like to see you tell that to Miss Oakley and Miss Smith, sweetheart, but make sure you have your hands raised when you do."

Maggie and Sheridan giggled in agreement.

"At *any* rate," Uncle Finn said with a conciliatory smile reinforced by a firm lift of brows, evidently anxious to steer the conversation away from Aunt Libby's suffragist tendencies, "you're learning to shoot now, Sher, so it's a moot point."

Clay cleared his throat. "Uh, sir, as I mentioned, I train many of the new hires to shoot as well as ride, so I'd be more than happy to offer my services to Sheridan as well."

"Oh my goodness, Clay, really?" Sheridan practically bounced as she straightened up on the chair, socking Blaze in the gut at the thought of his little sister growing up. "Uncle Finn bought me my first gun for Christmas—a derringer—for protection when I go to New York in the fall, but I don't know how to use it. So, would you really give me lessons?"

"*I'm* giving you lessons, Sher," Blaze said in a clipped tone before the dandy could even respond, "so no need to bother Mr. Morgan."

"I assure you, it's no bother whatsoever." Clay smiled at Sheridan before he shifted his gaze to Blaze with a calm look that belied the gleam of challenge in his eyes. "I give lessons all the time, so I truly don't mind."

"No, but *I* do." Blaze stared him down, his tone as tight as his jaw. "She's my sister and my responsibility, so I'll be the one teaching her how to shoot, Mr. Morgan, not some stranger."

"But, that's just it, Blaze," Sheridan said with a taut heft of her chin, her temper apparently warming along with his, "you're not out of that cast until right before I leave for New York, and I don't want to wait that long."

"Wait a minute." Finn peered at Blaze with a crease in his brow. "I thought Jake was giving her lessons?"

Blaze shifted uncomfortably in his chair as heat scalded the back of his neck. "Nope. He asked me to do it because apparently *someone*"—he burned Sheridan with a hard gaze, tempering it with a faint smile as strained as this confounded conversation—"gave him some trouble."

"What kind of trouble?" Finn asked with a scrunch of his face, pinning Sheridan with a look that caused her cheeks to blossom bright red.

Blaze stared his sister down. "You want to tell him or should I?"

Muscles wobbled in Sheridan's throat as she turned to face their uncle, a familiar lift of her shoulders assuring Blaze she would do everything in her power to safeguard Jake's secret.

And hers.

"Jake was downright crabby and mean with me, Uncle Finn, and he even made me cry."

Propping elbows on the table, Uncle Finn lifted his coffee halfway, tone dubious before he took a drink. "That doesn't sound like Jake. Did you do something to upset him?"

A blush swallowed her whole, clear up to the roots of her hair, and Blaze decided to save her sassy little butt.

Just like he was trying to do from the dandy.

Blaze raised his sarsaparilla in a mock toast. "Jake says when it comes to teaching Sher, she's like stallions in a stall, bucking him at every turn."

"He's right, Uncle Finn," Sheridan was quick to add, obviously anxious to deflect Finn's curiosity as to the true source of their conflict. "But I'm afraid Jake's the one who did most of the bucking, not at all happy about teaching me, so if it's all the same to you, I'd rather he not. And since Blaze won't get his cast off for a while and Clay offered—"

"Absolutely," Clay said all too quickly, first with a smile to Sheridan, then one to Finn. "I'd be delighted to teach Sheridan."

Blaze's jaw molded tight. *Oh, I just bet you would—*

"Thank you, Clay, but no," Finn said before Blaze could even open his mouth, relief seeping through his gritted teeth that Uncle Finn was finally taking control. "Sheridan's lessons are the responsibility of our family, son, so we will handle it."

Blaze all but smirked at the sudden sobriety in Clay's face, grateful that his annoyingly polite demeanor would get him absolutely nowhere with Finn McShane. "I wouldn't mind, sir, truly, and I'd love to repay you for your hospitality today."

"Not necessary, Clay," Finn said with a soldered smile, the firm press of his mouth a clear indication Mr. Fancy-Hat would not be teaching his niece to shoot. "I don't want to impose, so case closed, but thank you for your offer."

Battling the urge to gloat, Blaze ignored the sudden slump of Sheridan's shoulders, figuring she'd thank him one day.

Clay rose with a gruff clear of his throat, offering Finn a respectful nod. "Well, it's getting late, sir, and I should be heading back, but thank you for the home-cooked meal and the game. I assure you, it was a much-needed respite from endless weeks on the road, especially the company."

He scanned the table with a polite smile, gaze finally lighting on Sheridan with the faintest curve of his lips. "I look forward to seeing you all next Sunday at 5:00 p.m. for our dinner with Uncle Bill, Annie, and Frank at the arena."

"We'll be there, son, so thank you." Finn rose to shake the dandy's hand. "And please extend my thanks to your uncle as well."

"Will do, sir. Till next week, then." Acknowledging their goodbyes with a tip of his hat, Morgan descended the porch steps and disappeared around to the front of the house, leaving Blaze's mood as sour as his dinner.

Yeah, he had no doubt ol' Clay Morgan was looking forward to seeing them again all right, especially Sheridan, but there was one thing Blaze knew that the dandy didn't. He upended the last of his sarsaparilla with a hard gulp.

It sure in the devil would be the very last time.

CHAPTER EIGHTEEN

"IGUESS IT'S TIME," JAKE SAID to his horse, Midnight, on the heels of a long and weary sigh. Shoulders slumped, he swayed side to side in the saddle as he rode into town at a pace a tad beyond standing still.

The moment that pretty-boy dandy had showed up to play horseshoes, Jake knew he needed to get out of town—or in— as the case may be. There was no way he was going to stand by and watch that Morgan character fawn over Sheridan through horseshoes and dinner, not when Finn and Blaze were there to keep him in line.

So, he did the only thing he knew to do—threw the blasted game to take a personal loss and gain an emotional win. Which hadn't been hard to do since Shaylee was so new at horseshoes and Sheridan was pert near as good as Finn. Bowing out, he made his excuses to Finn and Blaze, telling them he had something important to take care of in town.

"What in tarnation can be more important than Angus's barbecue?" Blaze had demanded, taking Jake aside. "And Gert's homemade ice cream to boot?"

The memory of his conversation with Blaze made Jake sigh again as he rolled back and forth in the saddle while Midnight plodded into town, his body as limp as his mood. *What could be more important?*

Uh ... the truth? After all, if Jake told Sheridan he was seeing Megan Joy, then by gum, he had to make it right whether he wanted to or not.

"What the devil do you mean, 'it's personal?'" Blaze had said as he followed Jake to the barn after his elimination in horseshoes. He scowled, obviously put off that his best friend was keeping secrets. "I consider it 'personal' you leaving me to battle the dandy on my own."

"I *mean* it's a private matter that I'd rather not go into, Blaze, so just let it go."

Blaze grabbed his arm to whirl him around. The deep worry in his expression was like a sock in Jake's gut, confirming just how close the two men were. "Just tell me one thing, Sully—are you in trouble?"

Yes.

"No," Jake emphasized with a duck of his head, his direct gaze meant to allay Blaze's concern. He huffed out a noisy blast of air, wondering if he shouldn't just let his best friend know since everybody would find out eventually, given Megan Joy's and her mom's propensity to gossip.

He hesitated. "I promised Sister Fred I'd let Pee-wee and a few of the boys who earned it ride Midnight in back of the orphanage as an incentive to get their schoolwork done."

Blaze's eyes narrowed. "And that can't wait till next Sunday afternoon, when we usually work with the boys here?"

Jake felt heat snake up his neck, well aware the excuse was pretty flimsy. Most Sunday afternoons, he, Blaze, and other cowhands worked with some of the older boys from the St. Mary Louise Orphanage anyway. Roping, riding, and general cowhand work to help train them for eventual jobs on Silver Lining Ranch or any other.

Jake gave an awkward shrug, figuring he may as well take advantage of this errand to see Megan Joy too, since she lived right next door. *And escape the dandy's flirtation with Sheridan.* "Just killing two birds with one stone."

Blaze folded his arms. "Really." He arched a brow. "And just what other bird needs to die?"

Grinding out a groan, Jake swiped a hand down his face, almost wishing he wasn't such a stickler for the truth, not to mention loyalty to a friend. "I'm hoping to see Megan Joy if you must know," he said in a near growl, "and I'd rather keep it quiet." He turned his back on Blaze to stalk toward the barn.

"Megan Joy?" Blaze trailed him in with humor lacing his tone. "And keep it quiet?" He chuckled. "Hate to tell you, old buddy, but those are two things that don't quite go together."

Tell me about it. Snatching his hat from the hook, Jake jerked it on low to cover his eyes before nabbing the curry comb.

"Humph. About dang time you're showing interest in a woman," Blaze said as he snatched a piece of hay from a nearby bale and put it in his mouth. "Because heaven knows the ladies of Virginia City sure have an interest in you, Sul, and Megan Joy's definitely the pick of the pack."

Jake made a valiant attempt to ignore him as he removed loose hair from Midnight's body before brushing the underside of his pad. Putting the comb back, he slapped the pad on the mare's back, hoping his best friend would just up and go away.

No such luck.

"After all," Blaze continued with a hip cocked to the stall and the hay twirling in his mouth, "although both you and I have bucked the idea of marriage forever, I have to admit marriage has taught me that the right woman can turn your life around for the better."

Or the worse. Jake flipped the right stirrup and girth strap over the saddle before hoisting it over the pad. *Like Sheridan with me,* he mused, *turning my safe, comfortable life into a constant stress.* His mouth tightened along with the saddle's tie strap when he pulled it hard. *And me from a happy-go-lucky cowboy into a total grouch.*

"Who the devil said anything about marriage?" Jake groused, not wanting anybody—least of all his best friend—thinking he was going soft on the subject. From the moment he and Blaze had become friends, they'd had a bond, a kinship, a do-or-die commitment to never getting married. Heck, they'd even sworn it in an oath at the age of thirteen, cutting their wrists to mingle their blood. And even though

Blaze had broken that blood vow for Maggie, Jake had no intention of doing the same—*ever*—whether he was seeing Megan Joy or not.

He couldn't.

His gaze glazed into a cold stare over Midnight's saddle into the darkness of his past, where a memory too awful to share shivered both his body and his soul.

"Is it ... " His mother's voice had lowered to barely audible as she'd cast a cautious look Jake's way, his tiny body bruised as he lay on the doctor's table. "... hereditary?"

The fear in her voice had made the word sound like a curse, but his six-year-old mind didn't know why. His eyelids lumbered closed, as heavy as his heart. He'd never told anyone about that day lest the fear in his soul also push people away ...

And he never would.

Giving the tie strap a final tug, Jake slowly expelled a silent sigh, turning to stare at Blaze with true regret. He softened his tone, feeling bad about sniping at his best friend. "Look, I'm just hankering for a little female company from time to time, you know? Like you did with Rachel before Maggie? And I like Megan Joy well enough, so why not? Besides," he said with a pointed look, "can you think of a better way to put distance between Half-Pint and me, than me seeing another woman?"

"As a matter of fact, no, old buddy, so that's brilliant." Blaze slapped Jake on the back with a chuckle before heading for the door. "And a little sparkin' will do you good, Sul, hopefully to put the sparkle back in your eyes and a smile on your face, which has been missing for a while, you know?"

Yeah, he knew.

Blaze turned at the door to give him a wink. "So, go have some fun, my friend, but not enough to jeopardize your bachelorhood, you hear?"

Yeah, he heard. *And fun?* Jake grunted. "Fun" would be teaming up with Sheridan in horseshoes like he used to when she'd been just a scrawny kid in overalls from ages twelve to sixteen. *Not* spending time with a woman like Megan Joy, who had designs on him. Another bluster of air escaped his lips as he'd mounted Midnight for the ride into town. Fun had come so easily back then, he mused with a melancholy air, filling his days with the laughter and love of family.

He halted Midnight in front of the massive two-story Victorian a wealthy donor had left to the St. Mary Louise hospital for use as an orphanage, the sound of children's shrieks and laughter filtering from the backyard. His gaze immediately flicked to the modest Burdzy mansion next door, separated from the orphanage by a fancy black wrought-iron fence.

He sure hoped the Burdzys would be dining outside on their back deck on such a pretty day. Either way, he was pretty sure Megan Joy or her little brother would see him giving horse rides in the backyard of the orphanage and invite him over. Which would make it a whole lot easier than calling on Megan Joy out of the blue.

"Jake's here!" Pee-wee Portell shouted as he shot out the front door of the orphanage, unleashing a swarm of young boys right behind him. "Can I ride Midnight into the backyard, Mr. Jake, please?"

Jake grinned and shook his head, hoping Pee-wee's announcement of his arrival would bring Megan Joy running too. "You bet, bud, so hop on up." He reached down to haul the boy into the saddle in front of him, grateful his small stature was more in line with a ten-year-old than the wiry thirteen-year-old that he was. "Meet you boys in the back," he called to the others as he showed Pee-wee how to handle the reins. More shrieks and hollers filled the air while the horde of ruffians stampeded around back.

Pee-wee whooped loudly when Jake galloped to the woods at the rear of the property and back several times before finally halting in front of the deck. "Whoa, boy," he said with a chuckle, both to Midnight and Pee-wee, who was still kicking his heels to make Midnight go. Shooting a grin at Miss Mary Cramer, the sweet, silver-haired orphanage administrator, Jake carefully helped Pee-wee down. "Who's next?"

"Me, me, me!" they all shouted, and it didn't take long for Megan Joy's eight-year-old brother, Wes, to pop his head out their back door. "Megan Joy, look—Jake's here!" he yelled, slamming the door behind him as he clambered down the Burdzy's back steps to race toward the fence, practically vaulting it to join the others. "Can I have a ride too, Jake, please?"

"Wesley Albert Burdzy—you get back over here this instant!" his mother called, standing on the back deck with Megan Joy by her side.

"No, Ma, I want to ride on Jake's horse." Ignoring his mother altogether, Wes bounced up and down. "Can I have a ride, Jake, please? Please?"

"Wes! You come home right this instant, young man."

Jake glanced from Wes's hopeful face to his mother's stern look, and figured any boy who couldn't obey his parents didn't deserve a ride on a horse. Parents were one of the greatest gifts God ever gave a child, and a day didn't go by that Jake didn't ache with the missing of his own.

"Jake—when you're done giving rides," Megan Joy called, looking pretty in a pink calico dress, "we have a fresh pitcher of lemonade waiting for you."

"Yes, ma'am," he said with a tip of his hat, gaze homing in on Wes, who was jumping up and down like a jackrabbit.

"Hey, he's not here for you, *Burd*-zee," Pee-wee piped up, emphasizing the "Bird" sound of his name while the other boys mumbled their agreement. "Besides, you're not welcome here, Bird-brain."

Jake dismounted and gently gripped Pee-wee's shoulder, his voice low. "Don't be a name-caller, Pee-wee. It's a dark mirror that reflects the caller more than anyone else, and that's not who you are. So, why don't you tell Wes you're sorry, son."

Hands in the pockets of his patched overalls, Pee-wee stared at his feet as he kicked at a clump of dirt, "Sorry," he muttered.

Jake tousled his hair. "Good man."

"Can I, Jake, please, please?" Wes said again, disregarding Pee-wee's apology and the others altogether.

Jake turned and squatted before the little boy with a sad smile. "Sorry, Wes, but I can't give rides to boys who don't mind their parents. You see, parents are a blessing from above, son, and something these other boys don't have, so I'm not inclined to give rides to somebody who doesn't appreciate and respect their own." He paused to clasp the boy's frail shoulder. "Do you understand?"

Wes blinked and then nodded with a glaze of moisture in his eyes.

"Good." Jake patted his shoulder. "Because you see, when I'm done here, I'll be coming over to your house for lemonade with your sister, and I sure would be glad to see a boy who obeys his parents so I can give him a ride the next time I come over."

"Yes, sir."

"Good boy. Now, you head on home and apologize to your mother, you hear? And tell your sister I'll be over in about twenty minutes or so, all right?"

"Yes, sir," Wes said.

Head bowed, Wes nodded and trudged back to his own yard, hands buried deep in the pockets of his knickers while Jake watched, remembering all the times his own mother had tried to discipline him to no avail. A sharp twinge cramped in his chest. And his step-pa too, when he wasn't busy keeping law and order as the sheriff of Hellgate, Montana.

Jake battled a sudden sting of moisture that threatened at the back of his lids, throat as thick as the regret in his gut. A man who had tried to save him—discipline him—but couldn't.

Keeping instruction is the path to life; but he that forsaketh reproof goeth astray.

Dear Lord, what Jake wouldn't give to have them all back again—kin, parents, and a blood family to love.

But he couldn't. Because they were all gone.

Along with any desire to ever go astray again.

CHAPTER NINETEEN

"**W**ELL, THIS WAS AN ENJOYABLE day, don't you think?" Stifling a yawn, Maggie shut the door to the bedroom that she and Blaze had shared since they wed on Valentine's day, hardly able to believe they'd been married almost six months. A contented sigh drifted from her lips as she studied her husband, obviously fresh from his bath with a towel cinched around his hips and hair damp. With his back to her, he rifled through his bureau drawer for fresh long johns, giving her ample opportunity to drink in the raw masculinity that had drawn every woman in Virginia City since the day Maggie arrived.

Including me.

Sun-streaked hair unruly with wet curls was a perfect match for thick biceps, broad shoulders, and a hard-sculpted back that narrowed into slim hips. Nibbling the edge of her smile, she exhaled again as she leaned back against their door, hands still clutched behind her on the knob, quite sure her husband was the most handsome man in all of Nevada. "A *most* enjoyable day, indeed. Don't you think, Blaze?"

No answer.

"Blaze?" Maggie watched him slip into his long johns, never turning around as he proceeded to button them up, his silence all but deafening from the best friend usually prone to sharing his day with her every night in bed.

Among other things.

Without a word, he strode toward their bed and slashed the covers back on his side before dropping down on his back, eyes closed and a scowl on his face while he lay with hands folded on his stomach.

Maggie blinked. "Blaze?" Moving toward the bed, she paused before squatting to skim a palm down his bristled jaw. "Are you all right, sweetheart?"

"Apparently not, Maggie," he said in the closest thing to a growl she'd heard in six months of marriage. He abruptly turned on his side to shut her out, that broad, muscled back suddenly not as appealing as before. "Go to bed, and we'll talk in the morning."

She stood, jaw dangling as she strove to contain her temper. Fortifying with a calming breath, she quietly marched to her side of the bed and sat down to take off her shoes with her back to him. "Be ye angry, and sin not," she said in a soft tone, determined to get to the bottom of her husband's surly mood, "and let not the sun go down upon your wrath. Ephesians 4:26."

Rising, she promptly carried her shoes to the closet and retrieved her nightgown hanging on the inside of the door. "Neither give place to the devil. Ephesians 4:27."

A smile squirmed on her lips as she returned to the bed, his eyes pinched as tightly closed as his mouth while she faced him to unbutton her blouse. "And grieve not the holy Spirit of God, whereby ye are sealed unto the day of redemption, but let all bitterness, and wrath, and anger, and clamour, and evil speaking, be put away from you, with all malice. Ephesians 4:30-31."

She bit back a grin when she noted the mulish clamp of his jaw, well aware that Brendan Zachery Donovan could be as stubborn as he was handsome. Removing her blouse, she tossed it on the bed, taking careful aim to slide it down his face. "Be not quick in your spirit to become angry," she continued as she removed her skirt, unable to keep the tease from her tone as she lobbed the skirt onto his head. "for anger lodges in the bosom of fools."

"This is *not* funny, Maggie!" he hissed as he hurled her clothing right back at her, brows digging low while he jolted up.

"No?" Maggie methodically began to untie the laces of her corset. "Well, to be honest, Blaze, I wouldn't know if it's funny or not since you refuse to talk to me."

He slammed a fist on the bed. "You know blasted well what this is about, Maggie, so don't stand there and pretend that you don't."

Silently gathering up her blouse, skirt, and corset, she released a quiet sigh while she hung each item in her closet, completely aware that Blaze had been out of sorts ever since Clay Morgan showed up, and even downright curt with the man. But never once after six blissful months as man and wife did Maggie think he would ever take it out on her.

Anxious to make amends, she made her way to the bed to sit on her side, facing him with eyes lowered while she absently fiddled with the nightgown bunched in her lap. "Well, I know you seemed out of sorts over Clay Morgan all evening, Blaze, but I'm not exactly sure why you would be angry at me."

"Come on, Maggie, you're one of the smartest women I know, so I'll just bet if you try real hard, you can figure it out."

Gaze fixed on the nightgown, she fiddled with its silken tie, not anxious to talk about her part in bringing Clay Morgan to a family affair.

"Did you invite Clay Morgan to the ranch?"

Her head shot up, eyes as wide as her mouth. "No, of course not! Why would you think that?"

"Because Jake saw him fawning over you and Sheridan outside the arena, so I'm pretty sure somebody put the idea in his head. Was it Sheridan?" He leaned in, those sapphire-blue eyes she fell in love with now so cool, she felt a chill.

"Well, not *exactly* …" She quickly launched the nightgown over her head, stalling as long as she could by grappling it onto her arms.

"And what's that supposed to mean?"

"It means, Blaze …" Maggie wrestled both the nightgown

in place and her thoughts, striving for the best way to phrase something her husband would not want to hear. Her gaze finally rose to meet his as she buttoned the gown. "That Clay Morgan had a question for Finn, so Sheridan suggested Finn would be available Sunday afternoon."

"Tarnation, Maggie!" Blaze gouged stiff fingers through his hair. "Why the devil didn't you stop her?"

Maggie was barely aware she was picking at her nails. "I tried, Blaze, at first, honestly I did, but then I didn't see the harm—"

"That's because you don't know Sheridan like we do, Maggie, so you don't know how blasted vulnerable she is."

Maggie placed a gentle hand on Blaze's leg. "She's only vulnerable because you've made her that way, Blaze—you, Finn, Dash, and Jake, isolating her from the outside world instead of letting her grow up normally."

Blaze pushed her hand away. "Stay out of this, Maggie— Uncle Finn, Dash, and I all made a vow to Ma before she died that we'd protect Sher and Shay, so we know what we're doing."

"Do you?" Her voice softened into a plea. "Sheridan is a normal, red-blooded American girl who longs for the attention of boys her age, Blaze."

"Yeah, that's what I'm afraid of." He grabbed his pillow and punched it hard several times, slapping it against the headboard before finally plopping down, staring at the ceiling through slits. "Along with those red-blooded American males like I used to be."

Oh, Blaze. A reedy sigh seeped through Maggie's lips as she tenderly touched his shoulder, remembering all too well how Blaze took advantage of women before he found the faith that opened his eyes. "She's not you, Blaze," she whispered. "She's a bright and curious young woman, almost nineteen years old, who deserves the same chance to grow up as you and Dash had. To learn to defend herself just like both of you did. Which is why she's going off to college in the first place."

A tic pulsed in his cheek. "No, she's going off to college because Aunt Libby strong-armed Uncle Finn! Found out he made a blasted promise to my mother to get her girls an education like Dash and me, which a woman flat-out doesn't need."

Maggie jolted straight up, shoulders squared. "I beg your pardon?"

He stared her down. "It's all fine and well you have an education, Maggie, but you might as well admit it now— once you have my babies, that degree will be nothing more than a useless piece of paper."

"*If* I have your babies," Maggie bit out, her temper hanging on by a thread, "which at the moment, doesn't look too promising."

He brandished a blunt finger. "Look, Maggie—women need to be protected, and I made a promise to Ma before she died that I would do just that for both Sher and Shay. So, I'm just doing my job as Sheridan's big brother until a husband can take over down the road."

Maggie's chin lashed up. "Oh, yeah? Well, I did just fine protecting myself against you, Blaze Donovan, if you recall, and I say Sheridan deserves the chance to do the same."

"Oh, sure you did"—Blaze mocked her with a slow nod of his head—"like you did with Clint Keller at the rodeo dance last year, weeping your fool head off when he made a pass."

Maggie snapped, along with the bare thread of her temper. Slapping her arms into a rigid fold, she glared him down. "Yes, as a matter of fact, you bull-headed baboon. If you must know, I slapped him silly before you rushed in to play the almighty hero."

"Yeah, that's why you bolted out of the woods into my arms like a scared, little rabbit."

Maggie closed her eyes, counting to ten under her breath before she opened them again with a deep draw of air, determined to remain the adult in this argument. "Blaze," she said quietly, ducking to peer up into his eyes, "I admire your loyalty to Sheridan, truly I do, but you can't protect her from the world." Her gaze softened along with her tone. "Only God can do that, sweetheart."

"You're right, Maggie"—he rammed a thumb to his chest—"and He's using *me* to do it, along with Uncle Finn, Dash, and Jake, so I suggest you just drop it right now and listen to that Bible you're so fond of quoting. Because as my wife, it says you have an obligation to stand by me, not my little sister."

"But you're being ridiculous!" Maggie shouted, fists clenched at her sides to keep from shaking him silly.

"No, I'm being a responsible brother who knows Sheridan a lot better than you, darlin', so I'm asking you for the last time to trust me in this, not her."

"But, Blaze—"

He bludgeoned the headboard with his palm. "For the last blasted time, Maggie—she's *my* sister, so butt out!"

The harshness of his words halted her air as his face blurred before her, the sting of her tears burning in her eyes as she stared at the man who promised to cherish her all the days of her life. "All right, Blaze, I'll butt out," she whispered, rising from the bed with her pillow in hand as she moved toward the door, "out of this conversation, *and* out of your bed."

"Maggie, wait—"

But she didn't.

Instead she closed the door on her husband's words, swiping at her eyes while she hurried to Sheridan's room, suddenly painfully aware that something had just drastically changed.

Because the honeymoon was definitely over.

CHAPTER TWENTY

CLUTCHING HER PILLOW TO HER chest, Sheridan sighed, the wispy sound lingering in the air along with her memories as she curled into a ball of contentment, reliving one of the most romantic days of her life.

Her mouth crooked. *Of course* it was *only* one of *two* romantic days in her life—the other being the kiss with Jake—thanks to the men in her family, who were bound and determined to protect her from the male element.

She gave a lazy stretch as she plopped on her back, a near-giddy smile sneaking across her lips. But what they didn't know was that *she* was even more bound and determined to experience the romance she'd dreamed about since the age of four.

With Jacob Michael Sullivan.

But my oh my, who knew it was going to be this fun to make him jealous? A tiny giggle popped out while she stared at the ceiling of her moonlit bedroom, her grin growing as she thought of the scowl Jake had worn from the moment Clay arrived. Her chest gave a little heave as she expelled another quiet sigh.

Of course, since "the kiss," Jake pretty much scowled all the time these days anyway, at least around her. So, she wasn't sure if she should be happy or sad that she had single-handedly transformed the easy-going big brother with the perennial smile into the resident grouch of Silver Lining Ranch.

Her smile returned. But Clay had certainly ramped Jake's scowl up several degrees, a situation that convinced Sheridan once and for all that Jake cared about her more than he wanted to admit.

Which is exactly what she had to get him to do—*admit* his feelings for her. And she was pretty sure Mr. Clay Morgan was just the ticket, and a mighty handsome one to boot.

Tap. Tap.

Sheridan sat up in the dark with a pinch in her brow. "Come in."

The door slowly squealed open, revealing what looked like a shadow in a chemise. "Sher? I didn't waken you, did I?" Maggie's voice was quiet and low, tinged with just a touch of nasal.

"No, of course not, Maggie. Is ... everything all right?"

Sheridan heard her sister-in-law's sniff before she closed the door behind her, quietly making her way to Sheridan's bed. "No, not really," she whispered. "Blaze and I had a fight, so I was wondering if maybe I could sleep with you?"

Sheridan blinked, eyes spanning wide at both the moonlit trail of tears on Maggie's cheeks and her own shock that Blaze and she were fighting at all. "Oh, Maggie, absolutely!" She scooted over and lifted the quilt coverlet for her sister-in-law to slip in, her own heart aching along with her. "What on earth happened?" she asked as she reached to tug a clean handkerchief from her nightstand drawer, handing it over.

"Thanks." Burrowing deep beneath the sheet, Maggie took the handkerchief and dabbed at her face with another sodden sniff. "Blaze is mad at me because of Clay."

"What?!" Sheridan sat straight up. "Why?"

Maggie expelled a shaky breath. "He's angry because Jake saw us talking to Clay at the Wild West Show, so he thinks I had a part in Clay coming over. That I should have stopped you from talking to Clay in the first place, giving him the idea he could come to the ranch."

"Oh, Maggie, I am *so* sorry!" Sheridan laid a gentle hand on Maggie's arm. "I never meant to get you in trouble with Blaze. But I suppose that's a side effect of making Jake jealous since the two of them *are* in cahoots." She wiggled her brows. "And it did work like a dream, given Jake's nasty mood because goodness, I've never seen him so cranky and out of sorts."

Her smile dimmed a hair as she blew out a wispy sigh. "Except, of course, when he had to teach me to shoot, that is." Her chin rose with a definite pinch of pluck. "But with Clay in the picture now, I'm hoping that makes Jake Sullivan forget all about Megan Joy and focus a little more on me." She grabbed Maggie's hand. "Either way, I'm just sorry for getting you involved."

Sitting up against the headboard, Maggie blew her nose. "No, Sheridan, it's Blaze who should be sorry for not letting you live your own life or me living mine! Aunt Libby always told me a woman has to be strong and stand her ground in a marriage or the man will ride roughshod over her, and now I see she was right."

"So, what are you going to do?" Sheridan whispered, "besides sleep here tonight?"

Maggie sniffed. "And tomorrow night and the night after if I have to"—she paused, head tipped in question—"that is, if it's all right with you?"

"Of course it is!" A smile tickled Sheridan's lips. "Actually, it'll be fun—like a girls' giggle fest, although I doubt Blaze will see any humor in it."

"Good," Maggie said with a heft of her chin, a hint of a smile squirming on her lips. "It's time my husband discovers 'marriage is a partnership, not a dictatorship,' like Aunt Libby is so fond of saying"—she gave Sheridan a wink—"*over* and *over*, as a matter of fact. But thank goodness I've attended enough suffragist meetings with her back in New York to know just how important it is to not let a man bully me. So, I refuse to 'butt out' of your life like he told me to do."

"He said that to you?" Sheridan's mouth dropped open.

"Yes, but he's just going to have to learn that 'justice and liberty for all' means wives too." She pinched Sheridan's waist. "And sisters!"

Sheridan launched into her sister-in-law's arms. "Oh, Maggie, I just love you to pieces! Blaze may be a bully, but he's an awfully smart one for marrying you."

"Well, I'm not always so sure about that, but I can tell you one thing, sweet sister-in-law of mine," she said with a return squeeze laced with giggles, "he's going to be a *whole* lot smarter before we're through."

CHAPTER TWENTY-ONE

"I'M SO GLAD YOU CAME over tonight, Jake." Megan Joy's voice was a husky whisper as she scooted a bit closer on their back-porch swing, the full moon overhead highlighting both the sheen of her dark curls and the glimmer of hope in her eyes. "This was fun."

Rib cage expanding and contracting, Jake realized that she was right—it *had* been fun spending the evening with the Burdzy's. Drinking lemonade and playing whist with the family. Not to mention sitting on the back-porch swing with a pretty girl who actually smelled like lemon drops and offered him peppermint candy. His mouth suddenly watered at the thought of two of his two favorite tastes.

Sidling a wee bit closer, Megan Joy laid her head against his shoulder, and Jake's mouth suddenly watered for a taste of a whole 'nother kind. He tugged her a hair closer, the warmth of her body rousing his senses. Well, maybe it was time. After all, he and Blake had spent most of their teens kissing on pretty girls, something Jake discovered he had a real fondness for.

But the moment the gals they sparked got a little older, getting ideas about marriage in their heads? Well, both he and Blaze would step real gingerly, backing off from those same girls like they were bull patties in a cow pasture. That's when Jake decided all the sparkin' wasn't worth it, even though Blaze tried to talk him into canoodling with gals at the Ponderosa like Blaze did before Maggie.

Something about leading a gal on just didn't sit well with Jake back then, not to mention he was pretty sure his Bible frowned upon the kind of sparkin' Blaze used to do. And so, since he didn't particularly approve of Blaze's flirtations, Jake decided to concentrate on other things while Blaze was out foolin' around. Things like working with Sister Fred's orphans, or shooting, riding, fishing, poker, pool, or even horseshoes or cornhole with Half-Pint.

Half-Pint. He frowned.

The very reason he was here tonight. He thought of Clay Morgan flirting with Sheridan, and made up his mind right on the spot that Megan Joy was just what he needed. A pretty gal to nuzzle. A soft girl to kiss. A few moments that just might drive another woman—blue blistering blazes, Sullivan, she's a *little girl!*—right out of his mind.

"Did … you … have fun tonight, Jake?" The uncertainty in Megan Joy's question pierced him to the core.

Slipping an arm over her shoulder, he pulled her close. "Yes, ma'am, I surely did." His fingers toyed with the cap sleeve of her dress, his blood warming over the delicious lemon scent of her hair. "Especially right now," he whispered, suddenly wanting nothing more than to taste that tantalizing peppermint in her mouth. One hand caressing the nape of her neck, he carefully eased her head to face his with the other, eyes sheathing closed as he slowly bent to fondle her mouth.

"Oh, Jake," she whispered, and the soft sound of his name on her lips kindled a fire dormant way too long, enticing him to delve deeper into a kiss that lured a soft moan from her throat. "This is what I've dreamed about for so very long …"

"Me too," he said in a husky tone as he gently explored her mouth with his own. His body suddenly stilled when he realized that it's what he dreamed about too.

With Sheridan. Every night of his miserable life.

Expelling a guilty sigh, he pulled away to cup Megan Joy's face in his hands. "Megan Joy, I need to go home before we get carried away, darlin'."

"But … but will I see you again?" The fragile hope in her voice crushed him, piercing his heart with the shame that tonight, he was no better than Blaze before he married

Maggie.

"Megan Joy," he began, voice soft with remorse—

A terrified scream suddenly shattered the air.

Jake jolted up from the swing, heart racing at the sound of Miss Cramer's cry from the orphanage next door. "Thank you for a lovely evening, Megan Joy," he rasped as he all but leapt off the Burdzy's front porch, shooting a look of apology over his shoulder before he vaulted the wrought-iron fence. Legs pumping as hard as his pulse, he bolted up the back-porch steps and banged on the kitchen door. "Miss Cramer?"

He stared in the window, the house completely dark except for a thin stream of light in the hall. Reaching on top of the door jamb, Jake retrieved the hidden key he and Blaze used whenever they helped Mr. Murphy with various repairs. He unlocked the door and squinted into the dark. "Miss Cramer?"

"In h-here," a trembling voice called.

Jake found her crying in her office with her head on the desk. "Miss Cramer!" He rushed around to gently lift her to her feet. "Are you hurt?"

"Oh, Jake!" She fell into his arms, body wrenching with sobs that tore at his heart. "N-Nooo, b-but we w-were r-robbed ... every c-cent of the m-money S-Sister Fred gave m-me for this m-month's b-budget."

"Tell me everything," he said calmly while he gently sat her back down in her chair, squatting as he handed her his handkerchief. "Did you see who did it?"

"Not r-really because it all happened so fast," she said with a heave, fingers shaking as she swiped at her eyes. "He almost knocked me down running from the parlour out the front door, so I only s-saw the back of him."

"Tell me exactly what happened, then, ma'am."

Blowing her nose, she sagged back in the chair with a quiver. "I ... l-locked the door as usual and turned out the l-lights, then went upstairs to help Sister Marguerite and Sister Berta read to the children. But then I heard something ... almost like a crash downstairs. So, I went to check, and that's when I screamed because a man bolted from my office and out the door like a blur, almost knocking me over. I hurried to lock it, of course, but not before I saw him jump on a horse and ride away."

She peered up with red-rimmed eyes potent with fear. "It was d-dark, Jake, so I d-didn't really see him, but he appeared to be a big man—tall with heavy girth. And when I rushed into my office to make sure everything was okay, I ... I ..." Tears pooled as her chin began to quiver.

Jake gently rubbed her arm. "Go on, Miss Cramer. That's when you what?"

She nodded to a lower desk drawer with a lock that had been shimmied open, wood splintered at the top. "That's when I saw that the desk drawer in which I lock the orphanage funds was ... was ... b-broken into, and the money was g-gone ...."

Her words trailed into a forlorn wail, and gathering her in his arms, Jake rubbed her back. "It's all right, Miss Cramer. We'll find him," he whispered, "but first I need some information."

She nodded against his chest and attempted to compose herself as she sat up straight.

"Did you see what he was wearing?"

"Like I said, it was dark and it happened so fast, but it appeared to be a light suitcoat—gray, maybe?—that came to his mid-thigh or so because I saw it flap open when he jumped on his horse."

"Hat?"

Her head bobbed. "Yes, it appeared to be a common black derby, but I remember his hair was longer—just over his collar."

"And his horse? Quarter horse? Morgan? Appaloosa? Paint?"

She squinted in thought. "Well, I don't know much about breeds, Jake, but I do remember it was mostly white with what looked like two large markings of tan on the rear, one on either side of the tail, I think. And a mane that was white with black streaks."

Jake nodded. "Mustang. What direction did he go?"

"Toward town, I believe."

"Good. How much money did he take?"

More tears welled. "Fifty dollars—an entire month's allowance."

"In what denominations?"

Her chin trembled. "It was two twenty-dollar bills and one ten-dollar bill in an envelope marked with my name."

"Do you have any idea how he got in?"

She motioned toward a front window that had been busted in. "It seems he broke in through the window."

Jake expelled a heavy sigh as he glanced at the broken glass. "Mr. Murphy will have to replace that in the morning," he said, referring to the handyman that worked for the orphanage, "but for now, I'll move your bureau against the window." He shot a glance into the hallway. "Sister Marguerite and Sister Berta are with the children?"

"Yes. The children were frightened when they heard my scream, so I didn't want the sisters to leave them."

Rising, he strode toward the bureau against the wall and shoved it against the window, grunting with every heave. "Lock the door behind me and the back one as well. I'll return as soon as I can to check on you before I head back to the ranch."

"What are you going to do, Jake?" She followed him to the front door, arms clutched to her waist.

He expelled another weary sigh, wishing Marshal Tanner wasn't out on a posse. Deputy Wilcox was practically a kid without much clout and a poor aim to boot. "I plan to pay a visit to Deputy Wilcox, then a visit to the Bucket of Blood Saloon because I have a suspicion that's where our thief just might be." He opened the door and turned. "Just one last thing, Miss Cramer. Did you happen to notice any particular smell about the thief?"

She blinked several times, as if she couldn't believe she'd

failed to mention it. "Oh my goodness, yes! He smelled like ..."—she peered up with a scrunch of her nose—"like licorice."

"Sen-Sen," he said with a wry twist of lips, pretty darn sure Slick Sikeston—a notorious gunslinger and gambler— was their man. "Only a few men I know that chew it instead of tobacco. Lock the door and go to bed, Miss Cramer, and I'll check on the orphanage before I head home." He gave her shoulder a reassuring grip. "We'll get your money back, ma'am."

"Oh, Jake, you're a godsend!" Miss Cramer whispered, moisture gathering in her lashes once again. "And I can't thank you enough."

Nodding, he clambered down the front steps, a tic in his jaw as he stormed toward where his horse was tied up to the Burdzy's front post.

A godsend. He cut loose with a harsh grunt. Maybe tonight, but not in his past. Untying Midnight's rein, Jake gave his neck a quick scrub before mounting into the saddle.

And definitely not for a man who chewed Sen-Sen.

CHAPTER TWENTY-TWO

*T*AP. *TAP.*
Still giggling and talking in Sheridan's bed thirty minutes later, Sheridan and Maggie went completely silent at the sound of a knock on the door, gazes locking before Sheridan squeezed Maggie's hand. "Who is it?"

"It's Aunt Libby, darling. May I come in?"

Sheridan bounded from the bed in a virtual leap, swinging the door wide. "Oh, you bet, Aunt Libby, because we're having a girls' bedtime chat, and we sure could use your experience and expertise in dealing with hard-headed men."

"Ooooo, my favorite subject!" Libby hurried in with a devious rub of hands, plopping down on the bed in her nightgown. "I heard giggles on my way to the bathroom, so I'm glad I knocked on your door." She winked. "Especially since Finn is sound asleep."

"Me too," Sheridan said, returning to her side of the bed. She scampered into the middle, patting the empty spot on her right for Aunt Libby. "Snuggle in, Aunt Libby."

Maggie scooted over to make more room. "Yes, please do because you're just the person we need to talk to."

"About what?" Libby glanced from Sheridan to Maggie and back.

"*Wellllll* ..." Sheridan peeked at Maggie with a nervous bite of her lip before returning her gaze to her aunt. "Maggie and Blaze had a fight, so Maggie came to sleep with me tonight."

Concern immediately wrinkled Libby's brow as she searched Maggie's face. "Oh my goodness, Maggie, are you all right?"

"I am, Aunt Libby, but I'm afraid Blaze isn't." She put a

hand to her lips to stifle a giggle. "Or at least, I hope he isn't."

Libby pursed her lips. "Margaret Rose Donovan, I thought we agreed last year that you would call me Libby since we're dear friends."

"Whoops—sorry, Libby, but hearing Sheridan call you Aunt Libby brought back the habit." Maggie reached across Sheridan to give Libby's hand a quick squeeze. "You see, Sheridan, before I married your brother, Libby was my mother's dearest friend, not my actual aunt, but that's what I called her back then—Aunt Libby. But then last year, she became my dearest friend, too, so we decided to dispense with the title even though, after marrying Blaze, she's now also my aunt as well." She looped an arm to Sheridan's waist. "But aunt, nieces, or sisters-in-law, the best thing is we are all best friends now, right?"

"Right!" Libby agreed with a firm nod of her head, tucking her arm around Sheridan on the other side, uniting the three of them in a side-by-side hug. "Oh, how I love this—three strong women in the same house!"

"Uh, speaking of strong, Libby," Maggie began with a wink at Sheridan, "we have a bit of a woman's issue to discuss."

Libby actually clasped her hands to her chest with a little hop, looking far younger than her forty years with thick auburn hair trailing her shoulders and a little-girl grin on her beautiful face. "Oh, pinch me, *please*, because this has to be the best dream I've had in a long, long while. A woman's issue??" Her shoulders rose and fell in a delighted sigh as she crossed her palms over her heart. "Next to romance, there's nothing I love more than discussing women's issues, so let's have it, ladies, because I am a captive audience."

Sneaking a peek at Maggie for encouragement, Sheridan turned back to her aunt. "Uh ... well, then you are *really* going to like this discussion, Aunt Libby, I promise, because it's about a woman's issue that *involves* romance."

"Oooooo!" Libby shimmied into a cross-legged position. "I haven't had any of that since Finn and I got married last year, when we butted heads over his stance on women's rights before the mayoral election."

She rubbed her palms together with a wiggle of brows, making both Sheridan and Maggie laugh. Everyone was aware that Aunt Libby was a suffragist in the truest sense of the word, a situation that had almost derailed her marriage to Finn. "So, spill it, please, girls—what's on your minds?"

Maggie flopped back against the headboard with a noisy gust of air. "Well, as Sheridan said, I'm bunking with her tonight because Blaze and I had our very first argument."

Libby shifted to face them both, smile dimming. "About what, Maggie?"

Maggie tucked her knees to her chest and plopped her chin on top. "Blaze is angry at me because Clay showed up tonight."

"What?" Libby bowed her head, face in a scrunch. "Whatever for?"

Sheridan peeked up at her aunt as she picked at her nails. "Because I sort of, kind of invited Clay to come over today when we met him outside the arena, and Blaze is mad at Maggie because she was with me at the time."

"Yep." Maggie's mouth went flat. "Not only is my husband trying to control his sister, but he's also trying to control me, telling me in no uncertain terms I needed to 'butt out' of Sheridan's life."

"Pardon me?" Libby splayed a hand to her chest, green eyes narrowing into battle mode. "Ohhhhh, I see ... like nephew, like uncle apparently, bullying his wife around like Finn tried to do when we got married."

Libby's mouth compressed as she shook her head. "I will admit Finn has come a long way, but we can never let our guard down, ladies, in our fight for equality and independence." She reached to pat Maggie's hand. "I am so proud of you for standing up for yourself with Blaze, Maggie. The first lesson that man needs to learn is that 'marriage is a partnership, not a dictatorship.'"

Sheridan and Maggie exchanged a grin.

"And *you*, young lady," Libby continued with a thrust of her chin in Sheridan's direction, "are a woman of eighteen now—almost nineteen—so you also have to learn how to stand up for yourself with men. Which means you cannot let your brother—or your uncle—infringe on your God-given rights to life, liberty, and the pursuit of happiness, understood?"

"Yes, ma'am." Sheridan nodded, so very grateful for the strength and support of both her aunt and sister-in-law after growing up without any female influence.

"Which is exactly why I battled so hard with your uncle to let you go away to Vassar instead of attending the Normal School for teachers here in Virginia City," Aunt Libby said with a pat of Sheridan's hand. "Because as Maggie will discover tonight and you, at Vassar in the fall, when it comes to convincing our men"—she winked—"sometimes distance can be a very good thing."

CHAPTER TWENTY-THREE

"**U**H, AUNT LIBBY?" SCRAPING HER lip with her teeth, Sheridan peeked up at her aunt who sat Indian-style in front of her on Sheridan's bed, just like Kathy Jean and Sophia would always do. "I know you're the one responsible for me going away to Vassar, and I can't thank you enough. But ... well ... the truth is—I'm reluctant to go."

Aunt Libby stared, mouth parted in surprise. "Why, whatever for, sweetheart? Vassar is a wonderful school, and you'll finally have your freedom from your brothers and uncle for the very first time."

"I know." Sheridan lowered her gaze as she picked at her nails. "But ... but ... "

"She's in love with Jake," Maggie said quietly, reminding Sheridan just how little time she had to win Jake's heart. "And she's been hoping for Jake to return that love before she leaves for school—"

"To put my mind and heart at rest," Sheridan interjected, "so I can focus on my studies without worry—"

"*Which* is why we invited Clay to the ranch in the first place." Maggie gently rubbed Sheridan's back. "To hopefully make Jake jealous."

"*Ohhhhhhh ...*" Libby's eyes flared wide as she put a hand to her mouth. "Oh my, now I see ..." She ducked to peer up into Sheridan's face. "Does Jake know how you feel, Sheridan? And does he feel the same?"

Sheridan shot a quick glance at Maggie. "Uh ... yes, Jake knows how I feel, and he's given me some indication he might feel the same, but he doesn't seem inclined to follow through." Moisture burned beneath her lids. "In fact, he came right out and said it was something he neither wants nor will ever allow."

"*Some* Indication?" Libby glanced from Sheridan to Maggie and back. "Like what, sweetheart?"

Sheridan hesitated as heat roared to her cheeks, unwilling to admit to her aunt how brazen she'd been. But, then, what choice did she have? "Well, he ... he ..."—eyes tightly closed, she picked at a hangnail, not even wincing when she pulled it clean off—"k-kissed me."

Silence.

Sheridan's lashes lifted, rib cage constricting when she saw the gape of her aunt's mouth. She rushed to explain. "It's a long story, Aunt Libby," she said, words tumbling faster than her stomach, "but the gist of it is that Jake fell over a rock while he was teaching me to shoot, knocking him clean out, and I was so worried he was dead that I ... I ..."

She squeezed her eyes closed once again, unable to look her aunt in the face while she took in a deep gulp of air. "I ... um ... well, I kissed *him* first ..." The last phrase came out as a whisper of shame while she covered her face with her hands, convinced her aunt would be appalled at her unseemly behavior. And sweet mother of mercy, if Aunt Libby ever told Uncle Finn ...

"Oh, I see ..." Aunt Libby said in a hush. "So, you kissed him first, and then he kissed you back?"

Sheridan gulped and opened her eyes. "Well, not exactly. You see, I kissed him to see if he was faking or really knocked out, and he pushed me away, claiming he wasn't attracted to me. But I heard him moan, Aunt Libby, I swear, when I kissed him that first time, so I ... I ..." A knot ducked in her throat as she gave a tiny shrug. "Kissed him again, hoping to prove the attraction, and *that's* when he groaned and kissed me back so thoroughly, my bones felt like mush. But please, Aunt Libby, you have to promise never to tell Uncle Finn because I would absolutely *die* if he ever found out!"

Libby blinked several times. "Uh … I'm sure it's safe to say he would, too, sweetheart, as protective as he is of Shaylee and you." She swiped the handkerchief from Maggie's hand, fanning herself furiously while she loosened the top button of her nightgown. "Great balls of fire, Sheridan, it reminds me of my first kiss with your uncle when I wasn't much older than you."

"So, you, you …"—Sheridan swallowed hard—"understand?"

The handkerchief flapped to a stop mid-air as Libby's brows rose. "Understand? More than you know, young lady, because your uncle weakened me at the knees more times than I can count before we were courting, but I sure don't understand Jake."

Her mouth pursed in thought as her gaze drifted into a pensive stare. "It certainly seems from what you said that he's attracted to you, although I can almost hear Finn saying that any man would respond if a woman threw herself at him—"

Sheridan caught a harsh breath as heat toasted her cheeks. "Please, Aunt Libby, that's why you can't ever tell him because I would be mortified!"

"Oh, I'm sorry, sweetheart!" Libby gave Sheridan a quick hug. "Of course, I will never tell him, I promise. I didn't mean that the way it sounded, of course, but we do have to look at this from every angle, right?"

Sheridan's weak nod wobbled as Jake's words came back to haunt.

"Yeah, well that tends to happen, Half-Pint, when a girl looks and acts more like a painted gal at The Silver Pistol than the proper daughter of the mayor."

Libby ducked to pin Sheridan with a probing gaze. "Do you really believe in your heart that Jake cares for you that way, sweetheart?"

Sheridan's eyelids fluttered closed as she thought about Jake's kiss like she'd done a hundred times since—the tight clutch of his arms, the press of his lips, possessive yet tender, the hoarse groan of desire when his husky words had feathered her ear.

"God, please *give me strength—my heart can't take this ..."*

Her lids popped up as she stared at her aunt with wide eyes. "Yes, Aunt Libby, I ... I really do. Not just because of the kiss he gave me, which more than proved he was attracted to me, but because of the prayer he whispered in the throes of that kiss. He said, 'God, *please* give me strength—my heart can't take this ...'"

Maggie shook Sheridan's arm. "Wait—you didn't tell me that!"

"Because I just now remembered it. I don't know how to explain it, but it was almost like he was thinking it instead of saying it outright, you know? Which is probably why I didn't remember it, I suppose, almost as if I dreamed it. But I sure remember it now—the barest of whispers warm in my ear before he literally kissed the daylights out of me."

Maggie snatched her handkerchief back from Libby, commencing to doing a little fanning of her own. "Sweet chorus of angels, Sheridan, that's enough to make me go back to my room," she muttered.

Sheridan grabbed her aunt's hand, cupping it with both of her own. "Oh, Aunt Libby, don't you see? Why would Jake pray for strength not to kiss me if he didn't want to?"

"Well, he is a man, Sheridan, and you are a very attractive woman." Crossing her arms, Libby propped a fist to her chin, face scrunched in thought. "So, it is possible he didn't want to take advantage of the attraction from a moral and loyalty standpoint, I suppose ..."

"But he *did* say his heart couldn't take it as well, Libby," Maggie volunteered, her train of thought apparently in stride with Sheridan's. "So, to me that suggests his heart is involved as well, doesn't it?"

"It would certainly seem so," Libby said, "but what on earth is stopping him, then?"

Maggie met Sheridan's gaze before she arched a brow at Libby. "Our husbands, I suspect. We all know how overprotective both Blaze and Finn have been with Sheridan, practically keeping her under lock and key. They simply refuse to allow her to grow up as a normal young woman who interacts with young men, which is downright wrong."

"Agreed," Libby said with a firm nod of her head. "Which is why going to Vassar will be so valuable for her." Her eyes softened as they met Sheridan's. "But I certainly understand your hesitation to leave, sweetheart, because I felt the very same way when I was eighteen."

Her smile was soft as her gaze wandered into a faraway look. "Goodness, I remember being so smitten with your uncle the summer of my senior year when we'd worked together as festival volunteers, that I tried to talk my mother out of my going to Vassar at all. I even begged to go to Mill's Ladies College north of San Francisco to be closer to home, but my mother would have none of it because Vassar was her alma mater."

Her smile suddenly flattened as her lovesick look disappeared in a wry twist of her lips. "Which turned out to be a godsend because Finn 'McShame' as I often referred to him back then, stood me up for the festival dance by taking Jo Beth instead."

"Oh, Aunt Libby!" Sheridan put a hand to her mouth. "What an awful thing to do!"

"I thought so." Libby expelled a heavy sigh. "But your uncle used to be a bit of a womanizer back then, I'm afraid— and nothing like sweet, easy-going Jake, for pity's sake—so I can certainly empathize with your hesitation to go away. It's no secret that in the past, I've never been a great judge of men, but I have to admit that Jake certainly seems like a safe bet."

Libby ducked to offer a gentle smile. "And I do believe every woman deserves the right to make her own choices instead of having her bull-headed uncle and brothers dictate whom she may see." She patted Sheridan's leg. "But if Jake doesn't comply before September, keep in mind he'll still be here when you come back, honey, for Christmas and after you graduate."

Against her will, tears hit Sheridan like a flash flood, swelling beneath her lids. "Maybe not, Aunt Libby," she whispered, quickly swiping at her eyes. "He told me he's been seeing Megan Joy."

"What?" Aunt Libby blinked. "Since when? I just spoke with Debbie Burdzy a few days ago, and she never said a peep about it, and we all know she'd print it in the *Territorial Enterprise* if she could."

"Or her daughter would," Maggie said with a playful pinch of Sheridan's arm, obviously hoping to lift Sheridan's spirits.

Sheridan offered a wobbly smile of thanks to her sister-in-law before she turned back to Aunt Libby. "Even so, I know Jake. He hates to lie if he can avoid it." Her lips skewed off-center. "Even though I know he was lying through his teeth when he said he only sees me as a little sister."

She sighed. "But Blaze and Dash always used to make fun of him because he had such a lousy poker face, they claimed he couldn't lie to save his soul. Like one time when the boys went fishing and Blaze teased Jake because he refused to fish with worms, ribbing him mercilessly about being a scaredy-cat."

A faint smile pulled at Sheridan's lips at the memory. "Apparently some mean neighbor boy once dumped a whole bucketful of worms down Jake's pants when he was just three or four. Anyway, to shut Blaze up, Jake claimed, 'scaredy-cats don't eat worms,' then insisted he'd done so many times before, which certainly put an end to the teasing."

Sheridan's teeth tugged at the edge of her smile as she glanced from Libby to Maggie and back. "*Until* he was so riddled with guilt that he had to make it right by swallowing a worm whole right in front of Blaze, Dash, and me."

"No!" Aunt Libby gaped with an open-mouth smile while

Maggie giggled.

"Yep." Sheridan grinned and shook her head at the memory, tone softening whenever she thought about what a man of integrity Jake was, which just made her love him all the more. "Sweet, sweet Jake. The poor guy puked and heaved the rest of the night, which just made the teasing all the worse, I'm afraid."

She drew in a deep breath, her smile dimming when she slowly expelled it with a sudden slump of shoulders. "Which means if Jake told me he's seeing Megan Joy, Aunt Libby, I'm pretty sure he has every intention of making it right by doing just that."

Her aunt's voice was soft. "Which is why you want him to admit he cares for you before you go away."

"Yes, ma'am." Sheridan dropped her head back against the headboard while more moisture rimmed in her eyes. "What am I supposed to do, Aunt Libby? I won't be able to focus on my studies if I'm worried about losing Jake, and Maggie and I have prayed about it too. But we thought in the meantime maybe Clay could light a fire under Jake. But not if Uncle Finn and Blaze refuse to allow him to call on me."

"Mmm …" Aunt Libby shifted to sit beside Sheridan, following suit with her head resting back as well. "I see your dilemma," she said, finger to her chin as she stared straight ahead, eyes squinted in thought. "Well, I suppose I could talk to your Uncle Finn, convince him to let Clay teach you to shoot."

Sheridan spun to face her aunt. "You would do that, Aunt Libby?"

Libby smiled and gave her a quick hug. "Of course I would, sweetheart. After all, we women have to stick together, right?" She suddenly sat straight up with a gleam in her eyes. "Wait! Finn asked me to hold off on starting a suffragist club in Virginia City till after he runs for Senator William Stewart's seat in a little over a year, so I've agreed."

She wiggled her brows. "But he never said *anything* about

a suffragist club in the family, now did he?" You know—
'unus pro omnibus, omnes pro uno'? 'One for all, all for one,'
like in the motto of The Three Musketeers? Well, that can be
our motto, too."

Maggie silently clapped her hands. "Oooooo, 'The Three
Suffrageteers'—I like that, Libby."

Sheridan and Maggie exchanged grins. "Oh, me too!"
Sheridan agreed, lunging to give her Aunt Libby a hug.

Aunt Libby squeezed back with a squeal. "Oh, and I know—
we can call our secret club the Silver Lining independence
Platform—code name 'SLIP,'" she said with a giggle, "since
our very first goal will be to give our menfolk 'the slip' as to
what we are planning on Sheridan's behalf. Then, hopefully
one day, our little club will become the basis for the Nevada
Women's League I hope to start in the future."

"Oh, Libby, yes!" Maggie said, launching her arms around
both Sheridan and Libby in a giddy hug, giggles merging all
around.

Sheridan pulled back, eyes wide with hope. "So, when will
you talk to Uncle Finn, Aunt Libby?"

"Well ..." Libby paused to consider the question. "The
timing has to be perfect, of course, so I think after our dinner
with Clay, his uncle, Annie Oakley and her husband might be
the most opportune time." Arm hooked to Sheridan's waist,
she bent to press a kiss to her niece's head. "So, that will be
my task, and then we'll just take it from there, one step at a
time."

"Yes," Maggie said with an arm to the other side of
Sheridan's waist, giving her sister-in-law a playful pinch,
"and my task will be working on Blaze to broaden his
perspective on women's rights, both with his wife *and* his
sister."

Sheridan could barely contain her excitement, hands
pressed to her chin in prayer mode. "Oh, I am soooo excited,
and I can't thank you both enough!" Fairly quivering with
anticipation, she grinned at Maggie and then at her Aunt

Libby, brows lifted in question. "And what will my task be then?" she asked with a giddy wiggle of feet.

"Oh, that's an easy one." Maggie leaned forward to wink at Libby before she sealed it and each other with a unified hug. "It's your job to pray and look pretty!"

CHAPTER TWENTY-FOUR

JAKE COULD SMELL THE BUCKET of Blood Saloon *long* before he ever entered it, the stench of stale cigar smoke, rotgut whiskey, and grimy men roiling past the swinging doors into the dusty street along with a drunk or two. He'd gone by Deputy Wilcox's house first, and the kid was sound asleep just as Jake had suspected he'd be, so he'd asked him to meet him at the Bucket of Blood Saloon in fifteen minutes.

The tinny sound of piano music floated on the breeze along with the sour smell of sweat and vomit as Jake surveyed the horses tied up in front of one of Virginia City's most notorious saloons. He sure in the devil hated the idea of stepping foot in this cesspool where most of the troublemakers in town could be found, but if he was going to find Slick Sikeston, it would be here.

Squinting in the dark lit only by one dim street light, Jake wasn't ruffled in the least that Sikeston's mustang was absent out front. The notorious gambler and gunslinger wasn't called "Slick" for nothing, so Jake and Midnight moseyed around back, where a hodge-podge collection of horseflesh was tied up to the posts.

Including a pretty mustang with tan markings on its rear.

It was a contest over which pulsed through his veins more— adrenaline or anger—as he dismounted and tied Midnight up to a nearby tree in the back. Half-cocking his Colt 45, he spun the cylinder to double-check his load, then slid it back into his holster. Next, he searched Sikeston's saddlebag on the mustang to make sure the money wasn't there, although he knew the scum's gambling habit demanded a rich purse.

Moving toward the back door of the saloon like a shadow, he carefully stepped over a drunk snoring in the doorway and slipped into the crowd.

"My-my, now *where* in tarnation have they been keeping you, sweetheart?" A pretty woman in her thirties or so— or would be if not for the harshly dyed red hair and heavy rouge—eyed him up and down as he entered the main room. The neckline of her red dress was so low, Jake figured his face had to be a close match given the hot rush of blood in his cheeks. She slipped her arm through his and peeked up beneath sooty lashes. "So, what's your pleasure, Cowboy?"

"I'm looking for Slick Sikeston," he said, raising his voice over the raucous music and laughter, "so I'd be much obliged, ma'am, if you could show me where he is."

She caressed his waist with a pretty tilt of her head. "I can show you a whole lot more than that, honey, so when you're done with Sikeston, you come see me, all right? Name's Jackpot Janie, and I'll be more than happy to show you why." She gave his bicep a seductive squeeze. "And yours is?"

"Jake," he said in a stiff tone.

"Well, Jake"—she nodded across the room to a table in the back where a poker game was going on—"you're in luck because that yellow-bellied varmint just wandered in a little while ago, so he's all yours. But you come back to see me, you hear?"

"Thank you, ma'am." Jake forced a tight smile as he gave her a nod and eased on past, gaze homing in on Sikeston's table with a hard clamp of his jaw. "Sikeston," he said when he stopped in front of his table, voice none too friendly, "been looking for you."

"Well now, will you looky here." Cards in hand, Sikeston leaned back with a lazy smile, one arm casually draped over the back of the chair. "It's the Nevada State Shootout champ three years running, lookin' to take me on." He grinned, and a gold tooth gleamed in his mouth. "Hopin' to weed out the competition, are ya?"

Jake's jaw felt like it was ready to crack, his dislike of Sikeston as strong as the stink of body odor and beer. He'd beaten the nefarious gunslinger over and over in Nevada's State Shootout, so it was no secret to Jake that the lowlife braggart had something to prove and made no bones about it. "You robbed the St. Mary Louise Orphanage tonight, you bucket of scum, and I want every single dime back."

Grinning, Sikeston slowly laid his cards down and began to pick at his teeth, a dangerous glint in his eyes. "You got proof, Sullivan? Because I don't take kindly to false accusations."

In a blink of a lash, Jake had his gun drawn, aimed dead-center at Sikeston's ugly mug, clearing the table *real* fast. Chairs scraped and conversations hushed as Jake cocked his revolver. "I got all the proof I need, slime mold, right there in your vest pocket, so why don't you empty it for me?"

The cocky smile on the weasel's face took a sinister twist as he slowly rose to his feet, greasy strands of dark hair slithering over his collar. "Well, now, why don't we just settle this outside?"

"No need." Jake said with a hard smile, rounding the empty chairs to relieve Sikeston of his gun. He slid it across the table away from the lowlife before pointing his Colt straight at the blackguard's heart. Raise your hands and stand up—*now*."

Pure hate radiated from the lowlife's eyes as he slowly stood up, hands in the air. Jake frisked him real good, jaw calcifying when he found an envelope in his vest pocket with Miss Cramer's name on it.

"Well, well, looky here, Mr. Sikeston." Jake shook the envelope open and peered in, a smile gliding across his lips when he saw two twenties and a ten. "Looks like our orphans will eat for another month." The smile died on his lips as he stashed the envelope in his own vest. "What do you say we pay a little visit to the deputy, shall we?"

Gaze never straying from Sikeston's, Jake lifted his chin to call over his shoulder. "Miss Jackpot Janie?" he shouted, although the room was pert near still as a morgue.

"Here!"

Jake heard the rapid click of heels before Janie magically appeared by his side. "If you don't mind, ma'am, I'd be much obliged if you'd rip that string tie from this buzzard's throat and tie his hands with it real good and tight."

"With pleasure." Janie scooted around Jake just as Deputy Wilcox arrived.

"No need with ties, Jake," the deputy said, pert near huffing and puffing as he held up a brand-spankin'-new set of handcuffs. "I'll take it from here."

"Thanks, Deputy." Jake pulled out the envelope with Miss Cramer's name on it. "Found this in his vest pocket after Miss Cramer gave me a description, so I'll take it back to the orphanage on my way home if that's all right with you."

"Sure, Jake, and thanks." Deputy Wilcox glanced up with a glow of admiration in his eyes like Jake had seen from some of the youngest cowhands on the ranch, reminding him just how young and inexperienced Deputy Wilcox actually was.

Jake paused, his Colt still trained on Sikeston. "You sure, Deputy? Because I can stay—"

"No, sir. The orphanage needs that money, so I appreciate you taking it back to Miss Cramer."

"All right." Jake tipped his hat at Janie before searing Sikeston with a hard glare. "I'll talk Miss Cramer into pressing charges, you can bet on that."

Slowly holstering his revolver, Jake strode toward the door, avoiding the gawks and glares of patrons as he passed.

"Jake—*look out!*" Janie's cry rang out at the sound of a scuffle.

Jake spun and dropped low, gun drawn just as Sikeston took aim, handcuffs dangling loose on one arm while Deputy Wilcox lay dazed on the floor.

Squeezing the trigger of his Colt a split second before Sikeston, Jake blasted the gun from his hand. The firearm slammed hard against the wall, discharging a shot that scattered men like fleas on a dog dipped in lye. A bloodcurdling howl rose before obscenities peppered the air as Sikeston held his gun hand with a groan, fingers dripping with blood.

Deputy Wilcox lumbered up with a dazed look, somehow managing to secure the cuffs on both of Sikeston's wrists by the time Jake strode back to the table.

Holstering his Colt with a cold smile, Jake stared him down, his eyes as hard as Sikeston's. "That was a warning, you yellow-bellied sack of dung. The next time you take a shot at me, it'll be through the heart."

He turned to give a nod to Deputy Wilcox. "You know, Deputy, I do believe I'd like to follow you back for the sheer joy of watching this scoundrel locked up where he belongs, if you don't mind."

"Don't mind at all, Jake. Appreciate the company." He prodded his gun into Sikeston's back. "Get a move on, Sikeston. Got a lumpy cot just waiting for you in a cold, damp cell." More curse words hissed in the air as the Deputy poked Sikeston's back all the way to the front door.

Jake turned to Janie with a polite tip of his hat, offering a grateful smile. "Much obliged, Miss Janie. You saved my life, and I can't thank you enough."

"Why, sure you can, Cowboy," Miss Janie said with a sassy wink. "Just give it a little bit of thought."

Jake couldn't help but grin, truly grateful for Miss Jackpot Janie right about now. "I suspect ol' Slick would be mighty grateful as well if you tended his horse out in the back while he's indisposed. A mottled mustang in tan and white."

He paused assessing her through a playful squint. "And I do believe you would look mighty fine on that mare, Miss Janie, should he be held up a while, you know?" He delivered a wink. "Which is entirely possible for theft and attempted murder." Tipping his hat, Jake strode to the back door of the Bucket of Blood Saloon with a bucket of gratitude for Miss

Jackpot Janie. His grin suddenly spanned ear to ear when he realized that come morning, ol' Slick would have a bucket of hurt too.

CHAPTER TWENTY-FIVE

QUIETLY CLOSING THE DOOR AS she left Sheridan's room, Libby wasn't quite sure how she was going to sleep tonight—she was far too excited! She had no idea how three women could giggle and chat for almost an hour, but they had, and Libby hadn't felt this alive, this connected with other women in years. Not since she and Maggie's mother had attended their first suffragist meeting at the age of eighteen.

Some of her euphoria melted into a sad smile as she closed the bathroom door behind her. She couldn't help but remember the best friend she'd met when she'd moved to live with her Aunt Marie in New York the fall of her freshman year at Vassar. Maggie's mother—Helen Dunne—had lived on the same street, and the two had been inseparable ever since, even after Helen had married Maggie's father, Ryan Mullaney.

As an only child, Libby had reveled in her friendship with Helen—the kindest and most loving person Libby had ever met, and when Maggie had been born, she rejoiced to become the doting godmother who quickly claimed the unofficial title of "Aunt Libby."

Suddenly melancholy, Libby slowly opened the Colgate toothpaste jar and carefully applied some to her toothbrush, beginning the nightly ritual of scouring her teeth. Helen had passed on the year before Maggie and Libby had moved to Virginia City last year, leaving a giant hole in Libby's heart. Until Helen's daughter—sweet Maggie Mullaney—had filled it up with her love and friendship. No longer Maggie's "unofficial aunt," Libby was now Maggie's best friend as well. A smile suddenly tickled her lips as she took a swig of water before spitting it back out.

And fellow suffrageteer!

The thought put a bounce in her step as she quietly made her way back to her room, where Finn was snoring spread-eagle on their bed with sheet and cover kicked off as usual. Libby swore the man was a bloomin' furnace, able to heat up a bed in the dead of winter like a smoldering fire. She nibbled the edge of her smile as she carefully slipped beneath the sheet.

And a wife in any season with a fire of a whole other kind.

A sigh of contentment breezed from her lips as she shimmied deep into the bed, the memory of bonding with Maggie and Sheridan in their own private women's club warming her inside pert as much as Finn was able to do. She snuck a peek at his long body stretched out in a white short-legged sleeveless union suit that exposed powerful arms and legs corded with hard muscles even in repose, and felt a familiar shiver of heat. *Almost.* No question the chemistry between her and Finn had always been strong, but never more so than now in their first year of "remarriage."

Even so, she knew he wouldn't be all that happy about the Silver Lining Independence Platform they'd formed. She wiggled to turn on her side. But what he didn't know wouldn't hurt him, she surmised, admiring his well-sculpted chest matted with hair that peeked out of his partially unbuttoned union suit. Thickly coiled, the dark hair matched the stubble on his jaw, barely peppered with a hint of silver.

Scrunching her legs to her chest, she studied the man whose favor she needed to cull on Sheridan's behalf and hoped their honeymoon status would give her more leeway than she'd had before. A gentle smile lighted on her lips when an unusually loud snort escaped his mouth while his broad chest rose and fell in the rhythm of sleep. There was no question Finn McShane was as handsome today as he'd been when she'd first married him over seventeen years ago—the first time. Her mouth crooked.

And surely as stubborn.

No, that wasn't fair, Libby had to admit, well aware that Finn had mellowed considerably over the seventeen years they'd been apart. She knew now that his goals for women's rights were aligned with hers and every bit as strong. Her smile flattened a wee bit.

Albeit a whole *lot slower.*

"Libby, this is the wild and wooly West out here, darlin'," he'd explained after he'd been elected mayor, "where men move a whole lot slower when it comes to the notion of women's independence, so unfortunately, we have to take it slowly as well. But I promise you, sweetheart," he'd whispered as he'd nuzzled her ear, "we'll step up the pace on a woman's right to vote once I'm elected senator in a year or so."

A year or so. Libby picked at her nails as she worried her lip. Not too far away for women to obtain a long-denied right, surely, but definitely too late for Sheridan's right to choose the boys she may see. She huffed out a sigh while she pummeled her pillow to make it more comfortable. *Especially if one of them was the bait to draw Jake out of his shell.*

"Trouble sleeping, darlin'?" Finn slowly lumbered on his side to face her, his voice gravelly with sleep as he drew her close.

"A little." She straightened her legs to snuggle in. "Must be all the extra coffee I had at dinner, I suppose, making me as skittery as popcorn in Angus's skillet. My brain is refusing to go to sleep."

"Something on your mind?" Finn deposited a kiss to Libby's head while he gently massaged her back, lulling her eyes closed for a reason that had absolutely nothing to do with sleep.

"Just thinking about Sheridan, I guess," she said quietly, breathing in the clean scent of cedar from Angus's soap on Finn's raspy jaw, causing her stomach to skitter as much as her body. "It's hard to believe she'll be gone to college soon, you know?" She paused to press a light kiss to his throat, tone cautious. "Not much time to learn to shoot."

"No, but Blaze only needs a few weeks to accomplish that, so there's still time."

Libby absently threaded her fingers through the hair peeking through his open buttons, pretty sure Finn would rather wear nothing at all to bed given how hot he got at night. He flat-out refused to wear the typical red union suit most men wore with its long sleeves and long legs. Why, he'd just barely consented to the sleeveless/thigh-high version Libby had asked him to wear in lieu of sleeping buck naked like he used to. Heat swarmed her face and neck as she imagined him lying there with nary a stitch on, surely an indecency for even a wife! So he'd relented for her, but he always made sure he left the front halfway unbuttoned, he claimed, because of all the heat he generated.

She gulped. *Both in his own body and mine...*

"I have to admit," she continued carefully, "I was pretty surprised to hear Jake backed out of teaching Sheridan because she mentioned once that Jake always treated her better than her big brothers did, so it just seems strange, you know? The two of them not getting along."

"I know. I was surprised, too, but Jake's had to pick up the slack due to Blaze's injured hand, so maybe he was just having a bad day."

Libby burrowed in closer, pausing before she made her case. "Seems to me the perfect solution might be to let Clay teach her to shoot, then, since Jake and Blaze can't do it right now."

"Not necessary, darlin'." Finn rolled over on his back and brought Libby along, ratcheting up her pulse when he hooked her firmly on top. He nestled in to skim his mouth along the curve of her neck. "Blaze will get to it in time, so I have a much better idea."

"Uh ... what's that?" Libby whispered, swallowing hard when Finn's lips strayed to the neckline of her gown. Her eyelids fluttered closed over the warm chills he unleashed.

"What do you say we forget about Sheridan right now, because I'll just bet you can expend some of that extra energy on me." In the catch of her breath, he switched places, straddling her with a dangerous gleam in his eyes that confirmed he was now fully awake.

Lowering his body flush with hers, he gently nuzzled her lips, removing all thoughts of Sheridan when his mouth strayed to suckle the lobe of her ear. "So, what do you think?" he whispered, voice husky as it blew warm against her skin.

What did she think?

From the very first moment Finn McShane had first kissed her those many years ago, he'd had this annoying ability to scramble her thoughts and turn her body to mush, totally disarming her with the mere touch of his hand or his mouth.

What did she think?

She thought this man had entirely too much control over her, but oddly enough at the moment … She lunged to kiss him with the soft ache of a moan.

It didn't seem to matter at all.

CHAPTER TWENTY-SIX

"**H**OLY FROG SPIT!" EYES BUGGING wide, Shaylee absently yanked on the lace collar of the pink gingham dress she absolutely hated while Clay Morgan ushered Jake and the family into Buffalo Bill's personal dining tent. Round as a circus tent and cozy as a cabin, Mr. Cody's dining area was intimately aglow with candles in sturdy silver candlesticks that graced a long table covered with white linen and china.

"Oh my goodness, this is lovely!" Libby said with a hand to her chest, eyes agog over the intimately elegant surroundings, and she wasn't alone. No one had expected such luxury inside a tent, but the décor was surprisingly warm and inviting for so transient a structure. From the large and vibrant woven rug beneath the table fringed with leather, to the sconce-like oil lamps attached to each support post around the perimeter, they might have been dining in one of the finest restaurants in San Francisco. Softly illuminated colorful Navajo wall hangings complemented the colors of the rug cushioning the floor while the sweet scent of wildflowers—bright yellow stalks of native flora—were resplendent in a crystal vase on either end of the table.

Clay Morgan offered an ostentatious bow to Jake's way of thinking, his smile as bright as the blasted oil lamps. "Well, the truth is, Mrs. McShane, that Uncle Bill does a fair amount of entertaining when he takes his show on the road, enjoying the company of esteemed city officials such as yourselves or other celebrities, so he always insists on the finest for his guests.

"Holy snake snot, Mister Morgan, this is gorgeous!"

Shaylee said, apparently in agreement with her aunt on the elegant décor, albeit somewhat less dignified. "I ain't never seen a tent for eatin' like this before."

Jake laughed along with the others as Finn pinched the back of Shaylee's neck with a chuckle. "*Haven't ever* seen a tent this big, young lady, not 'ain't never.' And frog spit and snake snot are *not* holy for the umpteenth time, Shaylee Ann."

"Nor will there be any frog spit to be found, I promise," Morgan said with a broad grin, irritating Jake when he extended his arm to usher Sheridan to the table while Finn followed suit with Libby, Aiden with Maeve, Blaze with Maggie, and Dash with Shaylee.

Tired of being the grouch he'd become from the day Sheridan kissed him, Jake managed a grin for Shaylee, determined that no woman—or little girl, as he quickly amended in his mind, refusing to see Sheridan as anything but—would ever control his moods again. He leaned close to Shaylee's ear as he pulled out her chair. "You keep fidgeting with that dog-gone dress, Doodle, and Mr. Cody will think you have fleas."

A mischievous grin snuck across her lips. "Not as many as him, I bet, with all the animals he's rubbin' against day in and day out." Her smile went flat as she tugged on that stupid lace collar again. "And 'dog-gone' dress is right because it itches like a dog gone crazy with fleas. I hate dresses," she hissed under her breath, obviously far more partial to the overalls she wore daily than the Sunday best Libby made her wear to church. She scrunched her freckled nose and flipped a long auburn braid over her shoulder, ever the tomboy who resisted wearing curls, even at age fourteen. "They itch and when I'm on my own, ain't *nobody* gonna make me wear 'em ever again."

Dash sat down beside her with a wink, tugging on her pigtail. "Hate to tell you, Doodlebug, but you'll have to wear one at your wedding someday."

"Ha! Ain't getting' married, no way, no how," she said with a firm cross of skinny arms.

Jake chuckled as he placed a linen napkin on his lap. "I'd say that's a pretty safe bet with baggy overalls, dirt under your nails, and a tarantula for a pet."

"Boys stink," she announced, promptly tucking her napkin inside her lacey collar.

Dash bumped her shoulder with his own. "Not as much as you do, Doodle, when you roll around with the animals, especially Penelope." He leaned close to take a sniff, a grin peeking through. "You did take a bath after wallowing with that new piglet, didn't you?"

"Her name is Clarabelle, for your information, and of course I did," Shaylee said with an offended scrunch of her nose, as if she could smell said piglet. Her lower lip jutted out. "Aunt Libby made me."

"Then thank God for Aunt Libby," Dash said under his breath as he pinched the back of his sister's neck, exchanging grins with Jake.

"Good evening, everyone—it's a real pleasure to have you join us tonight."

Jake's gaze shot to the door of the tent to see that the gravelly voice belonged to none other than Buffalo Bill Cody himself, standing alongside Annie Oakley on the arm of her husband, Frank Butler. Jake immediately stood along with Blaze and Dash to make their way to the head of the table where Clay Morgan had seated Finn, Libby, and her parents.

"It's an honor to be dining with you tonight, Mr. Cody." Finn rose and pumped Buffalo Bill's hand with enthusiasm.

"Call me Bill, please," he said with a thrust of a goatee that was scattered with more silver than his black moustache, which curled up on the ends. Finn's six-foot-three was at least a half a head taller than the Wild West ringmaster's, but you'd never know it given the commanding presence of the famous showman who attracted crowds all over the world.

He was dressed as if ready for a show in a scarlet shirt

filigreed with silver piping and long fringed leather vest. Thigh-high black leather boots completed his ensemble along with a black Stetson cocked to the side atop shoulder-length black hair streaked with silver.

"Thank you for the invitation, Bill," Finn said, turning to Annie Oakley with a gracious bow before he shook Frank's hand. "And a real pleasure to meet both you and Mr. Butler, Miss Oakley. May I introduce you to my wife, Libby, her parents Maeve and Aiden O'Shea, and the rest of our brood."

Finn made the introductions while Blaze, Dash, and Jake approached to shake the men's hands, finally slapping Jake on the back last. "And this here is Jake Sullivan, our assistant foreman on the ranch. No blood relation, but I consider him part of the family nonetheless." He gripped Jake in a fatherly hug, pride gleaming in his eyes. "And, I might add, other than you and your sharpshooters, Bill, the best shot you'll see around these parts."

Buffalo Bill's dark brows lifted. "Well, young man, I believe I'd like to see that talent after supper if you're game."

Heat gorged Jake's face as he took a step back with an awkward grin. "I'm afraid that's more fiction than fact, sir," he said, never quite comfortable with praise. "Mr. McShane is a full-blooded Irishman, after all, so I'd definitely factor that in."

"As is Mr. Sullivan, I assure you, Mr. Cody," Blaze said with a friendly hook of Jake's shoulder, "who's obviously too modest to admit he's the Nevada State Shootout champ three years running with gold-plated plaques to prove it."

"That's right, sir," Dash said with an elbow to Jake's side, "including snuffing out flames on candles and knocking corks off of bottles at pert near 40 feet away."

Annie Oakley stepped forward to shake Jake's hand, so petite at a mere five foot, she looked more like a little girl with long brown tresses than a mature woman of twenty-six. "Goodness, Mr. Sullivan, I agree with Bill—we'd love to see a demonstration." She slid Bill a sideways wink before teasing Finn with a smile. "Who knows? Bill might just hire you out from under Mr. McShane."

"Or propose a challenge at least," Bill said with a wink of his own at Miss Oakley. "Annie will give you a go, won't you darlin'?"

"Oh, no ..." Shaking his head, Jake backed away with two hands in the air, fire ringing his collar as a hoarse chuckle slipped from his lips. "No, thanks, Mr. Cody. I know Miss Oakley's reputation all too well and have seen her in action, too, so trust me—I'm smart enough to decline."

"Wise man," Frank Butler said, looping an arm to Annie's waist with a proud flash of teeth. "I met this little filly in Cincinnati in 1875 when I was touring my shooting act. Lost $100 in a bet with this sweet young thing when she was only fifteen years old, besting me after I missed on the 25th shot." Annie smiled up at him, and he deposited a kiss to her head. "You might say I lost a whole lot of pride, but I won a whole lotta girl, so I'm a very lucky man."

Laughter filled the tent as everyone took their seats. Bill shook his napkin out and placed it on his lap as he studied Jake through a hard squint. "Sharpshooting is the lifeblood of this show, son, so I'd still be interested in seeing you shoot."

"So would I, actually," Morgan said with a friendly smile that Jake suspected was anything but. "How about a challenge, Jake, just between you and me? After all, I'm fairly good with a gun and have won an award or two myself before Uncle Bill took me on, so what do you say?"

"Yes sirree, Bob!" Buffalo Bill pounded on the table with a loud hoot, while everyone else cheered in agreement.

Jake hesitated, gaze flicking to where Sheridan sat pretty as a picture, excitement sparkling in those blue eyes as she pressed her hands to her chin in prayer mode. "Come on, Jake—it'll be fun, please?" she said with a slope of her brows, as if imploring him to agree.

"Do it, Jake!" Giggling, Shaylee shook his arm back and forth while all the others spurred him on as well.

Morgan leaned back and idly hooked an arm over Sheridan's chair, his eyes challenging Jake to far more than a shoot-out. "Unless, of course," he said with a polite smile, "you're afraid you won't win ..."

Jake stared him down while several of Bill's "Western Girls," as he referred to them, dressed in fringed leather skirts, boots, and vests, arrived to fill water glasses and tote platters of meat and vegetables piled high. No, he wasn't afraid he wouldn't win because he already knew he wouldn't.

At least not in the only challenge Jake cared about— Sheridan. Because he wouldn't allow himself to go there. And as sure as the tic in his jaw, he wouldn't allow the dandy to go there either. Ignoring everyone's prodding, his jaw hardened in resolve as he delivered a smile to the dandy every bit as strained as his own, giving a slight nod of his head. "You're on."

CHAPTER TWENTY-SEVEN

FINISH HIM OFF, JAKE. MOUTH pressed tight, Finn watched Jake raise his rifle just as Buffalo Bill hurled three coins in the air. Jake's body was a blur while he blasted all three in easy succession, unleashing a slow bleed of relief from Finn's lips and a loud roar of shrieks and cheers from his family.

Thatta boy, he thought with a wide grin, applauding like crazy. He couldn't be prouder if Jake were his own son and the truth was, sometimes Finn felt like he was, the two of them bonded by a painful past. He had no doubt whatsoever Jake was one of the best shots in Nevada, but for some reason tonight, a win had been particularly important to Finn.

Some reason? He watched while Clay Morgan extended a hand of congratulations, the smile on his face as stiff as Jake's when the two men shook. Finn's gaze flicked to where Sheridan stood with hands clasped to her chest, glowing more than the stupid candles on the table. He didn't know if her dreamy-eyed look was because of the truly enjoyable evening, pride over Jake whooping Bill's dandy nephew, or the dandy nephew himself. His jaw hardened. But it was definitely the last one that worried Finn the most, given what Blaze had told him this morning.

"What?" Finn had sat straight up in his cordovan leather chair after Blaze entered his study this morning before church, spilling the beans about Clay Morgan. "What do you mean we have a problem?"

"I *mean*," Blaze had said after quietly closing the door behind him, "that Clay Morgan is trouble. On the day of the Wild West show, Jake saw him drooling all over Sheridan when she and Maggie went to the privy. Then the night of Sheridan's graduation barbecue, Maggie and I had it out because I found out *they* invited the dandy to come when she *knows* how we feel about men sniffing around Sheridan."

Finn's eyes narrowed. "Thus the invitation to dinner tonight for the entire family."

"Yep." Blaze slanted back in the chair with a clasp of hands on his stomach, elbows stiff on the arms of the chair. "Both Jake and I were suspicious of him from the get-go, but now that we know he's got his eye on Sheridan, well, we just wanted you to know because he appears to be a real dandy, and a sneaky one at that."

Finn kneaded the bridge of his nose, surprised he hadn't seen it himself, either at the barbecue or at the dinner. But then Clay seemed a sociable man, dividing his attention equally among everyone. Finn usually had an innate sense about people—and men, in particular—but if Blaze's suspicions were true, it seemed for once his gut had failed him. He hated to admit it, but he supposed he'd been bedazzled like everyone else by the prospect of dining with Buffalo Bill Cody himself, never even considering that his nephew, in town for mere weeks, could pose any jeopardy.

"Yeah, sneaky," Finn said with a lengthy sigh way too weary for this early in the morning. But that's what Sheridan did to him these days, exhausted his energy worrying about keeping his promise to his sister. A promise of importance, not only because it had been his sister's dying wish, but one that Finn believed in as well—deeply. Sheridan's infatuation with love and marriage had never bothered him before until now, when she was way too vulnerable to girlish dreams that could turn into a woman's nightmare.

Like Peg.

Thoughts of his sister, Peg, produced an immediate ache, reminding him she was a woman who'd suffered and died too soon, something neither she nor Finn wanted for her daughters. Especially Sheridan, Finn mused, who was so much like her mother, blinded by the idea of falling in love, never seeing the pitfalls that could take her down. Well, Finn could see them clearly enough for them both, and he'd make darn good and sure Sheridan steered clear until she was older and ready to handle them.

No question the girl was smart as a whip in academics, her grades putting even Blaze and Dash to shame, but when it came to the real world? He frowned as Clay Morgan's easy smile and smooth manner suddenly popped into his thoughts, reminding him how the handsome dandy had beguiled all the ladies, including Libby and her mother Maeve. He seriously doubted if a book-smart innocent like Sheridan would *ever* be able to handle a man like that.

"Well, it's been a mighty fine evening, Mayor McShane," Bill said with a hearty clap on Finn's back, jolting his thoughts back to the present. He tossed a glance at Jake, who wore a sheepish smile as Finn's family surrounded him, dispensing lots of hugs and slaps on the shoulder. "I'd keep an eye on that one if I were you, Mayor, so I don't steal him away." He offered Finn a handshake. "Hope we can do this again the next time the show's in Virginia City."

"Count on it, Bill," Finn said with a firm grip, "but next time at my ranch, where I can hopefully return your warm hospitality."

And Sheridan is away at school.

Handshakes and hugs ensued as Finn and his family took their leave, waving and shouting their goodbyes on the way to their wagon and carriage. Finn helped both Libby and Maeve up into his phaeton to take Libby's parents home first while Blaze helped Maggie, Sheridan and Shaylee into the double-bench rig along with Dash and Jake to head on home.

Libby gently touched Finn's arm as he took the reins. "Sorry, Finn," she whispered, "but I think Mother and I should use the privy before we head out given all the sarsaparilla we drank tonight. Do you mind?"

"Capital idea, Libby." Aiden quickly jumped back down to

help his wife do the same.

"No problem, darlin'," Finn said as he lifted her from the carriage. He glanced over at the others in the wagon when Aiden and the ladies left. "See you back at the ranch after a visit to the privy." He shook his head while the wagon pulled away, smiling at all the shrieking and giggling coming from Shaylee and Sheridan as Dash and Jake clowned around.

"Excuse me, Mayor McShane?"

Finn turned around, body tensing as Clay Morgan approached with the same easy smile with which he had charmed everyone. He took his Stetson off. "Thank you for coming tonight," he said, nervously twirling the hat with his fingers. "I can't tell you what a pleasure it is getting to know upstanding town folk such as you and your family, sir, especially after being on the road for so long, away from our own families."

"It was our pleasure, son, so thank you for the invitation."

Clay paused, the hat stilling in his hands. "Sir, I'd like to offer my services again as far as teaching Sheridan to shoot—"

Finn interrupted him with a palm in the air. "Thank you, Clay, but as I told you before, the case is closed. Blaze will be teaching his sister to shoot."

Smile compressed, Clay nodded as a knot ducked in his throat. "Well, then, sir, I was hoping you might at least allow me to call on Sheridan for the brief time I'm in Virginia City."

"Why?" Finn cocked his head, eyes boring into his.

Ruddy color bled into the boy's face as the hat started whirling once again. "Well, because it gets a mite lonely on the road, sir, and I would like to get to know her better. She's bright, beautiful, and has a unique quality about her that I find myself"—his Adam's apple hitched several times in his throat—"drawn to."

Finn's smile thinned. *That's called innocence, Mr. Morgan, and you can be drawn all you want, but you're not going to get any closer.* "Well, I can certainly understand your appreciation of Sheridan's unique qualities, Clay, because I appreciate them, too, which is why her brothers and I take great pains to safeguard them."

"Sir, I assure you my intentions are completely honorable—"

"And I appreciate that assurance, son, but as Sheridan's guardian, I'm obliged to see to her welfare to the best of my ability. Unfortunately for you, that ability tells me it wouldn't be wise to expose my inexperienced and vulnerable eighteen-year-old niece to a handsome and personable young man when both of you will be parting ways very soon."

"But, sir—"

Finn cocked a brow. "That's my final word, Mr. Morgan."

"I see." Clay slapped his hat on with a tad of temper. "Well, pardon me, sir, but one would think a young woman soon to be nineteen who is going off to college would be old enough to decide for herself."

Hip cocked, Finn gave a slow nod as he perched hands loosely on his thighs. "One would think that I suppose, Clay, if one were a young man looking toward his own interests rather than that of a young woman's. But as the guardian of that young woman, not only do I think I know what's best for her"—Finn pinned him with an unflinching stare—"but I also have the power to insure it. Thank you again for a wonderful evening, and I bid you good night," he said with a polite doff of his hat, smile compressed as he mounted his phaeton.

And if I have my way—goodbye.

CHAPTER TWENTY-EIGHT

"**I** CAN HARDLY BELIEVE SUMMER IS half over, and you'll be gone in six weeks!" Kathy Jean said in a near moan while sipping on her ice cream soda at Lambert's Confectionary with Sheridan and Sophia.

Gobbling her own ice cream sundae way too quickly—her favorite, hot fudge—Sheridan smiled at the loud, sucking noise Kathy Jean made as she drained her soda, her friend's eyes as moist as the bottom of her empty glass. "We're going to miss you *so* much!" Kathy Jean wailed.

"Si, and based on what you said about the kiss Jake gave you at the beginning of the summer, something tells me we won't be alone." Sophia wiggled her dark brows in a jest that belied the sheen in her eyes.

Sheridan winced, the heat pulsing in her face from Sophia's tease at least countering the brain freeze she always got when she ate her ice cream too quickly. Kneading her temple, she quickly glanced at the other tables close by in front of Mr. Lambert's store window, hoping no one had overheard Sophia's remark. "Sophia, shhhh!" she whispered to the best friend who was starting to sound more and more like her sister all the time. Grabbing her napkin, Sheridan quickly fanned her face. "That is our secret and nobody else's." She offered a feeble smile. "Well, ours and Aunt Libby's and Maggie's, that is."

Sophia leaned close with a twinkle in her eye. "And Jake's?"

The napkin flapped wildly in Sheridan's hand as she tried to cool the heat that always invaded whenever she thought of Jake and his amazing kiss. She ducked close to both of her friends, voice barely a whisper. "*Yes*, but I don't want everyone *else* to know too, you goose, so please refer to him as 'he who shall remain nameless,' all right?"

The mischief in Sophia's black eyes gleamed bright as she locked her lips with a pretend key. "Si. When it comes to 'he who shall remain nameless,' my lips are sealed, chica." Hovering over her ice cream soda, she took a sip before delivering a mischievous smile. "But when it comes to the kisses of other hombres to make 'he who shall remain nameless' jealous?"—she winked—"not so much."

"*Sophia!*" Kathy Jean rasped as she made a quick sign of the cross while Sheridan commenced fanning, figuring Kathy Jean and she may as well be twins given the matching burn on both of their cheeks.

"And speaking of other hombres," Sophia said coyly, slowly twirling the straw in her glass, "How was dinner at the Wild West Show?"

Grateful to give her teeth a rest from the cold of bolting her ice cream, Sheridan pounced on the opportunity to tell her friends all about one of the most exciting evenings she'd ever had. Kathy Jean and Sophia appeared to hang onto her every word as she expounded in great detail about the food, the décor, and the thrill of sharing a meal with Buffalo Bill, Annie Oakley, and her husband Frank.

She was near giddy by the time she got to how Jake won the shooting match with Clay, this time her cheeks flushed with excitement rather than from Sophia's teasing. "Goodness, they were so evenly matched, going head-to-head snuffing out candles with revolvers and shooting corks out of bottles until finally Jake won on the 15th round of shooting coins in the air."

"Oh my goodness!" Kathy clasped hands to her chest. "I'm so excited Jake won!"

"Me too," Sophia said, her almond eyes in a curious squint while she homed in on Sheridan with a tilt of her head that could only spell trouble. "But I must admit, chica, I'm more interested to know if Mr. Clay Morgan won something too."

"*Sophia!*" Sheridan whispered with another flash of heat, her friend's wink confirming *exactly* what her friend meant. The napkin was now officially more of a fan than a cover for Sheridan's lap. "Sweet mother of mercy, Sophia Lopez, Clay Morgan is *just* a means to an end, and you know it."

No matter how attractive that means is!

Sheridan caught her breath when her stomach did a little flip, just like it had at the dinner when Clay had smiled and flirted, even squeezing her hand under the table. She shook the feelings off with a nervous jut of her chin, not about to let a few fluttery feelings get in the way of her love for Jake. She arched a brow. "To show Jake other men find me attractive and nothing more."

I hope.

"Si, but an awfully handsome means to an end, no?" She slowly sucked on her straw while she watched Sheridan closely, finishing her soda with a loud noise before she offered a smile. "And is it working?"

Sheridan paused, thinking how much nicer Jake had been since the Wild West dinner three days ago, sweet and easy-going, almost like his old self once again.

Before the kiss.

A weighty sigh parted from her lips. "A little, I think, because at least he's not scowling at me anymore, but I'm a long way from his declaration of love, I'm afraid." She dipped her spoon back into her ice cream with a sad pinch of brows. "And I'm running out of time to make him jealous enough to prove he cares—both to himself and to me. Not to mention how to do it."

"Wait …" Kathy Jean paused with a wide-eyed blink, a cherry halfway to her mouth. "I thought Maggie and your Aunt Libby were helping you with that. You know, talking your brother and uncle into agreeing to shooting lessons with Clay?"

"Believe me, they tried," Sheridan said with a wispy sigh.

Slouching over her sundae, she poked at the pecans scattered on top as if it were all their fault. "But Blaze and Maggie got in a huge fight over it, and Blaze is just *now* warming up again, so naturally Maggie's hesitant to bring it up again. And Aunt Libby tried too, but Uncle Finn didn't want to talk about it right then, she said, so she's waiting to broach it again soon."

Sheridan spooned a mound of ice cream in her mouth and winced, her love life as cold as the brain freeze had been—and just as painful. "In the meantime, I'm no closer to making Jake jealous than I was before, and my time is already half gone."

Clunk! Both Sheridan and Kathy Jean jumped in their seats when Sophia slammed her soda glass on the table with a heft of her chin. "Well, that settles it, then," she said, glancing around to make sure no one was listening. She lowered her voice as she bent in close. "You have no choice, chica—you have to kiss *him*."

Sheridan's mouth took a twist. "I already did that, Sophia, and it only made things worse, remember?"

"No, chica, not a kiss for 'he who shall remain nameless.'" Her lips curled in a sweet smile. "A kiss for 'the means to an end,' mi cielo, so 'he who shall remain nameless' finds out."

"Huh?" Kathy Jean blinked.

The whites of Sheridan's eyes expanded. "*What?!*" Palm splayed to her chest, she ducked in. "First of all, I'm *not* that kind of girl, Sophia Lopez"—the memory of lying prone on Jake while she kissed him senseless flashed in her mind and she gulped—"except with Jake. Secondly, in order to kiss someone, *chica*, a certain *someone* has to be around, and I haven't heard a peep from Mr. Morgan since the dinner three nights ago. And thirdly," she said with a hard swallow, "once the deed is done, how on earth do I make sure 'he who shall remain nameless' finds out?"

Sophia scrunched her nose in thought. "Well, first of all, you don't have to *be* that kind of girl because we just need you to spend enough time with Clay Morgan for him to kiss *you*," she said with a wink. "Secondly, you said he offered to teach you to shoot, so take him up on it by marching over there right now. After all, you're in town three times a week anyway to spend time with us before you leave, si? That's plenty of time for both shooting lessons and—"

Sheridan slapped a hand to Sophia's mouth, stopping the flow of her words. "And your third point? How do we make sure the right someone finds out?"

"Bah! The easiest of all." Sophia pursed her lips in a satisfied smile. "Since my sister works at the Ponderosa with your brother, I will just tell Lolita, and she will tell Dash, and we both know who Dash will tell, si?"

Sheridan's pulse stuttered. Yes, there was no question that Dash would tell both Blaze and Jake. A lump bobbed in her throat.

But also Uncle Finn.

"Uh, maybe this isn't such a good idea," she said in a squeaky voice, "what if Uncle Finn finds out?"

"So?" Sophia scrunched her shoulders, palms face up in the air. "You tell him you've been seeing Clay, and you like him very much."

"B-But … I *haven't* been seeing Clay," Sheridan sputtered.

"Of course you have, chica." Sophia winked. "The day you met him, at the barbecue, and at the dinner." She shrugged. "What can he do?"

Sheridan's jaw dropped. "Uh, lock me in my room?"

"Would he really do that, Sher?" Kathy Jean whispered, apparently shocked at the idea of Sheridan imprisoned in her room for the rest of the summer.

"Well, he never has before," Sheridan said with a scrunch of her nose, "but then I've never done much to make him angry before."

Sophia bent to study her with a squint. "Did he *forbid* you from seeing Clay?"

"Well, no, not exactly … but I don't think he would like it."

"Exactamente," Sophia said, "and neither would Jake."

Sheridan's body stilled. *No, he wouldn't, would he?* She hesitated, thinking it through. Maybe Sophia was right. After all, hadn't this been her plan all along? To make Jake jealous? For goodness sake, she knew he cared about her and had loved her from the age of four, but now she *also* knew that love was coupled with attraction. Wasn't *that* worth fighting for?

Wasn't *he* worth fighting for?

Her heart began a slow thud as she absently stirred the hot fudge into her melted ice cream. *Yes,* he was, and Sheridan truly believed that nothing would accomplish that more than Jake learning she'd been secretly seeing Clay and possibly falling in love.

Especially if a kiss were involved!

Her heart suddenly stalled for several painful seconds. But what if she *did* fall in love? With Clay or someone up at school?

"Promise me, Sheridan, that if this summer doesn't go the way you hope, you'll lay it aside for the rest of this year to enjoy your time away at school."

All air immediately suspended in Sheridan's lungs because all at once, she knew she had no choice. She only had six weeks to make the man of her dreams admit he was in love with her, and she had to do everything she could to make that happen.

She gulped. *Even* if it meant kissing Clay Morgan!

"Well?" Sophia clicked her fingernails on the table while Kathy Jean bit hers. "Are you willing to pursue any means to an end to win the heart of he who shall remain nameless?"

Sucking in a deep draw of air, Sheridan gave a nervous nod. "I think so."

"That's real good, chiquita," Sophia said with a lazy smile, gaze veering over Sheridan's shoulder, "because he happens to be standing right outside of that window."

CHAPTER TWENTY-NINE

GLANCING OVER HER SHOULDER, SHERIDAN felt another brain freeze she couldn't blame on the ice cream. There stood Clay Morgan, flashing the same crooked smile that had fluttered her stomach all night at the Wild West dinner. Tipping his hat, he gave a sideways nod toward the door before proceeding to enter Lambert's Confectionary, freezing her body with a cold chill colder than the hot fudge sundae she'd just consumed.

Or maybe it was a warm one.

Melting her into a puddle like the soupy ice cream at the bottom of her bowl.

"Ay-ay-ay!" Sophia whispered way too loudly for Sheridan's comfort, tracking Clay as he made his way to their table. "You spoke true, chica—that man is fabuloso!"

"Well, good afternoon, ladies," Clay said as he approached with his hat in his hands. "My name is Clay Morgan, and I'm with the Buffalo Bill Wild West show." He delivered a polite smile and a nod to both Sophia and Kathy Jean before his gaze lighted on Sheridan, warming considerably. "May I join you?"

"Uh …" Sheridan could only stare, her tongue completely uncooperative and obviously frozen along with her brain.

"Oh, absolutamente, Mr. Morgan," Sophia said with a wide smile that matched Clay's to a tooth, indicating the empty chair between her and Kathy Jean, whose face was now the color of Sheridan's vanilla ice cream. She inclined her head toward Kathy Jean. "This is Kathy Jean Rightler and I am Sophia Lopez, Sheridan's best friends, and I must say we have heard much about you—*ouch!*"

Sophia's eyes narrowed as she shot a pointed look at Sheridan, casually reaching beneath the table to rub her leg before she turned back to Clay. "Maria at the post office is a friend of my mother's, you see, and she's mentioned you quite often, that you visit every day."

Clay's husky laugh could have melted the ice cream if it wasn't already a pool of soup. "Yes, Maria and I have become good friends," he said with a firm nod, the twinkle in his eye almost winking. "I handle all the shipments for the show, of course, so that keeps me beating a path to her door, I'm afraid. It's a pleasure to meet you both, Sophia and Kathy Jean," he said with a polite smile before his attention settled on Sheridan. "I was actually on my way there when I saw you as I passed, Sheridan, so I consider that a stroke of good luck for me."

"Oh ... a ... r-really?" she stuttered, completely caught off-guard by the onslaught of goosebumps tingling her skin. She swallowed hard. *And just a plain ol' 'stroke' for me.*

"Yes," he said, casually fiddling with the brim of his gold-studded black Stetson, "I was wondering if perhaps I could offer you and your friends a tour of the show grounds some morning when the show is not in progress."

"Ay, caramba!" Sophia splayed a hand to her bosom, her excitement more than evident in the flash of white teeth that all but blinded Sheridan. "We would be honored, Mr. Morgan."

"Clay, please," he said with almost as many teeth as Sophia.

Even Kathy Jean, usually so shy and mute with strangers, gaped in astonishment with a fold of hands to a chest considerably less endowed than Sophia's, her face still as pale as death. "Oh, Mr. Morgan, that would be an absolute miracle! You have no idea how I've longed to see the inner workings of a traveling show."

Clay winked at Kathy Jean, effectively replenishing the blood supply in her face. "Well, I'd say it's a date, then, ladies," he said, homing in on Sheridan with brown eyes that seemed to deepen to the exact color of her hot fudge, making her hungry all over again. "Although I'd say the real miracle will be if Miss Donovan stays after for a personal shooting lesson."

"Of course she will," Kathy Jean said, grabbing Sheridan's arm and shaking it as if she were Sophia. "Won't you, Sher?"

Sheridan blinked several times, gaze flicking from Kathy Jean's giddy anticipation, to Sophia's pleading smile before meeting Clay's laughing eyes with an embarrassing gulp. "Uh ... okay."

"Great!" Clay said, rising with his hat in hand. "So, what morning works best for you, ladies?"

"Tomorrow!" Kathy Jean and Sophia shouted in unison while Sheridan could only sit there, as mute as her chair.

Brows raised in question, Clay ducked his head toward Sheridan, grinning when she gave him a dumb nod. "All right, ladies, then can you meet me at the front gate tomorrow morning at nine sharp?"

"Yes, yes!" Poor Kathy Jean actually hopped in the air with a clap of hands while Sophia tossed Sheridan a wink.

Clay questioned Sheridan with a jut of his brow. "Is that good for you, Sheridan?"

"Oh, absolutely!" Kathy Jean assured, apparently the new spokesman for the group. "Sheridan can ride in to town with her uncle, Mayor Finn, and her sister-in-law, Maggie, who works at St. Mary Louise Hospital, can't you, Sher?"

Sheridan's head slowly bobbed up and down, obviously her new mode of communication.

At least around Clay Morgan.

Until the kiss.

Her body went numb as all the blood in her limbs converged in her cheeks.

Clay chuckled and pushed in his chair, eyes fixed on Sheridan with enough heat to melt both her and all the ice cream in Mr. Lambert's ice cellar. "Well, then ladies, I will see you tomorrow. And let's keep this our little secret." He gave them a wink. "Don't want to make any of the other town folk jealous since we can't go giving tours to everyone, now can we? So, mum's the word, okay?" He tipped his hat to the ladies and then at Sheridan with a wink.

All Sheridan could do was blink, begging to differ with Mr. Morgan on one minor point. "Mum" was definitely not the word of the day. She slumped back in her chair, lashes dropping as if weighted with lead.

That would be "terrified."

CHAPTER THIRTY

"**WHOA!**" JAKE SAID AS HE pulled the reins of the wagon, slowing it to a stop in front of the train station. The warning whistle for the V&T Truckee Railroad's 8:10 to Carson City shrieked into the air along with a belch of smoke. "Right on time, Boss," he said with a smile to Finn, who was heading out on a three-day government business trip to the state capital of Carson City.

Finn checked his watch and nodded. "I can always count on you to be punctual, Jake," he said with a grin, grabbing his suitcase. He gave him a wink. "Now if you can just rub off on Blaze and Dash in that area, I will be one happy man. Particularly Dash, who won't see the sun for several hours or so with his crazy schedule at the Ponderosa."

Reaching into the back seat, he gave a quick squeeze to both Maggie's and Sheridan's knees. "Have a good day at work, Maggie, and Sheridan, enjoy your time with your friends. Oh, and I'd appreciate it if both of you would help take care of Libby for me, girls, because you know how restless she gets when I'm out of town."

Sheridan chuckled. "You mean help keep her out of trouble, Uncle Finn, don't you?" she said with a mischievous gleam in her eyes that reminded Jake of her Aunt Libby.

Finn jumped out and tipped his Stetson with a wide grin. "Exactly, Sher, so mum's the word, okay?"

"Yes, sir," Sheridan said, a blush suddenly swamping her cheeks. "Oh, and Uncle Finn?" She sat up on the bench with hands clasped in her lap and hope in her eyes. "Is it all right if I stay in town with Kathy Jean a few times a week for a while?"

The blush deepened as she picked at her nails, making Jake wonder why in the devil she was so nervous today. "Sister Fred was looking for volunteers, so I promised her that Kathy Jean, Sophia, and I would tutor the girls at the orphanage in math and grammar this summer."

Finn smiled and hefted his bag. "I don't see why not, as long as you clear it with Libby, all right? And I'm proud of you, darlin'." He gave a quick salute to Jake. "You'll pick me up on Saturday on the 2:10, Jake?"

"Yes, sir," Jake said with a return salute, "and once I drop Maggie off at the hospital and Sher off at Kathy Jean's, I'll head on over to the blacksmith to get the wagon wheel repaired because it's not long for this world, I don't think."

"Thanks, son. Goodbye, all." With a smile and a wave, Finn headed toward the train.

"Yah!" Jake said with a snap of the reins, steering the wagon in the direction of St. Mary Louise Hospital while Maggie and Sheridan chatted nonstop in the back. When Jake pulled up in front of the hospital, he hopped out to assist Maggie down. "I'll be by to pick you up at five, Maggie. Then once we get this wagon wheel fixed, you'll be able to drive yourself again, all right?"

"Thanks, Jakie." Maggie pinched his cheek with a playful smile. "You're a gem, you know that? Just like the brother I never had." She hurried around the wagon, blowing kisses to Sheridan. "Have fun today, Sher. See you both tonight." Sprinting up the hospital steps, she held a hand to her nurse's cap to secure it as she ran, obviously anxious to start work. Blaze said that she absolutely loved being a nurse, so much so that he worried how she'd feel once she had a baby and had to quit.

"Next stop, the Edwards' house on Sixth," Jake bellowed like a conductor on a train, so very glad his good moods were back.

"Good morning, Sheridan!"

Or were.

Jake bit back a scowl when Clay Morgan shouted out as he spotted their wagon from the boardwalk, obviously on his way to the post office given the stack of mail in his hands. Sheridan waved, and the dandy winked, pinking her cheeks all over again.

Anxious to clear her mind of Morgan, Jake glanced over his shoulder with a crooked smile, reins in hand. "I know you're top drawer when it comes to math, Half-Pint, and Kathy Jean with grammar, but I have to admit, I'm a wee bit nervous over what Sophia might teach them."

More color blasted her face as she jutted her chin in defense. "If you must know, Jake Sullivan, Sophia won second place in the math verbal quiz, so she's very smart."

Properly chastened, Jake offered an apologetic tone. "Sorry, Half-Pint. And let me just say for the record—so are you, because it's a mighty nice thing you're doing tutoring those kids when you could be spending your last summer home just having fun. Whoa!" He pulled up in front of Kathy Jean's house and hopped out, ready to lift her down.

Fiddling with a small velvet clip purse, she slipped the silver chain over her shoulder, then dropped it to the floor when she reached to pick up her umbrella. "Oh, drat," she whispered, retrieving the purse to sling it over her shoulder once again. Face beet red, she avoided his eyes as she turned to offer Jake her hands.

"You okay, Half-Pint?" he asked, face crimped as he extended his arms.

Those blue eyes met his just as he grabbed her, and the longing he saw in them jolted him clean to the bottom of his soles, flashing his body with a dangerous heat he hadn't felt since the day she had kissed him.

Suddenly aware she was dangling mid-air, he dropped her so fast, she teetered like a round-bottomed doll, ready to topple. He grabbed her arms to steady her and wished he could do the same for his heart when it lurched in his chest. "Sher, I'm so sorry. Are you all right?"

"No, I'm not, Jake," she whispered in a mournful tone, "and I think you know why."

Another flash of heat scorched his body, but this one gorged his cheeks with blood as well when he stumbled back, avoiding her eyes. "I'll pick you up at five-ten sharp," he said in a gruff tone, jaw hard as he mounted the wagon and snatched up the reins.

"Oh, and, Jake, just for the record?" Her voice wobbled with emotion as he spared her a sideways glance, her chin trembling despite the firm jut of her jaw. "I'm sorry too."

CHAPTER THIRTY-ONE

SHERIDAN SHOT A NERVOUS GLANCE over her shoulder as she, Kathy Jean, and Sophia hurried to make their nine o'clock appointment with Clay, never more grateful that the lot for the Wild West Show tents were well beyond the city limits, on the far edge of town.

Opposite the blacksmith, thank God!

"Eeeeek! I can't believe your uncle said you could stay with me each week," Kathy Jean said with a squeal, rushing to keep up with Sophia's long-legged stride while their friend all but dragged Sheridan toward the Wild West arena. A giggle popped from Kathy Jean's lips. "I am *soooo* excited!"

Me too. Sheridan bit her lip. *I think.* After all, the sooner she could get Clay to kiss her, the sooner she could make Jake jealous. *Right?* She stumbled along with Sophia, her brown twill—and most serviceable—dress fluttering in the breeze along with the feather on Kathy Jean's hat. Sophia had shaken her head when she'd seen Sheridan's choice of attire, berating her for not wearing something more feminine that matched the blue of her eyes. But Sheridan figured she'd be aiming for a target—not a man—so she wanted to be comfortable when Clay taught her to shoot.

Clay. She swallowed hard as she stared at the city of tents sprawled at the foot of the mountain range. They bloomed along with a scrubby collection of cactus and tumbleweed on rocky fields scattered with wildflowers. Beyond it all, the Sierra Nevada mountains stood guard, a majestic sentinel that for some reason always made Sheridan feel safe.

Except for today. With Clay Morgan. She gulped as Sophia nimbly dodged a rut blooming with spikes of pigweed.

"So, how many nights can you stay at my house each week?" Kathy Jean continued, one hand pinned to her small straw hat to make sure it stayed on. "Two or three?"

"Two—" Sheridan began.

"No, three," Sophia quickly amended as she towed Sheridan along.

Kathy Jean clapped. "Oh, goody! "For how long?"

"For a week or two I gue—"

"Till she *leaves* for college," Sophia interrupted, evidently intent on getting Sheridan that kiss and then some.

Giving a little whoop, Kathy Jean did a little jig in between strides, her calico dress blowing in the wind when she raced to catch up. "We will have *so* much fun!"

Sophia shot a grin over her shoulder with a waggle of brows that reminded Sheridan way too much of Lolita. "But not as much as Clay," she quipped, immediately dusting Sheridan's cheeks with a warmth that almost made her turn around. Instead she dug her heels into the dirt, effectively bringing her friend to a dusty halt.

"Sophia Maria Lopez!" Out of breath, Sheridan splayed a hand to her chest. "For the love of all that's decent, it's hard enough to do this without remarks like that, scaring me half to death."

Sophia whirled around with hands on her hips, impatiently tapping a toe. "Look, chica, do you want to make Jake jealous or not?"

"Of course I do," Sheridan said with a heft of her chin that matched Sophia's to a tilt, "but I don't know why a kiss has to be involved. Why can't we just make Jake jealous by having Clay teach me to shoot?"

"Ay-ay-ay!" Sophia threw her hands in the air with a shake of her head. She thrust a finger in the air. "One, you are a sheltered innocent who could certainly use the practice in kissing and two"—a second finger popped up—"teaching you to shoot will make Jake mad, yes, but not enough to push him into your arms since *he* does not want to teach you in the first place. And three," she said with a lift of both her brow and a third finger, "Jake knows you will be leaving in a month anyway, so he might choose to bide his time rather than make time, chica." She leaned in, her points underscored with a squint of black eyes. "By sicking Blaze and your uncle on you instead."

Sheridan blinked, a little disappointed that Sophia's logic made some sense, which was unusual in and of itself.

"Ah, but a kiss?" Sophia crossed her palms over her heart with a comical roll of eyes. "Now *that* can kindle a spark of jealousy, which can then ignite the flames of love in Jake's soul, fanning them into an inferno."

Slapping a hand to her bodice, Sheridan flapped the front of her dress for air, pretty sure Jake's soul wouldn't be the only thing on fire. "*O-kaaay*, then I hope it doesn't take forever because we all know it isn't Clay Morgan I want to win over."

Kathy Jean hooked an arm to Sheridan's waist, sympathy lacing her tone. "No, Sher, but I think Sophia may be right"—a pucker popped at the bridge of her friend's nose —"it may be Clay's advances that strike the match to singe Jake's temper."

"Not 'may'—*will*," Sophia stressed with a dip of her head, black eyes glinting with assurance.

Sheridan glanced from Sophia's confident gaze to Kathy Jean's apologetic smile and back, finally huffing out a sigh of surrender. "Well, I guess I can't argue with you both, *especially* since the sensible one"—she gave a nod over her shoulder toward Kathy Jean—"is in agreement." A tiny shiver rippled through her body. "Although I do worry you're rubbing off on her, Sophia Lopez, instead of the other way around, just like your sister is rubbing off on you."

"*Ay, caramba!* One can only hope," Sophia said with a dramatic pose, palms pressed in prayer as she fixed her gaze on the heavens.

By the time the girls reached the front of the tent city, it was three minutes before nine, allowing Sheridan a final moment of panic where she considered a sprint in the opposite direction. Or ducking behind one of half a dozen wagons in front, where men were unloading supplies.

"Ah, right on time!" Clay Morgan grinned as he strode toward them from the inner sanctum of the arena, where a blur of cowboys and Indians galloped in the main ring amid clouds of dust. "I like that in a person," he said, halting before her and her friends while her stomach flapped more than the American flag on a pole at the top of the tent. He glanced at the watch in his pocket and grinned, giving Sheridan a wink. "Or early, actually, which I like even better, given the company. Right this way, ladies."

Pressing a casual palm to the small of Sheridan's back, he took the lead while Sophia and Kathy Jean followed, all of them goggle-eyed as Clay highlighted points of interest and occasionally made introductions.

Sheridan's jaw ached from falling open! She and the girls were gob-smacked at the enormity of the production, with cast and staff numbering almost five hundred according to Clay, all living in wall tents festooned with flags. "Twenty-five cowboys, a dozen cowgirls, and one hundred Indian men, women, and children were all fed three hot meals a day cooked on twenty-foot-long ranges," he explained with a look of pride in his eyes, "and we generate our own electricity and even staff our own fire department."

Yes, Sheridan had seen the show on the day it opened, of course. But even so, she wasn't prepared for the amount of equipment, animals, people, vehicles, and staging needed for acts such as the bison hunt, train robbery, Indian war battle reenactment, and the grand finale—an Indian attack on a burning cabin. She shivered at the memory, which had appeared all too real, with war cries and flames of fire violating the starry sky before Buffalo Bill and his cowboys road in to the rescue.

"That's an inside glimpse of the inner workings of our

show, so how about a behind-the-scenes demonstration few people ever get to see?" Clay nodded to a young cowboy, who strolled forward with a wide grin. "Chet Randall here is one of our show-stoppers, ladies, and he's going to escort Sophia and Kathy Jean to a private practice for none other than Miss Annie Oakley herself while I teach Sheridan to shoot."

A collective gasp rose from all three girls who stared with mouths agape, the news managing to leave even Sophia speechless.

Clay paused, surveying them with a twinkle in his eyes. "Unless, of course, you'd rather not?"

"No!" Kathy Jean managed to squeak out, "we definitely want to!"

"*Ay, caramba,*" Sophia muttered with a quick sign of the cross, Annie Oakley being one of the women she admired most in the world.

"Good!" Clay clapped his hands together, causing Sheridan's stomach to jump. *Sweet Mother of Mercy—if he could do that with a clap of his hands, what could he do with his lips?* "Chet, I want you to take good care of Sophia and Kathy Jean here," he said with a nod at both of the girls before laying a hand on Sheridan's shoulder, "because they're good friends of my student here, all right?"

"Yes, sir. Shall we go, ladies?" Extending an arm to each, Chet shot a wink at both girls that instantly put a blush on Kathy Jean's face and a smile on Sophia's.

Sheridan gulped as Chet ushered them away.

And panic on hers.

CHAPTER THIRTY-TWO

A RMS CLUTCHED TO HER WAIST, Sheridan watched them go, almost wishing she could leave with them. She startled when Clay gently tugged her arm to face him.

"There's nothing to be nervous about, Sheridan," he said with a kind smile, as if he could see the skitters in her stomach. "Guns are safe as long as you know how to handle them."

A lump bobbed in her throat as she peered up, reminded all over again how handsome he was. *But will I be able to "handle" you?*

"Did you bring your derringer?" he asked, offering his arm to guide her to the entrance they just came in.

"No, not today." She balked, eyes spanning wide. "Wait— where are we going?"

He patted her arm with a reassuring smile while he hiked a thumb over his shoulder toward the main center ring. "I'm taking you to the shooting range set up behind the tents since practice is going on inside the arena, and we don't want to get run over. Same place as Chet took the girls, actually, only we'll be shooting on the opposite end away from Annie and the crowd she always draws so we won't be distracted, all right?"

She gave a shaky nod as she snuck a peek up at Clay while he continued to point things out on their way around the tent, thinking he might possibly be even better looking than Jake and her brothers. *Won't be distracted?* She gulped. *Not likely.*

"Okay," he said as he led her to a nearly deserted side of the tent. Only a young boy in his early teens waited near a makeshift table of plywood on sawhorses with several rifles and pistols on top. "I've got a selection of firearms here that I thought might be easiest for you, Sheridan." Slipping his coat off, he laid it neatly across the table and pulled a coin from his pocket, flipping it to the boy, who caught it handily. "There you go, Jimmy—thanks for keeping an eye on things."

"Yes, sir, Mr. Clay. Anytime." He loped away with a wave, causing Sheridan's heart to hammer double time.

She glanced around, hoping to see other people while he selected a rifle from the table, but although she heard shots from a distance, she and Clay seemed completely alone.

Her attention jolted back when she heard the cock of a gun while he inspected the chamber to make sure it was empty. Closing it again, he waved her over. "Okay, Sheridan, this is a Remington 76 and one of Annie's favorites, so she recommended it for you." He winked. "And it happens to be Teddy Roosevelt's favorite too."

"Wait …" Panic flared in Sheridan's chest. "Annie won't tell Uncle Finn about these lessons, will she?"

His smile softened as he slacked a hip. "No, ma'am—no names, I promise. All she knows is that I'm teaching a very petite person to shoot."

A slow bleed of air seeped past her lips as she offered a wobbly smile. "As you know, Uncle Finn was pretty adamant about Blaze teaching me to shoot, but since he didn't directly forbid me from working with you"—she gave a sheepish shrug—"I figure what he doesn't know won't hurt him, right?"

"My thoughts exactly," Clay said with a wink. He held the rifle aloft, carefully pointing out the barrel, shaft, chamber, bolt, sight, trigger, and butt of the Remington Model he'd chosen.

"I already know most of that," Sheridan said shyly when he finished. "Jake taught me about gun safety and terminology, types of guns, how to clean and load them, and stance before he quit on actually teaching me to shoot."

Surprise flickered in his brown eyes as he arched a brow.

"Did he now? Well, that certainly makes my job easier, then, because we can move right into target practice." Handing over the rifle, he nodded first at a box of ammunition on the table, then pointed at the bulls-eye target set up a distance away. "I thought we'd start out at 25 feet and move up from there with each lesson, so let's see you load and take a stance."

"Okay ..." She cautiously took the rifle from his hands and checked the safety before pulling the bolt backward to load the ammunition, clicking it closed with a shaky smile. Moving around the table, she took her stance, not exactly remembering what Jake had shown her since she'd been rattled at the time.

"Here," Clay said, coming up behind her like Jake had done to position her just so, his arms around her as he adjusted both her hold and the fit of the butt of the gun into her pocket. "Perfect," he whispered, the warmth of his breath tickling her cheek and tingling her body. The scent of musk soap taunted her senses as his whisper turned husky. "Do you mind if I ask you a question, Sheridan?"

"Uh, no," she said, head fixed over the gunsight while she peeked at him out of the corner of her eyes.

I think.

Stepping away, he studied her through a squint, arms in a loose fold. "I know Blaze said Jake quit teaching you because you gave him trouble, and I can't help but wonder what he meant by that? Because the truth is, you're flat-out one of the sweetest and prettiest girls I've ever met, so I can't imagine any man telling you no." He idly scratched the nape of his neck. "I guess I'm just a little curious as to exactly what kind of trouble you gave him?"

Blood swarmed her cheeks—all the way to the roots of her hair. She lowered her gaze and bit on her lip so hard, it hurt. "Uh ... well ... uh ..."

"Never mind," he said with a gentle squeeze of her arm. "It's none of my business, but I think I can figure it out. All I can say is I sure hope you smacked him silly."

She blinked, remembering all too well the slap she'd given Jake when he'd compared her to one of those women at The Silver Pistol. A muscle worked in her throat. "Uh ... as a matter of fact, I did," she said with a seed of a smile, still seeing Jake's glazed look in her mind.

Clay took a step back. "Good to know," he said with a teasing raise of his palms and a crooked smile, the twinkle in his eyes putting one in her own. Giving a nod toward the bulls-eye target a fair distance away, he slid her a lazy grin that shocked her when it fluttered her stomach more than she liked. "Well, Miss Donovan, since Jake got you started, why don't you show me what you know?"

"All ... right." Hunkering down over the rifle, she peered through the sight, more than a little flustered over the feelings he'd just provoked. Flutters, yes, but also surprise that just maybe Clay Morgan wasn't the wolf she'd been so worried he'd be. Finger quivering, she gave the trigger a slow squeeze, the jolt of the rifle not unlike the jolt he'd just given her.

What did she know? Well, she knew one thing for dead sure, given these unwelcome tingles.

I could be in a whole heap of trouble.

CHAPTER THIRTY-THREE

"**O**KAY, TONIGHT'S THE NIGHT." LIBBY threw her shoulders back with a firm thrust of her chin as she studied herself in the bathroom mirror, determined to fight for women's rights, even if it meant only one woman at a time.

Beginning with my niece.

She reached for the perfume bottle Finn had brought back from his trip to Carson City and dabbed a little behind each ear and wrist. Pausing with a nervous grate of her lip, she scrunched her eyes closed to do the same to the cleft of her breast, wishing she didn't have to resort to feminine wiles to change Finn's mind.

Expelling a silent sigh, she set the bottle down and assessed the lay of auburn tresses spilling down the lacey front of her thinnest cotton nightgown. Finn's favorite, of course, because it was the next best thing to nothing at all, he said.

Her smile took a slant.

But it worked, she supposed, so that's all that mattered. Right?

Especially for Sheridan.

Slipping her robe on, she doused the light and tiptoed down the hall to her room, lightly touching her fingers to her lips before pressing a good-luck kiss to Sheridan's bedroom door on the way. "Please, Lord," she whispered, help Finn to see the light and allow Sheridan more freedom."

With a silent twist of the knob, she entered her bedroom where Finn sat in their bed, obviously going over notes from his day given the open portfolio on the nightstand. He glanced up over the specs perched on his nose, and she shook her head with a smile, thinking Finn McShane even looked handsome in specs and an unbuttoned union suit.

She flashed him a bright smile while she quietly closed the door. "Still working?" Slipping her robe off, she hung it on the back hook before hurrying to climb into bed, Finn's propensity for wide-open windows allowing a pleasant, if not somewhat cool, breeze. "Brrr ...," she said as she shimmied beneath the covers, cozying up to him with a playful jut of her brow. "I wonder if you would have run for mayor if you'd known the long hours involved."

Smiling, he removed his glasses and set them on the nightstand. "Definitely, ma'am, because you see, I have a wife anxious to be married to a senator so she can wield him on behalf of women's rights." He stuffed his papers into the portfolio and laid it aside, turning out the light. "Which is when the real work begins, darlin', for the senator *and* the suffragist." He hooked an arm to her waist to slide her in close. "Come here, woman, and wield away."

"Speaking of women's rights—"

He stole her words with a kiss that almost stole every thought from her head while hungry hands swept the length of her gown. "Mmm ... my favorite nightgown on my favorite woman," he whispered, lips wandering to suckle the lobe of her ear.

"Uh, excuse me!" She slammed two flat palms to his chest with a crook of her brow. "I better be the *only* woman, Finn McShane, or you will be in *soooo* much trouble."

He sidetracked her with a husky chuckle while he slowly worked on the buttons of her gown, methodically unhooking each one. "I'm already in trouble, darlin', because I'm head over heels in love with a woman I'd do anything for."

"Anything?" she rasped, trying to ignore the warm chills when he feathered kisses along her collarbone while easing the nightgown off of her shoulder.

His soft laughter warmed her skin when he nestled his mouth into the curve of her neck, making his way down to the hollow of her throat. "Let me rephrase that—*almost* anything, Mrs. McShane," he corrected while he rolled her onto her back, descending with a chuckle he immediately deposited in her mouth with a kiss.

A soft moan rumbled in her throat as he melted her to the bed with the same kisses that had always muddled her mind, stealing her focus.

By the time Libby could think clearly again, she was lying limp and languid in Finn's arms a long while later, wondering how she'd ever lived without this man in her life. Every time they made love, she fell deeper and deeper, pretty sure she'd do almost anything for him too.

And his niece.

"Finn?"

"Mmm?" His thumb slowly grazed the thin nightgown back and forth on her hip as he held her, eyes closed and a half smile hovering on his lips.

"About that 'woman you'd do anything for.'" She pressed a soft kiss to the open swathe of his granite chest. "Did you mean it?"

"With all my heart, darlin'," he said, his sleepy tone hopefully boding well for a yes.

"Well ... Sheridan will be leaving in three weeks, and Blaze still has that cast on his arm, so I was kind of wondering"— she lifted her head enough to peek up while she absently twirled a finger around a patch of hair on his chest—"or hoping, really ... that you'd reconsider letting Clay teach her to shoot."

His eyes remained closed while the faint smile on his lips went flat. "Libby, we've been through this several times. Blaze's cast comes off next week, which is plenty of time for him to teach Sheridan what she needs to know."

Libby stifled a huff of frustration. "But, Finn, I just don't understand what you have against Clay Morgan. He seems like such a nice young man—"

"*Whom* Sheridan will never see again after he leaves, so

there's no sense in stirring the pot. Especially with a man who ogled her through dinner as if she were dessert."

Libby flattened her palm on Finn's chest lest she be tempted to yank out a hair or two. "Oh, for crying out loud, Finn, men have ogled pretty girls from the dawn of man, and you certainly did your fair share before we got married, as I recall."

"Yes, and that's how I can read what's on a man's mind when he sees a pretty girl." His eyelids edged up, reflecting a bit of the mule he always accused her of. "As her guardian, I am not going to let some fast-talking dandy—'nice young man or no'—sweet-talk her into something she's in no way ready for."

"You mean something *you're* not ready for," Libby countered, sitting up to give him the full benefit of her disagreement with a jag of her brow. "That girl is almost a woman of nineteen, Finn, which means you're going to have to learn to trust her."

"It's not Sheridan I don't trust"—he pummeled his pillow hard before shoving it beneath his head, lips compressed as he turned on his side. "It's the men she attracts. Case closed."

"That's a lie, Finn McShane, and you know it. Poor Sheridan hasn't even had the chance to attract a boy since you lock her away like Rapunzel in a tower. Which is an insult not only to Sheridan, but to yourself. You have to trust you've raised her right."

"Trust has to be earned, Libby," he said with a scowl, giving his pillow a final whack. "Like I earned yours." He closed his eyes.

She snatched her own pillow to give it a whop like she wished she could do to Finn. "Trust can't be earned if one isn't free to earn it, Mr. Mayor. And for heaven's sake, she'll be halfway across the country in three weeks, so you won't be able to control her there …"

Finn grunted, and Libby knew he planned to try and do just that. Mother had already told her he'd talked to her father about his old friend at Vassar keeping an eye on Sheridan while she was there during the day. As well as Aunt Marie, with whom Sheridan would stay.

Striving for a calmer demeanor, Libby laid her hand on his arm, her voice far more soothing than before. "Really, Finn, what does it matter if Clay teaches her to shoot? It's only for three weeks, darling, so what could possibly happen?"

"What could happen?" Finn's eyelids flipped up. *"What could happen?"* he repeated with clipped enunciation. "She could end up in a nightmare marriage like her mother did, saddled with babies instead of a degree, miserable and alone because her philandering husband travels too much."

He kicked the covers off on his side and bludgeoned his pillow again. "Or worse yet, pregnant out of wedlock and labeled a scarlet woman with her son a bastard until her souse of a husband finally upped and married her."

Libby caught a harsh breath, remembering all too well the rumors people told about Finn's sister when she'd moved away for a year, but Libby hadn't believed them because eventually her "husband" showed up. "I … I'm sorry, Finn—I didn't realize that."

Huffing out a weary sigh, Finn drew her into his arms, laying his head against hers. "Libby," he said quietly, "I promised my sister that I would make sure Sheridan and Shaylee got an education before they got married, and this is the only way I know how to do that, sweetheart."

"But she's going away to *get* that education, Finn, in three short weeks, so I don't understand—"

Clutching her arms, he held her at bay, his grip suddenly taut. "She's my blood, Libby, so let me handle this, all right?" His whisper sounded almost harsh, the fire in his eyes igniting her own. "I'm her guardian, and I know what's best for her."

Her chin lashed up. "Oh, sure you do. Just like you thought you knew what was best for me when we first got married. Well, you were wrong then, Finn, and you're wrong now."

"Libby, I'm warning you—this is important to me." His

voice was deadly quiet.

"And to Sheridan and me as well," she whispered, determined to do everything she could to give Sheridan the freedom she deserved. Her eyes pleaded. "Please, Finn— why can't we compromise?"

"We *did!*" he snapped, dropping her arms to pummel his pillow one last time, "on sending Sheridan to Vassar when I wanted her closer to home, remember? You got the last word then, Libby, and by God, I'll have it now." As if reining in his temper, he slowly drew in a deep breath, then gently buffed her arms, his voice considerably softer. "Look, Libby, this is my responsibility, and I take it very seriously, so please understand. She's my niece, darlin', so I get the final word."

"But that's just it, Finn, she's my niece too—"

His grip tightened. "This. Discussion. Is. Over," he bit out in a deadly tone that brooked no argument, "so let it go, darlin', *please.*"

"But—"

His hold actually pinched as a spark of once-familiar fire blazed in those hazel eyes that she hadn't seen in a long, long time. "*Not. One. More. Word.* Good night, Libby." Pillow balled in his hands, he turned on his side, his back a brick wall she would never scale.

At least not tonight.

A painful mix of tears and temper pooled in her eyes as she grabbed her own pillow and tossed it to her side of the bed, as far away from Finn McShane as she could possibly get.

Not one more word?

Gladly, she thought with a swipe at her eyes. He wanted the final word? Well, she'd give it to him. Curling in a ball, she made a vow of silence, determined to give Finn McMule exactly what he asked for. Not only tonight, but in the days ahead.

Not one more word.

CHAPTER THIRTY-FOUR

"**D**ON'T DO ANYTHING I WOULDN'T do!" Hand to her mouth, Sophia called from Kathy Jean's bedroom window, her whisper way too loud to suit as Sheridan hurried to Kathy Jean's front gate.

"As if that's even possible," Kathy Jean said with a giggle, still in her nightgown after the three spent the night together on this, their last week together. "She's had six shooting lessons, and he hasn't even kissed her yet."

Sheridan spun around at the gate, her cheeks on fire for any number of reasons: Kathy Jean's comment shouted to the world, her nervousness over seeing Clay again, or even the fact he hadn't yet kissed her, dragging this whole jealousy plot out so long, she was starting to want him to. "Kathy Jean Rightler, hush!" She huffed out a sigh, feeling guilty enough for her growing attraction to Clay without her friend announcing her failure from the rooftops. "Pretty futile at this point anyway, since I only have a week left to make you know who jealous."

"Don't say that, chica —today could be the day." Sophia waggled her brows. "Chet says Clay likes you *very* much."

Sheridan's smile slid sideways, pretty sure Sophia had made *way* more headway with Chet since they met than Sheridan had with Clay, given Clay's Wild West friend's fascination with Sheridan's best friend. "Well, if it isn't, it will be the last one, that's for dead sure." Her shoulders rose and fell in a heavy sigh. "Maybe that's the reason Uncle Finn and my brothers have tried so hard to keep me away from men—they're not worth the time and pain."

"Oh, they're worth it all right, mi amiga mujer," Sophia

said with a low chuckle, "at least according to Lolita, and something tells me you're about to find out. Adios, chica, and buena suerte."

Good luck? Mood deflated, Sheridan trudged down the street toward the edge of town, thinking she'd need a *whole* lot more than good luck to make strides with Jake before she left. She was certain finding out about Clay kissing her would have done the trick. Her mouth sagged along with her shoulders. But not if she couldn't make it happen. And now, with only a week left, it was almost too late ...

Almost.

She halted midway in crossing the dusty street, barely noticing the buggies and wagons passing by as she blinked. A slow smile wended across her lips when she suddenly realized "almost" carried a thread of possibility, a strand of hope that meant there was still time. And by hit or miss, hug or kiss, she intended to come up with something today to light a fire under Jake Sullivan.

"Good morning, Sheridan," Clay said as she rounded the tent to approach their usual target-practice area, where he was standing next to one of the prettiest palominos Sheridan had ever seen. "Ready for our final lesson?"

"I am, Mr. Morgan. And who's this?" She smiled and cooed to the palomino before looking up, head tilted in question while she petted his horse. "And are we going somewhere else for this lesson?"

"We are," he said with a small bow, dark eyes twinkling as he nodded over his shoulder toward the Sierra Nevada mountains. "I found a pretty lake a mile or two back, so I thought it would be nice to celebrate with a picnic after our lesson, just you, me, and ol' Silver Bullet here." He paused, as if her hesitation was of concern. "If that's all right with you, of course."

"Uh ..." Sheridan swallowed hard.

He took a step forward, arm extended toward the arena. "I can always ask Annie or one of the other ladies to join us if that would make you more comfortable."

She studied his handsome face, his expression as earnest as she'd ever seen, and suddenly relaxed with a slow bleed of air. "No, no, Clay, this will be nice. As long as we don't go too far." She caressed Silver Bullet's mane with another smile. "I love his name."

"It's right over the rise, I promise," he said, palm to his chest as he delivered a little-boy grin that swirled her stomach. "The perfect place for a picnic." He mounted, then helped her up behind him, making her most grateful she'd worn her split leather skirt. Leaning to rub the horse's neck, he flashed a smile. "And the perfect name for the horse who will take us there, since bullets have been our main focus these last few weeks, in the birthplace of silver, no less."

He was right, of course. It *was* the perfect place for a picnic, she decided, when they'd galloped a mile or two over the ridge to a small but pretty lake she remembered Uncle Finn taking them to years ago to fish. A copse of aspens shimmered in the breeze along one shore while the mountains rose beyond the other, the perfect setting for a picnic basket atop a Navajo-style blanket Clay had obviously set up ahead of time.

Helping Sheridan down, he tied Silver Bullet to a wispy aspen tree, chuckling when the palomino immediately started nibbling. "Looks like somebody's hungry," he said while he unloaded supplies from his saddle bag with a wink, which included a pistol, a rifle, and a number of empty tin cans and some string. "But we have work to do before we eat, Miss Donovan, because *this* is your final exam." Tying tin cans to the limbs of an aspen, he paused to angle a brow. "You did bring your derringer, yes?"

"Yes!" Sheridan said with a giddy press of palms, excitement coursing through her veins like adrenaline at the challenge of a final exam, something she'd always mastered in school. She promptly produced the pearl-handle derringer Uncle Finn had given her for Christmas from her pocket, holding it up with a proud smile. "And you'll be happy to know, Mr. Morgan, that Blaze was most impressed with my 'natural ability' at shooting when he was finally able to teach me last week." She winked. "Says I'm a quick study."

He chuckled as he walked to where she stood, the sound echoing across the lake. "Well, actually you are, Sheridan. A derringer isn't easy to shoot, but you handle it well."

She sighed as she aimed it at the tin cans he'd tied on the tree, both arms extended in a tight hold. "Better than the rifle, at least, which still deals me a fit on recoil."

"Let's take a look at that first," he said as he handed her his rifle, positioning her exactly where he wanted her to stand. "You're loaded and ready to go, so let's see you aim for the highest can."

Tucking the rifle butt against her shoulder, she took careful aim, cheek resting against the stock. She pulled the trigger, jerking hard at the recoil when she missed the can by a mile. She tried again with the same result. "See what I mean?" She unleashed a heavy sigh. "What am I doing wrong?"

"You're still leaning back too far in your stance," he said as he positioned her once again, reminding her of something he'd told her before. "You're doing this"—he encircled her from behind, his arms aligned with hers as they took aim together, leaning her back against his chest—"when you should be doing this."

He straightened and leaned forward the slightest bit, his body flush against hers for several erratic beats of her pulse. "You want to lean forward enough that your body is centered over yours knees and maintain a high grip on the gun like this." He covered her hands with his own while his finger hugged hers on the trigger, causing a lump in her throat at the intimacy of the action. Sure, Clay had always positioned her before, but never *this* close. "Then you slowly squeeze …"

Ping!

The shot hit dead on, sending the tin can into a wild spin along with her heart. "See?" he whispered, the sound almost husky in her ear before he stepped away. "Now, you try."

Fighting a gulp, she worked hard to match his stance, a warm chill skittering her spine when she felt the warmth of his palm pressing her forward. "Remember, Sheridan, you want to place the majority of your weight on the ball of the foot rather than the heel, all right?"

Nodding, she refocused and took careful aim, heart stopping as she slowly eased the trigger back.

Ping!

Euphoria burst in her chest when the can flew in the air, completely dislodged from the tree. "I did it!" she shouted, so excited she threw her free arm around Clay in a one-sided hug, her giggle ringing in the air. "I shot a bulls-eye!"

"Yes, you did, Miss Donovan," he said with a chuckle, taking the rifle from her hand to embrace her more fully. "In more ways than one," he said, his voice suddenly low and raspy as he pressed a kiss to her hair.

Pulse racing, she peered up, heart stopping altogether when he tenderly skimmed her mouth with the pad of his thumb before carefully laying the rifle aside. His shuttered gaze never left hers as he rose to cradle her face in his hands. "A bulls-eye right through my heart, Miss Donovan," he whispered, his black eyes, if possible, darkening even more as he slowly lowered his head.

Oh my goodness—this is It!

That was all she had time to think before his mouth grazed hers with the barest of touches. Warm tingles skittered through her, suddenly colliding with goosebumps when he deepened the kiss, drawing her close with a soft groan. "Sheridan, I care about you."

She could smell musk soap, peppermint, and a hint of bay rum, scents that teased along with his mouth as he feathered kisses along the curve of her throat. His words of fondness were soft and intent, warming her skin with a delicious tingle. Wonderful sensations all, except for one thing.

It wasn't Jake.

CHAPTER THIRTY-FIVE

"WHAT THE DEVIL AM I doing, girl?" Jake scrubbed Midnight's snout in a manner as listless as the malaise that had lingered from the moment Sheridan had kissed him at the beginning of the summer. His gaze numbed into an empty stare as he fondled the horse's mane. "I don't want to go to Megan Joy's for dinner. Tonight or any night, but her mother cornered me at church, so what could I do?"

Midnight nickered and nuzzled his hand, and Jake unleashed a weary sigh, grazing the mare's neck with a gentle rub. Because the truth of the matter was, it was his own blasted fault for telling Sheridan he was "seeing" Megan Joy in the first place, and all to keep from telling a lie.

When all the time he was living one.

Denying his feelings for Sheridan.

"No, *not* Sheridan!" he hissed while he stormed to the tack room for his saddle, slamming it over the wooden railing of Midnight's stall. "*Half-Pint.*" Jaw tight, he snatched the curry comb from the hook outside Midnight's stall and proceeded to groom her, removing loose hair from the mare's sleek body. He didn't want to see Finn's niece as anything other than the little girl who'd shadowed him from little on, the sweet little mite he'd do anything for. Nothing more than a near sister.

Yeah. He grunted while he combed Midnight with an intensity that mirrored his frustration. *But not 'near' enough.*

Finishing up with the comb, he exchanged it for a stiff-bristled brush to remove dirt and hair stirred up by the curry, expelling another heavy sigh while he worked in short strokes from front to back. All he could say was thank God Sheridan would be gone in another week, out of harm's way.

And mine.

"Hey, Sully—we have a big blasted problem." Blaze stormed into the barn with Dash ambling in behind, his mood apparently a mirror image of Jake's, given the scowl on his face.

Join the club. Brush in hand, Jake peered over his shoulder, figuring any problem his two best friends could toss his way would pale compared to the one he lived with day in and day out.

"We just found out Clay Morgan's been sparkin' Sheridan."

Except that. Jake could barely breathe, pulse rate climbing along with his temper. "What?!"

"Clyde heard it from Lolita, who heard it from Sophia, who apparently heard it from Sheridan," Dash volunteered, hands buried deep in his pockets as he strolled up next to Blaze, definitely the more even-tempered of the two brothers. But despite his easy stance, he had a cool fire in his eyes, although it was a mere flicker compared to the bonfire in Blaze's. "Clyde figured we should know."

A rare swear word hissed from Jake's lips as he hurled the brush against the wall, unnerving both Midnight and his two friends, who blinked in shock at the uncommon display of anger. "I'm going to kill him," he muttered, jerking Midnight's saddle off the railing before flinging it over the mare's back, fingers shaking while he cinched it up.

"Hey, calm down, old buddy," Blaze said, obviously tempering his own anger in an effort to help temper Jake's. That was something they'd both done for each other over the years, although Blaze seldom had to do it for Jake. Retrieving the brush, he hung it back on its hook before laying a reassuring hand on Jake's shoulder. "We're just as upset as you, Sully, but let's handle this without murder, okay?"

Mauling his face with his hands, Jake unleashed a loud blast of air, reining in the temper he seldom lost.

Except with Sheridan.

"I'm sorry, Blaze, but I knew that dandy would be trouble the moment I laid eyes on him, so something needs to be done. I swear I'll bash his head in for even looking Sheridan's way."

"You're right, Sul, but I'll handle this, okay?" Blaze ducked to peer up at his friend, gaze and voice quiet. "Because you sure in the devil aren't in any frame of mind to deal with it."

Jake finished cinching with a hard jerk. "No, I'll handle it. That guy has had my fist coming for a long time now."

"Nope." Blaze tightened his grip on Jake's shoulder. "With the mood you're in, you'll only stir up a hornet's nest that could backfire, earning Sher's sympathy for the polecat." He slapped Jake on the back and moseyed over to perch on the wooden railing of Midnight's stall. "Sher's only here for another week, so I'll just tell Uncle Finn that Morgan's been sniffing around whenever she's in town, and I think he needs to restrict her to the ranch this last week."

Jake gaped, jaw almost coming unhinged. "What? You're not going to tell Finn what the skunk has done?"

Blaze shook his head. "I don't think so. Finn might blow worse than you. I suspect he and Libby are butting heads because he's been in a pretty foul mood all week, chewing on my hide but good."

"Not to mention dinners have been *prettttty* frosty to say the least," Dash added with a squint of a smile, absently scratching the back of his neck as he leaned against the railing next to Blaze. "So much so, even Clyde's slop is starting to look mighty good."

Jake almost cracked a smile, well aware how much Dash hated taking his suppers at the Ponderosa on those rare times he had to work an afternoon shift.

"So," Blaze continued "the last thing I want to do is ruffle Uncle Finn's feathers even more by telling him Morgan made a pass at Sher." His shoulders rattled in a mock shiver before he pointed a warning finger at Jake. "So, promise you'll stay out of it and let me handle this, you hear?"

Jake scowled as he led Midnight out of the stall. "Yeah, I hear. I won't go hunting the yellow-bellied womanizer just yet," Jake said as he mounted his horse with a hard clamp of his jaw. "For now. But I can't guarantee I won't take a clip at the guy if I happen to see him in the street."

"Wait!" Blaze grabbed the side of Jake's rein. "Where the devil you going now?"

"Dinner at Megan Joy's," Dash said in a matter-of-fact tone, glancing at his watch before ambling toward his horse's stall.

"And how the devil do you know that?" Jake stared, miffed enough he had to go to Megan Joy's, without everybody else knowing it too.

"How do you think?" Dash said, grabbing a curry comb. "Mrs. Burdzy was practically handing out flyers to everybody who came into the store today." He winked. "Hope goulash doesn't give you heartburn."

Head bowed, Jake kneaded the bridge of his nose with a heavy sigh.

Nope, not goulash ...

"You know, old buddy"—a touch of tease lit Blaze's eyes as he let go of the rein with gritted teeth, sucking air through a clenched smile—"I'm no expert, but it seems if you're as adverse to marriage as you always claim, dinner at Megan Joy's might not be the smartest move."

No joke. "Yeah, well, it'll be the last time for a long while, I can tell you that," Jake mumbled, raking fingers through his hair. "Thank God Sheridan's leaving, because now I won't have to distance myself anymore by seeing another woman on a regular basis."

"Yeah." Blaze's smile dimmed considerably at the mention of his sister, the reminder of Clay Morgan's advances souring both of their moods all over again. His shoulders slumped as he plodded to the door, anger tingeing his tone once more. "Thank God is right, or I'd be tempted to bust Morgan's chops like you, kicking his sorry butt from here to their next stop."

"No, you wouldn't," Jake called, leading his horse out of the stall with a hard smile. "Because that job would be mine."

CHAPTER THIRTY-SIX

"**Y**EAH, WELL, I'LL BE RIGHT behind you, my friend," Blaze muttered under his breath as he watched Jake ride down the drive, wondering if he should have just let him teach Morgan a lesson. Because *nobody* taught a lesson better than Jake Sullivan, the once quiet and skinny orphan that all the other boys always made fun of.

Until Jake had shocked Blaze senseless—and everyone else—the day he knocked Reginald Crumley out cold. The burly bully of the eighth grade, Reggie had forced a kiss on sweet Grace Johnson behind the outhouse when Jake had been on his way to the privy.

Hearing Gracie's cry, Jake had taken Reggie on, jumping on his back and drumming his head like a Shoshone war chief. Attempting to flail Jake off his back, Reggie had screamed so loud, the whole schoolyard had gathered 'round, bug-eyed.

Who would have guessed that small and spindly Jake Sullivan could land one in Reggie's gut, knocking him clean out with the next clip to his jaw? Pert near half Reggie's size, Jake had felled Reggie like a dead tree, along with a few of Reggie's teeth, earning everyone's undying respect.

Nobody *ever* made fun of Jake Sullivan after that.

And sweet Gracie Johnson followed poor Jake around moony-eyed the next four years.

Shaking his head, Blaze walked toward the house with a faint smile. When Blaze saved Jake from falling off a cliff months later, that had sealed a life-long friendship for which Blaze would always be grateful. Because Jake was the calm and steady one to Blaze's fire and fury, the unflappable, solid-rock friend he could count on to never lose his temper when

Blaze always did.

Usually.

Picking up his pace, Blaze scowled as he mounted the steps of the log-hewn wrap-around porch two at a time, their dilemma with Sheridan coming back to haunt. Dad-burn-it— if he'd known about Sher meeting up with Morgan, he would have stomped on that dandy like a stinkbug. His mouth twitched. *Or sent Jake to do it.*

Barreling through the mammoth oak door with its intricate carving of Bar SLR, he let it slam good and loud behind him since everyone was gone. Tonight was Angus's night off and Finn's city council meeting in town, while the ladies spent the evening at Mrs. Poppy's for dinner and quiltin'.

Their border collie, Scout, came a-running from the back of the house, tail wagging enough to cause a stiff breeze. The welcome in the collie's dark brown eyes helped ease Blaze's grouchy mood. After a dusty day overseeing repairs on the south forty in the blazing heat, he usually enjoyed coming home. But tonight his uncle's magnificent hardwood entryway with its vibrant Navajo rug, colorful paintings, and unique pottery, failed to soothe. He had too blasted much on his mind to clear up.

Like, why is Sheridan hobnobbing with Morgan?

And just why *didn't my wife tell me?*

Well, he sure in the devil intended to find out, and glancing at the mantle clock in the empty parlour, he figured the ladies wouldn't be home for a while, and Finn even later than that. Just enough time for a quick dinner, an hour or so of paperwork and recording his logs, and then a nice long bath to wash all the grime off his tired body.

But the grime in his mind that was stoking his temper till it was almost red hot? He strode down the hall toward the kitchen with a tic in his temple, figuring a good long soak in the tub was just the ticket.

And an ice-cold one at that.

Blaze had bathed, shaved, and was reading in bed when

the ladies finally came home. The sounds of muted laughter, female chatter, and running water seeped under his closed door, in stark contrast to his own sullen mood while he waited for Maggie.

When she quietly entered their room, the whites of her eyes expanded in the dim light of the gas lantern on his nightstand. Her surprise was evident that he was still awake after a long day on the range that usually began at dawn. "You're still up!" she said with a smile, her obvious approval more of a statement than a question." She sniffed at the air as she laid her purse on her dressing table and hurried over to give him a kiss. "Mmm … and I smell Angus's cedar soap, so that means you're sweet-smelling and snuggly too."

She sat on the edge of the bed and nuzzled his jaw, the touch of her lips dispelling the heat of his temper with a heat of a whole 'nother kind. "And you shaved! Mmm … it would appear, Mr. Donovan, that you have something other than sleep on your mind."

"You got that right, Maggie, but I'm afraid you have the motivation all wrong."

She pulled back, hands still latched to his arms as she studied him with a pucker in her brow. "Are you angry with me?"

"Depends, Mrs. Donovan." He slapped his book closed and slammed it on the nightstand, crossing his arms to challenge her with a lidded glare. "On whether or not you lied to me."

Maggie shot straight up, hands on her hips. "I do not lie, Blaze Donovan, to you or anyone else."

He leaned in, a fire lit deep in his belly. And not the usual kind he always had in this room he shared with Maggie "You don't tell the whole truth, like the time you didn't mention Clay Morgan was coming to the barbecue to see Sheridan."

"Oh, for pity's sake—are we back to that again?" She strode to the closet to unhook her nightgown off the inside of the door, promptly kicking her pumps off. "I promised the last time we had this argument that I would always be totally honest with you regarding Sheridan and Clay Morgan, and I have ever since."

"Oh, sure," he said with an exaggerated nod of his head, "like forgetting to tell me he's been sparkin' her."

"What?" She spun around, fingers frozen on the middle button of her pin-striped shirtwaist, her wide-eyed shock a true Sarah Bernhardt performance.

"Oh, don't act like you didn't know, Maggie." Blaze hurled the coverlet away to jump up, staring her down in his long johns.

"I *didn't* know, you bull-headed baboon!" she shouted back.

Blaze paused, chastened by the fire in her eyes, which was about as rare as it was common for him. "You really didn't know?" His voice softened several degrees.

"No, I *didn't!"* She fumbled with the buttons to get her shirt off, obviously flustered when she opted to just fling it up over her head with shaky hands. "Who on earth told you that?"

He scratched his bare chest through the opening of his union suit, which he refused to button up in the summer. "Dash heard it from Sophia's sister. Seems Sheridan has been meeting up with Morgan on her visits to town."

Maggie slumped down on the side of the bed, nightgown dangling from her hand while her mouth dangled in shock. "I knew Sheridan wanted to make Jake jealous, but I never thought she would go that far."

"Well, she has, and it's got Jake, Dash, and me as hot as a lit fuse on a string of firecrackers, I can tell you that." He plopped down beside her on the bed, so hot, he was ready to stomp down to Sheridan's room and rail on her but good. But he knew Uncle Finn didn't need that aggravation tonight, so he'd deal with it in the morning.

Maggie whirled to face him. "Does Finn know? Because I'm pretty sure Libby doesn't, or she would have told me."

"No, Finn doesn't know—*yet.* But he will tomorrow when I tell him so we can clip Sheridan's wings real good." He released a heavy sigh, slipping her a sideways look. "And I don't plan to tell him the whole truth with the kiss and all because as cold as it's been between Libby and him lately, I don't want to send him over the edge."

Maggie bumped his shoulder with a trace of a smile as she unbuttoned her skirt. "Oh, not the whole truth, huh? Sounds like you think that's a good thing if it keeps the peace."

He slid her a shuttered look out of the corner of his eyes, voice low with tease. "Between me and Uncle Finn, Mrs. Donovan, not between me and my wife."

She stood up to step out of her skirt. "So, what are you going to tell him, then?"

He perused her chemise head to toe in a slow scan, suddenly not all that interested in talking to Uncle Finn right about now. Hooking an arm to her waist, he tugged her over, conveniently toppling her into his lap with a trip of her skirt. "I'm going to tell him Morgan's been sniffing around when Sheridan's in town with her friends," he said, feathering the curve of her neck with his mouth, "and that I think we should restrict her to the ranch this last week."

"Mmm …" Maggie dropped her head back to give him full access while he slowly untied the strings of her corset. "But she has her farewell overnight party at Kathy Jean's the last night before she leaves, you know, so I don't think it's fair to keep her from that."

"No, but it'll only be for one night," he said, flinging the corset across the room while he suckled the lobe of her ear. "And you can bet we'll make darn good and sure Mrs. Edwards keeps a close eye on the girls and turns Morgan away if he tries to show up. Because Jake, Dash, and I want to put an end to this confounded thing once and for all."

"Ha!" Maggie sat up with an arch of her brow, fingers idly skimming the rasp of his jaw. "You could have done that in a heartbeat, if Jake would just admit he's attracted to Sher as a woman."

"Come on, Maggie"—Blaze turned his head into her palm,

grazing it with a soft kiss— "Jake only sees Sher as a little sister."

"Horse apples!" she said, a little of the heat pulsing through Blaze's body suddenly sparking in his wife's eyes. She snatched her nightgown off the bed and started to put it on. "If that's true, then why did Jake kiss the daylights out of her then, huh?"

The moment the words slipped past her lips, she slapped a hand over her mouth, cheeks ashen while the nightgown dropped to the floor. "Uh-oh … I didn't mean to say that." She gulped as she pleaded with her eyes. "So, *please* don't tell Sher I told you, okay?"

But Blaze wasn't listening—or breathing, for that matter. All he could do was stare in shock as the blood drained clear out of his face. When his heart kicked back in, he retaliated with a hot flash of eyes. "That's a bloomin' lie—Jake said Sher kissed *him*."

Maggie hopped off his lap to retrieve her nightgown from the floor. "Yes, she kissed him all right, but the little fact you're missing, Blaze Donovan, is that Jake kissed her back—*passionately*, if you must know—so he needs to at least acknowledge he cares about her as a woman and *not* a little sister."

"Blue blistering blazes," he whispered, putting his head in his hands. He was hardly able to believe that Jake had kept this from him. Probably because he knew Blaze would have laid him out flat. He slowly shook his head. "Blue thunder, I had no idea! Jake and I have never had secrets before, but this sure explains his reluctance to teach her to shoot."

Maggie laid a gentle hand on his shoulder. "Just talk to him, Blaze. Find out why he's fighting it like he is, because Sheridan *knows* that he cares for her that way."

"I will," he said with a weighty sigh that depleted his energy as he lapsed into a vacant stare. "Dad-burn-it, Maggie, why does love have to be so complicated?"

A wispy sigh of her own drifted in the air as she sat beside him to rest her head on his shoulder. "Because human beings are complicated, my love, riddled with hurts and insecurities, and hopes that have been dashed. But the good news is, God *is* love, and when we follow His ways, He teaches us how to make it right."

He kneaded his temples with his forefinger and thumb. "I know, but blast it all, Maggie—why does it have to be so dad-gum hard?"

She pressed a soft kiss to his sandpaper cheek. "Because it's been my experience, darling, that anything worth it usually is." Giving him a tight squeeze, she stood up to put her nightgown back on once again, pausing to deliver a sassy wink. "You know, like me hooking you?" She grinned as her arms grappled to pull the gown over her head.

But not before he tossed her on the bed, flat on her back as she bounced with a gasp. "If that's the case, Mrs. Donovan," he said with a husky whisper, smile decadent while he plucked up the nightgown to sail it far away. "Then why in tarnation are you putting that silly thing on?"

CHAPTER THIRTY-SEVEN

"**T**ABLE IS SET. WHAT NOW?" Overalls splattered with mud, Shaylee dipped a finger in Maggie's bowl of icing and licked it with eyes closed, emitting a loud, long moan of satisfaction that made Sheridan shake her head with a smile.

"Great day in the morning, Shaylee Ann"—Maggie snatched the bowl out of Shaylee's reach with an off-center smile—"only *God* knows where that finger has been, sweetheart."

"Yep, and *me*." Shaylee wiggled auburn brows with a pixie smile, her fair, creamy skin dusted with a light spray of freckles that seemed right at home with the speckles of dirt on her face.

Aunt Libby froze midway through peeling a potato, a curl of skin dangling along with her mouth. "Shaylee Ann Donovan, *please* tell me you haven't been in the pen with that piglet."

Shaylee's chin nudged up, her love of animals evident in the sympathetic slope of her brows. "Her name is Clarabelle, Aunt Libby, and of course I have because who else is going to play with her? She's an only child, for heaven's sake, and in mourning to boot since her twin brother didn't make it, so I would think you'd be more sympathetic to her plight."

A smile flickered at the edge of Aunt Libby's mouth despite her obvious attempt to remain stern. "No one questions your regard for all creatures great and small, sweetheart, and we all find it most commendable. But even *more* so when you wash your hands after, so thank you for setting the table." She paused with a start, part of the peel plopping into her bowl. "You *did* wash your hands prior to, right?"

"Whoops." Teeth tugging her lip, Shaylee quickly bounded to the sink to wash her hands, drawing a groan from every woman in the room.

Shaking her head, Libby continued with her peeling once again, the edge of her lip tipping up. "And I *am* sympathetic to Clarabelle's plight, young lady. It's when it comes in contact with my dinner that I find myself less inclined." She motioned her head toward the door. "Dinner will be ready soon, so you best clean up."

"Yes, ma'am." Shaylee trudged from the room, a noisy sigh trailing her through the door while all three women exchanged glances that broke into chuckles.

"I know she's a late-blooming fourteen," Libby said as she sliced chunks of potato into a boiling pot on the stove, "but she'll be fifteen soon, and I honestly worry about her transition into womanhood the way she fights me on wearing a dress and curling her hair."

"I know." Sheridan finished turning the fried chicken in the skillet and put the lid back on. "Goodness, I was ready to become a woman at age eleven as I recall, wearing nothing but dresses and bows from that moment on, just to try and turn a boy's head."

"For all the good it did," Maggie said with a wry smile while she frosted the cake for dessert, "with prison wardens for brothers."

"And an uncle who won't listen to reason." Libby sat down at the kitchen table to shell the peas. "No matter how hard I try to feminize Shaylee Ann, Finn bucks me at every turn, stating that she has plenty of time to grow up, so we should just allow her to enjoy her childhood until nature takes its course."

Maggie chuckled. "Well, it appears nature has certainly done that, what with Shay spending all her free time tramping through the woods with squirrels and raccoons, then wallowing with pigs." She grimaced. "Albeit the wrong kind of nature."

Grating her lip, Sheridan peeked up from kneading the bread dough, praying her aunt and sister-in-law wouldn't be shocked at what she was about to say. "Uh, speaking of nature taking its course," she said in a frail whisper, gulping when Aunt Libby and Maggie paused to look up. "I um ... well I've been sort of, kind of"—her brows wrinkled in a near wince—"seeing Clay."

Libby caught her breath while Maggie offered a commiserative smile. "I know," she said with a note of sympathy in her tone.

"You *know*?" Sheridan said in unison with her aunt, the whites of her eyes as wide as Aunt Libby's for a whole different reason.

"Yes, because Blaze told me last night when we had it out—*again*."

Aunt Libby just sat there, peapod frozen in hand, as if just now realizing the impact of what Sheridan said. "Wait—you've been seeing Clay?"

Sheridan's cheeks warmed as she peeked up at her aunt. "Yes. He's been teaching me to shoot, which is why Blaze thought I was such a quick study." She glanced at Maggie and back. "I am so sorry I didn't tell either of you, but I didn't want to get you in trouble."

"And the saints be praised for that," Libby said with a droll smile, "because your uncle and I still haven't recovered from our last argument over Clay."

Sheridan put her palms to her cheeks. "Oh, Aunt Libby, I am sooooo sorry for all the problems I've caused for both you and Maggie. I hope you can forgive me."

"Of course I can, darling, because we're in this together. The Silver Lining independence Platform, remember?" Her mouth took a slant as she continued to shell her peas. "It's your uncle I can't forgive at the moment."

"It has been rather chilly at dinners lately," Maggie said with a sympathetic smile. Blaze said Uncle Finn has been a real bear and riding him hard." She paused. "What happened, Libby?"

Libby's heavy exhale lingered in the air. "Oh, we were discussing Sheridan's independence, and he told me flat out that he was her guardian, so he was going to have the last word." Her mouth compressed into a thin smile. She looked up beneath a sweep of lashes, looking for all her forty years, like a mischievous girl in her teens. "So I gave it to him."

Maggie put a hand to her mouth to shield a smile. "You know, Libby, you're going to have to speak to him beyond monosyllables eventually *and* forgive him."

Libby tossed her head, auburn curls bouncing with the motion, almost seeming to Sheridan at times as if Libby were the younger woman and Maggie the elder. "I know, but nothing says I can't make him wait so he thinks twice the next time, right?"

"Uh, do not let the sun go down on your anger?" Maggie quoted softly.

Libby shrugged and popped a pea in her mouth with an impish smile. "It's not going down on my anger," she said with a wink, "just my kisses."

Shaking her head, Maggie turned back to Sheridan, who was buttering a baking pan before washing her hands at the pump, carrying it and a bowl of dough to the table. "Well, no worries, Sher, because Blaze and I made up, so all is well in our relationship." She jagged a brow at Sheridan. "But from what Blaze told me about how Jake reacted to you seeing Clay, I'm not so sure about yours and his."

"So, he knows?" Sheridan asked in a rush, pulse going haywire at the prospect that her plan may have worked.

"Of course he knows," Maggie said with a pointed look that held the barest trace of a smile, "because *after* Blaze and I made up, he told me he had to talk Jake out of riding into town and confronting Clay. Said Jake swore he was going to bash Clay's head in for even looking at you. But Blaze convinced him it wasn't worth it since you're only here for another week. *Especially* since Blaze plans to watch you like a hawk. But, the good news is"—a smile twitched on her face—"apparently Jake was pretty darn riled, which sounds like jealousy to me."

"He was?" Sheridan clasped her hands to her chin in hope.

Maggie's lips skewed. "Yes, sweetheart, but unfortunately, he went to dinner at Megan Joy's instead."

Sheridan flopped down in the chair with a moan, clunking both bowl and pan on the table. "This whole jealousy scheme hasn't worked very well, has it? I care for Jake, he cares for Megan Joy, and Clay cares for me." Stabbing the dough with her hands, she proceeded to shape them into balls for dinner rolls, laying them side by side in the pan.

She unleashed a mournful sigh. "This is a fine mess I've gotten us in, isn't it? I've caused rifts between both of you and your husbands, Jake barely talks to me so even our friendship appears to be over, and Blaze will probably chain me to the house so I can't say goodbye to my friends or Clay." Practically mutilating the ball of dough in her hands, she slammed it into the pan. "Sweet soul-saving mercy, sometimes I wish I didn't have any men in my life."

Smiling, Aunt Libby reached across the table to lay a comforting hand on Sheridan's arm. Well, cheer up, sweetheart," she said with a playful squeeze, a definite gleam of trouble in her eyes, "because the good news is that in one week?" She winked. "We'll be leaving them *all* behind."

CHAPTER THIRTY-EIGHT

"**O**H, I'M GOING TO MISS you both *soooooo* much!" Sheridan flung her arms around her two friends as they huddled together on Kathy Jean's bed in their nightgowns, where all three had been talking and laughing for the last few hours.

"As much as you'll miss Jake?" Sophia asked with a dance of brows, popping a piece of popcorn in the air to catch it with ease.

"More!" Sheridan said with a shaky jut of her chin, downright miffed—and deeply hurt—that Jake had almost avoided her completely this entire last week she was home. "After all, you girls actually *want* to be with me."

"If you want my opinion, Sher," Kathy Jean said with a quiet smile, "I think Jake does, too, which is why he avoids you so much. It's safer, I suspect, than facing his feelings for you."

Sheridan slumped back against the brass headboard with knees bent while Sophia and Kathy Jean faced her sitting cross-legged, a bowl of popcorn smack dab in the middle.

"Well," Sophia said as she tossed another kernel in her mouth, never one for overly serious conversation, "I bet I know someone who *will* miss you, chica, and you, him."

Sheridan smiled, shaking her head as she nibbled a piece of corn. A tinge of sadness shadowed her as she finally admitted to herself that Clay Morgan had made inroads, no matter how small, into her heart despite her refusal to love anyone but Jake.

After that first kiss, she'd shot almost perfect scores, followed by a picnic where they had laughed and talked for hours, ending with a second kiss that had melted her more than the first, completely muddling her feelings for Jake. She exhaled softly. "Okay, yes, I'm finally willing to admit that I probably will miss Clay, too, both the lessons and the attention he lavished on me."

"And the kisses?" Sophia eyed her with a cat-and-mouse smile, as if awaiting to pounce on Sheridan's answer.

Sheridan's cheeks warmed as she deflected with a quick scoop into the popcorn bowl, grabbing a handful to immediately pelt some pieces into her mouth. She hesitated to give Sophia's question careful consideration and suddenly realized, that *yes*, much to her dismay, she *would* miss Clay's kisses! But not because she liked him, although she certainly did. But because his kisses made her feel attractive and pretty and like the woman Jake refused to see. All at once, confusion furrowed her brow when she couldn't help but wonder ...

But if I truly loved Jake, would I want to kiss another man?

Expelling the unwelcome thought in a noisy exhale, she tossed more popcorn, quickly gulping it down. Peeking up, she managed a sheepish smile. "Unfortunately, yes, I have to admit I will miss Clay's kisses as well, although there were only two." And yet, they'd made her feel like a woman for the first time in her life.

A memory flashed of Jake kissing her senseless.

She swallowed hard. *Correction. Second time in my life.*

"Si, but two kisses that have given Mr. Jake some much-needed competition, no?" Sophia grinned as she bounced a kernel off of Sheridan's nose. "In your heart at least, chiquita, if not in reality."

Popcorn to her lips, Sheridan paused, reflecting on Sophia's statement. Maybe her friend was right. Maybe this whole "making Jake jealous" scheme wasn't a failure at all. Because if she couldn't win Jake's love, then perhaps the love she *could* win—be it with Clay or whomever God ordained—would set her free from this painful little-girl fantasy that someday Jake would be hers.

She chewed on the popcorn with a faint smile. "I think you're right, Sophia, but unfortunately it's a moot point. With Uncle Finn restricting me to the ranch all week till tonight— my last night in Virginia City till Christmas—I'll probably never see Clay again." A whisper of a sigh drifted from her lips as her gaze wandered into a melancholy stare. "Even so, my time spent with him does comfort me somewhat knowing that if Jake doesn't want me, at least there are men who will."

"*And* men whose kisses can make you want them as well, si?" Sophia tipped her head.

"I suppose," Sheridan said slowly, her manner pensive. "Although I will admit that does bother me a wee bit."

"And why is that?" Kathy Jean asked, brows in a scrunch as she chomped on her popcorn.

Sheridan shrugged. "Because I'm in love with Jake, so I feel guilty because I don't understand how a girl can be attracted to two men at the same time."

"Bah," Sophia said with a dismissive wave of her hand, "Lolita says it happens to her all the time."

"But she's not in love like I am with Jake, Sophia, so it just feels"—Sheridan lifted a limp shoulder—"I don't know … wrong, I guess."

Sophia wagged a finger. "Only because your uncle and brothers have sheltered you like a nun, chica, allowing no interaction with men whatsoever, which is not good. So, do not feel bad about Clay Morgan because I think he was good for you in more ways than one."

Sheridan sagged against the headboard, hoping her friend was right. "I suppose …"

"Wait—did you hear that?" Kathy Jean raised a palm to still their conversation.

"Hear what?" Sheridan whispered.

Clink.

All but vaulting off the bed, Sophia darted over to the window. "Uh-oh," she said with a soft chuckle, "if you think you feel guilty now, chiquita, just wait till you see this."

Sheridan bounded off the bed along with Kathy Jean, the three of them peering into the Edward's backyard.

Where Clay Morgan stood in the light of the moon.

Wreaking havoc with Sheridan's pulse.

"How on earth did he know I was here?" Sheridan whispered, wondering how a man so handsome could look even more so in the moonlight. She put a hand to her flushed face. "Or even know which room I was in?"

Sophia pinched Sheridan's waist. "Because he's not only handsome and smart, chica, he is smitten. Besides," she said with a droll smile, "it is past ten, so we are probably the only light in the house, no?"

Kathy Jean nodded. "Most likely, because Mama and Papa go to bed early." Her eyes grew as she peeked out the window. "Oh no—he wants you to come out." Her whisper was a shaky rasp while Clay waved Sheridan down, Kathy Jean's anxious tone clear evidence she was not the bravest of the three.

But then, neither was Sheridan. "W-What do I do?" Sheridan stuttered, well aware it was wrong to even consider sneaking out.

"Ay-ay-ay!" Throwing her hands in the air, Sophia butted both girls out of the way as she threw up the sash, holding up a single finger. "Hello, Clay," she whispered loudly, "un minuto, por favor." She turned to latch two hands to Sheridan's shoulders. "You go down to see what he wants, chica, then come right back."

"B-But my parents wouldn't like that," Kathy Jean said, wringing her hands.

"Nor would Uncle Finn." Sheridan stepped closer to Kathy Jean.

Sophia arched a dark brow as she folded her arms, toe tapping. "And did that stop you before?"

Sheridan blinked, thinking Sophia had a point. "Well, no …" She glanced down at her cotton nightgown. "But I'm not dressed."

"*Sheridan ...*" Clay's whisper rose in volume.

"Shhh!" Sophia hushed him with another finger. "Un minuto, Clay." She turned back to Sheridan with a parental smile. "So, get dressed, chica, and go down to see what he wants, si?"

"Okay." A little-girl whisper parted from her lips as she hurried into Kathy Jean's closet to change back into her clothes. She stepped out with a hard swallow. "I'm ready. I think."

"*Please* be quiet," Kathy Jean begged, fanning her pink cheeks.

Sophia gave her a quick squeeze. "A kiss or two, then you come right back, si?" She winked. "After all, you are not Lolita Lopez, eh?"

No, she was *definitely* not Lolita Lopez. Or even Sophia for that matter, Sheridan thought as she tiptoed down the staircase, or her legs wouldn't be wobbling quite this much. Slowly unlatching the bolt on the kitchen door, Sheridan eased it open with nary a squeak, carefully closing it again as she stepped out on Kathy Jean's back porch.

"Oh!" Her surprise squeaked out when someone pinned her to the wall with a kiss that all but melted her into the siding.

"Holy thunder, do you have any idea how much I've missed you?" Clay whispered as he pulled back to cup her face in his hands. "Not seeing you for an entire week?"

She offered a wobbly smile. "A little."

He drew her into a tight hug. "I'm crazy about you, Sheridan, and I'm not about to let you go."

A little-girl giggle tripped from her throat as the scent of bay rum filled her senses. "You have to, Clay, because I'm leaving tomorrow."

"True," he whispered, pressing a kiss to her ear before he held her at bay, "but guess what I just realized?" He grinned like a little boy at his very first rodeo. "We have a six-month break after our tour in New York, where I just happen to have a cousin who's been begging me to stay."

She blinked. "You're going to be in New York?"

His grin, if possible, grew even wider. "From October till March of next year," he said with a wink. "So, you know what that means, don't you?"

Yes. Her breathing accelerated. *I'll have a suitor at Vassar.* She gulped. And not just any suitor. Her eyelids wavered closed as she thought of Clay's kisses. *One whose kisses can buckle my knees.*

And before she could even open her eyes, he did just that, scooping her up with a low chuckle as he swung her around and around. "Isn't that a dream come true?" Setting her back down, he kissed her long and deep, purling waves of that womanly feeling all the way through her, tingling both fingers and toes.

A dream come true? She emitted a tiny moan as Clay nibbled her ear. *Maybe.*

Even *if* it wasn't the one she'd really wanted.

CHAPTER THIRTY-NINE

A FARAWAY SCREAM PIERCED THE AIR, *and Jake's head shot up, fear breaking out in a cold sweat on the back of his neck. "Josie," he whispered, the sound of his voice drowned out by the shrieks and laughter of his friends as they swung on a wild grape vine into the river.*

"Noooooo!"

Jake's blood ran cold at the sound of his ma's echoing scream. Scrambling up the bank, he took off like a shot, chest heaving while he ran for his life.

"Josie!" he screamed, stumbling as he clawed his way back.

"Jake, I love you. Don't leave me, please!"

But he did.

"God, no!" His voice was a broken rasp when he found her tiny body, lying inert on the floor in a sea of broken glass. Once shiny black curls twisted about her, splayed and dusted with dirt against a delicate face so pale and still. Heaves wracking his chest, he swallowed her up in his arms and sobbed, the sound as battered and broken as she.

"I love you, Jakie," she whispered, and he wept against her neck. "Do you love me?"

The question grieved him, and jerking away, he stared at her with tears streaming his face, stunned that he suddenly held a towheaded four-year-old in his arms instead of his little sister. Her little-girl smile melted his heart as she held up a bruised finger. "Will you kiss it?" she whispered, and he did, vowing he'd do everything in his power to make sure she was always safe.

"I love you, Jakie." She planted a stubby, little hand to his

cheek and blinked, blue eyes wide with trust. "Do you love me?"

"I do, Half-Pint, now and forever." Cradling her tiny face in his hands, he closed his eyes to kiss her cheek, then sucked in a harsh breath when she turned, revealing a grownup Sheridan whose lips now aligned with his own. "Jake, I need you. Do you need me?"

"God help me, I do ..." Lowering his mouth to hers, he consumed her like a man dying of starvation, desperate for the taste of the one girl he craved ...

"Jake, I need you ..."

He groaned, slapping away the hand that rattled his shoulder.

"Jake! I need you—wake up!"

He jolted awake, finger on the trigger of his Colt as he shot straight up in his cot.

A curse sizzled the air. "Blast it all, Sullivan, put the dog-gone gun away!"

Blaze's face came into view, as blurry and foggy as Jake's mind at the moment. Breathing hard, he slumped back onto the cot with eyes closed, Colt limp in his hand. "Confound it all, Donovan," he groused, voice groggy with sleep, "what the devil are you doing waking me up in the dead of night?"

More curses defiled the air. "Keep it down over there. We're tryin' to sleep."

Blaze's voice was hot and low in Jake's ear. "We need you, Jake, *now*—in the barn. It's an emergency. About Sheridan!"

Jake's eyelids flipped up faster than the rolled shade on Burdzy's Emporium door at daybreak. "What about Sheridan?" he whispered, voice hoarse as he bolted up in the cot once again, his thin cover all but puddling onto the floor.

But Blaze was already out the door, sending shivers down Jake's body that he couldn't blame on the bare state he preferred to sleep in during the hot summer months. Jumping up from the cot, he dressed in seconds flat, heart pumping as much as his legs while he sprinted toward the barn.

"What's wrong?" he rasped when he skidded to a stop in front of Midnight's stall, where Blaze and Dash stood with grim faces. Chest heaving, he gulped in large quantities of air as he grasped the wooden railing with a stitch in his side.

Eyes deadly sober, Dash stepped forward with hands plunged deep in his pockets. "Clyde overheard Clay Morgan talking to someone tonight at the Ponderosa," he said in a somber tone too foreign for the brother with the perennial smile, "claiming he was about to hit the jackpot with the mayor's pretty daughter."

Jake's Adam's apple hitched hard, wishing he'd just messed up that pretty boy's face like he'd wanted to in the beginning. "Well, so what? She's leaving tomorrow for New York, so what more can he do?"

Dash's somber look did not bode well for Jake's peace of mind. "Said he can't wait for the show to go home next month for a six- month rest after the tour finishes in Texas." He paused, pinning Jake with a hard stare. "*In New York.*"

Burying a silent groan, Jake listed against the wooden stall, eyelids sinking closed as he kneaded the fury that instantly throbbed in his temple.

Blaze moved in to plant a heavy hand on Jake's shoulder. "Jake, you know I would never force you to do anything against your will, but this is Sheridan we're talking about here. We could lose her to this dandy who's on the road six months out of the year, flirting with women in bars and God knows what else. Is that what you want for her?"

A groan broke through as a headache began to pound between his ears. Hissing a rare curse under his breath, he veered into a cold stare with a hard clamp of his jaw. "You know I don't."

Blaze's grip on Jake's shoulder tightened, conveying the same worry Jake felt in his gut. "Listen to me, Jake. The only one that can stop this is you."

Jake glanced up, creases digging deep at the bridge of his nose. "How? She's an eighteen-year-old girl blinded by romance since the age of four. She's not about to listen to me if this dandy has swept her off her feet." He grunted. "Especially with the cold shoulder I've been giving her all summer."

Blaze and Dash exchanged looks before Blaze slapped Jake on the back, exhaling loudly while he perched on the railing. "Dash and I have talked it over, and we both agree there's only one way to reach her." His mouth compressed in a thin line as he nailed Jake with a penetrating look he knew all too well.

"Oh, no you don't," Jake said with a firm shake of his head, backing off with two palms in the air.

The plea in Blaze's tone was pathetic. "You have to, Jake. The only thing that will protect Sheridan from that smooth-talking dandy is to tell her you have feelings for her. Give her a little hope so she sends him packing."

Jake's jaw practically came unhinged. "You want me to *lie* to her?"

Blaze's eyes turned flinty along with his jaw. "Better than lying to me."

Fire scorched the back of Jake's neck, licking his collar while he licked his lips, which immediately parched as dry as his tongue. "What are you talking about? I didn't lie to you."

Dash moved to park on the railing along with Blaze, his tone far kinder than his brother's. "Maggie told Blaze everything about why you wouldn't teach Sher to shoot."

Jake fought a gulp, stomach roiling over what Maggie might know. "So what? I told him too." His gaze flicked to Blaze, pulse stuttering over the stony look in his friend's eyes. "Remember, Donovan? The day we were branding? I told you Sheridan kissed me, which is why I needed to stay away. Because I only see her as a little sister, remember? I told you that!"

Dash cleared his throat as he idly scratched the back of his head, peering up at Jake with eyes as soft as his brother's were hard. "Yeah, Sul, but what you *didn't* tell him was that you kissed Sher back, and pretty intensely from the sound of it. Apparently flat-out convincing her you have feelings for her that are anything but sisterly."

Blood pulsed in Jake's cheeks as he turned away to grip a hand to the next stall, unable to face his two best friends for the shame in his throat.

"Either way, Jake," Dash said quietly, "there's already a lie hanging in the balance here, my friend. So all we want to know is who you told the lie *to*"—he paused, the conviction of his words causing Jake to drop his head in his hand—"our little sister … or to us."

CHAPTER FORTY

JAKE FELT LIKE THAT PILE of manure in Midnight's stall, only at the moment, he was pretty sure he stunk way more, lying to the people he loved the most. Blue blazes, how he hated lying! He slammed his fist against the wall. Telling people one thing, then doing another.

Just like Pa.

He shook his head, shame burrowing in. Right next to the mountain of it that was already there. And the sad thing was he hadn't fully realized he was even doing it, making him as bad as Pa.

"Look, Sully," Dash said softly, obviously the designated spokesman so Blaze wouldn't rip out his tonsils, "everybody knows Sher has followed you around like a lovesick puppy since she was knee-high to a calf, and there's no question the girl's a flirt to boot, so nobody here is blaming you."

Blaze grunted, the sound as deadly as a rusty hacksaw.

"But if what Maggie told Blaze is true," Dash continued gently, "and you do have those kind of feelings for Sher, then would it be so awful to let her know?"

Jake spun around, jaw distending so much, he swore he heard it pop. "You want me to lead her on?!"

Dash shrugged. "If it protects her from an out-of-town scalawag, why not? Besides," he said with a pointed stare that appeared to sharpen along the lines of his brother's granite gaze, not unlike a shotgun ready to take aim, "if it *is* true, what's the harm?"

"What's the harm? *What's the harm?!*" Jake's voice squeaked like some prepubescent, pimple-faced kid. "Because marriage is *not* even a possibility, Dash," he said, wishing this was all just a nightmare and he was still back in his cot. His gaze whipped to Blaze with a plea of panic in his tone. "I've been telling you that for years, Blaze, you know that, so tell him."

Blaze crossed his arms, eyes narrowing. "Yeah, old buddy, I do know that, but what I don't know is why?"

"*What?*" Jake couldn't believe it. His best friend who'd insisted on a blood oath at the age of thirteen to never get married, was putting *him* on the spot? Huffing out his frustration, he slashed stiff fingers through his hair. "For crying out loud, Donovan, you know why! We all know how Finn feels about Sher steering clear of romance till she gets her degree. And you would have shot me and any other man who even looked at her cross-eyed, and I dare you to deny it."

"I don't deny it." Blaze studied him through hooded eyes, but apparently his tone was on the thaw. "But stacking up your character against some sweet-talking, out-of-town dandy we know next to nothing about, leaves me no choice but to go with the lesser of two evils."

"*Lesser of two evils??*" Jake stared him down.

"Yeah," Dash said with a shake of his head, stooping to pluck up a piece of hay and tuck it in his teeth. "The dandy's prettier, no doubt, but Sher's eyesight probably isn't too good, so no harm there."

Blaze scratched the back of his neck. "And the fact he snorts like a pig in slop when he laughs apparently doesn't bother her either ..."

"Real funny, you two clowns." Jake slacked a hip.

Dash pursed his lips, eyes scrunched in thought. "True, his feet smell worse than prairie poop when he takes his boots off, pert near turning a body blue, but Sher should be okay long as he keeps his shoes on."

Hands on his hips, Jake shook his head, not about to let these two troublemakers get the upper hand. "Look, this may be a laughing matter to you idiots, but it's not funny to me. I have no interest in getting married to anyone—*ever*—so you can just forget it."

Blaze actually resorted to begging, his voice almost a whine. "Come on, Jake, I didn't either, and you see what happened for me."

Jake's mouth cemented while he stared his best friend down with a tight press of his jaw. "Well, it can't happen for me, Blaze, and I have my reasons—some you know, some you don't—so just let it go."

Dash jumped down from the fence to casually stroll over with hands in his pockets. "So, don't marry her, Jake," he said with a light shrug. "Just tell her you have feelings for her, which you do, so it's not like it's a lie."

Jake stared, slack-jawed. "Lead her on with false hope? I just told you marriage is off the table for me, Dash, so that would be downright cruel."

Blaze grunted. "Not as cruel as some dandy of questionable character leading her on with hurt and heartache, taking advantage of her innocence. Or even a possible fortune-hunter, trapping her into a miserable marriage."

Sweat licked the back of Jake's collar. "We don't know that," he rasped.

Blaze's eyes went hard, a flicker of temper starting to burn all over again. "No, Sully, all we *do* know is he's been sneaking around with her, kissing on her, and doing only God knows what. Blue blazes, she's just an innocent—for all we know, he could ruin her forever." His gaze thinned to a knifepoint, voice murderously low. "If he hasn't already ..."

Clawing his forehead, Jake felt like putting a fist through the wall. "Then we'll tell Finn, and he'll stop her."

Blaze spiked a brow. "How? Finn's here and Sher'll be in New York. How is he going to stop a girl who's already defied him by sneaking behind his back? Besides, I already told you—this stalemate between him and Libby has put his teeth on edge. If we tell Finn about this, it'll be like poking a female grizzly in the spring."

"With a carcass bone honed to knife point," Dash added, "and a bloody one at that."

Blaze's jaw shifted as he cornered Jake with a desperate gaze. "Especially if there's something that would keep Sher's heart at home for dead sure. Because if this dandy marries her, Jake, he could settle her in New York away from her family, if he even marries her at all, where we'll seldom get to see her again. Is that what you want?"

"No," Jake whispered, shoulders sagging into a slump when he realized that Blaze was right—he was the only one that could stop Sher from making a horrible mistake. But then, he would also be the one making a horrible mistake by deceiving her. "I don't know, Blaze ..."

Blaze climbed down from the fencing to clasp a hand to Jake's shoulder. "Look, Jake, you don't have to promise her anything. Just tell her you have feelings for her that you have to sort out. Then break it off when the danger is past. It'll hurt her for a while, but not as much as a lifetime of pain with a man who's only home three months a year, and probably hobnobbing with women the rest of the time." His grip tightened as he ducked to peer up into his friend's face. "Please, Jake? For Sher, me, Dash, and Finn?"

Finn. The man who was a second father. And the redemption he so desperately needed for failing the first. His ribcage depleted in one long, painful breath, as if it were his last, the expiration of a vow he'd made so many years ago to one little girl after he'd failed another.

To always love her.

To always protect her.

To always make sure she never got hurt.

Gouging his temple with the pads of his fingers, he finally gave a slow nod.

Loud whoops bounced off the walls as Dash and Blaze slapped him on the back.

Blaze hooked him in a shoulder hug. "You are a life saver, old buddy. I'm going in to wake her up now to tell her you need to see her in the barn, all right?"

Jake's Adam's apple jerked hard in his throat as guilt soured his tongue.

"You won't regret this, Jake, I promise," Blaze whispered before he and Dash hooted and barreled out of the barn, leaving him on his own.

Eyelids sinking closed, Jake listed against the stall with a grunt.

Already do.

CHAPTER FORTY-ONE

" *A S LONG AS OUR HEARTS are aligned with God's ...
therein is the safest place to be ..."*

Maggie's words haunted as Sheridan sniffed, balling up the soggy handkerchief before she laid it on her nightstand.

Right next to the other two.

"Then why doesn't it feel like it, God?" she whispered, voice nasal from weeping. Casting a worried glance at the alarm clock, Sheridan tugged a clean handkerchief from her drawer, well aware midnight was far too late to be up when she, Maggie, and Aunt Libby had to board a train first thing in the morning. She'd always thought "the safest place to be" had meant marrying Jake because he'd made her feel so very safe from little on.

Until this summer.

Flopping back on her pillow, she stared at the ceiling through sodden eyes. Apparently "safe" didn't necessarily mean "happy," she decided because Jake didn't want her.

But Clay certainly did.

Pushing the wetness from her eyes, she reflected on her last moments with Clay in Kathy Jean's backyard. No, he wasn't Jake, but he might be the very one to help her let Jake go.

Against her will, more tears welled, and with a frail heave, she pressed the handkerchief to her eyes once again. But the sad truth was, she didn't *want* to let Jake go ...

Tap. Tap.

Sheridan shot up, hoping against hope it was Maggie so she could unburden her soul.

"Maggie?" she whispered.

"It's Blaze."

Blaze? Sheridan blinked, jumping up to snatch her robe from the closet just as his second whisper leaked through the door.

"Sher—wake up!"

She grunted as she wrestled into her robe, tying the sash with a jerk. *As if I could sleep!* Hurrying to the door, she opened it quietly, robe clutched to her neck. "Blaze, what's wrong?"

"Jake needs to see you—in the barn—*now,*" he whispered, chest heaving as if he'd run all the way.

Her heart stopped. "What??"

Finger to his lips, he nodded to her closet. "Go on, get your slippers on."

Still in a daze, she put on her slippers, and he tugged her out of her room, all but dragging her down the stairs till he clutched her shoulders in the foyer. "He wants to say goodbye, Sher, without the rest of the family around."

"*What??*" She blinked, hardly able to believe what she'd heard. *Jake?* Wanted to be alone with her? In the dead of night? To say goodbye? Her heart kicked back in like a mule buck to the head, making her dizzy.

Blaze wasted no time prodding her to the door. Silently opening it up, he pressed a kiss to her head. "Just go, Half-Pint—he's waiting for you."

Jake is waiting for me? She just stood there until Blaze nudged her down the steps with a hand to the small of her back. "Go! Do you want to see him or not?"

She started to hyperventilate as she stumbled down the last step, hardly able to believe Jake was waiting for her. *Her!* Breaking into a run, she sprinted across the moonlit lawn, heart seizing all over again when she skidded to a stop in front of Midnight's stall. Goose bumps popped at the sight of his broad back as he leaned over the fence, the light from a single oil lamp defining taut muscles strained with his weight. "Jake?" He turned slowly, and heat instantly pooled in her belly so strong, she swayed on her feet. "Did you ...

want to see me?"

"Yeah." A lump bobbed in his throat as he moved toward her like a man on a mission, those blue eyes penetrating her with an unwavering stare. Halting a foot away, he huffed out a heavy blast of air while he buried his hands deep in his pockets. "I … uh, wanted to say goodbye."

"Is that all?" she whispered, picking at her nails as she watched him with a vulnerable chew of her lip.

"No." He gave a gruff clear of his throat as if girding himself for what he was about to say. His pale blue eyes were guarded while he shifted from one leg to the other, a bronzed chest peeking through a half-buttoned shirt.

Sheridan could barely breathe, drinking in the man she had loved from childhood.

Slashing blunt fingers through nearly coal-black hair, he exhaled again before homing in on her with a tentative look. "I wanted to tell you that I"—his Adam's apple dipped several times while his voice came out in a husky rasp— "have feelings for you, Sheridan."

She gasped, the sound all but echoing in the silent barn. Tears pooled in her eyes as she took a step forward.

"No!" He held out a hand, palm up. "No closer please, because this is not easy to say."

She gulped, heart hammering so hard, she feared he could see it through her robe.

Chest rising with a deep inhale, he started to pace, his words as shaky as the hand he was tunneling through his hair. "I have"—he swallowed hard—"feelings for you, Sheridan, but I need time to sort them out."

"What kind of feelings?" she said softly, almost surprised how much stronger her voice sounded than his.

He paused, gaze flicking briefly to hers before he looked away, pacing once again. "I, uh … I'm attracted to you, of which you're already well aware," he said quietly, his pace slowing as if the admission had calmed him somehow. "And I want time to sort those feelings out while you're away at school."

"Why?" she whispered, pulse pounding in her ears so hard, she barely heard herself at all.

He halted to knead the bridge of his nose, head bowed. "Because I'm as confused as I am attracted, Sheridan, and I need to think it through, long and hard"—he peered up beneath thick dark lashes—"and pray about what I should do."

"You'll pray about it?" Hope threaded her tone.

He looked up, a pinch of offense riddling his brow. "Of course. That's a first resort for me, Sheridan, not a last."

She gave a shaky nod. "Good to know, because I've been doing that for years now."

She could have sworn he winced before he turned away, head bent.

"Jake?"

"Yeah?" He didn't turn around, so she walked to him.

"I'm in love with you," she said softly, and her heart hitched when his shoulders slumped all the more.

"That's just it, Sheridan, I don't think you are." He turned to face her head-on, his big-brother posture tightly in place. "I think you're confusing love with big-brother affection."

Annoyance prickled through her. "I don't think so, Jake"—her chin rose in defiance—"because never once do I remember either Blaze or Dash kissing me the way you did that day."

Blood gorged his face, and never had she seen him flush so hard, nor those beautiful eyes harden so much to pale-blue agate. His chin rose to counter hers, hard as sculpted stone "Nor I, with any female in town, be it a saloon girl or other."

Tears suddenly swelled, trembling on her lashes like her legs trembled on the floor. His words made her feel cheap and tawdry, and with a ragged heave, she turned to go.

"Wait!" He grabbed her from behind before she could take another step, whirling her around to swallow her up in a fierce hug. "I'm sorry," he whispered against her hair, rubbing her back while she sobbed in his arms. "Shhh … shhh, Half-Pint, don't cry, please. I'm sorry." He bent his head against hers.

Breathing in his scent, she slipped her arms around his muscled back, sniffing while she lay her head on his chest. "I love you, Jake, and deep down, I think you love me too."

A low groan rattled in his chest, vibrating in her ear. "I do love you, Half-Pint," he whispered with an agony she'd sensed in him many times before, "but I'm not sure it's in the way that you want."

She pulled away to peer up while she swiped the tears from her eyes. "I want you to love me as a woman, Jake, touch me and kiss me like you did that day, and then hopefully, someday, make me your wife."

His hold dropped as he took a step back. "That's just it, Sher—I'm confused. All these years you've been like a little sister to me, so it's just"—he plowed fingers through his thick hair, disrupting it enough that several dark strands dangled over his forehead—"hard, you know? And now there's these … these … *feelings* that I need time to sort out—"

"How much time?" she said in a rush, desperate for some kind of commitment to hang her hopes on.

He plunged his hands back into his pockets and shrugged. "I don't know. "You're so young, Sheridan, and I'm almost eight years older, for pity's sake."

"I don't care," she said in a near hiss, taking a step forward.

"No, but I do. Your uncle would fire me on the spot if he knew we were talking like this."

"No, he wouldn't!" She clutched his arms. "He would be fine with it, Jake, because he loves you, and you're already part of the family."

He grunted, dislodging her hold with a lift of his arms. "Not if I stand in the way of your schooling. You know that. Finn wants you to go to college, and he doesn't want *anything* to get in the way."

She grated her lip in thought, well aware Jake was right. For some reason Uncle Finn was bound and determined she get a degree because heaven knows they'd butted heads over it more times than she could count. *Some reason?* She sighed. Blaze had told her long ago that Ma had made Uncle Finn swear on her Bible that he'd see to her children's college educations, *including* the girls. She wrinkled her nose. Which was downright silly because everyone knows girls got married, for heaven's sake, *not* go to college.

Except me, apparently.

Unleashing a forlorn sigh of surrender, Sheridan looked up. "What about after I graduate then, Jake? I'll be twenty when I obtain my teaching degree, so you and I can just promise ourselves to each other till then."

He gently buffed her arms with a patient smile. "Let's just wait and see, Half Pint, okay? A lot can happen in two years." He tweaked the pigtail she always wore to bed.

Her rib cage squeezed along with a crease in her brow. Stepping back from his hold, she barricaded her arms to her waist with the barest jut of her chin, determined to make Jake give her more than an empty "wait and see." And she had a sneaky suspicion as to just how. Thoughts of Clay emboldened her as she pursed her lips into battle mode. "I don't want to 'wait and see,' Jake. I would like some assurance that you and I *will* marry someday—"

"Sher …" He was shaking his head before she could even finish her sentence.

"Because otherwise I'll be more vulnerable," she quickly explained, satisfied when a frown popped in his brow. Feigning nonchalance, Sheridan tossed her braid over her shoulder. "Aunt Libby says I'll have to be on my guard because there are so many eligible men who seek female companionship."

Catching the edge of her lip in her teeth, she peeked up beneath her lashes like Lolita had taught her, determined to use every ploy to get Jake to commit to at least *something*. "So, if I have a promise from you, no other man would stand a chance."

She almost grinned when he shifted his stance, huffing out a loud blast of air as he slapped hands low on his hips. "All right, Sheridan, friends for now with the *possibility* of more after you graduate, all right?"

A smile squirmed on her lips as her chin nudged up a hair, thinking Jake Sullivan was *such* a mule. "Not a friendship with the 'possibility' of more, Jake Sullivan, because I can have *that* with any male I meet in New York." She plopped her hands on her hips like him. "I want a *close* friendship where we correspond at least once a week and a definite *promise* of more, cross your heart and hope to die."

He stared her down, the nervous tic in his cheek keeping time with the race of her pulse before he gusted out a noisy sigh. "All right, you win," he said with a scowl, "cross my heart and hope to die."

Her grin slid sideways. "No, Jacob Michael, 'winning' would be a ring on my finger, mister, but a close friendship with the promise of more will work for now."

"*But* you have to swear you won't breathe a word of this to anyone in the family, especially Finn, Libby, or Maggie, or to Sophia and Kathy Jean either—*ever*. Because this is nobody's business but ours, Sheridan, all right? And as far as any talkin' you've done with Maggie or Libby in the past about your feelings for me? I want you to promise to put an end to it, telling them we are nothing more than friends, understood?" Spitting in his palm, he wiped it against his pants before extending his hand in the "spit swear" they'd made up when they were young. "Agreed?"

She eyed him with a tight purse of lips, gaze pensive as she considered his words, not thrilled about never being able to talk to Maggie and Libby about it anymore. But she might consider it if she could barter something as important in return. "All right. But I'll only agree on one condition, Jake Sullivan."

Arm still extended, he slacked a hip. "And that is?"

She spit in her palm and rubbed it against her robe before

shaking his hand with a smirk, figuring if he could use spit to seal a deal, she sure in the blazes could too. She jagged a definitive brow. "We seal it with a kiss."

CHAPTER FORTY-TWO

A KISS? ICE WATER SHOT THROUGH Jake's veins, right before it boiled into lava within two ragged beats of his pulse. He jerked back as if she scalded him with her words, battling a gulp when his gaze flicked to those lush lips and held.

Better than being scalded by a kiss.

"No way, Sheridan," he said with a jut of his chin, not about to go down *that* road again. "That's an intimacy reserved for two people who are in love, not friends."

She actually stomped a tiny slipper, the action barely producing any sound at all, but the intent of her hissed response was near deafening. "I *am* in love with you, you pig-headed mule, and I think you're in love with me, too, but you're too dad-burned stubborn to show it."

He blinked and took a step back, not used to such volatile words from his sweet, little Half-Pint.

She took a step forward, poking a tiny finger into his chest as she glared up, reminding him so much of that little six-year-old who used to bully her brothers in much the same way. *Or tried.* "And another thing," she said with more pokes, "we are *not* just friends per our agreement. We are *good* friends with the *promise of more*, and I can't think of anything *more promising* than a kiss, so those are my terms, take 'em or leave 'em."

Giving him the benefit of an adorable scowl, she stepped back with a staunch cross of arms, looking so much like that little girl he used to tickle out of her tantrums, that he bit back a smile, tempted to do it all over again. But she was no longer that little girl, and the thought instantly sobered him. Because sure as the sparks in those remarkable blue eyes, *that* wasn't the type of touching she was looking for anymore.

He distanced himself with another step back, opting to call her bluff. "I guess I leave 'em, then, Sher, because kisses are *not* what I want."

He felt an immediate ache in his chest when tears welled in her eyes.

Shoulders square, she lashed her chin up in anger, totally at odds with the tremble of those sweet lips he so longed to still. "Well, that's fine, then, Jake Sullivan," she whispered, pain threading her tone as she swiped at the wetness coating her cheeks, "because I have a feeling there will be plenty of men who will. Goodbye, Jake." Turning on her heel, she bolted for the door.

"Sheridan, wait!" But she didn't, and with a hiss of a curse under his breath, he darted after her, swooping her up before she got too far out the door.

"Leave me alone!" she screamed, battering his chest while she flailed and sobbed in his arms.

Petrified she'd wake up the entire ranch, he ducked back into the barn and set her against the wall, silencing her with a kiss that suddenly silenced all his denial as well. The lava was back as she slowly slid down with a soft moan, their mouths never parting while he bundled her in his arms, lost in the taste of the woman of his dreams.

God help me, I love her!

The stark realization both stunned and stoked, inflaming his desire for a woman he couldn't have. But he *could* have this one single moment, he decided, when he could pour all of his love and passion into protecting her from any other man. Arm to her waist, he jerked her close with a kiss that made her go limp against chest, infusing him with a possession he'd never felt for a woman before.

Butting her to the wall, he tunneled fingers into her hair to cradle her face in his hands, taking her mouth with a vengeance that mated her moan with his. "No other lips but mine," he rasped against her jaw, trailing to suckle the lobe of her ear. "Swear it, Sheridan, *now*—no other man but me."

"I swear," she whispered, her ragged breathing merging with his as she skimmed a gentle hand down his jaw, "no other man but you, Jake." A beautiful smile slowly curved on a mouth now swollen with his love as she peered up with a misty look, their bodies still pressed to the wall. Mischief suddenly lit in her eyes as she stood on tiptoe to seal the deal with that infamous tug of his lower lip, lodging a groan deep in his throat.

Right before he sealed the deal all over again.

CHAPTER FORTY-THREE

"A RE YOU EXCITED ABOUT SCHOOL starting next week?" Maggie smiled over her shoulder as she hung Sheridan's dresses in the closet of Aunt Marie's guest room while Aunt Libby laid folded items into the drawers. They'd just arrived this afternoon at Aunt Marie's main house in Poughkeepsie, New York. Home to Vassar, Poughkeepsie was also the summer and weekend home to New York society such as the Astors, Rogers, and Vanderbilts.

Two hours from New York City, Poughkeepsie was close enough to visit Aunt Marie's townhouse in Manhattan for weekend shopping and social events—*and* Aunt Libby's beloved suffragist and volunteer activities. Yet still far enough away to maintain the idyllic beauty of the Hudson River Valley. Sheridan sighed as she carried the last of her shoes to the closet.

And the perfect place to dream of Jake!

"Excited? Oh, yes!" But lining her shoes up in the closet just so, Sheridan realized her "excitement" had little to do with Vassar. "In fact, 'excitement' doesn't even begin to describe how I'm feeling right now." She grinned. "More like "euphoric, I'd say." Pausing in the closet with a dreamy smile, she closed her eyes to relive Jake's kisses in the barn a week ago, wishing she could tell Maggie and Aunt Libby about her and Jake's agreement. Unfortunately, he'd tied her hands but good with his unbreakable spit swear—*along* with her heart!

Upon their arrival, Aunt Marie had handed her a letter from Clay that had arrived along with letters from Uncle Finn for both her and Aunt Libby. But Sheridan hadn't even opened

Clay's yet, no interest whatsoever in seeing him again. Not with memories of Jake's kisses filling her brain and her heart!

She had no doubt that Clay's interest had sparked Jake's, but she had to admit that hurting Clay dimmed her joy somewhat, leaving an ache behind over what she had done. Resolute, she rose to her feet, vowing to write him tonight to break it off and apologize for any hurt she may have caused. Expelling a lovesick sigh, she put Clay out of her mind to focus on Jake while she all but floated out from the closet.

"Oh, just you wait!" Aunt Libby gushed, not only excited to spend time with Aunt Marie again, but also her many friends from Vassar and the National Woman Suffrage Association during the week she and Maggie were staying. "Why, my college days at Vassar were some of the happiest of my life, Sheridan, and they will be for you too."

"But not *the* happiest of your life, I'll wager," Maggie said with a wink, closing up Sheridan's empty suitcases to store them away in the closet.

Aunt Libby grinned ear to ear, her face so aglow, she looked closer to Maggie's and Sheridan's ages than her own. She pulled Finn's letter from her skirt pocket and waved it in the air. "You would be correct, Mrs. Donovan, at least since his letter arrived." She held it to her chest with a sigh that could have been a swoon. "I'd say our argument was almost worth it because it seems the man is wonderfully besotted, apologizing up one side of the letter, and missing me down the other."

Maggie chuckled. "Well, with two weeks of train travel and one week in New York, I suspect both of our boys will be pining for us before all is said and done."

Sheridan sighed. *And hopefully all three.*

Hands on her slim hips, Aunt Libby looked around the pretty room with its pale yellow floral wallpaper and wispy-sheered windows that overlooked a lovely view of the Hudson River. She glanced at her watch. "Well, since everything is put away, I suggest we not waste any more time dawdling since

Aunt Marie is serving tea in five minutes." She marched to the door to open it, waving Maggie and Sheridan through with a bright smile. "Shall we?"

Sheridan was still walking on air when they entered Aunt Marie's spacious parlour with its huge bay window overlooking a lush lawn and rambling gardens along the Hudson River. Part music room, part parlour, the room was a delightful setting for a tea with its watered-silk divan and cream tufted settees interspersed with French fluted tables.

Blue-and-cream striped wing chairs flanked a floor-to-ceiling fireplace paneled with cream wainscoting while the late-summer sun streamed through rich, velvet-swagged windows onto a pastel blue, cream, and green Oriental rug. The scent of roses and wisps of dried lavender filled the air from milk vases gracing the tables while the soft laughter of five elderly women filled the room.

"Ah, here they are now!" Aunt Marie said as she rose from the settee in a lacey, blue taffeta dress that set off her silver-white chignon perfectly. She was still beautiful, boasting the same creamy skin as her sister, Maeve, Libby's mother, despite being in her sixties.

Her taffeta dress rustled softly as she hurried over to hook an arm around Aunt Libby's waist, and Sheridan could instantly see the resemblance, hinting at what Libby might look like in twenty years. "Ladies," she said to the four other women with a note of pride, "this is my niece, Liberty O'Shea McShane, wife to the Mayor of Virginia City and co-owner of the Silver Lining Ranch, along with her nieces Maggie and Sheridan Donovan."

Ushering them into the room, Aunt Marie promptly introduced her four lady friends, Mrs. Rhiannon Feuerstein, Mrs. Sherida Stewart, Mrs. Carrie Booth Schmidt, and Mrs. Monika Cotrill, all of whom were dressed to the hilt in the most elegant summer dresses Sheridan had ever seen.

"So, young lady," Mrs. Rhiannon Feuerstein said once everyone had been served tea and scones, "what course of study do you hope to pursue?" Her tea cup paused at lips pinched in a faint line of disapproval, nose scrunched the slightest bit as if the pursuit of academia for women was offensive.

Sheridan stirred milk and sugar into her tea. "Education, Mrs. Feuerstein." Laying her spoon aside, she lifted her cup with a bright smile. "You see, from the age of four, I loved to play school with my dolls"—her eyes warmed with a twinkle—"or any live specimens I could badger into it as well, from my brothers and ranch hands, to our collie, kittens, and donkeys." Several of the ladies laughed—although Mrs. Feuerstein wasn't one—while Sheridan shrugged and lifted her cup in a toast. "So, I suppose becoming a teacher is the natural course of action."

"And Sheridan will make one of the best," Aunt Libby piped up, the sheen of pride in her eyes unmistakable.

"Humph." Taking a dainty sip of her tea, Mrs. Feuerstein wrinkled her nose enough to show her disdain. "Well, you do know teachers can't marry," she said, the gargantuan diamond ring on her finger and ostentatious emerald brooch on her silk dress evidence that she had done so and quite well.

Sheridan blinked, a vague memory of that ridiculous rule taking the starch out of her smile.

"There are certainly exceptions to that rule, Mrs. Feuerstein," Aunt Libby said, ever the advocate for women's rights as she shot Sheridan a comforting smile.

"The '1872 Rules for Teachers' expressly prohibits teachers from marrying," Mrs. Feuerstein stated emphatically, squinting as if she smelled something bad.

Aunt Marie bobbled her tea, obviously upset over the direction the conversation was taking. "Now, Rhianne—"

"*Female* teachers only," Libby said with a bite to her tone, the sudden square of her shoulders indicating her temper was now as warm as the tea in her cup. "*Not* male teachers, ironically, which is just another one of the many injustices men perpetrate on women."

Mrs. Feuerstein grunted, the sound strangely at odds with the bounty of diamonds gracing her person. "Rules are rules," she snapped.

"My, but we've had a hot summer, haven't we, though?" Mrs. Carrie Booth Schmidt said in a rush, dabbing a handkerchief to her neck. Sheridan sent a gentle smile to the sweet, silver-haired woman with the kindly face, grateful for her valiant attempt to steer the conversation away from a fistfight between Aunt Libby and the bejeweled snob.

Aunt Libby's china cup clinked back into her saucer with attitude while she leaned forward on the edge of her seat, a touch of fire in her green eyes. "That primitive document of balderdash, ma'am, *also* mandates teachers to clean chimneys, bring a bucket of water and a scuttle of coal to school each day, and forbids riding in a buggy with a man unless he is her father or brother."

"Now, ladies—" Mrs. Sherida Stewart began, wringing her napkin with a gentle pinch of her face while Aunt Marie upended her tea like a shot of whiskey.

"And another thing," Libby continued with a jut of an auburn brow, "although the ridiculous prohibition against married teachers is customary for this time, fine organizations like The National Woman Suffrage Association are working to change that.

Barely taking a breath, Aunt Libby forged on with a pointed look. "But, fortunately for my niece, that will not be necessary because asinine rules such as the *1872 Rules for Teachers*"—Libby hissed the document title as if it were a profanity—"are not strictly followed on the Comstock, thank God, evidenced by the several married female teachers in Virginia City over the years. A fact that not only reveals a necessity born out of the scarcity of women in the mining West, *Mrs. Feuerstein*, but obviously an elevated intelligence as well."

Brrrrrrnggg!

At the sound of her new-fangled doorbell, poor Aunt Marie

shot out of the settee like one of the tiddlywinks Sheridan used to play with when she was small. Exchanging glances, Sheridan and Maggie bit back smiles as Marie bolted for the door. "Oh, that must be Grace," she said in a flutter, leaving Mrs. Carrie Booth Schmidt, Mrs. Sherida Stewart, and Mrs. Monika Cotrill frantically fanning themselves with their handkerchiefs while Aunt Libby stared Mrs. *Frankenstein* down.

"Grace! I'm so glad you could come by." Aunt Marie quickly ushered in a pretty girl about Sheridan's age, all but dragging her into the parlour. "Sheridan, I wanted you to meet my next-door neighbor, Grace Carmody. This will be her first year at Vassar too."

Tall and willowy with shiny black curls piled high on her head, Grace extended her hand to Sheridan with a generous smile. Silky skin kissed with just a hint of a blush, complemented clear gray eyes as soft and gentle as a doe, the epitome of her name. "I'm so glad to meet you," she said, "because now we'll both know someone on our first day of school."

Shaking her hand, Sheridan grinned, peering up at what she sensed in her spirit might become a very good friend. "And thank God too," she said as she leaned close to deliver both a wink and a whisper, "because to be honest, I'm shaking in my boots."

Even Grace's soft laughter matched her name as she bent to give Sheridan a quick hug. "Me, too," she said with a giggle, "and I don't even own any."

Aunt Marie laughed as she cupped a hand to Grace's waist to introduce her to everyone else. "Ladies, this is my neighbor Genevieve Carmody's granddaughter from New York City, who will be staying with her while she's attending Vassar." Aunt Marie introduced everyone else to Grace, and Sheridan couldn't help a squirm of a smile when Mrs. Feuer*crab* grunted a hello.

"Have a seat, Grace, and I'll pour you some tea."

Grace glanced at the watch pinned to her bodice. "Oh, I wish I could, Mrs. O'Shea, but Grandmother has tickets for the John Philip Sousa performance tonight at the Collingwood Opera House, and we're going to dinner prior to, so I don't have much time."

"Surely you can stay for one cup of tea, dear, can't you?" Not one easily dissuaded, Aunt Marie prodded Grace to the divan where Maggie and Aunt Libby were sitting, promptly seating her between the two. "Cream in your tea, Grace? And sugar?"

"Yes, please." Biting her lip, Grace offered Maggie and Libby a nervous smile before her gaze locked on Sheridan's, both of them busting out in laughter with a hand to their mouths that drew an immediate scowl from Mrs. Feuer*snob*.

"So, young lady," Mrs. Feuer*snub* said with a familiar pinch of her nose, "what course of study do you hope to pursue?"

Aunt Marie jumped up like a jack-in-the-box, all but shoving the tray of pastries under Grace's nose. "Scones, sweetheart?"

"Thank you, Mrs. O'Shea, but Grandmother would scold if I ruined my dinner."

A nervous giggle popped out of Marie's mouth as she set the tray back down. "Yes, I suppose that does sound like Genevieve …"

Boom! Boom!

Sheridan's startled gaze—and everyone else's—shot to where Mrs. Feuerstein pounded a cane on the polished wood floor, a personal item Sheridan hadn't noticed before. She couldn't help it when her mouth twitched. Probably to whop people if they didn't agree with her.

Grace blinked at the woman, clearly taken aback. "Oh, yes, well, I'm enrolled in the Schools of Art and Music, Mrs. Feuerstein."

"Good heavens, you don't plan to go into burlesque, do you?"

"Rhiannon!" Aunt Marie went as pale as her cream tufted

settee, and Mrs. Schmidt gasped while poor Mrs. Cotrill dropped her teacup, which was—fortunately—empty.

Sheridan nervously gnawed on her lip when Aunt Libby sat up as stiff as Mrs. Feuer*stick's* cane, green eyes glittering more than the woman's gaudy emeralds. "What on earth kind of question—"

Brrrrrrnggg!

Aunt Marie launched up from the settee, surely setting the record for the most exercise during a tea as she rushed to the front door. "I'll get it!"

Grace rose as well, offering shaky smiles all around. "It was lovely meeting you all," she said with a nervous nod, first to the older ladies, and then to Maggie and Libby before she grinned at Sheridan. "Especially you, Sheridan, because I have a feeling we're going to become the best of friends."

"Me too," Sheridan said, rising to escort Grace to the foyer, where Aunt Marie was ushering in a tall, dark-haired young man who looked vaguely familiar.

Turning at the parlour door, Grace gave Sheridan a hug. "I'd love to chat tomorrow if you have time, Sheridan, so just let me know, okay? I live next door on the right." Glancing over her shoulder to where Aunt Marie was talking to the young man, she looped her arm through Sheridan's to lead her toward them. "And I want you to meet my twin brother, Gray, as well, because we're almost inseparable, so he'll be around a lot too."

On cue, the young man glanced up with an easy grin, striking gray eyes twinkling as much as the polished silver on Aunt Marie's foyer table. Over a head taller than his sister, he was her male version in almost every other way, from a fluid grace that was clearly masculine, to thick black hair parted on the side with a slight wave. But where Grace's eyes were soft and shy, Gray's were confident and bold with just enough mischief to hint at the barest trace of a rogue to his sister's genteel lady.

"Gray! Let me introduce you to my new best friend," Grace

said with a definite thread of excitement in her tone, promptly hauling Sheridan to a halt in front of her twin. "Sheridan, this is my twin brother, Mr. Grayson Carmody, who, I might add is far too charming for his own good or that of any lady. Gray, this is Sheridan Donovan from"—she blinked, head whirling to stare at Sheridan wide-eyed—"gracious, where are my manners, Sheridan? I forgot to ask!"

Sheridan laughed as she gave Grace's arm a quick squeeze, mischief lacing her tone while she lowered her voice with a nod toward the parlour. "That's okay. I believe they may have been stolen by Mrs. Feuer*rude*, who can certainly use them."

Giggling along with Grace, Sheridan extended a hand to Gray with a bright smile, his teasing eyes suddenly putting her at ease because they reminded her of Dash. "Sheridan Donovan from the Silver Lining Ranch in Virginia City, Mr. Carmody. It's a pleasure to meet you."

"My thoughts exactly, Miss Donovan," he said with a short bow, surprising her when he lifted her hand to kiss it instead of the handshake she was expecting. "And since Grace and I spend an ample amount of time together socially," he said with a wink, "it appears you're my new best friend too."

Grace bumped Sheridan's shoulders with an affectionate roll of eyes. "Which is far better than the alternative, Sheridan, because Gray is an insatiable flirt, so friendship is undoubtedly the safest course."

Gray wrinkled his nose as he looped an arm to his sister's waist, giving her a playful pinch. "Safest, yes, but considerably more boring, Miss Donovan. And please call me Gray, if you will. And may I call you Sheridan?"

"Please," Sheridan said with a comfortable smile. "We don't stand on formality out west, Gray, so that suits me just fine."

Hugging Sheridan's waist on one side and her brother's on the other, Grace giggled with a little hunch of shoulders. "We are going to have *soooo* much fun together, I just know it, and hopefully be friends forever!"

Grinning along with Grace, Gray sent Sheridan a wink over his sister's head that, true to Grace's words, seemed a tad too friendly. "Well, I'm certainly willing to do my part and then some, Gracie. How 'bout you, Sheridan?"

"Oh, absolutely!" Sheridan grinned right back, thinking that with his playful manner and rakish charm, Gray Carmody was a dangerous mix of both Blaze and Dash, making her most grateful she'd already committed her heart to Jake. "Friends forever," she said, warming more to the brotherly side of Grace's twin rather than the other, prompting her to toss a wink right back.

And nothing more.

CHAPTER FORTY-FOUR

" *JAKE!*"
  J   He spun around with his fishing rod slung over his shoulder, a low groan trapped in his throat when he saw his little sister dart out from the house in her bare feet, black curls bouncing on tiny shoulders as she scrambled to catch up. "Wait for me, please?"

"Aw, Josie." Cocking a hip, he gouged the bridge of his nose, wishing just once he could sneak out to go fishing without her tagging along. "Go home! Ma will wonder where you are."

Tears pooled in pale-blue eyes so like his own as she drew close, her tiny feet dirty from running on the dusty road. "But I want to come with you."

"You can't, Moonbeam," he said, employing one of his favorite nicknames since she was one of the few sources of pure light in his life. He scowled. Except lately, when Ma's fear seemed to poison Josie's mind like it did everything else, making his little sister downright needy. "So, go home, Beam, now!" He turned on his heel and took off in a sprint.

"But, Jake, I love you. Don't leave me, please!"

But he did, as fast as he could, running from both Josie and the guilt that ate at his soul. Chest heaving, he never slowed once ... until her shouts faded completely away ...

"Sully, wake up!"

Jake jerked up in his bed, fingers instantly locked on the trigger of his Colt as he blinked at Clint Keller, the ranch hand who slept in the next cot.

"You were dreaming again," Clint snapped, evidently getting as tired of Jake's nightmares as Jake was. "What the devil is wrong with you anyway? That's the third time this month."

"Sorry, Clint." Jake's voice was rusty with sleep while he mauled his face with his hands, not blaming Clint one bit for being testy. Heck, Jake was testy, too, over the once-familiar nightmares that had started up all over again for absolutely no reason.

No reason? Expelling a weary sigh, Jake tucked his Colt into the holster he kept alongside his bed and laid back down, eyes wide open as he stared at a knotty-pine ceiling he didn't even see. No, no reason at all.

Except those kisses in the barn over a month ago.

Dropping back into his cot with a grunt, Clint pummeled his pillow several times like he probably wanted to pummel Jake, shoving it under his neck to settle back in. "Why the devil don't you go sleep in the big house like Finn wants you to?" he groused. "You're practically family anyway, and then we could all get some sleep."

Practically family. Jake stifled a grunt. Yeah, that was the problem. Only his "practically family" had a far more sisterly bent than Sheridan's.

Except in his body.

Reality wrenched his eyelids closed with a weight as crushing as the regret that constricted the ribs in his chest. And "practically" sure wasn't family.

Nor ever be.

"God help the woman you marry," his mother had screamed at him more than once, and that was all he was trying to do.

Help the one woman he would marry.

If he could.

Rolling onto his side, Jake thought of all the letters they'd written over the last month—his one a week to her three and four—and he could honestly say he'd never been happier with his relationship with Sheridan.

Or more conflicted. Every letter revealed deeper insight into a woman he already loved, only serving to intensify a friendship that made him love her all the more. At least her absence alleviated some of his guilt, allowing him to enjoy her from afar without the worry of intimate involvement. He buried another grunt.

Who was he kidding? Between the dreams where she lived in his arms ... to the nightmares that lived in the dark recesses of his mind, he felt the intimacy deep in his soul, and it scared the daylights out of him.

The nightmares had been gone for years, and then started up all over again at the beginning of the summer when Sheridan first kissed him at the range. After that, one or two had haunted his brain like a warning until he made up his mind to stay as far away from her as he possibly could. He'd been fine then—in his sleep, at least—where he could kiss her and love her the way that he wanted.

And now he couldn't even do that.

Dark memories wouldn't let him.

A shiver whispered through him despite the warmth of his body, reminding him she'd be home for Christmas in only two months. He swallowed hard, well aware he'd have to distance himself all over again.

She wouldn't like it.

And neither would he.

But guilt would have its way.

And he, a semblance of peace.

CHAPTER FORTY-FIVE

I
DON'T WANT TO LEAVE. A long, wispy sigh drifted from Sheridan's lips as she glanced around the cozy candle-lit parlour, where she'd just spent the last day and night of her Christmas vacation with family.

Her holiday had been almost perfect. Aside from the long train ride to and from, every single moment of seven wonderful days at home had been filled with family and friends, food and fun.

She'd baked cookies with Shay, Libby, and Maggie, and exchanged laughter and presents with Sophia and Kathy Jean. Dinners were filled with giggles and tease over her brothers' antics while the table was filled with the bounty of Gert's and Angus's kitchens.

On Christmas morn, Uncle Finn read his traditional Christmas reading from the Bible, his rich voice husky and low with the true import of the season: Gratitude for the birth of the Savior and the love of family and friends.

Sheridan pressed a kiss to Shaylee's head while her little sister lay sleeping on her shoulder on the couch after a busy day of laughing, reminiscing, and playing games. The Christmas tree still stood in the corner for one more day, glass ornaments twinkling in the flickering light of oil lamps, candlelight, and a waning fire in the hearth.

Uncle Finn played chess with Aiden on one side of the large stone fireplace while Jake, Dash, Blaze, Gert, and Angus were embroiled in a rousing round of poker on the other. Next to Shay on the sofa, Aunt Libby and Maggie chatted quietly with Libby's mother, Maeve, who was sipping a late-night tea as she relaxed in Uncle Finn's chair.

Truly an almost perfect holiday.

Her gaze flicked to where Jake was laughing as he raked in a win, and the ache in her heart made it pretty clear where the "almost" came in.

Although Jake was considered family and had been an integral part of every dinner, game time, and church attendance during this Christmas, never once did he seek Sheridan out on her own. Oh, he smiled and teased and winked like he used to aplenty, almost reverting back to the easy camaraderie they'd once shared before she turned sixteen.

But his glances were never furtive, seeking her out alone. His smiles were never clandestine, meant for her eyes alone. And his attention was never directed her way, for her heart alone.

Her breathing shallowed as she fixed her gaze on his handsome face, willing him to glance up and give her some sense of connection, no matter how remote. Certainly their letters had deepened their friendship considerably, leading her to believe they'd made great strides in deepening their connection as well. And, yet, in seven whole days, he'd given her nothing more than casual association without so much as a whiff of flirtation, along with a Christmas gift of stationery and a silver ink pen.

Oh, Jake! Moisture stung at the back of her lids as the clock struck ten. *Please, I need more ...* And lowering her head to press another kiss to Shaylee's hair, Sheridan knew she couldn't leave without it.

"Now *that's* the kind of Christmas gift I like," Aiden bellowed, leaning back with a smug tug of his vest, a rare chess win over Finn putting a broad smile on his face.

"Congratulations, Aiden." Finn stood to extend a handshake, which Aiden promptly pumped with a satisfied chuckle while a collective groan rose on the other side of the hearth.

"Read 'em and weep," Jake said with a proud show of his hand that obviously earned him the lucrative pot of money in the middle of the table.

Issuing a loud moan, Blaze threw his cards down along with everyone else, shaking his head as he delivered a begrudging smile. "I swear, Sullivan, you are one lucky stiff."

Sheridan's mouth slanted. "Stiff" being the operative word, at least when it came to any intimate interaction. And as far as luck? She stifled a grunt. The "lucky stiff" was about to run out.

Because no way was Sheridan leaving without a kiss from Jake Sullivan. The last few had carried her through almost three months, so she'd need at least three or four more to get her through the next five until she was back home for the summer.

"Okay, woman, it's time to head up." Shooting a telling glance at Aunt Libby over his shoulder, Uncle Finn pushed in his chair with a tired smile. "Before you have to carry me. Because losing plum tuckers a man out." He slapped Aiden on the back with a wink. "As your father knows all too well."

Sheridan's heart stuttered when chairs scraped away from the table on the other side of the room, the poker game obviously taking its toll too. Dash gave a lazy stretch over his head. "Dad-burn-it, Sullivan. I'll have to work an extra shift to make up for tonight's loss." He slapped Jake on the back with a cocky grin. "Which I'll handily make up, no doubt, at this week's game at the Ponderosa," he said with a wink, referencing Jake's, Blaze's, and Dash's weekly competitions in cards or pool before Dash clocked in.

"No doubt," Blaze said with a wide yawn as he pushed in his chair, it being common knowledge that Dash was now the card sharp of the family due to frequent play with Angus and Gert, while Blaze was the pool hustler. "But only because Gert and Angus won't be there."

"Come on, Shay," Sheridan whispered as she gently jostled her sister awake. "It's time to go to bed, sweetheart."

Uncle Finn bent to pick Shay up, grunting as he carefully laid her over his shoulder. "I'll carry her, Sher." He bent to press a kiss to Sheridan's cheek. "It's so good to have you home, sweetheart, but you best head up, too, since you've got an early morning."

"Yes, sir," she said with a quick side hug, wishing for the umpteenth time she didn't have to leave. "But I've got a hankering for a quick bite of Angus's cobbler before I head up, Uncle Finn, since there's nothing like it back East."

"Okay, sweetheart. See you in the morning." He headed toward the door, glancing back to give his wife a wry smile as she dawdled with hugs for her mother and Maggie. "Libby, get a move on, darlin', or I'll lock you out." He flopped a back-handed wave. "G'night, all."

Rushing over to give Sheridan a hug goodnight, Libby rolled her eyes. "Humph! As if a lock would keep me out. See you in the morning, sweetheart." She paused to cradle Sheridan's face in her hands, eyes misty. "It's been so good having you home again, Sheridan. We miss you terribly."

"Me too, Aunt Libby," Sheridan whispered, battling a mist of tears as well.

"No crying!" Maggie warned with a stern finger, a telltale sheen giving her dead away as she squeezed Sheridan in a hug. "There'll be enough of that in the morning. Good night, Sher."

By the time the ladies moved toward the door, Maeve and Aiden were following along with Gert, for their final night at the ranch just like Sheridan.

Blaze caught up with Maggie, hooking an arm to her waist as he tossed Jake a yawn over his shoulder. "Sleep in Sully, because we'll see Sher off first thing at eight, then head out to the west pasture after to move some cows."

"Sounds good, Boss." Jake pushed his chair in and lifted a hand in a wave on his way to the door. "I'll lock the front door behind me."

Heart pounding, Sheridan jumped up, grateful the rest of the crew were already halfway up the staircase. Peeking around the parlour entryway, she waited until they disappeared, then bolted for the doorway through which Jake had just left. With a jerk of her coat off the coat rack, she sneaked out the door, quietly closing it behind her. Her pulse surged when she saw he was halfway to the bunkhouse.

"Jake!" Her call was a strangled cry, desperate to stop him before he reached the bunkhouse. She thought she saw him stiffen before he appeared to pick up his pace. In one erratic beat of her heart, her three days—and three months—of frustration bubbled up into an anger so bold, she didn't give a hoot whether he entered the bunkhouse or not.

She *would* talk to Jake Sullivan tonight—and in front of a bunkhouse of cowhands in their underwear, if need be. Hiking her skirts up, she broke into a sprint, reaching the bunkhouse just as the door closed in her face. Without the slightest compunction, she slammed it back open, causing it to ricochet off the wall with a resounding bang.

"Jake Sullivan—I need to talk to you," she shouted, not a bit put off by the bug-eyed looks of him and a bunkhouse of men. Ignoring the blood gorging his face and hers, she thrust her chin up with a tight fold of arms, not giving a whit what he or anyone else thought because she was done being patient. She stomped her foot. "And I mean *now*, mister!"

CHAPTER FORTY-SIX

JAKE COULDN'T BREATHE, BODY FROZEN to the wood floor like a saguaro cactus in a Nevada blizzard, along with the air in his lungs.

Sheridan actually stomped her foot again, snapping him out of his stupor. And *still*, all he could do was gape, hardly able to believe she'd darkened the bunkhouse door, something she—and her brothers—had been skittish about her ever doing before. Swallowing the shock in his throat, he tried to speak, but nothing came out.

"Fine." Blue eyes narrowing, she slammed the door behind her before plunking her hands on her hips. "We can talk right here, then."

"The devil we will," he rasped, voice still rusty from the sheer stun of Sheridan's boldness. Adam's apple jerking hard, he shot past her to open the door, hooking her arm on the way as he yanked her through, slamming the door for good measure. Dropping his hold, he stormed toward the barn without another word, pretty darn sure he'd never been this angry with Sher before.

An image of her kissing him senseless as he lay inert on his back suddenly came to mind, and the heat of his anger combusted with a heat of a whole 'nother kind. Stomping into the barn, he quickly lit a lamp and whirled around, waiting for her to catch up before he slid the barn doors shut with a loud slam. "Just what in the devil do you think you're doing?" he shouted, grateful he could vent his anger where nobody could hear him—or her—since she was pert near yelling at the top of her lungs as well, obviously as angry at him as he was at her.

"Trying to get a few measly moments to talk to you alone, Jake Sullivan," she shouted back, snapping tightly balled fists to her hips, "but you made darn good and sure that would never happen, didn't you?"

He leaned in, looming over her like a threat. "Just like you made darn good and sure to embarrass the devil out of me in front of the other hands, Half-Pint, which I may never forgive you for."

She stepped in, granite jaw jerking up to go chin to chin with his, making him wonder what the devil they were teaching her up there if his sweet, little Half-Pint was turning into her Aunt Libby. "And I am *not* your 'Half-Pint,' Jake Sullivan ..." she began with blue sparks in her eyes.

No kidding. He took a step back.

"I am supposed to be your 'good friend with the promise of more,' as you will recall, who has written you countless letters, but the only 'more' I've gotten since I've been home for Christmas is more of the same cold shoulder you gave me all summer."

Body swarming with frustration, he shifted with a noisy blast of air, gouging the back of his neck. "For pity's sake, Sheridan, we've been laughing and talking all weekend—"

"With a roomful of people!" she yelled, her voice as close to a shriek as he'd ever heard, "because you've been avoiding me, you bullheaded baboon, and I dare you to deny it."

He ground his jaw, thinking he liked her a whole lot better when she wore pigtails and mud at the age of eight, instead of slinging it at nineteen. "I don't deny it, *little girl*," he emphasized just to get on her nerves, "because this is exactly what I knew would happen, you spouting off that friendship isn't enough, and blast it all, Sheridan, that's all I'm willing to give."

Locking her arms to her waist, she stared him down—or up since she barely came to his chest. "That was *not* our deal, Jake, and you know it. You spit swore and sealed it with a kiss that all but plastered me to the wall, you stubborn Irishman.

That we would be good friends with the promise of *more*, and I don't think seeing you alone once every three to six months is too much to ask."

Eyelids sagging closed, he swallowed hard, well aware she had a point, but then, so did he.

Right on top of my pinhead.

Because he should have never promised her anything but friendship.

Expelling a quiet sigh, he kneaded the bridge of his nose before he finally faced her head-on, his gaze gentled by the tinge of hurt he saw in her eyes. "No, it's not, Sheridan, for normal friends, but you and I?" He wagged a finger between them, figuring honesty was the best policy and hoping she would understand. "We're not normal friends, Half-Pint, because there's too much attraction between us, you know? And it's just"—he shoved his hands in his pockets as he looked away, praying she would cut him some slack—"well, it's just too dog-gone hard for me to keep my hands off you when we're alone."

"I understand completely, Jake."

He peered up beneath buckled brows. "You do?"

She gave a little shrug. "Sure. We're crazy about each other, so it only makes sense."

"Now, I didn't say th—"

Folding her arms, she cut him off with a sharp jag of her brow, daring him to deny it.

He blasted out a loud gust of frustration as he sifted shaky fingers through his hair. "Okay, we are, which is all the more reason I can't be alone with you during this friendship of ours. I love your letters and staying in touch that way, but when you come home ..."

He shook his head, grateful she'd be gone for another five months till summer, and not exactly sure what he was going to do then. "It's just too hard on me, you know?" His heart expanded and contracted along with his ribcage as he exhaled another cumbersome sigh, gaze fused to his boots.

"So, do you … see my point, then, why we can't be spending time alone together?"

"Completely," she whispered, "and I totally understand."

He glanced up beneath half-lidded lashes. "You do?"

"Of course I do, Jake, because it's just as hard for me as it is for you, so limiting our time alone together only makes sense given we're only friends with the promise of more."

"Oh, thank God!" he whispered, the words drifting out on a huge sigh of relief.

"As long as we seal it with a kiss."

"*What?!*" He backed away with hands in the air. "You just said you understood."

"I do." Her chin nudged up. "You want a friendship till I'm out of school, Jake, and I want more, so it seems to me that a few minutes spent sealing it with a kiss each time I come home is right down the middle."

"No, ma'am." He shook his head as he folded taut arms across his chest. "That is *not* friendship, Sheridan, kissing each other like that."

"Maybe not with the normal kind of friendship," she said, chin tipped up in reflective mode, as if she'd given this a great deal of thought. "But I like to think of our relationship as 'friendship plus.'"

He grunted. "Plus trouble."

She arched a brow. "Maybe to you, Jake Sullivan, but to me, it's friendship plus hope, where there are no other men but you till I graduate like you demanded. Remember?"— she closed her eyes as she splayed a hand to her chest—"No other lips but yours?"

His mouth clamped tight as heat pulsed in his face.

"So, what's it going to be, then, Jake?" She tapped a toe impatiently on the ground while she leveled him with a challenging gaze. "Friendship plus? Or just plain friendship, where I'm free to see whomever I like in New York?"

Swearing under his breath, he turned away to slash stiff fingers through his hair, wishing he could throttle both Blaze and Dash right about now for hogtying him like this.

One quick kiss.

That's all it had to be.

"Fine," he heard her say on the way to the door, evidently tired of waiting on his response, "then our deal is off."

"Sheridan!" His tone was an order for her to stop, making her wait while he fortified with a deep ingest of air. Turning around slowly, he strode toward the door where she stood and aimed a threatening finger right in her face. "One kiss, and we're done, understood?"—he glared her down—"and *no* argument, agreed?"

She nodded, and he shook her with a firm clasp of her arms. "No, I want a spoken promise, you little brat, that one kiss is all it will be."

Her head bobbed up and down as she raised a tiny palm. "One kiss, I swear." A twinkle lit her eyes as she fluttered her lashes. "Unless you want more."

"Ha!" He jerked his hands away as if she'd singed his fingers, determined to make it short and sweet and nothing more. "I'm not that stupid, Sheridan Marie."

Refusing to touch her, he leaned in close to gently brush his lips against hers, every intention of pulling away.

Until she stood on tiptoe and finished him off, drawing his lips to hers like a steer to the slaughter. With a hoarse groan wedged in his throat, he pushed her to the door with only two thoughts in mind.

One. This definitely wouldn't be short.

And two. Yes, he really *was* that stupid.

CHAPTER FORTY-SEVEN

"**G**OODNESS, THAT WAS FUN!" SHERIDAN plopped down in the swing on Grace's grandmother's back porch along with Grace, the two of them worn out after a rewarding spring day at Mulberry Stables teaching orphans to ride.

Somewhere a mourning dove called to its mate, the soft *woo-he-woo, woo, woo, woo* drifting in the air along with the sweet scent of Grace's grandmother's cherry trees, now in full bloom. The weather was warm for late April, but perfect for teaching precious children to ride horses at a nearby horse farm owned by the family of their favorite teacher, Professor Stephanie Cassandra McCall, who also happened to be a distant cousin to Grace and Gray.

From the moment Professor McCall had discovered that both Sheridan and Grace were experienced with horses, she'd wasted no time in enlisting their help for her favorite pet project. And since Gray was also an accomplished equestrian like his sister, the three of them had quickly volunteered, forming a tight bond, not only with the many delightful children they were privileged to teach, but with each other as well.

After Christmas vacation, Sheridan was grateful for something else to occupy her mind other than Jake's tempestuous kisses, so Mulberry Stables became a godsend. It was one of the few places she not only felt at home, but where she could give of herself to children who needed her. For the first time in her life, she felt as if she were doing something important, sowing into the lives of underprivileged children who hadn't been as lucky as she. As much as she enjoyed attending Vassar, it was Saturdays that put a skip in her heart, giving riding lessons at the stables for orphans from The Children's Home of Poughkeepsie.

Well, that and any letter from Jake.

"You're a natural, you know," Grace said with a fond smile, reaching to give Sheridan's hand a quick squeeze, the two of them alone this Saturday since Gray had a prior commitment. "The children love you, especially Wendell."

Sheridan grinned just hearing the name of her favorite child from The Children's Home of Poughkeepsie, otherwise known as CHP. Wendell Paxton was a precocious ten-year-old boy with crossed eyes, small in stature, but large in spunk, taking on anyone who even looked at *him* cross-eyed. Sheridan had fallen in love with him at first sight, desperate to instill a love in this little boy that would help safeguard him against the ridicule that often came his way. "He's a special one, Wendell is," she said softly, smiling as she pulled a walnut from her pocket, holding it out so Grace could see the crude face Wendell had carved on it for Sheridan.

Shaking her head in wonder, Grace took the walnut and held it up to the light. "That's absolutely precious, Sher, and proves just how much of an effect you have on children." She handed it back with a gentle smile. "You were meant to be a teacher, my friend."

"I know," Sheridan whispered, fondling the walnut with a quiet smile before she slipped it back into her pocket.

And Jake's wife as well.

Sheridan startled, the thought taking her by surprise because it hadn't come from her. Her smile skewed. At least not *this* time. Back in Virginia City, Jake had just about consumed her every thought from the age of four on, but since she'd arrived in New York and started attending Vassar, things had slowly begun to change, especially since Christmas.

Her world had expanded to include good friends like Grace and Gray—with whom she spent most of her free time on weekends, since Gray attended Columbia University in the city during the week. A smile tickled her lips as she thought of Grace's twin—a dear friend and incorrigible rogue who wanted to be more than friends, given his doting attention on weekends and the comical roll of his twin sister's eyes.

"Gray," his sister would tell him with a patient smile heavily laced with affection, "Sheridan is spoken for, so you need to focus somewhere else."

"But I don't want to," he'd say with a little-boy sulk that always eased into a wink and a grin, making Sheridan giggle whenever he did. Gray made her laugh and feel pretty and she adored him as a friend.

But it was Jake who held the claim on her heart.

Even so, distance had brought a much-needed balance to both her thoughts and her feelings about the stubborn cowboy who refused to give her his. Because between the miles that separated them, her friendships with Grace and Gray, and invigorating studies, Sheridan couldn't deny she'd grown considerably over the last year, happily broadening both her mind and her heart.

A gentle smile flickered across her lips. *Especially* her heart—both through her volunteer work with children like Wendell from The CHP and via Vassar's Society for Religious Inquiry or VSRI.

A member organization of the Young Women's Christian Association, the VSRI focused on evangelical progress of Christianity throughout the world, as well as improving conditions for female students, teachers, and factory workers, something Aunt Libby heartily applauded.

But what had captured Sheridan's heart the most was the organization's desire to advocate for the rights of women of color, from African American and Native American, to Hispanic American like her dear friend, Sophia, who'd been ostracized in school by many merely because her skin was brown.

A wispy sigh drifted from Sheridan's lips as she thought about leaving her life in Poughkeepsie to go home for the summer in a few weeks, and she had no doubt she'd miss it all—terribly. Never would she have believed going away to school could expand her horizons like it had, opening her up to a wide and wonderful world beyond the fences of The Silver Lining Ranch and Virginia City.

Not just geographically, but spiritually as well for a number of reasons. First and foremost, her intense longing for Jake had nudged her into devouring the Bible Maggie had given her, capturing her heart with hope and promises she had never been able to get from Jake.

Trust in the Lord, and do good; dwell in the land, and feed on His faithfulness. Delight yourself also in the Lord, and He shall give you the desires of your heart.

Which is *exactly* what she'd been doing since Christmas— trusting, doing good, feeding on God's faithfulness, and delighting herself in Him.

Instead of Jake.

Her mind traveled back to the kisses Jake had given her the night before she'd returned to school, and for the first time in almost five months, she was shocked to realize she didn't want *that* to be her focus anymore.

Oh, she had no doubt she loved Jake, and there was no question his kisses were wonderful, as was getting to know him better through his letters. But months of soul—and Bible—searching had convinced her getting to know God was *more* wonderful, bringing things into true perspective.

Therefore I tell you, do not be anxious about your life ... but seek first the kingdom of God and his righteousness, and all these things will be added to you.

All these things.

Sheridan's eyelids weighted closed, knowing full well what that meant. The things she had spent a lifetime longing for and worrying about, like marrying Jake, and getting him to commit to her as the man she truly believed she was meant to marry.

She opened one eye in a squint, peeking up at a blindingly

blue sky scudded with clouds that drifted by as slowly as the river. *Isn't he, Lord?*

"Soooo ... what did Jake have to say in his letter this week?" Grace said with a light pinch of Sheridan's waist, as if she could read Sheridan's mind, which she was often prone to do. Smile soft, she studied Sheridan through gentle gray eyes while they swung back and forth on Mrs. Carmody's back-porch swing. The lazy roll of the Hudson River was a soothing complement to a day of frenzied activity filled with laughter and love. A bit of the imp crept into Grace's gaze as she awaited Sheridan's response. "Because whatever it was, it's stolen your tongue *and* your thoughts, my friend."

Sheridan peeked up at the dear friend who was the second biggest reason—after Jake—for Sheridan's deepened faith. Grace Carmody was true to her name for she was truly a touch of grace in Sheridan's life, much like Maggie and Aunt Libby had been at home.

Fiercely devoted to the Word of God, Grace challenged Sheridan's faith daily, whether through endless debates and discussions, to gentle words of truth that pierced Sheridan's very soul like one of Grace's favorite Scriptures:

Search me, O God, and know my heart: try me, and know my thoughts: and see if there be any wicked way in me, and lead me in the way everlasting.

Sheridan's smile took a slant. A Scripture one *definitely* had to pray sparingly. She scrunched her nose as she pinched Grace right back. "I swear you're a mind reader, Grace Carmody, which is not always a good thing."

Grace's chuckle floated into the air along with cherry blossom petals in a gentle breeze. "Except with a dear friend who tends toward the melancholy when she can't hash certain thoughts out."

Breathing in the heavenly scent of spring, Grace smiled as she stared into her grandmother's backyard, where newly budding redbud and dogwood trees painted a watercolor landscape of pale green, pink, and white. "So, tell me, my friend, what has you so reflective after a day of children, horses, and fun?"

Sheridan expelled a lingering sigh, figuring she may as well divulge her latest concerns because Grace would eventually wheedle them out anyway. "I've been thinking ..." she began.

Grace bumped her shoulder with her own. "A dangerous thing to do," she teased, making Sheridan smile.

"About Jake." Leaning her head back on the swing, Sheridan pursed her lips in thought.

"No!" Grace said, mouth aghast as she put a hand to her cheek.

Sheridan wagged a finger. "You know, Grace Carmody, I think you may just be a bigger tease than your brother."

Grace grinned. "What can I say? He's a bad influence." Sitting up, Grace wiped a palm over her lips, as if to wipe her smile away. "All right, all serious now." The gray eyes softened. "What about Jake?"

Sheridan shifted to face Grace on the swing. "I've been thinking—and praying, of course—about my relationship with Jake, and I feel like I've handled it all wrong."

"What do you mean?" Grace asked, turning to face Sheridan as well.

Picking at her nails, Sheridan peered up with a touch of heat in her cheeks. "Well, I've been trying to win his affection with kisses like my friend Sophia suggested I do." She gave a little shrug. "Which, I will admit, at least in the beginning, helped confirm that not only is Jake attracted to me, but he truly does see me as a woman and not just a little girl."

Grace nodded.

"But the last two times I've been alone with him"—chewing the edge of her lip, she looked away, barely seeing the beauty of Mrs. Carmody's yard for the guilt in her mind—"it was me who forced the issue with kisses, apparently tempting him beyond his control because, well"—she lifted a shoulder— "he gave in even though he didn't want to. Which I now realize wasn't right because if I really love him, why would

I tempt him?"

"So, you feel guilty about that." Grace offered a gentle smile, her words more of a statement than a question.

Sheridan nodded, bracing her arms to her waist as she shimmied back into the swing, gaze trailing into a distant stare over the river. "I love him, Grace," she whispered with a sudden sheen of tears, "as sure as the buds on those trees bursting into spring, but I've come to realize that the cost of love is steep." A lump bobbed in her throat as she expelled a shaky sigh. "Because it means putting *it* before one's self."

"Ah, yes," Grace whispered, her gaze following Sheridan's into the lush beauty of her grandmother's backyard, "like God did for us, with His Son." Her bodice rose and fell with a wistful sigh that matched Sheridan's own to a breath. "Unconditional love. The greatest gift we will ever receive— *or* give."

Sheridan turned to Grace once again, her voice almost breathless. "Yes, and the kind of love I want to give Jake." A shy smile curved on her lips as hope flooded her soul. "Until, that is, I can give him far more as his wife."

Grace arched a brow. "So, no more kisses?"

"Not unless they're his idea," Sheridan said with a firm shake of her head before huffing out a heavy sigh, "which will never happen, of course, because he's made it perfectly clear he only wants to be friends. So, I'll just write him to say that when I come home next month, we'll do things *his* way." Mischief tickled her lips as she wiggled her brows. "For *now*. But come graduation?" She winked. "It's full steam ahead."

Chuckling, Grace leaned to give her a hug. "You know, Sheridan Donovan, you've come a long way from that lovesick cowgirl I first met at your Aunt Marie's tea."

"Oh, you bet I have, and I plan to go even further yet," she said with a heft of her chin, allowing a squirm of a smile before she hugged her friend right back, "*and* whether he likes it or not—I intend to take Mr. Sullivan right along with me."

CHAPTER FORTY-EIGHT

"**D**AYLIGHT'S BURNING, BOYS." SQUINTING UP at the sun as it melted into a tree line burnished with the reds and golds of dusk, Jake smiled as he hooked a good-sized trout on his overloaded stringer. He glanced over to where Blaze and Dash were desperately trying to catch up with stringers only half full, and his smile eased into a grin.

With an extra-busy calving season this spring, the three of them hadn't been able to indulge in one of their old-time fishing tournaments for a long, long while, so Jake couldn't remember the last time he'd enjoyed himself this much.

An image suddenly popped in his brain of pinning Sheridan's hands to the barn wall, arms splayed wide over hers as he kissed the daylights out of her after Christmas.

A knot ducked hard in his throat. Okay, maybe he could. But at least he couldn't remember the last time he'd enjoyed himself this much *fishing* with his best friends. Dropping the heavy stringer back into the water, he snatched his rod and reel up and stood, snapping his line forward to settle his homemade fly upstream. "I think it's time to call it a day— *and* a winner."

Blaze peered up beneath a hooded gaze that didn't bode well for ending the tournament anytime soon. He rose after hooking one of his brand-new homemade feather flies onto his line. "Still plenty of daylight to wipe that gloat off your face, Sully." Smile dry, he made an easy cast downstream. "So I suggest you settle in, *boy*, and I'll show you how it's done."

"Uh, as far as 'showing,' Mr. Donovan," Jake said in a polite drawl, the innocent slope of his brows anything but, "would that be in winnin', sir, or losin'?"

Dash's chuckle rang out over the lazy ripple of the stream as he unleashed a graceful cast. "Nice one, Sul. I think the 'Boss' is getting' a *little* too cocky after his rare poker win last night."

"You mean poker win-*ning* streak," Blaze corrected while he moseyed a little closer to where both Dash and Jake were fishing.

"Hate to break it to you, old buddy"— Jake grinned when a glimmer of silver caught his eye, and recasting, he deftly dropped his line in front of it—"but two games does not a streak make."

Setting his hook hard, Jake flashed more teeth while he reeled his catch in. Holding the nice-sized trout up in the air, he tossed Dash a wink before shooting Blaze a grin. "Unless we're talkin' losin' streaks, old buddy, given that pitiful stringer of yours."

"I'll show you pitiful, Sullivan." Blaze's jaw set—along with Dash's hook, eliciting a loud whoop out of Blaze's brother when he reeled in a trout almost as pretty as Jake's. Scowling, Blaze recast in the same spot with a thin smile. "Pool tournament. Tonight. the Ponderosa before Dash's shift. So I can educate you boys on what a real winning streak is."

"You're on," Jake said with a chuckle, "because I'm feeling pretty good right about now and *real* lucky." He grinned outright. Especially given the letter he'd received from Sheridan almost a month ago, letting him off the proverbial hook by agreeing to his original terms. A "close friendship with the *possibility* of more" *without* kisses this time, a turn of events that had literally stopped the stupid nightmares for good.

Blaze slid him a half-lidded look out of the corner of his eyes. "So I noticed, Sul. All month, as a matter of fact, not a hide nor hair of the grump we saw after Christmas." He paused as he recast his line. "It wouldn't happen to have anything to do with Sher coming home tomorrow, now would it?"

Yes. Face flaming, Jake turned away to whip his line in the other direction, not particularly interested in discussing Sher. *But not the way that you think.*

Dash chuckled. "Come to think of it, Sul, you have been awfully chipper lately, so is Blaze right? You looking forward to our little sis coming home?"

"Of course I am." Jake's tone was definitely not as "chipper" as before while he moved further downstream and, hopefully, further from a conversation he did *not* want to have. "Just like the rest of you because Sher is family to me."

"Or could be." Blaze's teasing chuckle didn't set well, unlike Dash's hook, which reeled in another keeper.

Refusing to allow Dash's and Blaze's probing to ruin his good mood, Jake sloshed back to the bank to rifle through his wooden tackle box, his voice a whole lot calmer than his stomach. "Sher and I are just friends, Blaze, like I've told you a dozen times before." He glanced up with a squint. "Hey, Dash, did you catch that on a dry fly or wet?"

"Wet," Dash said as he hooked the fish to his stringer.

Blaze ambled deeper into the water, his rolled up blue jeans now soaked to the waist. "Well, I admit, Sul, if I didn't know what a stickler for the truth you were, I'd say you're all wet, my friend, and soggier than Dash's fly. Because it hasn't escaped my notice—or anyone else's—that you were fine all through Christmas till Sher left, then a downright crab until now, when she's fixin' to come home again." He held a palm up in the air. "But if you tell me you two are nothing more than friends, then I guess I have no choice but to believe you."

Shaking his head, Jake laughed as he exchanged his dry fly for a wet one. "I know how anxious you and Dash are to up the gene pool with me in the family, boys, but you're fresh out of luck because like I said"—he cocked a brow as he rose to his feet—"Sher and I are *just* friends and *nothing* more," he repeated for the umpteenth time, not only grateful that that was now the whole truth, but thankful he no longer had to worry about Sher pushing for more. Her letter had literally set him free, claiming she loved him too much to tempt him with kisses, so she was willing to settle for being close friends like he wanted.

For now. Those two words tacked on at the end of her declaration had definitely taken the shine off her letter, but for the time being? He was safe, able to keep the woman he loved out of harm's way until she got her degree.

And him out of harm's way too …

Till he got out of town.

CHAPTER FORTY-NINE

"**O**H MY GOODNESS!" SHERIDAN BLINKED at her friend Grace in her bedroom mirror, shocked anew that Grace's parents had actually agreed to let her spend the summer at the Silver Lining Ranch. *Thank you, Lord!* Mr. and Mrs. Carmody were celebrating their 25th anniversary on a whirlwind grand tour of Europe, leaving Grace and Gray to stay with Aunt Marie for the summer in Poughkeepsie. Unfortunately, as a member of the Columbia University rowing team, Gray had athletic commitments over the summer, much to his dismay, so he was unable to make the trip.

Whirling around, Sheridan bolted to the bed where Grace sat straight as a poker, face pinched as white as the hands she gripped tightly in her lap. "I am sooooo excited!" Sheridan said with a joyful shriek, bestowing another giddy hug on her newest best friend. "We are going to have *sooooo* much fun!"

"Hopefully," Grace said in a squeaky voice, "if I stop shaking."

Sheridan laughed as she squeezed her again. "There's nothing to be nervous about, goose. My family is wonderful and very easy to be around, I promise. And I have absolutely no doubt they will love you even more than I do."

Body stiff, Grace peeked at Sheridan out the sides of her eyes, apparently not convinced. "But I've never been away from home or from Gray for this long before," she whispered, "so I didn't realize how much I rely on him to carry a conversation." She blinked, eyes somber. "What if I clam up and can't say a word?"

"That won't happen," Sheridan said with a gentle rub of

Grace's arm. "I won't leave your side, I promise."

A hint of a smile twitched on Grace's lips while a touch of mischief lit in her eyes. "Not even to be alone with Jake?"

Sheridan giggled, a surge of warmth invading her cheeks at the prospect of seeing Jake again. "*Especially* not to be alone with Jake, you little stinker," she said with a playful pinch, suddenly as nervous as Grace. "I've already made up mind to avoid all alone time with Jake, so I promise you that my goal this summer is only to deepen and strengthen our friendship and nothing more—with family and fun only, not kisses."

Grace bumped her shoulder against Sheridan's with a chuckle. "Unless he kisses you first, and then all bets are off, I guess."

A long, wispy sigh parted from Sheridan's lips. "I wish, but I'm afraid Mr. Jake Sullivan will avoid being alone with me as much as I will with him." She patted Grace's hand and rose, hurrying over to the mirror to finish pinning flaxen curls loosely on top of her head in the more mature style she'd adopted after Christmas. "There," she said with a final pat, thinking she looked—and felt—so much older in just a little under a year.

She couldn't help but reflect on how Sophia had talked her into a scheme to get Jake's attention this same time last year, and it had certainly worked. But now she wanted far more than just his attention. Her heart fluttered. She wanted his love, and thanks to her faith that had grown as much as she, she now knew the only way to achieve that—if Jake was meant for her at all—would be God's way.

"Ready?" She spun around with a bright smile, some of the giddiness returning at seeing Uncle Finn and her brothers again—along with Jake, of course. Uncle Finn had been in Carson City for the day, and a cattle emergency had kept the others out on the south forty, so only Aunt Libby, Maggie, and Shay had met her at the station, assuring her all would be home for dinner.

"Ready? Not in the least." Fortifying with a huge intake of

air for strength, no doubt, Grace rose from the bed in a lovely lavender silk dress that made her look, for all her angst, like a classic Victorian beauty in a rose garden rather than on a ranch. "But I suppose that doesn't matter, does it?"

"No, ma'am," Sheridan said with a sassy wink as she hooked her arm through Grace's. "Shall we?"

Sheridan was grateful Aunt Libby had arranged for tea and light sandwiches and cakes on the back deck prior to dinner. The men would need time to clean up when they came home, so the lovely tea gave both Grace and her time to relax prior to their arrival. By the time Angus announced dinner, Sheridan could tell Grace had relaxed somewhat, the warmth between her and the ladies a much-needed blessing.

Male chuckles drifted down the hallway from the dining room as Sheridan hooked an arm to Grace's waist, giving her a quick squeeze of support.

Which ... Sheridan readily accepted right back from Grace when she laid eyes on Jake laughing with Blaze and Dash at the end of the dining room table. Chairs immediately scraped when the ladies entered, the men rising to crowd around Sheridan with welcome-home hugs. Her pulse picked up pace as Jake waited his turn with a relaxed smile like the Jake of old, his warm hug confirming that her commitment to friendship in her last letter had been the right thing to do.

Pulling away from his hug with a brace of her arms, Jake squinted at her. "You look good, Sher, but I'm not sure where my little Half-Pint went."

She searched his face with a tender smile. *She's right here, Jake, ready to love you whenever you say.*

Looping an arm around Grace's waist, Sheridan flashed a bright smile to the men. "Gentlemen, this is my dearest friend from Vassar, Miss Grace Carmody, who also happens to be the granddaughter of Aunt Marie's neighbor. And this, Grace," she continued with a twinkle and a nod toward the men, "is the rowdy side of my family—my uncle and owner of The Silver Lining Ranch, Mayor Finn McShane, my two brothers, Blaze and Dash, and our dear friend and assistant foreman, Jake Sullivan."

"It's a pleasure to meet you, Grace," Finn said with a welcoming handshake while Blaze and Jake followed suit.

But when Dash stepped in to envelop Grace in a warm hug, Sheridan had to bite back a smile at the two circles of pink that instantly bloomed on Grace's cheeks. "Welcome to The Silver Lining Ranch, Miss Carmody. Any friend of Half-Pint, is a friend of mine who deserves way more than a handshake."

"Uh ... thank you, Dash," Grace whispered over his shoulder, eyes blinking wide as she gave Sheridan a nervous smile.

Dinner was everything Sheridan had hoped it would be. Angus had fixed her favorite meal—fried chicken and dumplings with the promise of his famous apple cobbler for dessert. Aunt Libby's engraved initial silver plates—a gift from Uncle Finn for their wedding—glowed in the flickering light of silver candlesticks along with a silver bowl of her yellow cottage roses, which graced the massive polished log table. Complemented by dried bittersweet berries that matched the vibrant Navajo rug beneath, they lent a soft touch to a rustic room of burnished log walls graced with desert watercolor paintings.

As always, Uncle Finn was gracious and warm, and her brothers and Jake were in rare form with lots of good-natured ribbing and stories that kept the dinner fun. From laughter and love, to tease and trauma when Shaylee introduced poor Grace to her pet tarantula, Annabelle, Sheridan could sense that Grace's fears had promptly been put to rest. *After* the poor thing had turned as white as Angus's creamed cauliflower, of course, when her sister had plopped Annabelle's cage on the table between Grace's plate and her own.

"Animals do *not* dine at the table, Shaylee Ann," Uncle Finn had said with a patient smile.

"Why not? Dash does." Blaze elbowed Jake, and their

laughter put a grin on everyone's faces, including Dash's.

"But Annabelle is nocturnal, Uncle Finn," Shaylee explained in her never-ending quest to make Annabelle part of the family. "So she won't be a bother, I promise. She's only active at night and sleeps during the day."

"Also just like Dash." Jake grinned as he elbowed Blaze right back.

Grinning, Sheridan leaned close to Grace. "Dash works nights at the Ponderosa Saloon, so he sleeps part of the day," she explained with a chuckle, the wry twist of Uncle Finn's mouth an indicator of his feelings about Dash's job.

"Hey, Grace," Shaylee quickly continued, conveniently ignoring her uncle and brothers, "can you believe that female tarantulas live up to 30 years, while males only live for seven?"

"I sure can. Probably nags him to death," Blaze said with a grin, ducking when Maggie tried to whack him with her napkin.

Dash reached for another piece of chicken with a lazy grin. "Or 'cause the female chews on the male till he croaks, Blaze," he said, "so I'd go easy on the little woman, or it might give her ideas."

Laughter bounced off the walls, and Sheridan grinned when Grace giggled along with the rest, so grateful for her family. With a shy scuff of her lip, she snuck a peek at Jake out of the corner of her eye, smiling when he plucked two chicken legs off of Blaze's plate to toss them onto Angus's, who'd sat down last and was rifling through what was left on the platter. Grinning, he glanced up and met her gaze, fluttering her stomach when he shot her a wink.

"Shay." Uncle Finn motioned toward the front door with a flicker of a smile. "Out on the porch please, Doodle, because as fond as we all are of Annabelle, she's not exactly good for digestion."

A heavy sigh blustered from Shaylee's lips as she lumbered up with a scowl, Annabelle's cage firmly in hand. "Okay, but she's gonna think nobody likes her, Uncle Finn, and she's liable to get depressed."

"No, she won't, Shay," Sheridan said, sympathy lacing her tone as she offered her sister a sweet smile. "Dash is happy all the time, and nobody likes him."

Dash's jaw dangled open in a shock as more laughter made the rounds, a chicken leg halfway to his mouth. "Et tu, Half-Pint?" he said with a hurt pinch of brows before his trademark grin eventually peeked through.

"So, Sher," Uncle Finn said as he took a slow sip of his coffee after dessert, "Libby and I have a host of activities planned in the evenings throughout Grace's stay, but what do you girls plan to do during the days?"

Adrenaline pulsed through Sheridan's body when Grace's gaze met hers, the twinkle of excitement in her friend's eyes on par with Sheridan's own. Reaching to squeeze Grace's hand, Sheridan grinned at her uncle. "I wrote Sister Fred a while back to ask about possibly volunteering to tutor the boys and girls at the orphanage in math, grammar, and music. You know, like Sophia, Kathy Jean, and I did last year? And she was overjoyed."

"And so are we!" Grace said with a little bounce, hands clasped to her chest like a little girl at Christmas.

"Not as excited as those little boys are likely to be," Dash said, looking directly at Grace with a grin.

Sheridan bit back a grin when Grace's cheeks dusted pink, surprised at the way Dash was flirting with her best friend.

"Oh, Sher, that sounds wonderful!" Libby gushed, and I want to help, too, so may I come along?"

"Absolutely, Aunt Libby! Sister Fred will be thrilled, and so will we."

"Oh ... and I can drive all of us into town each morning on my way to work," Maggie said, hands clasped to her chest, their excitement obviously catching. "It'll be *so* much fun!"

A low chuckle rolled from Jake's lips as he lifted his coffee in a toast. "Well, now, I think I may be jealous, ladies," he said as he took a drink, tumbling Sheridan's stomach when he shot her a wink over the rim. "Because as fond as I am of ranch life for a whole host of reasons"—he grinned as he nodded toward Blaze, slapping him on the back with a scrunch of his nose—"riding to work with this one sure isn't one of them."

CHAPTER FIFTY

GREEN EYES TWINKLING AND CHIN high, Aunt Libby turned the pages of an invisible book with great drama on the back porch, where the family was playing charades by lamplight in a circle of spindle-back chairs. The sweet scent of toasted marshmallows still floated in the air from the bonfire they'd enjoyed after Angus's barbecue supper, competing with the heady scent of Aunt Libby's roses.

"A book, a book!" Sheridan shouted as she bounced up and down on her chair like she was nine instead of nineteen, charades one of her favorite games the family had played all summer.

Holding up six fingers, Libby peered at her team with wide eyes.

"Six words," Grace called.

Libby held up one finger to indicate first word before she began to spin around and around.

"Spinning ..." Maggie shouted, bouncing on her chair as much as Sheridan while Grace and Shaylee shot up from theirs.

Libby managed to shake her head while circling.

"Whirling!" Grace called, but Aunt Libby just shook her head again, making Sheridan grin when she giggled to a stop with a definite wobble.

"Dizzy!" Sheridan was on her feet.

"I'll go along with that," Uncle Finn said with a lazy smile, arms folded as he leaned back in his chair, legs stretched out and crossed at the ankles. "But then most women are."

Obviously ignoring her husband and the chuckles of the

men, Libby tried a different tact as she spun her fist in a large circle.

"Around!" Grace shrieked, jumping up and down as high as Shaylee.

Tapping her nose with a huge grin, Libby lifted two fingers.

"Second word!" Shaylee yelled.

Libby pinched index finger and thumb together to indicate a small word.

"The!" Sheridan was on her feet with fists in the air. "Around the World in Eighty Days!" she screamed, and Libby threw her arms around her with a loud cheer while the other girls joined in.

"Uh-oh, record time—eight seconds." Jake announced with a wince, checking his watch as the appointed timekeeper for the game. He glanced up with a pained grin. "Which means we have to beat their time or the ladies win."

"Pure luck," Blaze said with a lazy smile at Maggie, as he rose to take his turn for the men's team.

Finn sat up while Dash did the same, competition suddenly bright in their eyes. "Well, let's hope some of it blows our way, gentlemen, because this is the last round, and I need my rest."

"Which you won't get, darling," Libby said with a challenging jag of her brow, her propensity to win at all costs making Sheridan grin, "*if* the ladies don't win."

Chuckling, Finn met his wife's jag with a jut of his own. "Well now, that can be a good thing or a bad thing, Liberty Bell," he said with a teasing drawl, utilizing the nickname he knew would ruffle her feathers. He shot her a wink. "Depending on how you look at it, darlin'."

Face flaming along with the lanterns, Aunt Libby marched over to Jake to extend her palm with a smirk. "Hand the stopwatch over, Jake, because I think it's best I time this one since you're part of the men's team and subject to bribery."

Finn cut her off at the pass, towering over her with a dangerous gleam in his eyes. "Not a chance, Mrs. McShane, but I promise you, darlin'," he said as he playfully prodded her back to her chair with a kiss and a wink, "you'll be a winner either way."

Shaking the jar that contained the slips of paper Sheridan had prepared for the game, Maggie sashayed up to Blaze with a pretty smile that was a threat all its own. Without question the sweetest female in the family, Maggie was a surprisingly poor loser at games, something her husband loved to tease her about. Eyes narrowed in warning, she promptly removed the lid for him to pick the word or phrase for the men's final turn. "I'd wish you luck, darling, but I think we both know it's safer if you don't have it."

Maggie's threat elicited chuckles around the circle as Blaze fished a folded paper from the jar. "No doubt about that, Mrs. Donovan, because my uncle didn't raise no stupid children."

"No, but *his* mama did if we don't win this game," Libby muttered as she seared Finn with a menacing look that was purely for show.

"All righty now." Blaze opened his folded piece of paper and grinned ear to ear. "Well, now, I do believe this should be a favorite of yours, Uncle Finn."

Libby groaned, prompting a giggle from Grace and Sheridan.

Tucking the piece of paper into his back pocket, Blaze splayed a palm to his chest, extending an arm with great fanfare as he pretended to sing.

"Song," Jake said with a grin.

Blaze held up six fingers.

"Oh, thank God they have as many words as we did," Libby said.

Raising clasped hands over his shoulder, Blaze proceeded to lash his arms down as if he were swinging a pick axe.

"I've Been Working on the Railroad!" Finn shouted in a rush, and Blaze let out a loud whoop that all the men echoed while the ladies groaned.

Jake slapped Blaze on the back with a loud chuckle.

"Thunderation, Donovan, that's a new record at two seconds, my boy, so the men now have a winning streak of four games running."

Slapping hands to her hips, Aunt Libby stamped her foot with a pretend scowl. "No fair. Finn was a railroad man, so he had an unfair advantage."

"As do you, darlin', with me," Finn said with a laugh, reeling Aunt Libby in for a kiss. "Because you can wheedle me into just about anything, Liberty Bell."

"Except charades," Dash piped up with a lazy grin, helping Jake and Blaze set the table and chairs back in place.

Everyone laughed as Sheridan glanced at her watch. "Hey, it's only ten o'clock, so who's up for fresh lemonade and a game of hearts?"

"Sorry, sweetheart." Uncle Finn led Aunt Libby to the door. "We've got a busy day tomorrow, I'm afraid, darlin', what with church and lunch at the Gold Hill Hotel. It was a fun evening, everyone, but you might want to consider making it an early night." He shot a grin over his shoulder as he gave Libby's waist a teasing pinch. "Because we've got a to-the death horseshoe tournament in the afternoon, so you ladies'll want to get up *nice and early* to practice. G'night, all." Good-nights rang out as Finn ushered Libby inside.

Chuckling, Blaze moseyed over to hook an arm to Maggie's waist with a cocky grin. "*Real* nice and early if you ladies want to catch up with us men, so we're going to pass, Half-Pint, because I'm beat." He pressed a kiss to Maggie's head. "After all, it's hard work winnin' all the time."

"Well, don't worry, darling," Maggie said with a brisk pat of his cheek before she slipped from his hold with a smirk, "I'll see to it you get plenty of sleep." She hurried over to join Grace, Shay, Dash, and Jake at the table while she blew him a kiss. "Sweet dreams, darling."

Sheridan jumped up to retrieve a deck of cards from the game chest Uncle Finn had built at the edge of the porch. "Yay, Maggie!"

Blaze blinked. "Wait—you're not coming with me?" His brows sloped up in a little-boy sulk.

"Soon, sweetheart," Maggie said as she blew him a kiss. "I think I'll play one or two hands of 'hearts' first"—She arched a teasing brow—"you know, so you have time to humble yours?"

"Very funny." Blaze's mouth took a twist. "Okay, but don't be long, all right?" He offered a backhanded wave before he disappeared through the door.

Sheridan giggled as she plopped the deck of cards on the table in front of Dash. "Why don't you get the game started, Dash, and I'll go make us some fresh lemonade."

Grace and Maggie immediately started to rise as if to help, and Sheridan stared them both down with a firm arch of her brow. "No, you two stay and play. I am perfectly capable of making lemonade on my own, thank you, so you girls need to redeem our female pride by putting these two"—she nodded to Dash and Jake with a smirk—"in their places."

Dash opened the deck of cards with a wide grin. "I'd make that lemonade real nice and sweet if I were you, Half-Pint," he said, shuffling the cards with all the ease of a card shark at the Ponderosa Saloon, "because I guarantee that when you ladies lose?" He had the nerve to send Grace a brazen wink. "Things will be sour enough."

CHAPTER FIFTY-ONE

"*THINGS WILL BE SOUR ENOUGH.*"
Sweet mother of mercy, Jake sure hoped not as he swooped up the cards Dash had just dealt and handed them right back while he rose from his chair. "Deal me out this round, will you, Dash?" he said, pushing his chair back in with a smile. "I think I'll go help Sher." Ignoring the blinks of surprise from both Maggie and Grace, Jake ambled toward the back door with a set of his jaw, hoping to do exactly what Sheridan had told Dash to do.

"Putting these two in their place."

Sher. Him. Their friendship.

Because now was the perfect time, after a solid month of good times and easy fun between Sher and him during family games, outings, dinners, and tournaments, be it fishing, croquet, cards, cornhole, or horseshoes. They'd laughed, talked, teased in total comfort the entire time, forging a friendship as far away from "friendship plus more" as Jake could possibly want. Where he could love her from afar without the promise of more. A friendship that was finally rock solid.

And strong enough for the truth.

Marriage was not an option.

Ever.

And a truth he hoped would keep the sweetness of their friendship from turning sour because God knows he didn't want to lead her on.

Easing the screen open without a squeal, he entered the kitchen, grinning at her off-key singing interspersed by grunts as she put everything she had into squeezing those dad-gum lemons, just like she did with everything these days. Her studies, her family, her friends, her friendship with him—with sweetness and love flowing as freely as lemonade into a glass.

He paused to study her from behind, amazed at how much she had changed in just six month. Her flaxen hair—usually trailing her shoulders—was now swept up on her head in a riot of curls, exposing a creamy neck that called to his lips, begging for a single touch of that silken skin. A cornflower-blue calico dress the color of her eyes hugged a tiny waist before flowing into gentle curves that proved she was no longer that little girl he so longed to protect.

Shaking the attraction off, he cleared his throat, the need to "protect" still foremost in his mind. "I came to help."

She whirled around with the knifc in hand, and he grinned outright as he took a step back with both palms in the air. "Or I can leave."

She giggled, and the sound warmed his heart just like it did the first time he ever saw hcr at the age of four, peeking out from behind Finn's trousers when Blaze first brought him home. "No, stay—please." Stepping aside, she waved a hand at the remaining four lemons on the cutting board with a sparkle in those blue, blue eyes. "I could definitely use a little brawn right about now, Mr. Sullivan, so wash your hands, and squeeze away."

Already am, he thought as he cranked the pump hard, annoyed at the way his heart squeezed in his chest at the thought of ever hurting this girl that he loved.

No. He swallowed hard. This *woman* he loved, he was finally willing to admit, scrubbing his hands with lye soap like he wished he could scrub his past, making him worthy to be more than a friend.

"This has been a fun summer so far, hasn't it?" she asked as she plopped a serving tray on the counter before tugging glasses from the cabinet.

"The best," he readily agreed, unable to remember a

summer when he'd been this happy, spending time with Sheridan, her family, and her friend without having to worry about more. Picking up a half lemon, he ground it to a pulp on the glass citrus squeezer as if it were the annoying attraction he felt for her, squeezing it out of his system once and for all. But tonight would be the start, he hoped, when he completely dispelled the idea of anything more—in *both* of their minds.

His smile quirked. "*Except* for your killer instinct in cornhole and horseshoes that is, Half-Pint, which nicks my male pride more often than I like."

Her chuckle filled both the kitchen and his heart as she retrieved the sugar crock from the pantry, hurrying back to clunk it on the counter. "Well, goodness, Jake Sullivan, I have to do *something* to keep you on your toes, don't I?" she said with an imp of a smile, but her unspoken message was loud and clear as it braised the back of his neck.

If I can't kiss you.

Bleeding every single drop of juice from each lemon, he stepped aside to let her mix in the sugar, arms crossed as he cocked a hip to the counter. "Well, you definitely do that, Half-Pint, but then you always have, darlin'."

She peeked up at him with so much love in her eyes, he froze on the spot, along with his tongue. He'd called her sweetheart and darlin' all of her life, but suddenly now, it felt way too intimate. "So, how's the tutoring going?" he quickly asked, moving to the pump under the guise of washing lemon juice off of his hands.

Chuckling, she measured out a cup of sugar. "Good, if you don't count the pregnant bull frog Pee-wee Portell brought to show Grace." She shook her head as she poured sugar into the pitcher. "The poor thing screamed like a little baby, shaking so hard, she about jumped out of her skin." She slid him a sideways grin. "And Grace too."

His laughter bounced off the walls as he dried his hands, more than familiar with the scream of a frightened frog, which did, indeed, sound like a startled infant.

Giggling, she promptly explained that the bullfrog was only one of a string of "gifts" Pee-wee had brought to Grace over the last few weeks. From a possum to a snake, that sweet boy had presented each with a proud puff of his chest, obviously smitten with his new teacher. And sweet Grace—as kind as she was—would simply ooh and ahh with great admiration, hand quivering against her chest while all the blood drained from her face.

They laughed so hard, Sheridan spilled part of the lemon juice all over the counter, so he grabbed a few more from the fruit basket to squeeze while she entertained him with the rest of the details. "God bless that woman," he said with a shake of his head as Sheridan cleaned up the spilled juice.

"Oh, He has," Sheridan said with a giggle, "because she told me she's having the time of her life." Mischief gleamed bright in her eyes while he poured the fresh lemon juice into her pitcher, and sliding him a grin, she placed it under the pump. "But somebody needs to tell that boy that wildflowers go a whole lot further with girls than wild frogs!"

Their laughter merged in the cozy kitchen as he worked the pump for her, reminding him just how much he enjoyed their easy friendship. "I'll be sure to have a talk with the boy when I take Midnight to the orphanage next week for a little R&R." He winked as he stepped back to let her stir. "Sister Fred's brilliant 'Riding Reward" program, you know, where the kiddos earn rides 'through the dark, scary fairy-tale forest' behind the orphanage while I tell them spook stories, which has done wonders to shape those boys up." He grinned. "Although most of the girls prefer prince and princess love stories like you always used to."

Her smile melted into the same hero worship he'd always seen from little on, but this time it was the gentle respect of a woman. "If I've never told you before, I really admire what you and Blaze do for Sister Fred and the orphanage, Jake, reaching out to those boys like you do, not to mention all the building and repairs you help Mr. Murphy with."

He buried his hands in his pockets, not comfortable with her praise because he sure didn't deserve it. "We can't touch what you, Grace, Kathy Jean, and Sophia do for those kids, Sher, and on your summer break too."

She shrugged as she stirred. "We love doing it, no question, and Grace and I want to be teachers, so it's good training as well." Laying the spoon aside, she paused to peer up at him with a tenderness she seemed to reserve just for him. "But I can tell, Jake Sullivan, that you're going to be a wonderful father someday."

Heat scorched the back of his neck as he took a step back, avoiding her eyes while he stared at the floor. "Sher …" Sucking in air like sustenance, he looked up to face her head-on, insides as shaky as an aspen leaf in the wind because her friendship was the most precious thing in his life. He cleared his throat.

Now to keep it that way.

"Yes, Jake?" Her body stilled like his, and he was pretty darn sure that neither of them were breathing as he cradled a gentle hand to her face, hoping and praying she would understand. "I need to tell you something, darlin'."

CHAPTER FIFTY-TWO

S HERIDAN FROZE.
    Oh my goodness—this is it!
The moment she'd been waiting for.
Praying for.
Living for!
And sweet mother of mercy, she couldn't breathe!

"Hey, you growin' those lemons in there?" Dash's tease drifted in through the screen door along with everyone's laughter, and it broke the tension when Jake jerked his hand away from her face to yell right back.

"Hold your horses, Donovan—I spilled half of the juice I squeezed, so we had to start over." He gave her a wink.

Sheridan grinned, grateful for the opportunity to breathe again. "Thank you for taking the blame," she whispered, remembering all the times he'd done exactly that over the years to save her from her brothers' or uncle's teasing. "*Again.*" Her grin softened into a tender smile. "You've always taken such good care of me, Jake."

His smile faded as his Adam's apple hitched in his throat, those dark eyes as serious as she had ever seen. "And I always will, Sheridan, which is what I wanted to talk to you about." His gaze flicked to the screen door and back as he took her hand in his. "Come on," he whispered while he tugged her out of the kitchen and down the hall to lead her out on the front porch, quietly closing the door behind them. "What I have to say is private."

Sheridan's heart was pounding so hard in her chest, she thought everyone might be able to hear despite all of Jake's caution. "Yes, J-Jake?" Her voice came out as a croak so hoarse, the silly bullfrog had nothing on her.

Nodding toward two rockers, he gently prodded her to sit while he did the same, turning his chair to face her before hunching on the edge with hands clasped. "Sheridan," he said quietly, pausing to inhale a deep breath as he avoided her eyes, "I think you know I love you, which is why your friendship means everything to me."

Her heart swelled with joy as she leaned to touch his arm. "Oh, Jake, I love you, too!"

Giving her hand a gentle pat, he pulled away to sit upright, the wary look in his eyes causing her heart to stall in her chest. "I won't deny there's a ..."—a knot ducked in his throat—"powerful attraction between us, Half-Pint, because that would be an outright lie, and I will never lie to you—you have my word on that."

She gave a shaky nod, her breathing suddenly as shallow as her hope when he cradled a tender hand to her face, the pain in his gaze inflicting some of her own. "Which is why I have to be honest with you, Sher, and tell you that despite my love and attraction for you, I have no intention of ever getting married—"

Her harsh gasp cut him off as she cupped both hands to her mouth with a pool of tears in her eyes.

Falling to his knees before her, he gently pried one of her hands from her face to grasp it tightly, the pained plea in his tone matching that in his eyes. "Oh, darlin', don't cry, please. It has nothing to do with you, Sheridan, but everything to do with a vile past I refuse to inflict on any woman, much less a woman I love like you."

"Oh, Jake ..." There was no way she could stop the flow of her tears as they spilled down her cheeks. A horrendous ache in her heart wrenched a sob from her lips as she slumped over, body quivering while she put her head in her hands to weep.

"Aw, Sher ..." With all the tenderness he'd always shown, he scooped her up in his arms and held her tightly while he rose to sit back down in his rocker with her in his lap, his soothing voice and touch doing little to alleviate her pain. "I love you too much to give you a hope that can never be, darlin', and too much to ever let you go as a friend, so please—forgive me and be my friend, Sheridan, and only my friend."

"B-But I … don't understand. W-Why?" she whispered, voice nasal with fluid and grief.

Cradling her face once again, he softly grazed her cheeks with his thumbs. "Because I don't deserve you, Sheridan, and because I'm a damaged man, sweetheart, in every way, and I refuse to subject you to that."

"*Please* explain it to me, Jake," she stuttered, gripping his shirt with desperate fingers, "because I don't understand. How? Why?"

He skimmed a hand down the side of her face to gently glide his thumb back and forth on her chin. "It's a long story, Sher, and we don't have time to go into it now, but someday, I promise. Till then, I need you to know that I love you and will always be here for you"—his throat convulsed along with her heart—"but as a friend, Half-Pint, and only a friend."

He ducked to peer up into her eyes, his anguish etched into every pore of his face. "So, I'm begging you, Sheridan, because I need to know, for my peace of mind and yours … can you … *will* you … accept that?"

She stared at the man she'd loved since the age of four and knew she would love him forever, but with a love far purer than any she had hoped to have. A love dictated by the very God she now served.

"*My command is this: Love each other as I have loved you.*"

Eyes swimming with saltwater, Sheridan gave a shaky nod.

Relief eased the tension from his face as he expelled a quiet sigh. "Promise me, then, Sher," he whispered, "because I need to know our friendship will be safe. Promise you'll let all notions of anymore go, please, so we can be the friends we were meant to be."

The friends we were meant to be.

Instead of the marriage that was meant to be.

Lifting a quivering palm to his face, she caressed his stubbled jaw while his handsome image blurred before her, knowing full well she would do just that. Because if she couldn't love Jake Sullivan the way that she wanted, then she would love him the only way that she could.

"Unconditional love. The greatest gift we will ever receive—or give."

Grace's words settled into her spirit with a peace that belied the awful grief in her heart, and laying her head against his chest, she hugged him with all of her might while saltwater dampened his shirt. "I promise, Jake," she whispered, voice hoarse and heart heavy, "cross my heart and hope to die."

And God help her—part of her would.

CHAPTER FIFTY-THREE

ALL READY FOR BED, GRACE quietly closed the door behind her before disrobing and hurrying over to where Sheridan was lying practically comatose, staring at the ceiling. "Okay, what's wrong?" she whispered, sitting down on the edge of the bed while she studied Sheridan with worried eyes.

"What makes you think something is wrong?" Sheridan asked with a tender look at the friend who was now more like a sister, attempting to inject at least some life into her dead tone.

Grace crooked a dark brow. "Uh, because you haven't been right since you and Jake returned with the lemonade? Both of your moods were suddenly as sour as if you'd forgotten to sweeten your own drinks."

Sheridan tried to smile, but the attempt was completely obliterated by the tears that pooled in her eyes. "Jake and I had a talk," she said quietly, battling the quiver of her jaw as she fixed her gaze back on the ceiling.

Hurrying around to the other side of the bed, Grace scurried in close, facing Sheridan with a hand to her arm. "What about?"

A brittle laugh escaped Sheridan's lips that quickly erupted into a sob. "Well, I *thought* it was going to be the answer to all my prayers, with him telling me he wanted to take our friendship to more." She swiped at her eyes as she issued a grunt. "He even got down on his knees. But it was only to tell me that yes, he loved me, but he had no intention of ever getting married and didn't want to lead me on."

"*What?*" Grace sat straight up, a bit of a spark in those

usually serene gray eyes. "Why the devil not?" she said in a near hiss, her rare swear word almost making Sheridan smile. *Almost.*

Sniffing, Sheridan lumbered up to sit against the headboard while she dabbed at her eyes with a damp handkerchief. "Oh, something about his 'vile past,' making him a 'damaged man.'" Handkerchief fisted in hand, she thumped the bed in frustration. "But we're *all* damaged people, Grace, no matter our past, aren't we? For pity's sake, my father passed shortly before my mother died when I was four, damaging our family so much, my brothers and uncle practically smothered me to death, keeping me under lock and key most of my life. Even so, we become new creatures in Christ according to my Bible, don't we?" She grunted again. "But apparently not according to Jake's."

"He wouldn't tell you what it was, his awful past?" Grace gently kneaded Sheridan's shoulder.

"No. Just said we didn't have time to go into it, but someday he would."

A rare grunt popped from Grace's lips, echoing Sheridan's. "Seems to me 'someday' ought to be right now, Sher, if he's been kissing on you like he has."

Sheridan's nightgown rose and fell with a melancholy sigh. "I know, Grace, but I promised him I would leave all that behind for the sake of our friendship."

Grace shimmied back against the headboard like Sheridan, arms in a fold that indicated her dear friend was not letting go so easily. "For the sake of the friendship I understand, Sher. But how about for the sake of the 'friend'?"

"What do you mean?" Blotting her face with the handkerchief, Sheridan studied Grace with a tip of her head.

"I *mean*"—Grace turned to face her directly, eyes in a squint as if thinking the situation through—"you're in love with Jake, and he's in love with you, and yet something awful from his past is keeping you apart." She gave Sheridan's hand a squeeze as concern clouded her eyes. "Does that seem right to you?"

"Well, no, of course not because I'm in love with him," Sheridan said with a swipe of her eyes, shoulders slumping all the more. "But what can I do? I can't *force* the man to marry me."

"No ... that's true," Grace said with a slow nod, "but you *can* force him to be the friend that both you and he deserves."

"How?" Sheridan's lips took a wry twist. "It's not like I can ply him with kisses anymore."

"No, but now you have something even better. A solid and caring friendship that allows you to probe and pray, becoming iron sharpening iron to help him face the truth, like the Bible says. The truth of a painful past healed by the truth of God's Word so he's free to be the man—*and friend*—God intended him to be." She ducked to peer up into Sheridan's eyes with a tender smile. "And maybe—just maybe—the husband as well?"

As iron sharpens iron, so a man sharpens the countenance of his friend.

"But what if Jake is right? What if I'm not meant to be his wife, Grace?"

Grace shrugged. "Then you have a dear friend who is now healthy and whole, ready to be happy with the woman who is." Her smile was gentle. "Either way you win, Sher, which is *always* the case with unconditional love."

Sheridan's eyelids drifted closed, peace lighting on her spirit—along with a bit of an ache—telling her that Grace was right. She loved Jake. And she wanted him to be happy—whether that meant with her or with someone else. But whichever it was, there was one thing of which she was absolutely certain.

A man like Jake was never meant to be alone.

"Agreed." Huffing out a sigh of surrender, Sheridan lifted her lashes to offer Grace a determined smile. "So, where do I begin? In order to sharpen iron, one has to get to the truth, and I seriously doubt that can happen unless Jake and I can be alone." She hiked a brow. "*Which* he goes to great lengths to avoid, as you well know."

"Oh, yes. "Grace giggled. "Which is exactly why quite a few jaws dropped when he hopped up to help you with lemonade."

Her smile slid off-center. "Ah, yes—the sour to my sweet." She sighed. "Well, I'll just have to add a little sour to his sweet by insisting he tell me about his past—*alone*." She scrunched her nose. "Maybe I can coax him into fishing at his favorite fishing hole like we used to." Her mouth went flat. "Before I grew curves."

Grace grinned. "Well, we have a whole month before we head back to school, so we'll just put our heads together to come up with a plan. And we can start right now."

"Tonight?" Sheridan stifled a yawn. "After Jake stomped on my hopes and dreams, Grace, I'm not sure I have enough energy left to plan anything but sleep."

"Oh, don't worry," Grace said as she plopped back on her pillow with a chuckle, "I promise that the first step—*and* the most important one—doesn't take any energy at all." Wiggling deep under the covers she reached to take Sheridan's hand, giving her a light squeeze. "We pray."

CHAPTER FIFTY-FOUR

"**S**O, CHIQUITA ..." SOPHIA PEEKED up beneath sooty lashes as she slowly peeled an orange on the back porch of the St. Mary Louise Orphanage. Following a morning of tutoring, she, Grace, Kathy Jean, and Sheridan were just finishing up the roast beef sandwiches the orphanage cook had provided for their lunch. "Have you seen him yet?"

Sheridan glanced up, her appetite suddenly fading away along with the shrieks and laughter of the children playing in the backyard. She shot a furtive glance first to where Jake was giving rides on Midnight through the woods behind the orphanage for Sister Fred's 'Riding Reward" program. Her gaze then shifted to Miss Cramer and a few of the sisters who sat at the other picnic table Jake and Blaze had just built for Sister Fred. She expelled a quiet sigh, not particularly interested in talking about Clay Morgan at the moment, but figured it was inevitable with Buffalo Bill's Wild West show back in town. Her mouth took a twist. *And* Sophia's relentless badgering that Sheridan needed to move on from Jake.

"Seen who?" Grace's eyes flicked from Sophia to Sheridan and back with a crimp in her brow.

"Clay Morgan," Kathy Jean whispered as she leaned in, obviously not wanting anyone else to overhear their conversation.

"Clay Morgan ...?" Grace repeated with a pinch above her nose, peering at Sheridan through a squint. The scent of her banana mingled with that of Sophia's orange and fresh sawdust from the brand-new tables. "You mean the beau that came to see you several times at your Aunt Marie's? The one who wouldn't take no for an answer?"

"Si." Sophia sucked on an orange slice with a sober face. "The one whose heart she broke like Jake broke hers."

Sheridan silently winced, her guilt still tender over using Clay to make Jake jealous in the first place. "Yes, Clay was rather persistent when he arrived in New York, but he quickly understood that Jake and I had a commitment," she calmly explained to Grace before turning to arch a brow at Sophia. "And I seriously doubt I broke his heart, Sophia Lopez, because Clay Morgan can practically have any girl he wants."

"Except *you*." Sophia popped an orange slice into her mouth with a smirk.

Grace sent Sheridan a wink as she peeled her banana further down. "Mmm ... that sounds familiar."

Shaking her head with a smile, Sheridan popped the last of her sandwich in her mouth and swallowed it whole. "And, *no*, Sophia Lopez, I haven't seen him yet, nor do I expect to because I'm pretty sure he doesn't want to see me either."

"Mmm ... how sure?" Sophia studied the slice of orange in her hand as if it were one of the frog specimens with which she taught the children biology.

Sheridan paused with a scrunch of her nose. "And what's *that* supposed to mean?"

A noisy sigh blasted from Sophia's lips as she leveled a firm look at her friend. "It means, chica, that when Chet came over last night, he told me Clay would like to see you. And, since he who shall remain nameless only wants to be friends, I think it would be good for you to see hi—"

Sheridan was shaking her head before Sophia could even finish. "No, ma'am. My heart is sore enough right now over Jake, Sophia. The last thing I want is to even *think* about another man right now, so please don't encourage it."

"Whoops." Sophia tugged on her lip with a guilty look. "Too late."

Sheridan blinked, stomach bottoming out. "Oh no, Sophia—what did you do?"

Sophia scrunched her face in apology. "Well, when Chet

said Clay wanted to see you"—she gave a little shrug—"I *may* have … *sort of* … mentioned he could see you after tutoring the children this morning …"

A weak groan trailed from Sheridan's lips as she put her head in her hands. "*Sophhhhia* … why on earth did you do that?" She peered up with pleading eyes. "I'm in no frame of mind or heart to deal with another man right now."

"But that's just it, chiquita," Sophia said with a thump of her fist on the table, black eyes sparking with anger over the heartache Jake had put Sheridan through. "You *are* in the frame of mind and heart because you need to realize Jake is not the only bull in the barn. And Jake," she emphasized with a stern jut of her jaw, shooting a narrow gaze into the woods where Jake just disappeared, "needs to realize that too."

Jake. Sheridan froze. *Was here.* Which meant that … *Jake. Clay. Together.* Sheridan shot up so fast, she shivered the table, Maggie's words coming back to haunt.

"Jake swore he was going to bash Clay's head in for even looking at you."

"Oh my goodness—I have to go—*now!*" Sheridan's hands shook as she fumbled cleaning up the remainder of her lunch.

Grace stilled her with a gentle hand. "Maybe not," she said slowly with a questioning tip of her head. "Maybe this is part of the plan we prayed for regarding yours and Jake's friendship." Her lips suddenly curved in a faint smile, the calm in her gray eyes somehow calming Sheridan too. "You know, iron sharpening iron?"

Sheridan stared, suddenly aware that Grace was right. Jake was being a mule about opening up to Sheridan regarding his past, but another jolt of jealousy might be just the leverage she needed to coerce him to confide in her at last.

The sound of horse hoofs from the street in front of the orphanage suddenly broke the tension in her chest, and sucking in a deep draw of air, Sheridan sat back down and finished gathering the remains of her lunch. "Well, then." Releasing a slow exhale, she glanced toward the woods once again before she gave everyone at the table a shaky smile. "Let the games begin …"

CHAPTER FIFTY-FIVE

"**G**EE, MR. JAKE," EIGHT-YEAR-OLD BUSTER Bixby said with a gap-toothed grin over his shoulder, "if I'd known this was going to be this much fun, I would have studied a whole lot harder, a *whole* lot sooner!"

Jake grinned as Midnight ambled along the mossy-edged path Jake had cut through the woods behind the orphanage, little ol' Buster swaying back and forth in the saddle in front of Jake like that tick-tock doohicky thing on Miss Cramer's piano. "Well, Buster, you keep earning those good marks from your teachers like you have, and you'll earn yourself a right exciting gallop through these woods next time, with a fairy-tale spook story to boot, you hear?"

"Yes, sir," Buster said with a little hop in the saddle, the feel of excitement in the little guy's spindly body making Jake wish he could have little Busters of his own someday. The thought suddenly darkened his mood like the lush canopy of trees overhead darkened the woods.

Talk about fairy tales!

Trotting out of the dark into the sunlight of the backyard helped chase the gloom away, and clutching Buster closer to his chest, Jake shouted his usual "Yee-haw!" as he bolted from the woods in a wild gallop, Buster's whoops and hollers bringing a grin to his face.

"Who's next, Miss Cramer?" he called when he deposited Buster at the steps of the back porch, the little guy instantly darting into the backyard with a backward wave to join his friends in a stickball game.

Miss Cramer rose from the picnic table with a swish of crumbs from her hands, her smile as bright as the blazing sun overhead. "You're done for today, Jake, so come on up and have some lunch. Mrs. Bellweather made extra roast beef sandwiches, so I have two set aside for you, young man."

"That sounds mighty good, Miss Cramer, thank you." Jake dismounted and tied Midnight up to the post of the brand-spankin'-new deck he and Blaze had helped Mr. Murphy build, which ran the entire length of the orphanage. Nudging his hat up, he mounted the steps with a rumble of his stomach, suddenly realizing how hungry he was.

"Wait!" Sophia fluttered her lashes at Jake in a tease. "And what do *we* have to do to get a ride, Mr. Jake?"

Jake grinned as he shot her a wink. "Well, I'd say all you have to do, Miss Lopez, is smile at pert near any cowboy you see, and it's a done deal." He paused on the top step, a faint furrow digging in above his nose. "Where's Sheridan?"

Jake's stomach tightened when Grace exchanged glances with Sophia and Kathy Jean.

"Oh, Mrs. Bellweather said Sheridan had a visitor out front, but I'm sure she'll be back soon," Miss Cramer explained in a cheery voice, dusting off the bench beside her for Jake to sit down. "Come, Jake, sit down and eat. You have to be starving."

Well, he *was* … but not anymore.

"Any idea who?" he asked in a casual tone, taking his hat off to ruffle his hair, the growling in his stomach turning into growling of a totally different kind.

"A nice young man from The Wild West show who was most polite." Miss Cramer reached for the lemonade to fill him a glass. "I bet you're ready for a cold drink of this."

"Actually, Miss Cramer"—Jake put his Stetson back on with a firm tug, sauntering back down the stairs—"Blaze is expecting me back at the ranch soon, ma'am, so I should head back, but thank you for the kind offer."

He shot Grace, Sophia, and Kathy Jean a wink as he mounted his horse. "But I'll just bet you'll find some takers on those extra sandwiches among those ladies over there."

Tipping his hat, he reined Midnight around toward the side of the house with a wave. "Have a good day, ladies," he said while the ladies bid him goodbye.

Because I sure won't.

"Clay, no, please—"

At the sound of Sheridan's strained voice, Jake spurred Midnight on with a sharp squeeze of his legs, rounding the corner of the orphanage where Clay Morgan was kissing her while she tried to squirm free.

"Take your filthy hands off of her!" Jake's harsh hiss carried a thousand threats as he leapt from the saddle and stormed up the stairs of the front porch, yanking Morgan around so fast, Sheridan emitted a tiny scream. Chest heaving, Jake stared him down with blood in his eyes, his voice pure venom while his fingers twitched for revenge, temper hanging on by a thread. "You ever lay another hand on her, Morgan, and I'll break it and every finger you have, got that?"

Morgan's eyes were black and bitter as a slow smile curled on his lips. "I've laid many a hand on her, Sullivan, and each and every one was worth anything you care to dole out."

Fury exploded in Jake's brain, and jerking Morgan out of Sher's range, he plowed an iron fist into the dandy's jaw, toppling him over the bannister into the bushes.

"Jake, *no!*" Sheridan's cry rang out in terror, but Jake barely heard as he vaulted over the bannister, ready to finish the lowlife off.

Morgan was on his feet before Jake even hit the ground. "What's the matter, Sullivan?" he said with a come-on wave of his fingers, his feral look indicating he was itching for a fight as much as Jake. "Afraid she'll give me more than she gives you?"

Snap! His vision went black with rage as he tucked his head and rammed into the dandy with a violent roar, slamming him flat on his back.

"Jake, stop—*please!*"

But he couldn't. His body wouldn't let him as he straddled

the dandy, bloodying his pretty face with blow after blow until all he could see was the vile man who had once done the same to him.

"Jacob Sullivan—*stop it this instant!*" Miss Cramer's shocked command finally registered through the fog of outrage in Jake's brain, and rib cage heaving, he rolled off of Morgan, body numb at the damage he had done.

Clay Morgan lay groaning on the ground with eyes closed, his face sporting blood, bruises, and swelling that was just starting to show.

God help me, what have I done?

Sheridan and Miss Cramer rushed down the steps as Jake tried to help Clay up, but Clay only thrust him away, stumbling up with a handkerchief to his lip.

"I'm sorry, Morgan," Jake said in a low voice raspy with regret.

"Not as sorry as you will be, I can promise that." Clay swayed on his feet, and one of the sisters rushed up to give him a damp rag that he dabbed on his face. "Thanks, Sister," he muttered, handing it back while Sheridan slowly approached.

She laid a gentle hand on his arm with tears in her eyes. "Clay, I am so sorry."

"Me too, Sheridan," he said with the barest semblance of a smile, face mottled as he bent to retrieve his Stetson from the ground. Placing it on his head, he slowly made his way to his horse, mounting as if every bone in his body ached as much as his face. With a limp tip of his hat, he turned and rode away, leaving a lump in Jake's throat as big as the one Clay Morgan now sported around his eye.

Retrieving his hat from the ground, Jake turned. His heart stopped when he saw Sheridan's friends and the sisters hovering over Pee-Wee, Buster, and the rest of the orphans on the side of the house, eyes wide with a fear he recognized all too well.

His gut cramped as moisture burned at the back of his lids.

"Not as sorry as you will be, Sullivan," Morgan had said, but he was wrong.

Because Jake doubted he could ever be any sorrier than he was right now.

Or more ashamed.

CHAPTER FIFTY-SIX

TWO WEEKS. THAT'S ALL HE had left. And then he could breathe easy.

And hard, when she left and took his heart with her again. A long, silent sigh seeped through Jake's lips as he played a game of hearts with Sheridan, Dash, and Grace in the parlour on family game night.

A summer breeze fluttered the sheers, ushering in the sweet scent of roses along with a symphony of crickets and katydids, beautiful music that merged with the family's laughter and love. Resigned to the fact that he was about to lose, Jake laid his Queen of Hearts down.

Just like he'd do in two weeks' time. When Sheridan and Grace left for school.

His Queen of Hearts. He peered up beneath lowered lashes at the woman who had stolen his and knew that as difficult as it would be to see her leave again, it was better than the alternative

The risk of falling deeper in love.

He'd already seen the damage his feelings for Sheridan had done over a month ago when he'd whaled on Clay Morgan at the orphanage, and then Sister Fred had whaled on him when she'd found out. She was the one who'd opened his young eyes to a deeper faith that had kept his demons of temper buried deep beneath the surface all these years. And the shame he felt at her scolding over his violent display in front of the children he loved made him vow to never let it happen again. Not to mention Sheridan, who now begged all the more for him to reveal his past.

But he couldn't. Not yet. It was bad enough he had to live

with it. He didn't want the woman he loved to live with it too.

Jake had returned to the orphanage the next day to apologize to every single child and teacher, then had ridden to the Wild West arena to do the same to Clay and his uncle. Buffalo Bill had taken it in stride, but Jake doubted Clay Morgan would ever forgive him, and he sure didn't blame him. Heck, Jake couldn't even forgive himself for what happened, nor fully understand it either, how he'd lost control like he had. All the more reason to never even consider getting married, because like he'd told Sheridan, he was damaged goods. And now everyone else knew that too.

Although Finn hadn't condoned his actions, Jake sensed he was relieved that Jake could do what he hadn't been able to do for his niece: keep Clay Morgan away. And Blaze and Dash had clapped him on the back like he'd just won a shooting contest against Annie Oakley herself, which made Jake feel all the worse.

He didn't want to win at fights.

He wanted to win at peace.

Sheridan's little-girl squeal broke into his morose train of thoughts when she won the game once again. All but bouncing on her chair, she preened while she recorded everyone's score, and the proud smile she always provoked kicked up the edge of Jake's lip. "Uh, do they teach any humility classes up there in that fancy school of yours, Half-Pint, because I think you may be in dire need."

The little brat just lifted her nose in the air with a giggle, lips pursed in a sassy smile. "What can I say, Sully? During long study times, Grace and I have become most proficient at the game of hearts."

His smile went flat. *No joke.*

"True," Grace said with a wink and a nod as she neatly cupped her cards in a stack to place back on the deck, "although it sure hasn't helped me tonight."

"Good game, Squirt." Dash threw his cards into the middle of the table and leaned back in a stretch, hands over his head.

"Well, we could always give Sher a rest from winning with a game of charades," he said, motioning his head to where Shaylee, Maggie, Blaze, Libby, and Finn had just finished up with a game of The Mansion of Happiness. Shaylee's favorite, The Mansion of Happiness was a board game where Sabbath-breakers were sent to the whipping post.

Like I should be. Jake chucked his cards on top of Dash's with a wry smile.

For being stupid enough to fall in love.

"Oooooo, charades sounds perfect!" Sheridan finished adding the scores with a flourish before glancing up with a flutter of lashes. "Grace came in second, Dash after that, *and Jake*"—she had the nerve to drawl his humiliation out as she wrinkled her nose with a sassy smirk—"lost *baaaaaaad*!"

Big surprise. Leveling a mock scowl at her, he made her giggle when he aimed a stern finger as well. "One game of charades will wipe that smirk right off your face, young lady, guaranteed."

"Cross your heart and hope to die?" She wiggled her brows, and he just shook his head with a hollow laugh, thinking she was closer than she knew. Because he definitely was crossing his heart in going against what it truly wanted, and there was no doubt he was dying too.

Now. And even more so in two weeks' time.

Dash slapped Jake on the back with a wide grin as he rose to his feet. "Let's just see who dies in a game of charades to the death, shall we, Sul?" He slid Grace a wink that promptly dusted her cheeks with a pretty pink. "After all, I believe the men have a winning streak of five games running, if I'm not mistaken."

"Why, I believe you're right, Dash," Jake said in an innocent tone as he pushed out his chair to stand up as well. He stretched arms high overhead while he shot Sheridan a crooked grin. "Because it's obvious we men are masters of acting things out."

Especially me. He fought the pull of a scowl. *At least lately.*

"Okay, family—who's up for charades?" Dash called out, and Shaylee bounded into the air with a shriek of assent while the others laughed and rose from their game table.

"Sounds like a plan." Finn looped an arm to Libby's waist to press a kiss to her head. "As long as coffee and sweets are involved."

"Have to admit, Libby," Finn said later after he and everyone else had polished off most of the oatmeal cookies Libby had served, "those were the finest oatmeal cookies you've ever made, darlin'."

"Hear, hear!" Jake said while the other men heartily agreed.

"Why, thank you, gentlemen." Libby laid a pad and pencil on the table along with a jar of prepared slips of paper for the game. She then set an ornate brass hourglass front and center, although Jake had his trusty stopwatch to measure exact time.

Smiling, she sat down with Maggie, Grace, Sheridan, and Shay on the extra-long, cowhide leather sofa Finn had special ordered for her from San Francisco. "I have to admit, Finn, when I first arrived and discovered the ladies did the cooking on Sundays because that was Angus's day off, I was more than a little bit worried since I'm not much of a cook." She scrunched her shoulders with a giggle as she snuggled with Shaylee. "Of course, I wasn't much of a wife either, and look how that's changed." She blew a kiss to her husband before she wrinkled her nose. "Mostly."

Finn's laughter boomed in the parlour as he settled back into his easy chair next to the loveseat occupied by Dash and Blaze. "I think we all have a little 'mostly' in our lives, Libs, so I'm sure not complaining."

Jake couldn't help but agree as he lounged back in a chair nabbed from the dining room, hands cupped to the back of his neck while his legs stretched out with boots crossed at the ankles. He buried a grunt.

Some of us more than others.

His gaze flicked to where Sheridan and Grace were chatting up a storm, thinking he'd "mostly" been a good friend to

Sheridan this summer, but not all. And it was the other side of that coin that inflicted more than a little guilt that he'd dodged her several attempts to get him alone in order to dig into his past. But Sheridan was the last person he wanted to expose his past to. Blast it all, he was ashamed enough to keep it hidden from the rest of the family, much less the woman he loved.

"Okay, ladies first," Shaylee shouted as she jumped up to hold out the jar to Sheridan.

"Why, thank you, Doodle." Sheridan hopped up to dig into the jar like she was digging for gold, eyes squeezed shut and teeth tugging at her lower lip as if it were life and death. Jake grinned. Which was pretty much how the woman did everything, with her whole heart and soul. The grin faded a hair.

Especially loving me.

Unleashing her usual squeal of excitement that seemed to accompany every joy in her life, she promptly stood at the front of the group and gave a dramatic bow. With great flair, she carefully turned the pages of a book like a scholar, chin high and a smile twitching on those beautiful lips.

"Book!" Maggie shouted, and Sheridan instantly tapped her nose to indicate she was correct.

Holding up three fingers to signal three words, Sheridan thrust a single finger in the air to identify it as the first one. Suddenly she put her head in her hands and began to sob, and the sound actually constricted Jake's stomach, because it was something he never wanted to hear or see.

"Cry!" Maggie guessed, all but leaping into the air.

Elation burst across Sheridan's beautiful face like the blinding light of the sun after a dark storm, and touching her nose, she hoisted two fingers.

"Second word ..." Shaylee hovered on the edge of her seat.

Shoulders scrunched, Sheridan looked flat-out adorable as she touched her index finger and thumb together right in front of her nose to signal a small word.

"A ... the ... in ..." Libby was shooting rapid-fire.

Sheridan shook her head, dislodging several golden strands from the topknot of curls perched on top of her head. "And!" Maggie said in a near squeal, and Sheridan slapped a finger to her nose, not wasting any time as she popped three fingers up.

"Cry and ..." Maggie appeared to be a nervous wreck, fists clenched white while she leaned forward so much, Jake was surprised she didn't fall off the couch. He grinned, remembering Blaze's stories about how competitive his wife was.

"Crime and Punishment!" Grace could have given Maggie a run for her money as she vaulted into the air with arms flailing high, unleashing wild squeals from all the ladies when Sheridan shrieked and jumped as well.

"Twenty seconds," Jake announced with a grin, pretty darn sure the men could topple that.

"Oh, and it's so appropriate!" Libby crossed her palms to her chest in near ecstasy, sending her husband a smug flutter of lashes. "Because arrogance is the 'crime' the men have committed, and losing is their 'punishment'!"

"Oooo, good one, Aunt Libby!" Sheridan gave her a hug.

"Move over, ladies," Blaze said with a lazy smile, moseying over to pluck a paper from the jar, "and we'll show you 'punishment.'"

Tap. Tap. Tap.

Finn glanced into the foyer, nose in a scrunch as he checked his watch. "Who in the devil could that be at this hour?" he said, ambling up to answer the door.

"Oh, goodness, Finn, I hope nothing's wrong." Libby hurried into the foyer while both Blaze and Jake followed behind.

Finn opened the door to a tall, good-looking man who looked to be in his early twenties, dressed to the nines in the latest styles of the day. Taking his bowler hat off his head, he flashed a perfect set of teeth. "Good evening, Mayor and

Mrs. McShane, I presume?"

"Yes, I'm Mayor McShane, and this is my wife, Libby."

The man offered a polite nod to Libby. "It's a pleasure to meet you, ma'am, and Mayor McShane, I have to say it's especially good to meet you." He extended an arm in a handshake.

Finn's voice held a note of curiosity as he shook the man's hand. "And why is that, Mr. ...?"

"Carmody—Grayson Carmody, sir, Grace's twin brother?" Grinning, he pumped Finn's hand like he was drilling for oil. "And why? *Because*, sir," he said with a confident thrust of his chin, "I'm the man who plans to marry your niece."

CHAPTER FIFTY-SEVEN

WHAT THE DEVIL? FINN STARED at the man who'd just blown up his evening as thoroughly as a stick of dynamite dipped in nitroglycerin. "Come again?" he said, his voice a near growl as he slowly eased Libby behind him. He blocked the door with his full girth, palms flat to the jambs while he shifted his stance with an impatient cock of his hip.

The dandy just grinned as if he didn't have a lick of sense, no earthly idea that Finn was seriously contemplating throwing him out on his ear. "I'm Grace's brother, sir," he repeated again, slower this time as if he suspected Finn didn't have a lick of sense either. "Sheridan invited me to come stay for the summer along with Grace, but prior commitments kept me away."

"Gray?" Inching past her brothers and Jake, Sheridan ducked under Finn to literally launch into the man's arms with a squeal, skirt billowing when the confounded dandy whirled her 'round and 'round on the front porch.

"Sugar Lips!" he shouted with *way* too much familiarity, causing a tic to pulse in Finn's jaw. The dandy deposited a kiss to Sheridan's hair, squeezing his niece like Finn wanted to squeeze him. *Around the neck.*

Sugar Lips???

"Oh my goodness, Gray—what on earth are you doing here?" Grace sneaked through on Finn's other side, joining in a three-way hug so tight, they may as well have been hog-tied.

"Conveniently sprained a muscle," he said with a wink to his sister, "so I could escort my two favorite girls home."

"*Ahem.*" Finn gave a gruff clear of his throat, refusing to move until Libby prodded him aside.

"Oh, for heaven's sake, Finn, ask our guest in," she said, promptly extending a hand. "Welcome, Gray. We have loved having Grace here, so it's a pleasure to meet you too."

Speak for yourself, Libby. Mouth tamped tight, Finn backed up to allow his wife to drag the dandy in while Sheridan and Grace hovered as close as shadows.

Hooking her arm through the dandy's, Sheridan stood straight and tall with a proud puff of her chest, the top of her upswept curls barely coming to the man's shoulders. "Everyone, this is Grace's twin and one of my dearest friends, Grayson Carmody, better known as Gray."

Gray winked, completely ignoring Finn's tight-lipped scowl—and that of every other male in the room as well, given his nephews' and Jake's hard-sculpted jaws. "Or the evil twin to my sister's saintly one."

"Unfortunately true." Sheridan chuckled as she pinched the dandy's cheek before extending a hand to introduce each person in the foyer. "Gray, these are my brothers Dash and Blaze," she said with pride while Gray reached to shake both of their hands, seemingly oblivious to the coolness of their manner. "Then my sister-in-law Maggie, Blaze's wife, and my little sister Shaylee"—she gave an affectionate nod to both Maggie and Shay while Gray offered a bow that included a wink for Shaylee—"and last but not least, our dear friend and assistant foreman of the Silver Lining Ranch, Jake Sullivan."

Jake stiffened when Gray offered a handshake with a measured smile, awkward seconds passing before his assistant foreman complied with a chilly nod.

And then before Finn could demand what the dandy meant by his hair-trigger comment about marrying Sheridan, Libby quickly scuttled him away to the parlour. Promptly pushing him down in the middle of the sofa, she offered both oatmeal cookies and a cup of coffee. "I can't tell you how much we've enjoyed having Grace here this summer," she prattled on, opting to sit on the end of the sofa while Sheridan and

Grace flanked the dandy on either side. Finn, Blaze, and Dash slowly returned to their seats like gunslingers ready to draw while Jake opted for a rigid stance behind his chair, feet straddled and arms crossed.

"You must have missed her terribly!" Libby continued.

Gray hooked an arm to both Grace's waist and Sheridan's, depositing a kiss to each of their cheeks. "More than air, Mrs. McShane, which is why I decided to come to escort them home."

Grace threw her arms around her brother, her face aglow as she gave him a big hug. "I still can't believe you're here, Gray," she said with a sheen of moisture in her eyes.

Finn masked his shock when the dandy's eyes misted, too, before they closed in a clearly affectionate embrace. His voice lowered to a gruff whisper. "I was going crazy missing you and Sher, sis, so I had to come."

Sheridan shifted to face Gray, her knees touching his leg while she laid a hand on his arm, causing Finn to hike a brow. "Wait—how did your competitions go?" she asked in a breathless voice.

"Competitions?" Finn's voice was brusque, a competition of his own going on between Jake and him as to whose jaw was grinding more.

Sheridan glanced up with a bright smile beaming so much, the dandy could have been her brother instead of Grace's. Finn's teeth milled tighter.

Or her beau.

"Gray is the captain of Columbia University's rowing team," she announced with enough pride in her eyes to blind all the men on Finn's side of the room. She turned back to shake the dandy's arm. "So, how did they go?"

The dandy squeezed Sheridan's waist, adding another pulsing nerve to both Finn's face and Jake's. "Took first place in the single sculls division, Sher, so you and Grace must have been saying those prayers you promised—"

"Columbia University," Jake interrupted coolly, "that's in

New York City, I believe." His hands pinched white on the back of the dining room chair he'd sat in earlier. "That's a fair piece from Poughkeepsie, as I recall. So I guess you don't get to see Grace as much as you like."

"Oh no, it's just a two-hour drive," Grace volunteered with a smile as glowing as Sheridan's, as if to relieve Jake's concern. "Gray comes to Poughkeepsie every weekend or we go there, so we're always together, which is why Sher and I missed him so much."

"And I, them," Gray said with another intimate squeeze of both his sister's waist and Sher's, getting on Finn's last nerve.

"Sheridan." Finn's tone was terse as he stared his niece down, determined to tackle this problem point blank. *Like I'd like to do with the dandy.* "This young man claims he wants to marry you, darlin'. You mind telling me what that's all about?"

The silence was deafening as four sets of male eyes cauterized his niece while the females on the other side of the room merely gaped in shock.

Hand to her mouth, Sheridan blinked several times as her cheeks bruised bright pink, gaze connecting with Grace's while the dandy just sat there, grinning like a fool.

And then in a spate of giggles that seemed to infect all the females in the room, Sheridan and Grace burst into laughter that Finn didn't find one bit funny.

Swiping at the tears in her eyes, Sheridan shook her head while she patted Gray's arm with a look of affection. "Gray and I are good friends like Grace and I are, Uncle Finn, with barely any difference."

Jake's low grunt matched Finn's silent one to a T. *Maybe to you, darlin', but not according to the lecherous look in that dandy's eye.* Finn's mouth compressed as he suddenly thought of his sister, Peg. *Like a lamb to the slaughter.*

Grace tweaked the back of her brother's neck with a giggle. "She's right, Mr. McShane. I'm afraid my brother tends to be a bit of a tease and a flirt, so he likes to stir the pot with comments like that, but I promise you, Sher and he are dear friends and nothing more."

"Where are your bags, Gray?" Libby intervened quickly, a flick of warning in her eyes to Finn before she lavished a warm smile on Grace's brother.

The smile Gray returned to Libby was as warm as the one he'd given his sister, not a trace of the dandy to be found. "At the Gold Hill Hotel, Mrs. McShane, where I intend to stay for the week until we head back East again."

"Absolutely not," Libby said with a firm lift of her chin, straining Finn's jaw all the more. "You are Grace's brother and Sheridan's good friend, so that makes you our friend, too. *And* a guest in our home." She turned to grill Finn with a determined look. "Isn't that right, Finn?"

Finn's lips fused tighter than a tick on a dog.

"Finn?" Libby waited with a lift of her brow. Blue blazes, they were all waiting, and the count was 50/50 on which way they wanted him to go.

Expelling a noisy breath, Finn scorched the dandy within an inch of his life. "Certainly, Mr. Carmody, our home is your home, so by all means, go collect your things. We'll have a room waiting when you come back, where you can settle in nice and close, to keep an eye on your sister." His smile was a silent threat.

While I keep an eye on you.

CHAPTER FIFTY-EIGHT

*T*HUNDERATION, GRACE, WHERE ARE YOU??
Sheridan paced back and forth in her bedroom, nightgown flaring with every pass as she bit the last of her pinky nail clean off. Halting midway, she closed her eyes to relive the scene in the parlour, when Uncle Finn had jolted everyone in the room with his bombshell question.

"This young man claims he wants to marry you, darlin'. You mind telling me what that's all about?"

A low groan scraped from Sheridan's throat as she continued on, rambling back and forth while she went to work on her second pinky with a vengeance. *What on earth had prompted Gray to say such a thing?*

Yes, he teased Sheridan like that all the time in New York, but she was used to it, merely dismissing it as his usual flirty, but lovable self. A man who despite his roguish and devil-may-care manner, truly loved and protected his sister at every turn, and now Sheridan too.

Which is why Sheridan and Grace had taken one look at each other and burst out laughing, because the idea of Sheridan and Gray being anything other than friends was sheer lunacy. But for Gray to tell her uncle such a thing in front of her brothers and Jake? A shiver rattled her body that skittered clear to her toes, the memory of Jake's hard-chiseled scowl burned deep in her brain. *What on earth had the man been thinking??*

The doorknob squeaked, and Sheridan spun around, body paralyzed as she watched Grace quietly enter the room and close the door behind her. "What did he say?" she whispered, the sound harsh in the dark quiet of the moonlit room.

Grabbing Sheridan's hand, Grace pulled her to the bed and scrambled in while Sheridan followed behind, the two girls sitting cross-legged to face each other head-on. "He said he did it for you," she whispered, moonlight highlighting the sympathy in her face.

"What?" Sheridan sat straight up. "What does he mean, he did it for me?"

Expelling a weary sigh, Grace inched back against the headboard with arms hugging tented knees, propping her chin on top of her nightgown with a little groan. "Well, I suppose it's partially my fault, Sheridan, because I wrote Gray about how upset you were when Jake said he never planned to marry, and apparently that upset Gray quite a bit too."

"For heaven's sake, why?" Sheridan asked, palms splayed wide.

Grace tipped her head with an affectionate smile. "You know why, Sher. He's convinced he's in love with you and wants to see you happy."

A grunt tripped from Sheridan's lips. "Well ostracizing half of my family is not the way to do it, Grace, and you know it."

"I know, and that's what I told him, but he's determined to light a fire under Jake to either marry you or"—Grace chewed on the edge of her lip with a soft slope of brows—"get out of his way so he can have a shot."

"What?!" Sheridan shifted to plop back against the headboard with a groan. "That's crazy. Gray and I are like brother and sister, and you and I both know it."

"Maybe to you, Sher," Grace said quietly, "and maybe to me until tonight. But after talking to him right now?" A sad, whispery sigh parted from Grace's lips. "I had no idea that his feelings for you were that deep, my friend, because Gray is always 'falling in love' as we both know. But this?"—she shook her head with a hint of a sheen in her eyes—"My heart aches for him, Sheridan, because I think he may actually be falling in love with you, and I know you can't return that love the way that he wants."

Sheridan blinked, the idea that Gray could actually be in love with her sending goose bumps skittering across her skin. Buffing her arms, she glanced up at Grace with a soulful smile. "I love Gray, Grace, you know that, but I'm *in love* with Jake and always have been, and Gray knows that, too, which is why I always thought his feelings for me were merely a case of wanting what he couldn't have."

"Me too," Grace whispered. Brushing the wetness from her eyes, she sat up, shoulders square against the headboard. "And it still might be, Sher, because heaven knows a girl has never turned him away before, so that may be all it is."

"I hope so." A mournful breath quivered from Sheridan's lips as she squeezed Grace's hand. "Because I would never want to hurt your brother. I care about him way too much, Grace. You and Gray have become two of my dearest friends.

Grace squeezed back. "And you, ours, Sher. *Which*," she said with a nervous grate of her lip, "is why Gray insists on helping you with Jake."

Sheridan's brows scrunched. "What do you mean, help me with Jake?"

Grace lifted a shoulder. "By laying it on thick with Jake, your uncle, and your brothers, convincing them he poses a problem to their plans to keep you away from all men. He seems to think that might break down Jake's barriers, forcing him to love you like 'you deserved to be loved'—his words exactly."

Moisture pricked beneath Sheridan's lids. "Oh, God bless him! But I doubt that will have any effect, Grace. Both you and I already told everyone in the parlour that Gray and I are only friends, so I'm not sure what purpose that will serve other than make half of my family dislike him intensely."

Brows raised, Sheridan put a hand to her chest. "*Especially* Uncle Finn! Oh my goodness, I've never seen him so tense as when he called me into his office for a private chat tonight after everyone else went to bed. Heavens, he even made me swear on the Bible that I didn't have romantic feelings for

Gray, if you can believe that." Her nose wrinkled. "Besides, I already tried the whole jealousy thing once before with Clay, remember? And it made me feel awful, like I was using Clay and lying to Jake."

Grace scooted around to lean a shoulder to the headboard, face wrinkled in thought. "But that's just it, Sher. Gray thinks it will have an impact based on Jake's, your uncle's, and your brothers' reaction to him tonight. You know, like they wanted to string him up?"

Sheridan nibbled on the edge of a shy smile. "Gray did seem to upset them pretty badly."

"Yes, and he doesn't want *you* to have to do a solitary thing but be yourself and totally honest—not lie or manipulate or feel like you're using him because it's his choice to do this for you, Sher—out of love."

Sheridan shook her head, amazed at Gray's willingness to help her win Jake. "But even if Gray's plan docsn't work, Grace, I'm just not sure I'll ever feel anything more than deep friendship for your brother."

Grace patted Sheridan's arm. "I know that, Sher, and so does Gray, and he told me he's okay with that." A sparkle lit in her friend's eyes. "But I think it's only fair to warn you that my brother is not only a confident man, but a determined one as well, my friend, so he doesn't plan to give up hope until he sees another man's ring on your finger."

"Well then, who knows?" Sheridan said with a lift of her palms. "I've always believed Jake and I were meant for each other from little on, but if I'm wrong about that? I suppose I could be wrong about ever falling in love with Gray too." She shrugged. "And I can honestly say now that I'm more than willing to marry whomever God ordains, if that's anyone at all"—affection warmed in her eyes for the lovable rogue twin she now saw as a brother—"even if it *is* dear, sweet Gray."

A gentle smile flickered across Grace's lips. "I think you would be good for him, Sher," she said quietly, "because you're the first girl who's ever been able to tame the rogue in him."

"That's because I'm a challenge, Grace, that's all, just like you told me at the onset, remember? You warned me that Gray would make a better friend than a beau, and I should avoid falling for him like every other girl seems to do, so I did. Which was easy to do since I'm so in love with Jake, of course"—she punctuated it with a lovesick sigh—"whose kisses branded both my lips and my mind." Her smile shifted to dry. "Or used to."

"Well, speaking of *those* kisses ..." Grace leaned in with a soft clap of hands. "Do you want to hear what Gray has planned to get them back?" She wiggled her brows.

Sheridan hunched her shoulders with a nervous grin, brows knit in concern. "Uh-oh ... knowing Gray, I'm almost afraid to ask."

A low, throaty giggle popped from Grace's mouth as she lowered her voice, a gleam of trouble glinting in her eyes that strangely enough, reminded Sheridan of Gray. "Well, I wouldn't worry if I were you, Sher, because it's not *you* who has to be afraid, my friend." She winked, making Sheridan grin outright because it was so out of character and far more reminiscent of her brother. "It's Jake."

CHAPTER FIFTY-NINE

"**S**O, CARMODY, HOW ARE YOU at cornhole?" Blaze said casually as dessert was finishing up on the back porch, his curt use of Gray's last name a key indicator that Grace's brother hadn't made any inroads with the male element at Silver Lining Ranch.

Jake stifled a smile, well aware Blaze was desperate to take the dandy down, and there was nobody better at cornhole than his best friend. Finn and Sheridan were the champs when it came to horseshoes, no question, but cornhole was Blaze's game through and through along with pool, which is why he suggested a cornhole tournament after dinner.

Gray glanced up from teasing with Sheridan—*as usual*—and flashed a cocky smile. "Pretty good, actually, *Donovan*," he boasted, and it was all Jake could do to keep the spit in his mouth instead of spewing it on the floor like he wanted. The idiot had the nerve to wink. "Alpha Delta Phi champ, as a matter of fact."

Oh, of course you are. Jake kept the spit in his mouth with great effort, eyes narrowing as he stared the dandy down. Since Carmody had disrupted everyone's peace of mind with his arrival four days ago, the prissy college boy had managed to rile the male folk, if possible, even more than the night he'd announced he wanted to marry Sher.

Because not only had he managed to charm the socks off all of the women, but he was pert near perfect in just about anything he set his hand to, which flat-out got on Jake's nerves. From cards and horseshoes, to riding and charades, the polecat appeared to have as much brains as brawn, making Jake itch to see how the varmint would measure up with a gun in his hand.

"Good," Blaze said with an abrupt push away from the table, "because I'm the Silver Lining Ranch champ, so I'm anxious to see what you got."

"My pleasure," Gray said with a gleam of challenge in his eyes, hooking an arm over Sheridan's shoulder, "as long as I can have Sheridan as a partner."

Blaze's gaze flicked from Gray to Jake and back. "Actually, Jake already planned to ask Sher to be on his team, didn't you old buddy?"

"Sure did." Jake rose too, not missing Finn's pointed look as he pushed in his chair. The same look Finn had given him the night the dandy had arrived, when he'd called Blaze, Dash, and him into his office after everyone else had gone upstairs.

"Carmody's trouble, boys," Finn had said as soon as Jake had shut the door, the hard angle of his jaw a sure sign he was as unhappy with this new development as Jake was. "And we need to fix it—fast."

"And how exactly do you propose we do that, Uncle Finn?" Dash said as he perched on the corner of his uncle's massive burlwood desk. His thin smile slid to the left. "Besides a gunfight with Jake?"

A harsh laugh tripped from Finn's mouth as he cuffed the back of his neck. "Don't think I didn't consider it, boys, but I'm a mite worried how the womenfolk might take it." Expelling a weighty sigh, he sank back with a swoosh of leather and a clasp of hands, elbows taut on the arms of his chair. "I've done everything I can to protect that girl—from asking a professor friend of Libby's to keep an eye on her at school, to asking Aunt Marie to keep me informed of any young men who came to call." He grunted. "Although God knows that woman is in league with Libby when it comes to allowing Sheridan her freedom, so it's no wonder she didn't mention Grace's brother."

Looking like he'd aged years in only a day, Finn kneaded

his temple with his eyes closed. "And Sheridan swore to me last night right here in this office that Gray and she are nothing more than friends, so that should be some reassurance I suppose."

Friends. Jake gulped as memories of pushing Sheridan to the wall of the barn to kiss the daylights out of her came back to haunt. His mouth compressed. *Unfortunately, not as reassuring as one might hope.*

"But Carmody is just so blasted smug and defiant," Finn continued, "that I just can't help but worry because Sheridan has absolutely no experience with men whatsoever ..."

Jake averted his gaze as his facial muscles tightened. *Except with me and that Morgan character ...*

"So, I can see him worming his way into her heart," Finn said, "which we simply can't risk with another year of her school to go, agreed?"

"Agreed," they all echoed in response.

"So, what do you propose, Uncle Finn?" Blaze sat forward, hands loosely clasped between his knees.

Finn blasted out a noisy sigh. "Well, as much as I hate to resort to this, I think the severity of this situation warrants it, so if Jake will agree—"

Jake's head shot up, mouth gaping as wide as his eyes. "Sir?"

Sympathy carved extra lines in Finn's weathered face along with fatigue. "It's no secret that Sheridan's always had a fondness for you, Jake, and I know you two have become real good friends over this summer especially, so I was thinking ..."

He met Jake's gaze head-on, a rare petition deepening the light brown of Finn's eyes, the father figure who had restored much of Jake's hope and peace from a painful past. "That maybe you could, you know"— face puckered in an awkward manner, he bobbed his head lightly back and forth as if trying to come up with the right words—"pay a little more attention to her."

Jake blinked, fighting the drop of his jaw. "You want me to ... *flirt* with Sheridan?"

Blaze's chuckle merged with Dash's as the two of them grinned at Jake. "Well, I know you're no ladies' man, Sullivan," Blaze said with a smirk, "but Sher *has* always hankered after you, so a little flirting on your part might be just what she needs to tether her to home." He winked. "You know, like you always did when she was small? Flirting your fool head off and all those kisses during her dad-gum weddings Dash and I were forced to attend?"

Jake seared Blaze with a glare that only made him and Dash laugh.

Finn held up a palm. "Now, let's not get carried away here, boys," he said with a chuckle that carried a sliver of threat, "paying a little more attention will do just fine, Jake."

Jake's lips compressed, pinching back a grunt. *Wanna bet?*

"So, what do you say, son—are you willing to help us out here?"

Son. Swallowing hard, Jake gouged a thumb to the socket of his eye to ward off a headache.

There was a hint of desperation in Finn's voice. "You know, just enough to give our girl a little hope for one more year until she comes back home to us, safe and sound?"

"Come on, Jake," Dash tossed in with a wide grin, "as gun-shy as you are about women, you could use a little practice."

Jake cauterized both Dash and his brother with a nasty look, triggering even more laughter from his two 'ex-best friends' before he homed in on Finn with a deep draw of air. "Yes, sir, I would be happy to—"

"Liar," Blaze said with a chuckle, earning another scorching look from Jake.

Giving a gruff clear of throat, Jake met Finn's eyes once again. "—but only for you, sir."

"I appreciate that, son, more than I can say. I know you won't disappoint me."

The scrape of Carmody's chair jolted Jake back to the

present as the dandy rose to his feet, lacing his fingers through Sheridan's to tug her up as well. "Hate to disappoint you, *old buddy,* but 'plannin' ain't doing, cowboy, because Sheridan already promised to be my partner in the next tournament." He hooked an arm to Sheridan's waist, his challenging gaze never straying from Jake's as he leaned to press a kiss to Sheridan's hair. Isn't that so, Sugar Lips?"

Pink suffused Sheridan's cheeks as her gaze flicked to Finn with a nervous smile while she eased from Gray's hold. "Uh, about that nickname, Uncle Finn," she said with a nervous tug of her lip, "Grace and I made Sophia's mother's recipe for Mexican wedding ball cookies one day, and I got powdered sugar on my lips"—she gave a feeble shrug—"so Gray's teased me with that nickname ever since."

Finn took a slow sip of his coffee, his gaze cool. "Seems a bit too intimate for just friends, Sheridan Marie."

"Uh ... anyway," Sheridan said, quickly turning back to Jake with an apology in her eyes while she picked at her nails, "I did promise Gray to be partners with him in the next game, so maybe the next one after that?"

The smug look on Carmody's face lit Jake's fuse to white hot. Gaze flicking to Finn's scowl and back, he nudged his Stetson up with a slow smile straight out of the Blaze Donovan handbook. "Well, actually, Half-Pint," he said with a hand over his heart, "you're leaving me in two days' time, darlin', and I won't get to see you again till Christmas while college boy here"—he gave a stiff nod to Carmody—"will get to see you all the time. So, I was hopin' to spend as much time with you as I can before you go."

The blue eyes did a slow blink—once, and then twice— before a soft blush dusted her cheeks, and suddenly oblivious to everyone else around the table, Jake homed in on the woman he loved, willing her to read the deep affection in his eyes. "Please, Sheridan? For me?"

A knot ducked in her throat as she nodded, and Gray looped an arm around Grace's shoulder with a heavy sigh. "Well, I guess it's you and me then, sis," he said, directing a polite smile to Libby and Finn as everyone rose from the table to commence with the tournament. "Dinner was wonderful, Mayor and Mrs. McShane, as usual, so thank you again."

He motioned his head toward the cornhole platforms already set up in the backyard. "But it appears it's time to 'fling' for our supper, so to speak." Escorting both Grace and Sheridan down the wide set of steps that flared out to a well-kept meadow, he lobbed a cocky grin over his shoulder that spun Jake's spurs all the more. "And may the best man win."

"Count on it," Blaze said as he draped an arm around Jake's shoulder, cutting loose with a low chuckle that helped ease a touch of Jake's chagrin. "Because truth be told, old buddy"— Blaze gave his best friend an encouraging wink. "He already has."

CHAPTER SIXTY

"IT'S HARD TO BELIEVE YOU'RE leaving again in two days." Jake's voice was soft and low as he shredded a dandelion till his fingers stained yellow.

Sheridan bit back a smile, thinking Gray Carmody was a genius, given Jake's possessiveness all week. "I know," she whispered, a bit of melancholy settling in at leaving him and her family once again. Propped against a thick California oak, she sat beside Jake while they watched Gray and Grace go head-to-head with Blaze and Dash in the final leg of cornhole.

The sun slowly bled into the horizon with a scarlet tinge as she leaned her head against the smooth cracked bark of the tree. Boots crossed at the ankle, she absently threaded fingers through the wispy meadow grass on either side of her skirt.

Jake's sigh was quiet as he threw the frittered puffs of dandelion into the air, work-roughened hands dropping to rest just inches from hers, twice her size as they tunneled into the grass too. "I'm … going to miss you, Sher." She caught her breath when his pinky inched over to tangle with hers, pooling heat in her belly. "Are you going to miss me?" His voice was low and gruff with emotion, shallowing her air.

Oh, Jake, with all of my heart! "Of course I am," she said softly, her words as breathless as she while she trained her gaze on Gray and Grace, too afraid to peek at Jake lest he see the lovesick look on her face. All at once, Gray glanced their way and gave her a wink, and her lips tipped up in a gentle smile, making her wish her uncle and brothers could know him for the lovable friend that he was.

"Are you … you know … as close to him as you are to

me?" There was a thread of hurt in Jake's tone that pulled her gaze to his, her heart thumping at the possessive look of love in his eyes.

A look of love so potent, she was compelled to lift a hand to skim her fingers along his stubbled jaw. "Oh, Jake, Gray is a dear friend whom I've definitely grown to love, but I'm *in love* with you, the dearest friend I've ever known."

His Adam's apple jerked hard as he cupped his hand over hers with a gentle squeeze. "Me too," he whispered, eyes caressing her face with such tenderness, a shiver of warmth skittered her skin. His gaze dropped to her lips, and heat purled through her so strong, she thought she might faint.

He glanced up to where Gray was cheering his sister's successful throws, and that hard-sculpted jaw calcified a hair. "Do you … think you could ever fall in love with him?"

She followed his line of sight to Gray and knew she should answer quickly to put his fears to rest, but the warmth and want he'd just unleashed begged for putting her own fears to rest as well. Fears of never being able to let another man in her heart, just like Jake would never let her into his. Of never getting married because her heart was already taken by someone who never would.

"I have to be honest with you, Sher, and tell you that despite my love and attraction for you, I have no intention of ever getting married—"

"Sher?"

She jerked her attention back, pretty sure the worry etched in his handsome face matched hers to a wrinkle. "I don't know, Jake," she whispered, gaze dropping to where his massive hand covered hers. The same hands that had always held her, comforted her since she'd been a little girl. And, she thought with a dangerous thud of her pulse, the same hands that had set her skin on fire with every hungry touch. She slowly looked up, heart wrenching in her chest. "Because nobody knows the future."

A loud whoop broke her reverie, and quietly slipping her

hand from beneath his, she looked up to where Gray was twirling Grace high in the air, their laughter all but echoing off the mountain walls.

"Looks like they won," Jake said with a flat smile, the same regret she heard in his voice producing a dull ache deep in her heart.

"Yes, it definitely does." She took his extended hand as he helped her up, forcing a bright smile that masked the sadness she suddenly felt.

And we lost ...

CHAPTER SIXTY-ONE

"THUNDERATION, SULLY, YOU *HAVE* TO!" Blaze stood there, hands perched low on his thighs and a dad-gum ridge in his brow that matched the plea in his tone.

"No, Blaze, I *don't*," Jake snapped, taking careful aim on the tin cans lined up at the ranch's shooting range at Silver Lake, where Blaze and Dash had tricked him into an hour of target practice to 'vent their frustration' over Carmody's threat to Sher. He picked off his six on the log farthest away with his usual precision, but Dash and Blaze's strong-arming stole some of the satisfaction he always derived from blasting the cans to smithereens.

Just like he wished he could do to their blasted request.

"But you're our only hope, Jake," Blaze continued, following him around while he retrieved more ammunition from the wagon. "After Sher leaves tomorrow, she's as good as gone from this family if she ups and marries that dandy, who's nothing but a womanizer. Believe me, I can spot 'em a mile away."

"And Blaze knows what he's talking about, too, because as we all know, he used to be one." Grinning, Dash finished his turn at a row of cans closer in than Jake's, nailing six out of six since he had fine-tuned his shooting skills in case they were needed as bartender at the Ponderosa Saloon. He moseyed back to reload, his grin veering toward dry with a near scowl. "Not to mention Grace told me how 'thrilled' she'd be if Sher married her brother because he, and I quote, 'needs to settle down instead of flitting around with every woman he meets.'"

Jake glanced up from the wagon, hand frozen on his Colt

45 as he squinted at Dash. "She said that?"

"Yep." Dash casually reloaded his Smith & Wesson, gaze never budging from Jake's. "*And* that hopefully Sher would help tone down his gambling problem too."

A rare curse defiled the bright sunny day as Jake slammed a fist to the wagon, his memory of their conversation at the cornhole tournament rearing its head.

"Do you ... think you could ever fall in love with him?"

"I don't know, Jake," she'd whispered with a pained look in her eyes, *"Since nobody knows the future."*

A low groan scraped past his lips as he gouged taut fingers through his hair. Sher would *never* fall for a clown like that. His heart skipped a beat.

Would she?

Swallowing the fear in his throat, he opted for the calm and steady approach. "I don't like him either," he said quietly, unwilling to toy with Sheridan's feelings any more than he already had, "but Sher's smarter than that, and I think she'll do the right thing." He nodded toward the targets. "You're up, Donovan."

Blaze gripped Jake's arm, obviously not interested in target practice.

Jake stifled a grunt. *Unless the target is me.*

"The right thing?" The whites of Blaze's eyes expanded, as if he were about to blow. "Then, tell me, Sully—did she do the right thing by sneaking off and kissing on Morgan?"

Jake's eyelids slammed closed, battling the jealousy that Blaze had just stoked all over again. His voice was as tight as his fists, the fight in him rearing its ugly head once again over thoughts of Morgan's lips on Sher's. But he'd vowed to never go there again, to where the hate and bitterness took control, so he forced his fists to relax, flexing his fingers. "She swore to Finn that they were just friends."

"And you *believe* that?" Blaze ripped his hat off and hurled it onto the wagon. "That snake belly told Finn he plans to marry her, for crying out loud!"

Jake stared at the gun in his hand, suddenly seeing Carmody's face in the sight as the dandy's words circled in his brain like a threat.

"I'm the man who plans to marry your niece."

He squeezed his eyes shut, wishing he'd never fallen in love with a sweet, four-year-old little girl. He tried to swallow, but his throat was too thick with emotion. "Even so, she has a right to marry whomever she wants."

Blaze jerked Jake's arm, whirling him around. "And that's *you*, Sully, whether you like it or not, which means you are— once again—the one who can keep our sister safe."

His Adam's apple ducked hard in his throat as the memory of their last few kisses scalded the back of his neck. His voice was barely a croak. "I wouldn't bet on it."

Dash hooked an arm over Jake's shoulder, his voice a whole lot calmer than his brother's. "Come on, Sul—you love her—you told us so. Would it be so hard to sacrifice what you want to keep her safe?"

"Yes!" He slung Dash's arm off his shoulder, eyes on fire as he glared him down. "Because I do love her, confound it, which is why I don't want to lead her on, Dash, breaking her heart in the end. You both know I don't want to get married, so doing what you're asking me to do would just hurt her."

Blaze's chin nudged up, his voice deadly low. "Better than some sweet-talkin' Casanova hurting her, Jake, don't you think?"

A harsh groan ached in Jake's throat as he slashed shaky fingers through his hair. He was no good for Sheridan, but nobody knew that but him because he couldn't tell anybody why.

"I pity any woman you marry, Jacob, because it's the kiss of death ..."

The kiss of death. His mother's words stabbed, a premonition of each and every kiss he and Sheridan had shared, reminding him all over again of the promises he'd made.

To himself.

To God.

And to Finn.

"Outside of Blaze and Dash, there's no one I trust more to protect Sheridan, so don't let me down, you hear?"

And he wouldn't.

A long, weary sigh of surrender seeped through his lips. Which meant Blaze and Dash were right, because first, he needed to protect her from the dandy.

And *then* he'd protect her from himself.

Mauling the bridge of his nose, he finally leveled a threatening finger at both Blaze and Dash, his words grinding through gritted teeth. "This-is-the-last-time," he bit out, swearing to himself he would leave Silver Lining Ranch if that's what it took to keep these two clowns from forcing his hand. "Then I tell her at Christmas that I can't marry any one *ever*, because I refuse to go on hurting someone I love, you hear?" Jaw locked, he extended his hand. "And I'm not doing it until you both shake on it."

Blaze and Dash exchanged looks before Blaze released a noisy sigh, returning Jake's grip. "All right, Sully, you got it," he said quietly, shaking Jake's hand before stepping aside to allow Dash to do the same. "That leaves only five months left we have to worry about, so that's as good as we're going to get, I guess. At least you bought us a year and a half of insurance, so this'll have to do." He gripped Jake's shoulder with a sympathetic smile. "All we ask is you just work your magic, old buddy, whatever the devil that is."

Jake buried a grunt. *You don't want to know, old buddy.* Sloughing off Blaze's arm, he stepped up to the shooting line and obliterated each and every one of Blaze's unused cans so fast, the smoke of burned powder tainted the air.

Stalking back to the wagon, he unloaded the casings from the cylinder and jammed his revolver into his holster before striding toward Midnight to mount up. Staring both Blaze and Dash down, he bludgeoned a stiff finger in the air. "But I want you to know that I'm going to make good and sure your sister knows you two put me up to this the entire time because I'm darn sick and tired of being the heavy with someone I love, you got it?"

"Yeah, we got it," Blaze muttered as he and Dash watched Jake, their once easy-going friend, jerk his horse around and gallop away, kicking up plenty of dust in his wake. A long weary sigh drifted from Blaze's mouth as he and Dash stared into the cloud of dirt. "But what we don't get, Sully," he said with a hard clamp of his jaw that matched his brother's to a rock, "is if you love her so dad-gum much, why in the devil don't you marry her?"

CHAPTER SIXTY-TWO

GOD HELP ME, I DON'T want to do this. Jake stood at the back entrance of the barn in the dark, staring up at a moon so bright, he didn't even need to light a lamp.

And yet, God help me I do ...

Somewhere a hoot owl called to its mate, the haunting sound in perfect sync with Jake's somber mood as he expelled a melancholy sigh. Because truth be told, there was a part of him—the lonely part—that was more than willing to pretend a little longer that Sheridan could actually be his.

But he knew better, even if Blaze and Dash did not. Because there was another part of him—the larger part—that despised destroying all the progress they'd made being just friends, as much as he despised getting her hopes up again.

He paused to listen while a heady warmth swirled through his body. Somehow he sensed her coming long before she actually entered the barn because he'd always had a sixth sense when it came to Sheridan, his body a compass and she his true north. Blaze had promised to knock on her bedroom door and send her down like he'd done the last time so Jake could say "goodbye."

Or in Jake's mind, the prelude to *goodbye* ...

"Jake?"

He spun around and for the hundredth time this summer, he marveled at how the little girl he always loved had blossomed into a woman, almost overnight. Yes, her body had burgeoned at sixteen, but it hadn't been till this summer that he saw the emergence of the woman behind the little girl. "Sorry to pull you out of bed at this late hour, Sher, but I"—he couldn't fight the bob of his throat—"wanted to say goodbye more privately ... more personally than with the whole family hanging around."

"I'm glad," she said with that sweet and tender smile that somehow always seemed the same, whether from the little girl or the woman, it was uniquely Sheridan. Robe modestly buttoned all the way to her neck, she moved into the barn until she stood beside him at the back door, joining in on studying the moon and stars with arms hugged to her waist. "It's beautiful out tonight, and Grace and I were just gabbing in bed, so this is nice—a chance to talk alone before I leave."

"I agree." Gently taking her hand, he led her out the back door to where he'd place two bales of hay against the barn wall, facing the Sierra Nevada mountains. Majestic boulders jagged high into the indigo sky like inky shadows, where moonlight illuminated craggy patches of snow. "I thought we could sit and drink in the Sierras while we talked," he said quietly, the majesty of their powerful beauty creating a reverence that somehow seemed appropriate for what he wanted to say. "Since I'm pretty sure Poughkeepsie has nothing like this."

Her chuckle was as soft as the moonlight while she sat beside him on her own bale that he'd covered with a horse blanket, leaning back against the wall with knees tented and arms propped on top. "Not even close, although the Hudson Valley is very pretty, but with much tamer and low-lying mountain ranges." A sigh drifted from her lips. "But I sure am going to miss the Sierras, my family, and"—she turned to offer a gentle smile—"you, my friend."

Friend.

Something Jake desperately wanted but now had to sacrifice for the greater good.

Sacrifice? He smothered a grunt as he reached to twine her hand in his, resting them on the bale between them. As if being near Sheridan, loving Sheridan, could ever be a sacrifice. No, the true sacrifice would come at Christmas, when he would have to tell her the truth *again*—once and for all—dashing any hope he might stir tonight, along with their precious friendship.

"I'm going to miss you, too, Sher," he said quietly, the sweet smell of hay mingling with her light lavender scent to embed a beautiful memory in his mind.

Forever.

Voices soft and low, they chatted easily about everything, just like in their letters—books recently read, national politics, school, the ranch—and Jake wished more than anything they could always be this way. His chest rose and fell in a melancholy mood. But things would have to change—first tonight—and then again come Christmas.

All at once, he realized that if he was being forced to do this against his will, then by heaven's gate, he wanted to enjoy *every* single moment. If Blaze and Dash had strong-armed him into tethering Sher's heart to his in order to bring her back home, he made up his mind right then and there to make the most of it. His jaw stiffened along with his resolve. By channeling all of his love into the effort, no matter the loss to come later.

Because just once in his sorry life, he wanted to experience her love freely.

Without regret.

Without guilt.

And without restraint stopping him from letting her know just how much he adored her.

"Sher, I want you to know that our friendship is one of the most precious things to me in this world, and I have enjoyed every single moment we've had this summer"—he gave her hand a gentle squeeze as he captured her gaze with his own—"except one."

She blinked, her peaceful smile dimming as her brows sloped up in concern. "What's that, Jake?"

He softly skimmed the palm of her hand with his thumb. "Remember when I asked if you thought you could ever fall in love with Gray?"

She nodded, throat shifting as she stared at his hand over hers, her breathing suddenly shallow.

His finger slowly grazed the length of hers. "You said you didn't know, and I have to admit, Sher, that bothered me a lot."

Her gaze rose to meet his, as skittish as that sweet, little doe he found trapped in barbwire out on the south forty just last week. "Why?" she whispered with a hard duck of her throat, "if we're just friends?"

His heart melted at the little-girl look in her eyes, the same one he fell in love with when she was just a mite with dirt on her face. He absently traced up and down the shape of her fingers, and his pulse ricocheted when a shiver traveled her body. "Because we're not just friends," he whispered, "are we, Sher?"

He heard the catch of her breath. "W-What are y-you saying, J-Jake?" she whispered, her voice as hoarse as his when he turned to face her, taking both of her hands in his.

"What I'm saying is"—his heart swelled with the truth of his feelings, and slowly tugging her to him, he held her close, eyes squeezed tight while he lay his head against hers, breathing in the lavender scent of her hair—"that I ache inside at the thought of you loving anyone else."

She pulled back to search his eyes, cupping his jaw in her tiny hand. "But what does that mean, Jake?"

Heart pounding, he cradled her face, thumbs grazing her cheeks as he studied every beautiful feature. "It means that for once in my life, Sheridan Marie, I want to be able to tell you—and show you—exactly how I feel without fear of what it may mean down the road."

He swallowed hard as he traced the shape of her lips with his thumb. "Gently, reverently, like my feelings for you. So will you let me, Sheridan? Will you let me show you what's buried deep in my heart? What I would act on in a heartbeat if I wasn't a broken man?"

All air seized in his throat for several painful seconds when water welled in her eyes, and then before he could draw in his next breath, she flung herself into his arms. Clinging to his neck, she lunged to kiss him, the taste of her lips completely ruining him for the slow and gentle kiss he'd meant to give when it unleashed a groan from deep in his soul.

"God help me, Sheridan, I love you," he whispered, joy pumping through him as he buried his lips in the crook of her neck, feasting on the silk of her skin, the soft lobe of her ear, fingers lost and tangled in flaxen waves, as if he couldn't get enough.

And God help him, he couldn't because Blaze and Dash had opened the floodgates to a love long denied, and with everything in him, Jake wanted this woman to know that she possessed him body and soul and always would.

No matter their fate.

"Oh, Jake, I love you too," she rasped, her breathing as fevered as his as she clung with all of her might.

He eased back to gently palm her hair away from her face, pulse ricocheting at how right this all seemed in the moment. As if he'd waited for her all of his life, and she him. Wonder purled through him while he slowly nuzzled her mouth, caressing her skin, her throat with a tenderness that belonged only to her.

Her tiny mew of pleasure completely undid him, seducing him with the need to explore more deeply, and forgetting all else, he did, the taste of Sheridan and peppermint sweet to his senses. Chest heaving, he cradled her face in his hands, both fire and fear licking through him when he realized he would do anything for this woman.

Including living without her.

A smile trembled on her beautiful lips, swollen with the need they both shared with each other. Reaching to graze a shaky finger down the curve of his jaw, she peered up with a sheen of hope in her eyes. "So, what does this mean for us, Jake?" she whispered.

Adam's apple ducking hard, he brushed the tenderest of

kisses to her lips, eyes closed as he lingered to memorize the moment. "It means that right now, Sheridan, in this fragile moment, I want you to know that my heart will always be yours."

He carefully swept golden strands over her shoulder, aching to the depths of his soul that this miracle couldn't last forever. "And although I long for you and continue to pray for you regarding the path that's ahead for us both"—he gently tugged her closer, resting his head against hers as he softly stroked her hair—"you were right when you said nobody knows the future, darlin', because life gives no guarantees." His ribcage squeezed with the most painful heartache he'd ever known. "So forgive me darlin', *please*—because neither can I."

Her body stiffened before she wound her arms around him as if she would never let go. "Then what do you want from me, Jake?" Her voice was a hoarse whisper.

Squeezing his eyes shut, he gripped her as hard as she gripped him, heart constricting with a love as potent as his regret. He swallowed hard as his voice broke on the lie.

"I want you to wait."

CHAPTER SIXTY-THREE

"**S**O … DID GRAY'S PLAN work?" Grace closed the book in her lap as she sat up in bed, eyes wide while she watched Sheridan quietly enter their bedroom.

A lovesick smile tiptoed across Sheridan's lips as she silently clicked the door behind her. "Like a charm," she said with a lovesick sigh, unbuttoning her robe before hanging it up in the closet.

Giggling, Grace snuggled back down under the covers. "I knew it would, and so did Gray. It was pure genius on his part to tell me to mention his 'gambling problem' to Dash in passing"—she actually winked—"even if it was only pitching pennies at the age of eight, as well as his 'flitting' around with every woman he meets."

Sheridan smiled as she slipped into bed, tugging the covers up to her neck like Grace. "Your brother is brilliant, no doubt about that."

"So, tell me," Grace said as she rolled on her side, elbow propped to the pillow. "Did he promise anything more?"

Sheridan's wispy sigh lingered in the air as she stared at the ceiling, not sure if she should be happy or sad about the outcome. "No, he was evasive as ever, but at least he kissed me good and proper like before." Her nightgown rose and fell as she clasped her hands to her chest. "But I do believe I can make it all the way to Christmas on those kisses alone."

Grace chuckled. "Well, after what I told Libby about Gray, I wouldn't be surprised if there's a promise or two from Jake in your stocking come Christmas, my friend."

Sheridan glanced over with a crimp in her brow. "Why? What did you tell Aunt Libby?"

Grace nibbled on the edge of her smile. "Just what Gray told me to tell her, although I will admit, I did lay it on a little thick, saying I was so grateful for you in Gray's life because with his reputation for gambling and womanizing, he really needed a good influence from a girl."

Sheridan's jaw dropped open in a chuckle. "Well, that should put the fear of God in Uncle Finn, I hope." Her smile faded a hair as she expelled a weary breath. "But goodness, what I wouldn't give to talk to Maggie and Aunt Libby about all of this, though, because I hate keeping secrets from them." Her smile compressed. "But that mule of a man made me spit swear not to tell the family or Sophia and Kathy Jean anything about our relationship."

Mischief twinkled in Grace's eyes. "But that didn't include me."

Sheridan grinned. "Nope, not you, thank God, or Gray either," she said, so very grateful for the two dear friends with whom she could share her feelings.

"So, how did you leave it with Jake?" Grace asked, excitement tingeing her tone.

Sheridan stared at the ceiling, the memory of Jake's words suddenly bleeding some of the joy from her voice. "He wants me to wait," she whispered.

"Wait?" Grace studied Sheridan's profile with a thread of confusion in her voice. "What do you mean 'wait'?"

"It means he doesn't want to risk losing me to Gray," she said quietly, thinking that should assure her of his love, but somehow it didn't.

"So, wait for what—till you graduate before he can promise more?"

"I'm not really sure, Grace," Sheridan said softly, Jake's words still haunting her mind.

"You were right when you said nobody knows the future, darlin', because life gives no guarantees. So forgive me darlin', please—because neither can I."

No guarantees.

No promises.

"What do you mean, you're not sure?" Grace probed, two indents above her nose.

Sheridan turned on her side to face her good friend, matching her posture with an elbow to her pillow. "I mean that although he told me he loves me and that his heart will always be mine, he said that life gives no guarantees for the future."

"Ha!" A rare grunt popped from Grace's lips. "Which means *he* gives no guarantees for the future, pretty much giving him what *he* wants in having you stay away from other men while he gives nothing in return."

"That's not exactly true"—Sheridan absently fiddled with the corner of her pillow, wandering into a melancholy stare. "He finally gave his love to me tonight ..."

"With words and kisses, Sheridan," Grace said with a shake of Sheridan's shoulder, "which does not a marriage make, and ultimately, that's what you want, right?"

Sheridan squinted at her friend. "Yes, of course, but I also want to make Jake happy."

"Of course you do," Grace said with a tight clasp of Sheridan's hand, "but there's only one way to truly make Jake happy, my friend, as we've discussed many times before, and that's with 'the plan,' remember?"

The plan. To heal Jake's heart from the pain of the past. Sheridan's rib cage suddenly relaxed with a peace that Jake's words and actions hadn't been able to bestow. *So he could finally embrace the joy of his future.*

Even if that wasn't with her.

Hope stung in her eyes as she lunged to squeeze her dear friend in a tight hug. "Oh, Grace, what on earth would I do without you?"

A soft chuckle floated in the moonlit room as Grace embraced Sheridan right back. "Why, the very same thing you'd do *with* me, my sweet friend, right now." She gave Sheridan's waist a playful pinch. "First pray ... and then plan."

CHAPTER SIXTY-FOUR

"**G**OT A MINUTE, SIR?" JAKE stood at the mayor's office door in City Hall, hat in hand as he assessed the stacks of papers on Finn's desk. "I can come back if you're busy ..."

Finn waved him in with a tired smile, the dark circles under his eyes confirming that the loss of his town marshal last week in a bank-robbery shoot-out had taken its toll. "No, Jake, come on in, please. I could use a break," he said laying his spectacles on his desk before he sagged back with a heavy sigh, gaze trailing off into a distant stare laced with grief. "I never fully realized just how much Cyrus handled on behalf of Virginia City or what an amazing asset he actually was to our town."

Jake lowered into one of several rickety chairs in front of Finn's well-worn desk, the sorrow in Finn's tone akin to that in Jake's chest since he'd first heard the news. "How's Abigail doing?" he asked just above a whisper, well aware that Marshal Cyrus Tanner's widow had literally broken down when Finn had told her. She'd been confined to bed after Doc Ritter gave her something to help her sleep.

"Not good." Finn massaged the bridge of his nose as he sagged into his chair, glancing up with the same hollow look he'd worn since the tragedy had taken place. "Her sister is taking her back to Ohio where her family lives, leaving on the train tomorrow."

"I'm glad. This town can't hold many good memories for her after all the times Cyrus has been hurt over the years. It's too bad they never had children of their own, but at least there's nothing keeping her here now." Jake expelled a cumbersome sigh as he quietly twiddled with his hat, Abigail's loss reopening wounds of his own from a past all too similar. He swallowed hard as he numbly stared at the floor. "Family will be good for her."

"Yeah," Finn said, resting his head on the back of his chair with a sad smile. "Abigail told Libby once that it was just as well the good Lord didn't see fit to send them any children. Claimed Cyrus's job was so dangerous, it was hard enough on her, much less a child."

"Yeah." Jake's eyelids lumbered closed while emotion thickened in his throat.

"So." The casters of Finn's chair squealed as if he were wheeling closer. Glancing up, Jake watched as his boss and mentor laid forearms on his desk with hands clasped, suddenly all business. The intensity of his gaze probed as if he already knew why Jake was there. "What can I do for you, son?"

Jake drew in a bolstering breath as he met Finn's direct gaze. "I'd like to apply for Cyrus's job," he said quietly, never surer that *this* was exactly what he needed to do.

Finn never even blinked. "Mind if I ask why?"

Carefully placing his hat on the edge of the desk, Jake leaned back to sit straight up, elbows resting on the arms of his chair and hands folded like Finn. "Because first and foremost, sir, you need a marshal. Secondly, because I'm one of the fastest guns in the state. And thirdly, because"—he looked away—"I need to forge a life of my own."

Finn paused, and Jake could almost feel the penetration of his mentor's unwavering stare. "Are you unhappy at Silver Lining Ranch, Jake?"

"No, sir." He focused on his hat as he twirled it slowly, reluctant for the man he respected more than any other to see the near-lie in his eyes. "I just think it's time to be on my own"—he paused to swallow hard—"both with a job and with a home."

"I see." Finn's chair squeaked once again, indicating he

was settling back in for a talk. "This wouldn't have anything to do with Sheridan's departure, would it?"

Jake's head jolted up, fire licking up the back of his neck. "No, sir," he said firmly, Finn's intense scrutiny making him squirm enough to look away with a duck of his throat. *Maybe.* Bowing his head, he kneaded his forehead with the ball of his hand. *Okay, mostly.*

He gave a gruff clear of his throat before he met his gaze again. "I will admit, it's a little lonely with Sheridan gone, sir, because as you know, she and I have gotten to be close friends. Add to that the fact that both Blaze and you have recently gotten married, and well"—he cuffed the back of his neck with a strained smile, hoping to deflect his awkwardness with a little humor—"sometimes there's so much ... well, you know, *togetherness* ... going on that I feel like a rooster at a hen party."

Finn smiled. "There's always Dash, you know, so you don't have to feel like odd man out, Jake."

A smile tugged at Jake's lips, relaxing him somewhat. "That's true, sir," he said with an idle scratch of his temple, his smile sliding into a grin, "because if ever there was an 'odd man out,' it would be Dash Donovan. I swear that boy is married to his job, so he's not even around half the time."

"No, that's true," Finn said with a slow nod, smile fading somewhat as his eyes trailed into a melancholy stare, his regret over Dash's chosen profession as evident as the lines of fatigue in his face. His gaze flicked up beneath weary lids. "Does Blaze know about this? Your interest in leaving the ranch?"

Jake almost winced, knowing this would be a blow to his best friend. "No, sir. I thought I'd check with you first, to see if you'd even consider me for the job."

A harsh chuckle erupted from Finn's mouth while he kneaded the deep crimp above his nose. "Consider you?" He shook his head as he offered Jake a lax smile laced with affection. "If I had my pick of any man in the state, son, you'd be at the top of the list. What I didn't consider, however, is you ever being interested. Truth be told, you're like a son to me, Jake, and a brother to my nieces and nephews, so I just assumed you were happy being a part of our family, part of the Silver Lining Ranch."

"And I *have* been, sir," Jake said in a rush, leaning forward to grip taut fingers on the edge of Finn's desk, "from the moment you took me in. Happier than I ever dreamed possible." He inhaled sharply as he sat back again, expelling it in one, long, depleted sigh as his gaze bore into the front of Finn's desk, seeing only the past he'd sought to leave behind. "And certainly happier than I deserved."

"Jake."

He looked up, cursing the burn of moisture at the back of his lids.

"You're one of the finest men I know, son, and a better influence on my two nephews than I could have ever hoped to be, although God knows I tried."

"No, sir—your nephews revere you."

He smiled. "Yes, I know they love and respect me, but my faith has always put them off, Jake, and you know it. At least till Maggie brought Blaze around. But you?" Jake looked down at his hat, unable to bear the quiet look of respect in Finn's eyes because God knows he didn't deserve it. "You earned their respect from the moment you arrived, with a quiet faith that quickly earned mine as well, and I want you to know, son—you will be sorely missed."

Jake's head shot up, his parted lips emitting uneven breaths. "Sir, are you saying—"

"That the job is yours if you want it, Jake, providing you answer one question first."

"Yes, sir?" Jake stared, his breathing growing more ragged by the moment.

Finn paused, his wise eyes searching Jake's face with true affection. "Have you prayed about it?"

Jake blinked, not exactly sure how to answer that. Had he

prayed about staying away from temptation with Sheridan? *Most definitely.* Had he prayed for an answer to side-track any notion of marriage with her? *Unequivocally.* But had he prayed about applying for the sheriff position and leaving Silver Lining Ranch? He gulped. *Not exactly.*

He scuffed the back of his head. "Well, I've certainly prayed about these unsettled feelings I've been having, sir, like I expressed to you earlier, so when Cyrus"—his Adam's apple hitched in his throat over the fact that Cyrus was actually gone—"well, I mean ... when his job opened up ... I just saw it as an answer to my prayers."

His gaze lifted to lock onto Finn's, the gratitude in his heart bringing an unwanted sheen to his eyes. "Because it's no secret that losing a marshal in a town like Virginia City is a difficult situation for you at best, sir, and a dangerous one at worst. So I see this as the opportunity I've prayed about for years, to somehow thank you for all that you've done for me in my life."

The sudden glaze in Finn's eyes left Jake undone, and steeling his jaw, he battled his emotion with a firm heft of his chin. "So, let me do this Mayor McShane, *please*—for you and for me—because you saved my life, sir, in more ways than one, and I'd like a chance to pay you back."

"You've paid me back a thousand times over, Jake, with your unbridled love and respect, so this is hardly necessary. But I am in dire need of a marshal, and you are just what I want, so how about we give it a trial run for six months or so?"

Jake bounded up from the chair to extend his hand, heart pounding in his chest. "I can't thank you enough, Finn, because you're saving my life once again."

"Somehow I doubt that, son, but we'll just consider this an equal trade, all right? I need a marshal, and you need a break from the ranch, so I consider this a gift from heaven."

Jake expelled a silent sigh. *You have no idea, sir.*

Finn reached across his desk to rifle through a stack of

papers, finally pulling several sheets from the stack. He slid them across the desk to Jake. "I've already sent word to several U.S. Marshal and sheriff friends of mine regarding my need for a marshal since Deputy Wilcox didn't want the job, but that's easily fixed with a letter. So, here's the application I need you to fill out, Jake, along with the job description and salary." He gave a nod toward the papers Jake picked up. "You'll be as surprised as I was at just how much Cyrus did for this town. Not only did he keep the peace, but he hired deputies, formed posses, conducted hangings when warranted, and last but not least," he said with a faint smile, "served as county tax collector, not to mention working closely with me on many city matters."

Excitement rushed through Jake's veins like adrenaline as he studied the papers. "It sounds like just the change of pace I've been looking for, sir, so thank you."

"No, thank *you*, son." Finn pulled a calendar out of his desk drawer to study. "Let's give you a week or so to settle things up with Blaze at the ranch, then plan on starting two weeks from today, all right? You can bring those papers with you all filled out if you will."

"Yes, sir."

"That'll give us time to have Cyrus's house spruced up a bit before you move in, but you can plan on doing that on Saturday."

Jake blinked. "Sir?"

Finn grinned. "One of the few perks in your job, Jake, and believe me, you'll more than earn it." He scratched the back of his neck with a fond smile. "That cottage off F Street on the edge of town wasn't much to look at before Cyrus and Abigail moved in over fifteen years ago. But now it's a right pretty little cottage thanks to all the work they did, although I suppose it could use a fresh coat of paint on both the house and fence."

He shot Jake a wink. "But it does have a double bed in a private bedroom, which is a sight better than sleeping in a bunkhouse cot with twenty smelly hands, I'll wager. You won't have to put up with the other boys' snoring anymore, but you *will* have to make your own meals. Although," he said with a hint of a twinkle in his eyes, "I'm sure the single ladies in this town will be more than happy to provide an endless stream of casseroles and what not, so I'm not too worried about you."

Jake stared, suddenly worried enough for the both of them.

"Unless, of course," Finn continued, you want to trek out to the ranch for an occasional dinner because you're always welcome, Jake, so I hope you know that. You're family, son, blood-related or not, which means you're expected for family dinner every Sunday as usual and holidays, too, understood?"

Jake offered a grateful smile. "Thank you, sir."

"Well …"—Finn slapped two palms on his desk—"I think that about covers all you need to know for now, so unless you have any further questions, I'll let you get back to the ranch for a far, far more difficult job." He winked. "Giving Blaze your notice."

CHAPTER SIXTY-FIVE

"*WHEEEEEEEE!!*" SWEET WENDELL PAXTON SQUEALED with delight as Gray swept him up in the air horizontally, bracing the little guy's chest and belly while the boy spread his arms like a bird. Autumn leaves of gold and scarlet floated down from several oak and maple trees overhead while Wendell floated in the air, a contest as to who was laughing louder—Wendell or Grayson Carmody.

Grinning in front of Professor McCall's phaeton, Sheridan stood side by side with her teacher while Gray delivered his promised reward if Wendell passed his riding test on his final lesson of the year. Five other children literally jumped up and down inside the teacher's vehicle, cheering the little boy on while everyone's laughter rose in the air along with Wendell.

Shaking her head as Gray dipped him up and down in waves while they both whirled 'round and 'round, Sheridan grinned, not sure who was more the little boy—Wendell or Gray.

"All right, Mr. Donovan," Professor McCall said with a chuckle, "I think Mr. Wendell is sufficiently dizzy, and if he's not, Miss Donovan and I certainly are."

With a final dip and a noisy "whooshing" sound, Gray landed Wendell on the ground in front of the phaeton. The children's giggles merged with Sheridan's and the professor's when the poor little guy stumbled around like a drunken cowboy at the Silver Pistol Saloon, with Gray not far behind.

"Gee whiz, thanks, Mr. Carmody—that was fun!"

"It was, wasn't it?" Gray said with a grin, tousling the little boy's red hair till it stood straight up on end. Sheridan bit back a smile. Not unlike Gray's at the moment, after an afternoon of working with orphans, spending more time giving them horsey rides at a gallop than teaching them to ride.

"Well, thank you, Miss Donovan and Mr. Carmody, once again for an excellent lesson," the professor said as Gray hoisted Wendell up into the phaeton with the other children, "and please tell Miss Carmody that we dearly missed her and hope she gets well soon."

"We will, Professor McCall." Sheridan reached up to give Wendell a quick hug goodbye, the little guy squeezing her so tightly, she almost hated to let him go.

"I won't see you again till after the holidays, young man," Sheridan whispered in his ear, so you have a wonderful Thanksgiving and Christmas for me, all right?"

"I love you, Miss Donovan," Wendell whispered back, and it was all Sheridan could do not to melt into a weepy puddle.

"Grayson," Professor McCall said with a stern heft of her chin despite a trace of a twinkle in her eyes. "I insist you take Miss Donovan inside for a cup of Cecilia's famous hot cocoa before you take her home, is that clear, young man?"

"Yes, ma'am." Gray stood to attention in front of his distant cousin, his eyes sparkling as much as the teacher's.

"Then I will see you both next Saturday for our usual lessons and *you*, Miss Donovan, in class on Monday. Good day to you both."

Sheridan waved, then blew kisses to the children. "Goodbye, Profes—*OHHH!!*" The breath suddenly whooshed from her lungs when Gray swooped her up like he had Wendell, causing giggles of shock to bubble up while she extended her arms to fly.

The heat of exhilaration pulsed in her cheeks, both from the brisk October air *and* the clasp of Gray's hands beneath her lower rib cage and stomach. She could hear the children's laughter and clapping before the phaeton disappeared around the corner, and when Gray finally stopped, she was completely out of breath.

"Grayson Horatio!" she shrieked when he set her down,

his hands welded to her waist to steady her while their bodies met, nearly flush. "You are incorrigible, mister!"

"But exciting, Miss Donovan, yes?" He made no effort to release his hold as he grinned down at her, so close, it put a crick in her neck just to look up.

"For Wendell, yes, Mr. Carmody," she responded with a dry smile, pulse clipping double time at his close proximity. Her palms pressed flat against his rock-hard chest to push him away.

Gray and Grace were affectionate people, both with each other and their grandmother, *and* with Sheridan, so she was used to his hugs and casual kisses to her head or cheek. *When Grace was around.*

But she'd never been alone-*alone* with just Gray before, and his nearness suddenly left her more than a little unsettled. "But for a grown woman flapping in the air like a duck?" She gave him a firm shove, dislodging his hold from her waist with a giant step back, hands plunked to her hips. "I think it qualifies as manhandling, sir."

"Well, I *am* a man, Miss Donovan," he said with a wink as he offered his arm to escort her inside the white estate house blanketed in ivy, where Professor McCall lived, "and heaven knows I love to handle women, so your point is well taken."

Lips pursed to restrain a smile, Sheridan wagged a finger in his handsome face. "Behave, Grayson Carmody, or I shall report you to your sister."

Laughing, he gave her finger a gentle tug before hooking a loose arm over her shoulder to usher her to the elegant country house surrounded by colorful oaks. "Let's go torment Cecilia till she gives us hot cocoa."

"Ha!" Sheridan said as they entered the paned, white wooden door beneath the pillared portico. Reminiscent of an elegant farm home, the estate house boasted blue shutters adorning two stories of windows and wings on both sides. "Torment for me, you mean, watching you fawn and flirt all over that poor girl." She unbuttoned her coat as she sniffed the air, the mouthwatering smell of fresh-baked cookies rumbling her stomach.

"Why? Jealous?" Gray slipped her coat off her shoulders before she could do it herself, studying her with a mischievous smile while he hung it up.

"Uh, I think 'nauseated' might be a better word." She turned to offer a smirk while he hooked his own coat onto the coat rack by the door, her arms folded in schoolmarm mode. "Tell me, Gray, do you ever get tired of flirting with females?"

"Well, I could ..." he said with a teasing lift of brows that belied the seriousness in those gray eyes, "if the right female ever looked my way." Giving her shoulders a light squeeze, he prodded Sheridan into the parlour with a hand to the small of her back. "Now you go settle into the parlour, Miss Donovan, while I fetch our hot cocoa and cookies."

"*And* flirt ..." Sheridan reminded him with a smug smile, pretty sure Professor McCall's pretty third-year college-student housekeeper harbored a crush on Gray.

Despite the blazing fire, Sheridan felt a shiver, and hurrying into the cozy parlour, she stood as close to the hearth as possible. She briskly rubbed the arms of her white shirtwaist while her thoughts turned to Jake's last letter, where he talked about a run-in with a gunslinger as the new marshal of Virginia City. Another shiver rattled her body at the thought of Jake in harm's way, but she shook it off with a quick prayer for his safety as usual since he'd written her about his new career.

"Cold?"

She whirled around, not expecting Gray back so soon, toting a tray with two steaming cups and a plate of cookies. "A little, but I suspect that hot cocoa will warm me up fast enough."

"Or the fire." Setting the tray down on the table, he snatched a cream knitted throw from the blue floral Victorian sofa and spread it out in front of the hearth before setting the tray down beside it. Dropping down, he stretched his legs out with a low groan, then patted the blanket beside him. "Or me ..."

"Gray." She offered him a patient smile, head dipped in maternal mode. "When are you going to realize that we are better as friends than a couple?"

He peered up beneath thick dark lashes as he patted the blanket beside him. "When I see a wedding band on your finger, Miss Donovan, and not a moment sooner. Sit, Sheridan. You have my word I will behave, and I never break my word."

Releasing a quiet sigh, Sheridan sat as close to the hearth— and as far away from Gray—as she could, relaxing in the warmth of the fire because she knew she could trust him.

Gray Carmody may be an insatiable flirt and womanizer, but he was honest to the core, something he didn't show to a lot of people. But he had to her, over and over, throughout the year and a half she'd known him. She closed her eyes as she sipped Cecilia's cocoa, the creamy concoction absolutely the best she'd ever had. "Mmm ... this is delicious."

"It is," Gray agreed, taking a sip of his own. "And the cocoa is too."

She couldn't help it—she grinned. "Goodness, my friend, you certainly know how to woo a woman."

His smile was wry. "Apparently not, Miss Donovan, or we'd be more than friends." He set his cup down to offer her a snickerdoodle cookie from the tray, wrinkling his nose a tad. "Snickerdoodles are good, I suppose, but Mexican wedding balls would be better, Sugar Lips."

Sheridan examined the cookies with great focus, looking for the lightest one she could find. "You do realize you aged my uncle ten years with that nickname, don't you?"

"Yes, and Jake too, I hope," he said with a wink. "Because then he'd be pushing forty and way too old for you."

She paused, snickerdoodle to her lips. "Gray?"

He glanced over with a leisurely chew of his cookie. "Yes, Sheridan?"

She studied his handsome face, thinking he was, if possible, even more handsome than Jake. "I'm glad we're good friends, because I can tell you what I really think."

"Uh-oh." He brushed cookie crumbs from his lips with a sheepish grin. "Am I in trouble?"

"No, not at all, you goose. I love both you and Grace like siblings."

He winced.

"Gray." Her tone was tender as she laid a gentle hand to his arm. "Grace told me you flit from girl to girl because it all comes so easily to you—catching a woman's eye—and you just get bored because there's no challenge."

Knees bent, he crossed his arms on top as he stared into the fire. "That's true, I suppose."

"In fact, my friend, she told me the only challenge you've ever had is me."

He slid her a sideways peek tipped with a smile. "That's true too."

"Well, don't you see?" Sheridan shifted to face him. "If I were to fall for you, too, the challenge would be gone, and I'd lose one of my dearest friends forever because you would just flit away."

He stared at her for several moments, his gaze searching her face as if deciding how to respond. "I don't think so, Sheridan," he said quietly, the boyish Gray suddenly nowhere to be found, "because I didn't fall in love with you as just another woman, my friend. I fell in love with you as a dear friend I'd do anything for."

Sheridan blinked with a sudden sting of tears, reaching to touch his hand. "Oh, Gray …"

"Okay," he said with a quick squeeze of her hand, promptly letting go to offer the plate to her for another cookie. The affectionate sparkle was back in his eyes as he gave her a wink, masking his deeper feelings so well, she might have imagined them. "This whole conversation has gotten entirely too serious. I suggest you stay here to finish your cocoa while I go 'torment' Cecilia into packing up a bag of cookies for

Grace, so we can go 'torment' my better half."

Sheridan grinned, her heart expanding in relief—and gratitude—for Gray's sensitivity to an awkward situation. "You mean flirt her into it, don't you?"

Grinning back, he jumped up and brushed crumbs from his lap. "Exactly, because believe it or not, Sheridan Marie, it actually works with some women."

"Most, I'll wager," she quipped with a chuckle, wondering for the very first time if she could ever fall in love with a dear friend like Gray.

His smile was smug as he adjusted the lay of his vest. "Most maybe, but definitely not all as you have so aptly shown."

His words tugged on her heart as firmly as he tugged on his vest, curving her lips into a gentle smile. "Only because I fell in love with a stubborn man back home first, Gray Carmody, or I suspect I'd be as hog-tied as all the other women you dazzle with your charm."

He leveled a taut finger, eyes squinted in a mock glare despite the playful smile that hovered on his lips. "Exactly, Miss Donovan, so I want you to make it perfectly clear to that blind dolt that if he doesn't marry you first, I am next in line with a bona fide offer, understood?"

"Yes, sir," she said with a sassy salute, teasing him right back.

The humor in his manner faded as he searched her eyes with true affection, his voice sobering into a husky whisper. "I'm not joking, Sheridan," he said quietly, and I want you to make good and sure he knows that, my friend, that I've flat-out asked you to marry me, all right? Because if I can't secure the love that I want for myself"—he arched a dark brow, the jest in his tone at odds with the sobriety in his eyes—"I at least want to help secure it for you."

CHAPTER SIXTY-SIX

HANDS PLUNGED IN HIS POCKETS and head down, Jake paced back and forth on the empty train-station platform rehearsing what he wanted to say to Sheridan when she arrived home for Christmas. Others waited inside the train station since the day was bitter cold, but you sure couldn't tell by him, not with sweat ringing his collar and hands damp with the memory of the last time he'd seen her.

"What do you want from me, Jake?" Her voice had been a hoarse whisper, lips swollen and wet from the kisses they'd shared.

"I want you to wait."

He halted mid-pace, gaze trailing into a bleak and guilty stare while snow flurries swirled around. "It's time to tell her the truth," he had argued with Blaze and Dash just last week, determined not to lead Sheridan on anymore. To tell her there was no hope for a marriage between them, and then finally tell her why.

A shiver rattled through his body that had nothing to do with the frigid temperatures. He almost wished he'd just spilled it all in one of the many letters they'd written back and forth like Sheridan repeatedly begged him to do. But he just couldn't put pen to paper with awful memories like that. It was bad enough that they were gouged into the walls of his mind.

"Afternoon, Marshal," Earl Holly said, jolting Jake from his thoughts. Face ruddy from the cold, Virginia City's station master for the Virginia and Truckee Railroad peeked out of the station door with a near-toothless smile. "Just got word the train's running a little late—'bout ten minutes or so. You may want to wait inside where it's warm like everybody else, or you're liable to catch your death out there, cold as it is."

Jake's smile went flat. *Catch his death.* Pretty much already did that way back when, before he'd ever come to the Silver Lining Ranch. The demise of everything he held dear.

His family.

His dreams.

His hope for a future.

"No, thanks, Earl, I'm not really all that cold. Got a lot on my mind, so I'm just walking it out."

"Still worried about that no-good Sikeston fellow?"

Jake smiled, Slick Sikeston the least of his worries. He'd thrown the gunslinger into a cell when he stirred up trouble at the Bucket of Blood Saloon last month, shooting up the place and nicking a few patrons in a drunken brawl. Pure trouble, Sikeston was the *same* mean-mouthed lowlife who'd robbed the orphanage a while back *whom*—Jake scowled— sweet Miss Cramer declined to prosecute after Jake caught him. Ever since, ol' Slick harbored a grudge against him, so he didn't take kindly to Jake locking him up for a full week, swearing he'd get even. Jake expelled a weary breath that swirled up like smoke. "Nope. I doubt we'll see Sikeston anytime soon. Threatened to throw his ugly mug back into the clink if he stepped one foot in Virginia City again."

"Whoo-eeee! I'll tell you what, Jake, the town's feeling a whole lot safer with you behind that badge, son. Poor old Cyrus was tough enough, I suppose, but everyone could see he was startin' to wear out when it came to these young pups like Sikeston, just itching to strut their stuff." He winked. "'Course it sure don't hurt you're the Nevada State Shootout champ, I'm guessin'."

"Thanks, Earl. All that gun practice at the Silver Lining Ranch paid off, I guess," he said with an awkward cuff of his neck, "but now that I'm wearing a badge, I'd like to play down that title since there are too many gunslingers out there looking to prove they're better than me."

Earl's laughter puffed into the cool December air. "No doubt about that, son, so you stay safe, you hear?"

"Exactly what I'm trying to do, Earl," he said with a polite tip of his hat before the old stationmaster clicked the door closed.

Safe.

For both Sheridan *and* me.

Ten minutes later on the money, a faraway whistle pierced the air as Jake looked up, steam billowing into the sky like angry thunderclouds. He grunted, wondering if it portended a storm in his friendship with Sheridan as well. He hoped not, but he wouldn't blame her if it did.

Chugging away, the train grew from a dot on the horizon to a shuddering mass of steel belching smoke as acrid as the taste of regret in his mouth. Its whistle shrieked as it bore down on the station, the smell of smoke and coal wrinkling his nose.

Both the train and Jake's pulse screeched to a stop at the exact same time, and when the passenger door squealed open with a loud clank, his breathing did too.

"Watch your step, miss," the conductor said as he helped a shapely woman with a green coat and matching velvet brimmed hat. Head down to watch her step while the conductor assisted, the feather on her hat snapped in the brisk breeze.

The woman's head rose, and Jake caught his breath—what was left of it—when he recognized Sheridan, looking far older and far more sophisticated than he ever expected.

No longer a little girl, but a woman. He swallowed the lump in his throat.

The one who owned his heart.

Shaking the thought off, Jake strode forward to swoop her up in a mighty twirl, not giving a hoot about the curious looks of the handful of other passengers disembarking the train. He was so darn happy to see her again, he kicked all negative thoughts off the fence, relishing this moment for what it was.

The homecoming of a dear friend.

"Welcome home, Half-Pint!" he shouted over the hiss of the steam engine, laughing at her squeal when he spun her around and around. A gust of wind almost absconded with her hat while she tried to hold it on, skirt billowing wide before he put her back down. He grinned when she wobbled, quickly bracing her arms to hold her steady. "Almost didn't recognize you under all those fancy duds."

Giggling, she literally launched back into his arms to hug him all over again, turning the tables on his heart by making *it* dizzy. "Oh, Jake, I missed you so much!"

"Well, now, I doubt that with Grace and *Gray*"—his voice lowered to gruff as he dragged the dandy's name out—"occupying all your time, *Sugar Lips*."

A pretty pink tinted her cheeks that he couldn't blame on the cold, making him wish he hadn't given in to the snide remark that clearly indicated jealousy. Quickly turning away to snatch up her suitcase that the conductor had set on the platform, he opted for tease to deflect the annoyance he felt. "So," he said, hooking a casual arm over her shoulder while he ushered her to the rig, his smile way too broad and stiff, "did the dandy pop the question yet?"

She peeked up with an odd look, confusion framing her eyes along with a thick fringe of light brown lashes while her lips parted, as if to speak.

"Howdy, Miss Donovan, and welcome home!" Earl called, leaning out the door of the station. "Mayor McShane and the Mrs. wanted me to be sure and welcome you home since they couldn't do it themselves, being they don't arrive back from their trip to Carson City till the next train."

Flashing the stationmaster a bright smile, Sheridan offered a wave. "Thanks, Earl, and Merry Christmas to you and your family!"

"You too, young lady, and same to you, Marshal." He nodded toward the rig where Jake had several blankets piled on the front seat. "You best get that young woman home right quick, Jake, before she turns cold as ice."

"Will do, Earl, and Merry Christmas." Rushing Sheridan to the rig, he helped her up, then put her suitcase in the back before hopping up to take the reins. "I'd wrap up real good and tight in both of those blankets, Sher, to keep warm because it's going to be a real cold ride."

Cold as ice.

Yah!" he said with a snap of the reins, suddenly feeling the frigid temperatures for the first time all day. Because deep down he had a sick feeling that once he told Sheridan why he refused to marry, their friendship would be much the same.

And "cold as ice" would only be the tip of the iceberg.

CHAPTER SIXTY-SEVEN

*S*OMETHING WASN'T RIGHT. SHERIDAN COULD feel it to the tips of her frozen toes, and the thought chilled her heart as much as the icy weather chilled her body to the bone. Yes, Jake tried to hide it with a bright smile and a joyous swing in the air, talking nonstop as they pulled out of the station. But Sheridan knew him better than he knew himself, sensing something brewing deep down inside, boding an ill wind as wicked as the weather.

"Jake?" Touching a hand to his arm, she stopped him mid-chatter with a gentle smile. "Can we stop by your house? I would love to see it, and I have a house-warming present for you."

He paused several seconds, his hesitation more than clear.

"And the train was so cold," she continued in a rush, shivering for good measure, "that I'd like a chance to warm up while we talk."

"Sure." Jake gave a nod and a stiff smile as they headed toward the edge of town, where Cyrus and Abigail Tanner had lived as far back as Sheridan could remember. He chattered all the way there, a hint of pride in his tone about all he had done to make the place his own.

She was still in shock—and more than a little grief—over the fact that Jake had left the Silver Lining Ranch to take the marshal job. But then a spark of hope had flickered in her heart that maybe—just maybe—he did so to settle down good and proper in his own house before he would take a wife.

Of course, she'd been more than a little alarmed when he'd first written he was taking the marshal job in the first place, given the prior marshal's demise, but everyone knew Jake was the best shot in Nevada. So Sheridan just decided they would both put their trust in God if that's where He wanted Jake to be.

And me?

Excitement suddenly bubbled within, merging with her newly strengthened faith that everything *would* work out in the end, and she felt her malaise slowly fade away. After all, she thought with a new swell of hope, she had an entire week for God to work his magic before she had to leave for school again.

Hopefully, engaged to the man of her dreams!

"Oh, Jake ..." she whispered when he pulled the rig up in front of the white-picket fence, completely charmed by the pretty, little cottage where Abigail's extensive garden was wintering till spring. "It's beautiful!"

He grinned, no mistaking the gleam of pride in his eyes now as he cast a loving glance at the small but tidy cream clapboard house with its rust-colored door. The same color trim was carefully painted around a three-window bay topped with a steel half dome. "Well, it's not Finn's ranch house by a long shot, but it sure beats sleeping with twenty hands who snore and smell. All it took was a few coats of paint inside and out, and it's good as new."

Hopping out, he tied the reins to the fence post and hurried around to help Sheridan down, palm to the small of her back as he guided her to the house.

"Oh, wait!" She whirled around, darting back to the rig to pull his gift out of her suitcase, then followed him up the steps to the front porch, sliding past him as he held the door open.

"It's small, but it's cozy," he said, closing the door again, "and it'll take a few minutes to warm up, so you'll want to keep your coat on." Striding to a modest stone fireplace, he squatted to add a small log to the banked fire in the hearth, coaxing the flames to life like Sheridan hoped to do with their relationship.

"Oh, Jake, it's wonderful!" she breathed, sweet chills warming her more than a crackling fire ever could because *this* was where Jake lived and slept. Clutching his wrapped gift to her chest, she slowly perused the comfy parlour and snug kitchen with delight, stopping short of entering a neat bedroom where a cast-iron double bed sported a patchwork quilt in masculine colors.

"Can I warm you up with a cup of coffee?" He moved a spindle-back chair from the kitchen table to smack dab in front of the hearth.

"No, the fire is perfect and more than enough." *Although a kiss would be better* ... Settling into the chair with her wrapped gift in her lap, she waited as he repositioned his own spindle-back chair in front of the fire also, albeit too far from hers.

He finally angled to face her dead-on. "It's good to have you home, Half-Pint," he said, and the minute the words were out of his mouth, she knew it wouldn't be good news. She long since figured out that Jake called her Half-Pint whenever he wanted to distance himself, and the pinch of his lips told her she was right.

"Here." She stood to awkwardly thrust the gift at him before sitting back down, clasping her hands tightly in her lap. "I brought you a house-warming gift," she whispered, hoping and praying it would provide the springboard she needed to delve into Jake's soul.

"Thanks, Sher, but you didn't have to do that ..." Shaking his head, he nudged a finger beneath the open end of the brown wrapping paper.

"But that's just it, Jake"—her voice was barely a whisper—"I did have to do it because I felt like God wanted me to."

He paused to stare at her for several seconds with a half-smile, a wrinkle above his nose indicating his confusion. "*O ... kay.*" Carefully removing the paper, his smile grew as he held up a picture frame backwards, tossing the paper aside. "How did you know I need pict—" His words tapered off when he turned it around, Adam's apple ducking hard in his throat.

"I made it myself," she said quickly, hoping to deflect the unease of his sudden silence. "Grace's grandmother taught us needlepoint this semester, so when I heard you moved into your own house"—she shrugged, the motion awkward—"I wanted you to have this to hang on your wall."

Nodding slowly, he swallowed hard once again, and before he looked down at the sampler, she could have sworn she saw a sheen of moisture in his eyes. "It's … beautiful, Sheridan," he said quietly, his voice gruff with emotion. He slowly skimmed a finger along the Scripture she'd sewn, and with a silent prayer, she begged for God to use it to heal his heart.

"As far as the east is from the west, so far hath he removed our transgressions from us." Her whisper filled the silence between them like a prayer as she watched the man she loved to the depth of her soul, longing for him to be free even if it meant freedom from her. "I thought it would be a good place to begin, Jake … to talk about your past."

Eyes fixed on the sampler, he gave a short nod before his gaze rose to meet hers. "This is … the best gift I've ever gotten, Sheridan, and I thank you from the bottom of my heart." Rising, he carefully set the framed sampler in the center of the cedar mantle, head bowed as he rested his palms beside it. "This won't be easy for me to say," he whispered, keeping his back to her, "*or* for you to hear, Sheridan, but it's time." He was silent so long, she opened her mouth to speak …

Until he slowly turned. It was as if he'd aged ten years in the span of only ten seconds, shoulders slumped while he sagged back into his chair. "My father owned every vice a man could have—drinking, carousing, gambling, abuse, stealing, you name it—and I hated him," he began, his voice taking on a monotone quality that made him suddenly seem so far away, as if he were traveling into the past while he stared glassy-eyed at the fire. "And he hated me. He was the sheriff of Bannack, Montana, but don't let the title fool you. He was a hardened criminal through and through, the mastermind behind hundreds of robberies and murders across his territory."

She gave a harsh catch of her breath, but it was as if he hadn't heard, continuing on in a lifeless drone that seemed to sap all energy right out of his soul.

"Why Ma ever married him I'll never understand, but rumor has it she had no choice. Some said she was loose, others said he raped her." His words twisted like a knife in Sheridan's heart. "But either way, I was the result, and there isn't a day goes by that I don't regret having Ace Conroy's blood in my veins."

"Oh, Jake ..." Hand to her mouth, there was no way she could stop the tears that welled as she rose to go to him.

"No—stay back!" Tone harsh, he held up a palm with eyes as wild and hard as the tale he told, his face contorted into a man she didn't even know.

Hunching over the edge of his chair with his head in his hands, he continued, his voice so distant and flat he might have been talking to himself. "Oh, he put on a real good front for the town folk, of course, to hide a heart as black as night. But at home, he was Satan incarnate, a drunken devil who wailed on me and my ma for pure sport. Never on our faces, mind you, or wherever folks could see, but black and blue underneath all the same."

"Oh, no ..." Tears streamed Sheridan's face as she stared at him, numb with grief.

"I was full of rage from little on, crazed with hate and fury—at him because he was so vile, and then at Ma because she married him. And the only way I could strike back was to make him look bad, to reflect the evil in him by being evil myself. Awful things I ... don't want to go into, but all fueled by pure hate. Too awful for a boy so young, I can tell you that. Got so bad, Ma hated me as much as she hated him, because I was his demon seed, she'd say, and somehow I knew that deep down inside she was right."

"Oh, Jake, no—you're not!" Sheridan rasped, her words nasal with grief for a little boy so brutalized and betrayed.

He looked up, and she sucked in a harsh breath at the total despair in his eyes. "But that's just it, Sheridan, I *am*."

"No!" She rose, hands fisted hard at her sides, the stark warning in his face the only thing keeping her from rushing to his side. "You are *not* your father, Jake Sullivan!"

"No, Sheridan, I'm his son." He stared at her with a hopelessness so potent, a darkness shivered across her very soul. "And," he continued in a tone as vacant as his eyes, "the sole reason my mother and sister are dead."

CHAPTER SIXTY-EIGHT

HE WAS RELIVING IT ALL over again. Just like his nightmares, only this time he was wide awake. In his dreams, he always woke up screaming, pulse racing and body layered in sweat, but although his heart hammered in his chest and parts of his shirt were damp, this time he didn't have the luxury of waking up or even screaming out loud …

Only in his soul, a man lost forever …

Sheridan sat there like a statue. She might have been dead except the rapid rise and fall of her chest, horror wet in her eyes, but something else, too, that he in no way deserved.

Compassion?

"What h-happened, Jake?" Her voice was hoarse, her words a papery whisper.

The shivering began—inside, if not out—when his gaze drifted back to the fire into a time he would never forget, and he knew now that this was his punishment, his own personal hell to pay for what he had done. A piece of his life he could never change, never escape.

Never be free.

"Jake?"

The flames of the fire licked the logs like sweat licked the back of his neck while his lips curled into a hard smile. "But that spawn of Satan finally got what he deserved when Montana Vigilantes figured out why the high and mighty Sheriff Conroy never could catch the marauding bandits that terrorized Bannack and Grasshopper Creek. Turns out the so-called upstanding sheriff was the ringleader for a ruthless gang of highwaymen who committed hundreds of robberies and murders across territorial Montana. So, the Vigilantes captured and lynched him from a tree in the center of town, making my ma and me watch while people clapped and cheered."

A nerve twitched in his cheek when Sheridan gasped, but he didn't look at her. He couldn't. The horror in his mind was bad enough; he sure didn't need to see it in her face. "Turned out lots of people in town hated him as much as Ma and me, but the problem was, they hated us too. When the local preacher told folks I was bad seed from the spawn of Satan, they banished us from the town. Ended up in the town of Hell Gate, where we changed our name to Sullivan so no one would know we were related to the monster who gave me life.

"Oh, Jake ..." Her voice broke on a heave.

"I was only six at the time," he whispered, gaze lost in the flames as his voice faded to near numb, "but I'd lived a lifetime of hell by then, so Hell Gate was almost a pleasure after that. Ma had no trouble getting work in one of the saloons, what with the goldrush and all the miners flooding the town, which left me alone a lot, so I fell in with a rough crowd."

A harsh laugh erupted from his lips. "Thunderation, I *was* the 'rough crowd,' the son of the infamous Sheriff Conroy to some of his gang who still lived in Hell Gate. Took me under their wing right quick, and before I could blink, I was following in my old man's boots with stealing and drinkin' at the ripe old age of eight."

He chanced a glance at Sheridan and wished he hadn't. She looked so much like that little girl of four he first fell in love with, her body small and hunched in the chair with arms clasped to her waist so hard, it could have pinched off her air. Blue eyes stared back in grief, rimmed red and raw from silent weeping.

He rose from the chair and started pacing, barely aware he was clenching and unclenching his fists over and over. "And then things changed for the better, only I was too angry inside to know it. One of the Montana Vigilantes that finally cleaned up Hell Gate by catching the rest of my pa's gang, became sheriff and married my ma."

His tone softened as the memory came back. "He was a good man, a godly man, but I was too far gone with hate and bitterness to accept him, no matter how hard he tried. Actually treated me better than my own ma, who almost couldn't stand the sight of me because she said I looked too much like my pa."

He gave a listless shrug. "That and I was nothing but trouble, a foul-mouthed hellion who refused to mind. But Dirk"—he paused to shoot Sheridan one of the few glances he'd sent her way since he'd begun, the barest hint of a smile on his lips—"that was my stepfather's name, you know, Dirk Wheeler. Well, he was the one who taught me to shoot, insisting I needed to know how to watch over my ma and new baby sister whenever Dirk was away, which was a lot in the wild Montana Territory back then."

Jake returned to his chair, hunching over with hands clasped as he gazed at the fire with a tender smile, not seeing it, but the little sister he had loved. "Josie was the one bright spot in my life back then, a beautiful little girl with glossy curls black as night and a pretty little smile that was pure sunshine to my soul." His lips curved higher as he spoke, almost feeling that very sunshine flooding his soul while her memory danced in his mind. "I called her Moonbeam because she took to cuddling with me at night from the age of three, so we could watch the moon and stars together while I made up stories about them."

He glanced up at Sheridan, heart constricting over how easy it had been to transfer the love he'd felt for Josie over to a little girl with hair like corn silk. Blue eyes that adored and revered him like Josie always had. "You reminded me of her, Sheridan, from the first moment I saw you, and I suppose that was why I fell in love with you at first sight." He swiped at the moisture in his eyes, barely aware it was even there.

"And I, you," she said softly, but his smile died along with his hope as he turned back to the fire.

"Josie was the world to me," he whispered, gaze trailing into the same painful past he relived so many nights in his dreams. "Until the week Dirk asked me to keep watch over her and Ma while he would be away on a posse. Word was that some of Ace Conroy's gang members vowed vengeance on the families of the Vigilantes who'd hung their brothers, and he didn't want to take any chances. Told me flat out not to leave the house for any reason except to empty the chamber pot, and that I was to keep guard day and night with my rifle."

A spark popped in the hearth, but Jake barely heard it. The flames blurred into an inferno while saltwater welled in his eyes, his own personal hell as alive and real as the day it had happened. "But I was an eleven-year-old hooligan, selfish to the core. So when Dirk didn't come back for three days, and my friends came by to talk me into fishing"— emotion swelled in his throat until he could barely breathe—"I did," he rasped. "Then yelled at Josie to boot, for trying to follow."

His eyelids weighted closed like they were made of lead as he swiped at his face, slick with regret. "I can still see her, so wounded and hurt while tears rolled down those tiny cheeks." A sob caught in his throat as he put his head in his hands, heaves wracking his body. "I … I … heard shots … and then screams … b-but I was t-too late. When I g-got back, bullets had riddled the c-cabin, and they …" His voice broke on another sob, all the grief he'd buried over the years flooding from his eyes.

"Oh, Jake, no …" Sheridan's arms surrounded him then, and he hung on tight, eyes squeezed shut as he wept from his very soul. "God help me, I didn't deserve to live, Sheridan, but I did, instead of them."

He glanced up, then, a man in the crosshairs of contrition as he bludgeoned a thumb to his chest with wild eyes. "It should have been *me* that died that day. It should have been *me* riddled with bullets, not them. And as God is my witness, there isn't an hour goes by that I don't wish"—his voice was a whisper, hoarse and nasal with grief—"that it was."

CHAPTER SIXTY-NINE

*N*O! THE THOUGHT OF NO Jake in this world pierced
Sheridan's heart anew as she knelt beside him to cling
with all of her might, wishing more than anything she could
set him free from his agony. But there was only One who had
the power to do that, and she had no doubt whatsoever that
somehow, someway, that was exactly what God intended to
do.

But till then … she could show him God's love through
her own …

"Jake," she whispered, eyes closed as she rested her head
against his shoulder, "I fell in love with that very boy, and
now I love the incredible man you've grown to be in spite of
a beginning no child should ever have."

Sitting up with a sniff, he fished his handkerchief from his
pocket to swab his face before expelling a weighty sigh. With
a sad smile, he gently cupped her face, the love in his eyes as
raw and real as the grief he'd just revealed. "I love you, too,
Sheridan, which is why I need you to understand why I can't
promise anything more than friendship."

"But that's just it—I *don't* understand!" Sheridan stood,
dislodging his hand from her face as she locked arms to her
waist, hurt brimming in her eyes. "We love each other, Jake,
and we're attracted to each other too—*a lot*—so explain to
me, *please*, why we can't fall in love and marry like normal
people do?"

He slowly rose to his feet like a man twice his age and
gently buffed her arms. "Because I'm *not* normal, Sheridan,"
he whispered. "I am a damaged man, who doesn't deserve
the happiness of a family of my own, not after destroying that

very happiness for three people I loved in my life, cutting their lives off far too soon. I'm sorry, Sheridan, but I refuse to carry that guilt into a marriage."

"Three?" Sheridan paused, confusion digging deep at the bridge of her nose.

"Yeah, three," he said quietly, gently guiding her to sit back down in her chair before he did the same, head bowed and hands clasped between parted knees while he stared aimlessly at the floor. "Josie, my ma, and my stepfather, Dirk."

"I ..."—Sheridan blinked, suddenly aware she hadn't even considered why Jake had ended up in Sister Fred's orphanage in the first place, before coming to the Silver Lining Ranch—"I don't understand. What about Dirk?" she whispered, almost afraid to hear his answer.

Silence prevailed for several moments while the fire crackled and sparked. "He's dead. Just like my ma and sister. And all because of me."

Sheridan gasped, and his glazed stare was suddenly back, telling her he was no longer present, but somewhere else in his dark and deadly past, where demons haunted and hopes were denied. "He ... he ... was devastated when he finally came home that night and found ..." His voice cracked as his Adam's apple jerked hard in his throat, more tears swimming in his eyes. "I ... was c-curled up in the c-corner in shock, h-holding my little s-sister while Ma still lay lifeless where I'd found her." He swiped at his face hard, gaze never straying from the floor where the tragedy, no doubt, played all over again in his mind. "H-He had to pry ... Josie ... out of my arms b-because I w-wouldn't let g-go ..." A sob choked from his throat, but when Sheridan rose, he jabbed a shaky palm in the air to stop her, sodden eyes those of a haunted man. "No, Sheridan—let me finish, *please*."

She slowly sat back down, heart breaking over the trauma caused to someone she loved.

His breathing was shallow as he continued, absently wiping his face with the sleeve of his coat. "He was such a good man, but I would never acknowledge that, never let him love me like he tried. He asked me what happened and I lied, too ashamed to tell him I wasn't there when it occurred. Wasn't there protecting my family like I was supposed to, like he'd asked. And all because fishing"—he said it like a curse, harsh and bitter—"was more important at the time ..." His voice faded along with his presence as he traveled back into the past, the only sound that of his labored breathing and the hiss of the fire.

"What happened to him, Jake?" she whispered, and it was as if he'd only heard in his subconscious because he was still faraway when his low drone finally continued.

"I guess I was in shock for days because I wouldn't talk, eat, sleep unless Dirk forced me. All I could do was stare, playing over and over in my mind the moment I could pull the trigger of my shotgun and murder the men who murdered my ma and sister."

A shiver shook through him as he rose to stand by the fire, laying a shaky hand on the mantle while he numbly stared into the flames. "Dirk was worried about me, I know, because he wouldn't leave for days at a time, but finally he had to go back to town to do his job, and that's when I left."

"Left?"

"To find my ma's and sister's killers. It was Ace's gang that killed them after all, and I knew I could find out who from the few gang members who'd escaped the lynching, some of whom relocated to Missoula. And I did," he said in a voice as dead as his family, the edge of his lip curling with a hate like Sheridan had never seen in him before, except the time he beat up on Clay. "Rattlesnake Reno," he hissed, "Frank Reno's little brother who was even meaner than him, the both of them jealous of the control Ace wielded."

Head bowed at the mantle, his shoulders sagged, if possible, even more. "When Dirk and the Montana Vigilantes strung Frank up, Rattlesnake and his gang vowed to get even, so I vowed to get even right back. Only a snot-nosed punk didn't stand a chance against the likes of Rattlesnake and his ilk, so they turned the tables on me, tying me up and sending a note to Dirk. Said he needed to come alone if he wanted to ever see his stepson alive again."

Sheridan could only stare in horror, barely breathing as his voice carried on, a low and foreboding hum like the one in her brain.

"And he did," he whispered with a slow shake of his head, as if he couldn't believe anybody would love him enough to do just that. "Rattlesnake's lookouts confirmed that Dirk was alone. 'Send the boy out first,' Dirk called from behind the protection of a boulder. Rattlesnake shoved me out the door with my hands bound and bleeding behind my back, no less than six guns trained on me while I stumbled across the yard. 'You try to run, Wheeler,' Rattlesnake yelled, 'and both you and the boy are dead.'"

Jake's body trembled as he stood before the fire, and Sheridan knew he was weeping again while he clenched a fist on the mantle. "'Jake, run to me!' Dirk shouted again, and I did, tears streaming as he swallowed me up in those big arms that had tried to love me so many times before."

Several heaves wracked Jake's body before he spoke again, his words hoarse and halting as if every one cost him a breath. "'Go,' he told me, cutting my bonds before hugging me tightly, nodding toward where he'd tied up his horse. 'Through the pass to Rattlesnake Creek, where a posse is waiting, then go back home. And wait for me with your gun trained out the window, you hear?'"

"'Yes, sir,' I said, hugging him back for the first time in my life. 'And I'm so sorry, Dirk, for running away, but I just wanted to make them pay.' 'I know,' he said in my ear, and to this day I can still feel his love in that kiss he placed on my head, his genuine caring in the touch of his hand rubbing my back. 'And they will. But I need to know you're safe first, so you go, son, now, all right?' Nodding, I pulled away, but not before he called out one last time. 'Jake,' he said, and I turned to see a love in his eyes greater than any I'd ever known. 'From now on, it's you and me, son, and we're family. I love you like you're my own, and I don't ever want you to forget that, you hear? Because today—*right now*—is our new beginning, understood?'"

"'Yes, sir,' I said, barely able to see him for the tears in my eyes. So, I did what he asked for the first time in my life—and the last—because I left to get the posse. But I didn't go home. I waited a while, then followed them back, trembling behind a rock while the shooting went on and on …"

Head bowed, Jake seemed to waver in front of the mantle, body sagging as the horror of his story lingered in the air like the fumes from the fire. "I remember praying for one of the few times in my life, like Dirk always tried to teach me to do, only it didn't work, Sheridan."

His hand trembled to his eyes, as if to block out the revulsion of that awful day. "When the smoke cleared, the gang was all dead and half of the posse"—his shoulders shook with several sobs as he dropped his head, voice lowering to a pained rasp along with it —"while Dirk hung from a tree behind the cabin, swinging in the breeze."

CHAPTER SEVENTY

BILE ROSE IN JAKE'S THROAT as always when he thought of that day, choking his air until his sobs finally broke through, ravaging his body as he mourned on the mantle.

He heard Sheridan's gasp of horror, and this time there was no stopping her. She ran to embrace him from behind, and he knew from the frantic grip of her hold that she longed to help absorb some of his pain.

The moment he felt her touch, he turned and clung like a man who was drowning, weeping in her arms like that lost little boy still trapped inside his own personal hell. His saltwater dampened her neck as they stood there, quivering in place until his grief was spent, and only then did she lead him to the sofa against the far wall facing the fire.

"*No* one should ever have to go through something that brutal, Jake, much less a child." Just a mite of a woman, and yet she bundled his weary body in her arms like an angel sent from above, desperate to soothe by rubbing his back like Dirk had done for him that awful day, whispering her love all the while.

Like salt in a wound of love betrayed.

When his body finally stilled, he slumped back against the sofa completely drained, eyes glassy as they stared at the ceiling in a daze. "Who does that?" he whispered, a thread of disbelief lacing his tone. "Who lays down his life for a kid like me not even his own blood, a sinner who ruined his life, spurned his love?" He felt the tragedy of it all etched into every line of his face even while his voice sounded far away, shadowed in awe.

Greater love hath no man than this, that a man lay down his life for his friends.

Sheridan laid a gentle hand to his arm. "A Savior sent by a loving Father," she whispered, "and a man named Dirk sent by a loving God, to redeem a little boy hell tried to claim but never could. Dirk gave up his life so *you* could be free, Jake, just like God's Son did for each of us. So, *please*"—her tone quivered with the need to reach him—"don't let Dirk's death be in vain." Her voice trailed off into a frail plea. "Nor that of God's Son."

He turned to search her face for the priceless treasure she was, and slowly lifting his hand, he tenderly traced the curve of her jaw. "I'm not," he whispered, his resolve shielded by the softest of love. "Dirk laid down his life for me, Sheridan, and that's what I intend to do for you."

"No ..." She shook her head violently, the motion splashing more tears down her cheeks. "Because if you do, Jake, you'll be laying my life down too."

"No, I won't," he whispered, scanning her face to commit it to memory because after today, he intended to keep his distance. "You're bright, beautiful, and good, Sheridan Donovan, and someday some lucky man will sweep you away as the girl of his dreams."

He tucked a finger to her chin with a gentle smile. "Just *not* before you get your degree, understood? Because I promised your uncle and brothers I would make sure no man got too close until then"—his smile faded into regret—"which is exactly why I've been leading you on all this time, Sheridan, which I swear I didn't want to do. But Blaze and Dash strong-armed me over and over, every time another man even got close. Heck, even Finn got into the act after Carmody pulled that stunt about wanting to marry you."

Leaning back, a grimace lined his lips, his manner more than a little sheepish. "In fact, it's time that you know one of the biggest reasons I've shied away from you all this time, Sher, even though your uncle asked me to keep it quiet. You see, after you turned sixteen, Finn actually pulled me aside and made me swear to help keep all romance and other men away till you graduated. Something about a promise he made to your mom before she died. And since that's only five months away now, Half-Pint, I figure I've done my job, and it's safe to tell you."

"But that's just it, Jake," she said with a thump of her fist on the sofa, "you *didn't* do your job! You *didn't* keep 'romance away'! You just made me fall deeper in love with you. Every smile and every kiss—"

"I know," he said quickly, cuffing the back of his neck as blood gorged his cheeks, "and I'm sorry, darlin', really I am, but your brothers convinced me it was for the best, and even Finn asked me to divert your attention from Carmody by flirting with you."

He rubbed the back of his neck, wishing he'd never allowed his best friends to talk him into all of this. "But they all figured the hurt could be a whole lot worse if you'd fallen for womanizers like Morgan or Carmody, Sher, so I went along."

Sheridan clutched his hand. "But your promise to Uncle Finn is over in five months, Jake, you said it yourself, so I don't understand what's stopping you now, even with the horrible past that you had."

"Sher." He took both of her hands in his own as he ducked to meet her distraught gaze. "After Dirk"—a muscle convulsed in his throat—"died, the town of Hell Gate turned on me just like Bannack turned on my ma and me. Word got out that I was to blame, not only for my sister's and mother's deaths, but for Dirk's and a half dozen other men in the posse as well. During the shoot-out, I heard Rattlesnake shout that I was Ace Conroy's kid, and they should lynch me up just like my pa and step-pa."

He felt his jaw turn to rock as he finished up his sad story, ignoring the stream of tears that slipped down Sheridan's face. Almost as if he were numb to her grief for the vile vent of emotions bottled up far too long. "When the preacher from

Bannack heard about it, he rode all the way to Hell Gate to warn the town, telling them if they knew what was best, they'd banish me because I had Ace Conroy's blood in my veins and was a demon from hell, just like my pa. He riled everyone up so much, some of the town folk even started talking about a lynching."

He barely heard Sheridan's groan as his gaze trailed into a distant stare over her shoulder. "I was only eleven at the time, but smart enough to know I had to leave. So, I took my shotgun and Dirk's horse, and I didn't stop till I got to Virginia City, miles away from any memory of Hell Gate or Bannack."

He swallowed hard as his gaze finally met Sheridan's soggy one. "Sister Fred took me in at the orphanage, and I saw the same love in her eyes that I'd seen in Dirk's, so I worked myself to the bone for that woman, and I listened this time when she talked about God, like I never listened to Dirk."

"And that's when Blaze brought you to the ranch," she whispered, "when I was only four."

His smile was sad as he tenderly brushed her hair over her shoulder. "You reminded me so much of Josie," he whispered, voice hoarse as moisture stung in his nose, "and I fell in love at first sight."

She nodded, and the motion toppled more tears from her eyes, her voice as soft and sweet as the first time he'd heard it so very long ago. "Me too. But I still don't understand why we can't be, Jake. You and I were meant for each other, and we both know it."

Heart aching, he softly skimmed her arms with his palms, wishing more than anything that he could love her the way they both wanted. But he could never do that to her.

Or the children they might bring into this world.

"I already told you, Sheridan, I'm a damaged man, and I won't do that to you or any children we might ever have."

She broke free from his hold to cradle his jaw in her hands, brows sloped in pain. "We're *all* 'damaged' people, Jake, until God sets us free, and 'if the Son therefore shall make you free, ye shall be free indeed.'"

He stepped back, causing her arms to fall. "I wish it were that simple."

"It *is* that simple!"

"Not for me," he whispered, inching away to sit on the edge of the sofa as he faced her again, taking her hand in his. "One time when my father whaled on me, he beat me unconscious. Fearing I would die, he took me and my mother to a doctor in another town. She told me later that the doctor waited until my father went to use the privy, then took her aside to ask a number of questions, finally telling her that he feared my father had a mental disorder that was hereditary."

"What?" Ridges furrowed Sheridan's brow.

"He said he'd seen cases where men were violent for no reason, showing no remorse or empathy even for family, a tendency to lie and manipulate, deceit and reckless behavior, and breaking the law. He warned her to leave, but then my pa came back, and nothing more was said."

Entwining her fingers with his, he studied their hands together, knowing they could never be joined that way. "Later, when my ma was angry at me, she told me Pa had a disease that I obviously inherited too. Since then, I've read a lot and have discovered my father was more than likely a psychopath, a new term for a person with no conscience, no chance for a normal life, exhibiting all the symptoms he had. And although it appeared I also leaned that way as a youth according to my mother and the people of both Bannack and Hell Gate," his gaze rose to connect with hers, "I have never exhibited any behavior like that since Sister Fred or your uncle took me in."

"Of course not!" Sheridan said, gripping his hand all the tighter. "You've never been like that with us, Jake, *never.*"

"No, that's true …" He slowly rubbed his thumb along the base of her wrist, shame flushing the back of his neck over that day at the orphanage. "Although Clay Morgan might beg to differ with you on that one, darlin'." He slowly raised his gaze to hers, sorrow pooling in his eyes against his will. "But my children could be, Sheridan," he whispered, "which is reason enough that we can't be."

"I don't care!" she shouted, fingernails digging in to his skin. "We can handle whatever comes if we do it together with God by our side. 'Though one may be overpowered by another, two can withstand because a threefold cord is not quickly broken,'" she quoted, the desperation bleeding into her voice.

He caressed the line of her face with the side of his hand, his smile as soft and tender as his voice. "No, darlin', we can't, because something else still stands in the way."

"Something else?" Her voice was barely a whisper.

Jake drew in a deep breath, determined to put an end to Sheridan's false hopes once and for all. "I'm the marshal of Virginia City, Sheridan, and when I took the vow before your uncle to safeguard this city, I also took a vow to safeguard you. I watched both my father and stepfather die as lawmen and Cyrus Tanner too, and I will never subject any woman to that life of fear and foreboding—*ever*."

A sob broke from her lips, and the sound slashed right through his heart as he gathered her close, rocking her gently while she wept in his arms. He pressed a kiss to her hair. "I love you more than anything in this world, Sheridan," he whispered, his voice gruff with an agony unlike any he'd known before, "so I hope we can always be friends. The Bible tells me that 'greater love hath no man than this, to lay down his life for his friends,' and that's all I'm doing, darlin', so I'm asking you for the last time, *please*"— he pulled away to cradle her face in his hands, unable to stem the water that flowed, "just let me go."

CHAPTER SEVENTY-ONE

" *JUST LET ME GO.* "

J Like a funeral dirge, Jake's words played over and over in her brain as Sheridan silently wept in her bed, mourning a death as real and wrenching as the anguish in her heart.

The death of her dream.

The death of her hope.

The death of a love she'd prayed for since she'd been a little girl.

So final. So foreboding. So full of heartbreak beyond anything she'd ever known.

Because it was over. Her quest for the love of her life was over. And there was nothing more to do.

But grieve.

Neither had spoken on the way back to the ranch, other than his quiet request for her silence regarding the awful details of his past, but then there was really no more to say. So, he'd just carried her bag to the front porch and pressed a kiss to her head, hugging her tightly for what felt like the very last time. "I've got a lot to do in town this week, Half-Pint, so I won't see you and your family till Christmas Eve," he'd whispered, "but I hope you enjoy your time with them this week." And with that, he'd driven the rig into the barn, mounted his horse, and simply ridden away.

Never was Sheridan more grateful that Uncle Finn and Aunt Libby weren't home yet from Carson City and Maggie was still at work because all she'd wanted to do was escape to her room and cry.

Of course, Blaze and Dash had come running from the

barn to welcome her home, swooping her in the air just like Jake had done. Shaylee all but squeezed the stuffing out of her while Angus fawned with boasts of making her favorite dinner. She'd noted a slight pause in each of their manners, no doubt concerned over her red-rimmed eyes, but she just convinced them it was tears of joy over seeing them again and all she needed was a rest before dinner.

A rest.

To cry her eyes out.

Before she saw everyone again.

Glancing at the clock, she was relieved she still had several hours to clean up, and expelling an exhausted sigh, she stared at the ceiling, wondering how on earth she was going to hide the ache in her heart from her family.

Of course, ever since Uncle Finn had remarried Aunt Libby two years ago, it helped that her aunt made sure that each and every holiday and birthday was chock full of fun and laughter with a well-planned itinerary of games, contests, and silly presents. A seed of a smile shadowed her lips. So hopefully, it wouldn't be too difficult to fool the people she loved most.

The people she loved most. The ache resurged with a vengeance.

All but one.

And then, as if she hadn't spilled a million tears already, more swelled beneath her lids, and closing her eyes, she prayed for God to heal Jake's grief—and hers.

Tap. Tap.

Eyelids flipping open, she was pretty sure that would be either Maggie or Aunt Libby, and glancing up at the ceiling, she felt the hint of a smile flicker at the edge of her lips. "Fast work, Lord." Sitting up in the bed, she quickly swiped at her eyes with her limp handkerchief and stashed it beneath her pillow before smoothing out her dress. "Come in," she said brightly, conjuring up a happy smile.

Which … immediately crumpled into a pathetic sob when both Maggie and Aunt Libby popped their heads in.

"Oh, Sher ..." Maggie rushed in while Aunt Libby quietly closed the door before hurrying over as Maggie scooped Sheridan into a protective hug. "Honey, what's wrong? Blaze said you didn't seem yourself, so you went up to rest, but this is way more than exhaustion, isn't it, Sher?"

Giving a weepy nod over Maggie's shoulder, more sobs broke through when Aunt Libby joined in on the hug, the three of them wrapped in a safe cocoon of family and love.

"Move over, sweetheart," Aunt Libby said with a bump of Sheridan's hip, the two of them sitting side by side against the headboard while Maggie sat cross-legged in front. "This has to do with Jake, doesn't it?" Her aunt hooked a gentle arm to Sheridan's waist.

"Uh-huh."

"I thought so," Maggie whispered, "because that's the only time I've ever seen you cry, Sher, when Jake is involved. That and the fact that Blaze just told me you and Jake have been in a secret relationship for the last year and a half."

"What?" Aunt Libby spun to face Sheridan head-on. "Is that true?"

Sheridan nodded with a chew of her lip. "It is, Aunt Libby, and I apologize for not telling you and Maggie about it because I really, really wanted to. But Jake swore me to secrecy."

"*Because* he didn't want to lead you on in the first place, but Blaze and Dash forced him to," Maggie added with a stern arch of her brow.

"What??" A hint of fire lit in Aunt Libby's eyes.

Lids narrowing, Maggie pursed her mouth. "Seems my husband and his brother took it upon themselves to tamper with Sheridan's affections using Jake as the bait, and all because Finn asked them to keep all men away until Sheridan was finished with school."

"*What??!!*" Aunt Libby's eyes bugged wide, her temper flaring along with the color in her cheeks as she glanced from Sheridan to Maggie, hand to her chest. "So, *my* husband

and *yours* have been manipulating an *actual* romantic relationship between Sheridan and Jake to set Sheridan up for heartbreak?"

"Yep." Maggie's lips went as flat as her tone. "Blaze just confessed everything to me last night because he knew Jake was going to lower the boom today, and he was worried about Sher."

Libby grunted. "A little late for that." She shifted to face Sheridan, caressing her arm with a worried look. "When did all this happen, sweetheart?"

"Right before I left for school the first time," she said with a melancholy sigh.

"Because Blaze and Dash heard that Clay Morgan was planning on pursuing Sheridan in New York," Maggie explained, "but they didn't tell Finn because you and he weren't speaking at the time, and they didn't want to upset him further."

"Yes, I remember that well." Libby's face wrinkled in a scrunch. "And I also remember how upset Finn was over Gray Carmody, so I wouldn't be surprised if he bullied Jake, too, before you returned to school after summer vacation."

"He did," Sheridan said quietly, "but Jake felt so badly about leading me on, he told Blaze and Dash he planned to tell me the whole truth during this Christmas break since I only had five more months of college left."

"The whole truth?" Maggie ducked her head to offer Sheridan a tender look.

Sheridan nodded, eyes glazing over once again. "That he's in love with me, but he can never marry me."

"What? *Why?*" Aunt Libby sat straight up.

Sheridan gave a listless shrug of her shoulders. "For a whole host of reasons beginning with me being too young for him and seeing me as a little sister—"

"*Which* he obviously dispelled quickly enough," Maggie said with a rare clip to her tone, obviously as miffed over the whole situation as Aunt Libby.

A sad smile lined Sheridan's lips. "Over and over as a matter of fact, buckling my knees every single time, and his too, from the intensity of his kisses. But he said he made a promise to Uncle Finn when I turned sixteen to keep me away from romance till I graduated—"

"Ha! Doesn't sound like he did *that* too well." Libby sat back with a firm fold of her arms.

"No, he didn't." Sheridan huffed out a heavy breath. "And I told him so. Every conversation, every letter, every magical kiss just made me fall deeper in love, and him as well, apparently."

"Then I don't understand what the problem is, Sher," Maggie coaxed. "Especially if he's free to pursue you in five months' time."

Ingesting a deep breath for strength, Sheridan forged on, filling them in on every one of Jake's reasons—or 'excuses' as she saw them—from his guilt over a horrific past that she only hinted at per his request, to his concerns over the health of future children or subjecting a woman to his dangerous life as a sheriff. A shocked silence prevailed when she finished, all eyes as misty as hers had been when Jake had told her his story not three hours ago.

"Oh, poor Jake!" Maggie's voice was raspy with pain. "Even though you haven't given us details, no one should ever have to go through a traumatic past, especially a child."

"No," Sheridan agreed, heart grieving all over again for the man that she loved.

"*Nor*," Aunt Libby stressed with a sudden jut of her chin, "should anyone have to go through the horror of that for the rest of their lives either."

Sheridan looked over at her aunt. "What do you mean?"

"I mean that my heart breaks for Jake for all the pain he's endured, and it aches for you, Sheridan, for all the pain that it's caused. But it would ache forever for this family if we allowed evil to prevail over good, believing a lie instead of a promise from God."

Sheridan blinked. "What promise, Aunt Libby?"

Libby's eyes flooded with tears as she squeezed Sheridan's hand. "For I know the thoughts that I think toward you, says the Lord, thoughts of peace and not of evil, to give you a future and a hope.' A '*future and a hope*,' Sheridan," she stressed with a shake of Sheridan's hand, "which is what he gave me with Finn despite my obstinance—"

"And me with Blaze, too, despite his!" Maggie's eyes lit with excitement, shining with tears of faith.

"And I have no doubt whatsoever that he wants to give that to Jake as well." She reached to caress Sheridan's face with a gentle hand, her gaze as flooded with faith as Maggie's. "And to you, too, my darling niece."

Sheridan's heart began to thud wildly in her chest, the idea that God had a hope and future for Jake, peace instead of evil, quickening her own faith as well. Moisture stung beneath her lids out of pure joy rather than grief when Scriptures suddenly flooded her mind as quickly as saltwater flooded her eyes.

But I will restore you to health and heal your wounds, declares the Lord.

Surely there is a future, and your hope will not be cut off.

For you, O Lord, are my hope, my trust, O Lord, from my youth.

"From my youth," she whispered, closing her eyes to see a little towheaded child on her knees every single night, praying for a boy whose heart was connected to hers.

Through his own tragic youth.

Paving a way for a 'future and a hope.'

Lashes popping up, Sheridan clasped both Maggie and Aunt Libby's hands, peace purling through her along with a rush of hope. "Oh, Aunt Libby, you're right—I can't allow Jake to live with the horror of his past any longer, not when God can give him a future and a hope"—a giggle slipped from her lips as she splayed a palm to her chest—"with me!"

CHAPTER SEVENTY-TWO

TAP. TAP. IT WAS A tossup as to what was jumping more as Sheridan knocked on Uncle Finn's office door after dinner—her nerves or her heart.

Aunt Libby and Maggie had convinced her that since Uncle Finn was one of the biggest—and one of the first—obstacles that had kept Jake away from Sheridan all these years, it was only fair he'd provide the solution.

"I've told that man all along that as a grown woman, you should have the right to choose whom you will marry, but would he listen?" She'd issued one of the frequent grunts that always accompanied any argument about women's rights, locking her arms across her chest as she sat on Sheridan's bed.

While Aunt Libby had expounded on the controlling stubbornness of men in a rather taut voice, Sheridan had peeked up from picking her nails. "I suppose he was just trying to protect me," she said softly, "and honor my mother's request."

Maggie huffed. "But to coerce your brothers and Jake into spying and plotting against you—his own flesh and blood!—for the sheer purpose of manipulation and control?" A shiver shimmied Maggie's shoulders as she got into the fray with a pretty hefty grunt of her own. "It was sinister and sneaky and flat-out wrong, Sheridan, and I think Libby is right. Finn needs to fix this, and *you* need to tell him so."

"Tonight!" Aunt Libby had underscored with a firm dip of her head, gaze as pointed as her tone. "After dinner."

Gulp. Sheridan had never stood up to Uncle Finn before because she loved and respected him too much and always figured he knew what was best for her. But despite the skitters in her stomach when both Aunt Libby and Maggie had first broached the idea, Sheridan knew in her heart this was the right thing to do.

For her. For Jake. *And* for their family.

So Aunt Libby had laid out the plan, and Maggie had led them in prayer, all up in her room before dinner, which had had, thank God, enough fun and laughter to help calm her nerves.

Till now.

Raising her sweaty fist again, she knocked a second time, harder than before.

Knock. Knock.

"Come in." Her Uncle Finn's tone sounded gruff, hardly easing her fears. Finn McShane was one of the kindest, godliest men she knew, but as the mayor of Virginia City, he'd been under more stress lately. Ever since his marshal was murdered almost six months ago, you could hear the strain in his clipped tone, as if he were too busy to talk. And she'd seen it in the fatigue lining his face at dinner, too, even though Jake had seamlessly slipped into the role of marshal. Sheridan swallowed hard. Probably another reason for his strain—and Sheridan's—since there'd been an uptick in disturbances in town lately.

Gingerly turning the knob, Sheridan peeked into the office where her uncle was working at a desk piled high with papers, his usually neat tie loosened and spectacles perched low on his nose. "I hope I'm not interrupting," she said with a shy smile, even though she knew that she was. But true to his nature, her uncle immediately tossed his pen on the desk and leaned back in his chair with a tired smile, ready to give her his all.

Now, if only he could ...

"You are *never* an interruption, Sheridan Marie, and you need to always remember that. You and your happiness and that of this family is my primary concern."

"That's what I'm counting on, Uncle Finn."

He immediately sat up with a wedge above his nose. "Why? Is there a problem, sweetheart?"

"You might say that." Voice soft, she quietly closed the door before making her way to one of the chairs in front of his desk, slowly sinking into it with a timid smile.

"Are you all right?" He leaned in with a wealth of worry etched in his brow, clearly ready to tackle any problem she might have.

"Physically yes. But emotionally?" She looked up beneath a sweep of heavy lashes, grateful for the prayers Aunt Libby and Maggie were saying on her behalf right this moment. "I've never been worse."

He shot up from his chair and quickly rounded his desk to take the one beside her instead, clutching her hand in his own. "Sheridan, what's wrong, sweetheart?"

Inhaling deeply, Sheridan turned to face her uncle head-on with a firm square of her shoulders like Aunt Libby had instructed her to do.

"Trust me, Sheridan," her aunt had said, "with a controlling man like your uncle, you need to strike while the iron is hot, darling, with immediate control of the situation."

And that's exactly what Sheridan intended to do—strike while the iron was hot. Steeling her spine as well as her posture, she met his own formidable chin with a hefty lift of her own. "I'm in love with Jake, Uncle Finn, and I want to marry him."

"What?" Her uncle dropped her hand like it was that blasted hot iron with which she'd just struck, jerking back to stare at her as if she'd lost her mind. She battled a heavy sigh.

No, only my heart.

"Are you crazy?" he continued, thick dark brows pinched low.

"Yes, Uncle Finn, I am," she said as calmly as she could, quite sure her aunt's and sister-in-law's prayers were in play or she'd be withering from her uncle's glaring frown. "Over

Jake Sullivan, and I need your help to talk him into marrying me."

"What?" This time he shot straight up from his chair, towering over her like a tree about to timber. "You're being ridiculous, young lady. I cannot and will not force a man to marry you."

She jumped to her feet, tempted to stand on the stupid chair to counter him eye to eye. "You can if he's in love with me."

"What?!" Her uncle slapped hands to his hips as he stared her down. "Just what in the devil makes you think that? Far as I can tell, Jake Sullivan sees you as nothing more than his little sister."

Plunking hands to her hips like him, she bent in with a spark in her eyes that would have done Aunt Libby proud. "Then I hate to tell you this, Uncle Finn, but if that's true, then Jake Sullivan has been doing an awful lot of sparkin' with his little sister."

Her uncle's face went as white as his shirt, hazel eyes suddenly as round as the gold buttons on his pinstriped vest. "Sweet mother of mercy," he rasped, mind obviously going way past "sparkin'." "That isn't why you want me to force him—?"

"Oh my goodness, no!" she choked out, her face whooshing as red as his was white. "I just mean Jake has been kissing on me with no little passion, Uncle Finn, and he's even admitted he's in love with me."

"Blue blessed thunder," he whispered, sinking back into his chair with a glazed look, his sagging jaw clearly as limp as his body. "How long has this been going on?"

Sheridan returned to her seat as well, her prior spunk tamed somewhat by her uncle's obvious shock. "Since the night before I left for college. Blaze came to my bedroom late to tell me that Jake wanted to see me in the barn. I found out from Jake later that both Blaze and Dash coerced Jake into leading me on because they discovered Clay Morgan planned to pursue me in New York." She lowered her gaze, careful to avoid any mention of Clay kissing her. "Because *you*" she said, looking up with the softest bit of accusation in her tone, "wanted *them* to keep me away from all men."

A bit of color replenished his cheeks as he shifted awkwardly in the chair. "It's true that I wanted to"—a lump bobbed in his throat—"forestall any potential romantic relationships until after you acquired your degree, sweetheart, but in no way do I condone what Blaze and Dash did ... or Jake for that matter."

"But you *did* ask Jake to flirt with me, did you not, Uncle Finn? To divert my attention away from Gray?"

A ruddy rash crawled up his neck. "I ... suppose, but for crying out loud, sweetheart, the last thing I wanted was for you to fall for a womanizer like that."

"I understand, Uncle Finn," she said with a dip of her head, pinning him with a pointed stare, "but I want *you* to understand that I'm in love with Jake, and *he's* in love with me. And you need to know that *you* are one of the biggest reasons he refuses to act on it." Borrowing a page from Aunt Libby's book about dealing with men, she calmly folded her hands in her lap and arched a brow. "So, I want you to fix it."

Her uncle's eyes narrowed, as thin as the gold clip on his tie. "I don't like your tone, young lady."

Chin nudging up, she bit back a smile at his curt manner, remembering Aunt Libby's statement that ruffling his feathers meant she'd leveled the playing field, her cue for softening her stance while staying her ground. "I know, Uncle Finn, any more than I like you and my brothers manipulating my life behind my back, robbing me of my independence, so I apologize. And no disrespect intended, sir, but you *were* the one who started this whole conspiracy when I turned sixteen, and you *did* say that happiness and that of this family is your primary concern."

Expression sober, Sheridan clamped her lips together to thwart a giggle on the rise, the grinding of her uncle's jaw confirming she was on point according to Aunt Libby. Jaw firm, she patiently waited while he stared her down in that imposing way that had always disarmed her as a child.

A loud bluster of air finally escaped his lips as he all but gouged the bridge of his nose with his fingers. "Confound it, Sheridan, I promised your mother you would get a degree before there was even a hint of romance in your life, young lady, and I aim to keep my word."

"Understood, Uncle Finn, but I'm only five months away from a degree, sir, and you need to know that there's been far more than a 'hint' of romance going on under your nose—"

"Enough!" He rose and stormed around his desk, palms pressed white on its littered surface while he leaned in with a commanding air. His jaw was as stiff as his tone. "I refuse to mettle in Jake's life."

Jumping up, she followed suit, leaning in as she slapped palms to his desk. "I see, just mine, is that it?"

"Precisely," he said, all tooth-grinding edging up considerably as he avoided her gaze while he dropped in his chair. He snatched up his pen in a clear dismissal, scrawling his signature on letters his secretary at City Hall had obviously prepared. "Come back with a degree in your hand, Sheridan, and maybe I'll consider discussing it."

"No!" She thumped a fist on his desk, determined she would not go back to school without a commitment from Jake.

Her uncle looked up from his papers, the whites of his eyes circled in shock. "Blue smoke of Hades, I knew sending you to that suffragette school would ruin you. You sound just like my wife."

"Thank you," Sheridan said, curbing the squirm of a smile lest she annoy her uncle further per Aunt Libby's advice.

"It *wasn't* a compliment!" He snapped.

"I heard that, Finn McShane!" The door flew open with a loud crack to the wall as Aunt Libby marched in along with Maggie and Shaylee, with Blaze and Dash hot on their heels.

Striding right up to the front of his desk, she hooked one hand to Sheridan's waist while she leaned in and pointed the other right in her husband's face. "And you are in big trouble, mister."

CHAPTER SEVENTY-THREE

"WHAT IN BLUE BLAZES IS going on?" Finn shouted, springing up from his chair like he'd just been bucked by a bronc.

And a filly at that.

"We are having a family meeting, Finn McShane," Aunt Libby said with a thrust of her chin, the action as common as air, "because *this* is a family, sweetheart, not a dictatorship. So, where do you want to have this meeting—here in your office or in the parlour?"

"Dad-burn-it, Libby, I don't want to have it at all—"

Ignoring his gruff tone, she glanced over her shoulder at Blaze and Dash. "Boys, will you be kind enough to bring in a few chairs from the dining room so we can all sit in comfort?"

"Blaze, Dash—halt!" Finn yelled. "Forget the blasted chairs. They're not necessary"—he bent in with palms splayed like before, cauterizing Aunt Libby with a threatening glare—"because we are *not* having a meeting!"

All the females in the room turned to burn Blaze and Dash with a look that quickly sent them on chair retrieval.

"Libby, please …" Finn's voice had lost some of its edge, his fatigue suddenly far more pronounced than earlier. His hazel eyes bore dark circles beneath that Sheridan hadn't noticed before as he pleaded with his wife. "You and I can talk with Sheridan, sweetheart, but this is not a family affair."

Smile tender, Aunt Libby rounded his desk to give him a tight hug, pulling away to blink up with a sheen of moisture in her eyes. "Actually it is, Finn," she said quietly, "because Jake is family, and he needs us now more than ever before."

"What do you mean?" he said as Dash and Blaze each brought in two chairs, lining them up in a semi-circle in front of Finn's desk.

Sheridan perched on the edge of her chair as she beseeched her uncle with a pained look. "Aunt Libby means that Jake is suffering inside—horribly—Uncle Finn, over a past that has tormented him his whole life, which is one of the reasons he gave me for not marrying me despite being in love with me."

"What kind of past?" Blaze asked, a criss-cross of worry lining his brow over a best friend who was more like a brother.

"Too horrible for you to even imagine, Blaze." Tears pooled in Sheridan's eyes as she stared at her brother. "Which is why he's never told anyone. And he only told me as one of *many* reasons to convince me we could never be." She swiped at the moisture on her face. "He asked me not to relay any details, so I won't, but suffice it to say it was painful enough that he sobbed in my arms for a good long time."

Blaze's Adam's apple jerked hard as he gave a curt nod.

"What other reasons?" Uncle Finn asked, his voice thick with emotion, drawing Sheridan's gaze to his own. Tears instantly stung in her eyes at the hard cut of his jaw, a sure sign he was fighting his feelings for a man who may as well be a son.

Love lodged in her throat as she glanced at her uncle, tenderness welling inside because she knew how much he cared. "He's got a whole saddlebag of them, Uncle Finn. Everything from being too old for me … to seeing me as just a little sister—"

"Ha!" Aunt Libby rolled her eyes. "Which is a bald-faced lie, and everyone in this room knows it, especially you two," she said, pinning both Blaze and Dash with an incriminating look, "since it was both of you who bullied Jake into leading Sheridan on in the first place."

"Wait—everyone knows what?" Shaylee glanced from Aunt Libby to her brothers and back with a pinch of brows, obviously hurt that she'd been left out of family secrets.

Maggie leaned close to Shaylee's ear. "That Jake's in love with your sister."

"Holy frog spit!" Shaylee shouted, her eyes practically bugging out of her head. "How do you know?"

"Because he kissed her!" Everyone in the room shouted in unison, except for Shaylee and Finn.

"Ewwww ..." Shaylee slapped a hand to her eyes. "I'm too young for this."

"So is Half-Pint," Uncle Finn muttered under his breath, earning a rapid-fire glare from his wife. He homed in on Sheridan once again. "What else?"

"Well, as I already mentioned, he thinks his vile past makes him unfit to have a family."

"Why the devil would he think that?" Finn demanded.

Sheridan offered her uncle a sad smile. "Because he's been told that over and over since he's been small, by his parents, town folk, ministers, doctors, you name it."

"Doctors?" Dash looked at her with a crimp in his brow.

"Yes," she whispered, heart aching over the true reason Jake wanted nothing to do with marriage. "Jake's father was such a violent man, that a doctor once told his mother he believed Jake's father had a mental illness. An illness that is"—she swallowed hard as tears swelled in her eyes, voice tapering off to a whisper—"hereditary."

The room went completely silent, Sheridan's heart pounding so hard, she was certain everyone could hear it.

"Who was this doctor?" Uncle Finn asked.

Sheridan gave a small lift of shoulders. "I don't know, Uncle Finn. That's something you would have to ask Jake."

"One man's opinion does not a diagnosis make," Maggie said quietly, "and there's certainly no evidence of any mental disorder in Jake."

"Unless you consider smelly feet a mental disorder," Dash quipped, obviously trying to lighten the tense mood, "since he sleeps in his boots half the time."

"And pert near snorting snot when he laughs too hard."

Blaze offered with a lazy smile.

Face somber, Uncle Finn expelled a weary breath, apparently too tired for humor. "Anything else?"

Sheridan nodded. "Both his father and stepfather were killed in the line of duty ..." she said, voice trailing off as she sent her uncle a soulful look.

"Line of duty?" Finn squinted at her.

She swallowed the lump in her throat. "They were both sheriffs," she whispered, "so between that and Cyrus losing his life in that robbery, Jake refuses to subject any woman to the dangers of his profession."

"I see." Finn sagged back in his chair with a tired sigh, head bowed and eyes closed as he rubbed his temple with the pads of his fingers. "Well, I can certainly understand your concern about Jake's state of mind, Sheridan, and I definitely share it, so I will be happy to talk to him about *that* further ..."

"But?" Libby hovered on the edge of her seat like Sheridan, with the same pinch in her brow.

Finn glanced up, offering his wife a weary smile. "But I can't force a man to marry my niece no matter how much I may want him in the family, Libby. I love and respect Jake as much as all of you, which is exactly why I refuse to twist his arm into something as important as this."

Libby issued a grunt. "Too bad you didn't have the same reservations with Sheridan," she muttered, "arm-twisting Jake and your nephews to manipulate her life."

"Might I remind you, *Libby*," Finn said in a patient tone that bordered dangerously close to the edge, "that I am Sheridan's guardian, responsible for her well-being while Jake is a grown man out on his own."

"And I'm a grown woman, Uncle Finn"—Sheridan's chin notched up—"who could very well be 'out on her own' in five months with a teaching degree in hand."

"Fine." Finn picked up his pen once again with a mulish press of his mouth that Aunt Libby often mentioned. "When that happens, young lady, you come back and we'll talk."

"No!" Libby shot to her feet, chin elevating to new heights. Finn's brows scrunched low. "No?"

"That's right," Libby said, battle-ready with a staunch pluck of hands to her hips. "Jake is an important part of this family, Finn, and his well-being affects all of us, especially Sheridan, so this needs to be addressed to all of our satisfaction *tonight*. Or else."

Uncle Finn's jaw went slack ... *right* before it hardened to steel. "Or *else*? And what the devil is *that* supposed to mean?"

Sheridan sprang from the chair, shoulders back and head high. "It *means*, Uncle Finn, that Gray Carmody has asked to court me," she said, ignoring Shaylee's gasp and the open-mouthed stares of both her brothers and uncle, "and if I don't have a commitment from Jake before I leave"— she swallowed hard, Aunt Libby's assurance that this would work spurring her on—"I plan to say yes."

"Over my dead body!" Finn shouted with another bang of his fist.

"Precisely, sweetheart," Aunt Libby said with a sweet smile, "and I'm too fond of you to see that happen, darling, so please don't risk losing Sheridan over this." Her brows rose in a veiled dare. "*Or* me."

"Uncle Finn," Maggie said quietly, the plea in her tone clearly an attempt to diffuse the situation. "Gray Carmody is very charming and very persuasive, with a wealthy family he adores on the *other* side of the country, so we could very well lose Sheridan altogether."

"To a womanizing dandy who gambles," Blaze pointed out, joining forces with the ladies.

"And I miss Jake." Shaylee's lower lip inched into a pout. "So if he married Sheridan, he would be around a lot more like before, right?"

"You've got that right, Doodlebug." Dash scratched the back of his neck with an evil grin. "Besides, I miss Jake too"— he smacked the back of Blaze's head in a jest—"because he's a whole lot more fun than this clown, especially since Jake isn't around anymore."

"So." Aunt Libby slipped around Finn's desk to loop an arm to his waist, peering up with a plea. "Are you going to show this family just how much you love them and fix this?" She stood on tiptoe to press a gentle kiss to his jaw, lashes fluttering. "Or are you going to sleep in the spare bedroom?"

Titters circled the room as Finn seared his wife with a half-lidded glare. "I never stood a chance, did I?"

"No!" A chorus of dissent rose to the rafters.

Finn's mouth went flat as he jerked Libby close with a hard hook of his arm. "I didn't think so, but I'm telling you all right now that yes, I will present your case, but I refuse to put a gun to the man's head, understood? Because in the end, it's Jake's decision, not mine." He angled a stiff finger at Sheridan. "And *you* have to finish school and stay away from courting Gray Carmody no matter what Jake decides, agreed?"

"Agreed," Sheridan said with a cleansing sigh, blowing both Finn and Libby a kiss before hugging Maggie with a loud squeal.

Knock! Knock! Knock!

Finn looked at his watch as Blaze jumped up to answer the door. "What now?" he muttered, huffing out a heavy sigh.

Deputy Wilcox rushed into Finn's study with Blaze hot on his heels, both of them wearing the same grim press of their jaws. "Sorry to intrude, Mayor McShane, b-but there was a gambling g-game gone awry at the Bucket of Blood involving Slick Sikeston."

Wringing his hat in his hands, he glanced around the room before fixing his gaze square on Finn with a hard bob of his throat. "And Jake has been shot."

CHAPTER SEVENTY-FOUR

"**S**O ... YOU NEED ANYTHING else?" Sheridan said with a bright smile, fluffing Jake's pillow for the tenth dad-gum time as he lay in the guest room at the Silver Lining Ranch. Checking her watch, she bent to press a kiss to his cheek before he could dodge it, the twinkle in her eyes not boding well for his efforts to keep her at bay. "Maybe Christmas cookies? A glass of milk?"—she clasped her hands behind her back like a little girl, giving a tiny shrug. "*A wife?*"

He rolled his eyes, lips pinched to keep the dad-burned smile away, but it wasn't easy. She'd hovered over him like a mama hover fly for the last three days—changing his dressings, waiting on him, reading to him. Not that he didn't like it deep down. Because he did.

That was the problem.

Especially when she applied liniment to his bare chest in slow easy circles that set both his skin and blood on fire. Bending so dog-gone close, the scent of lavender almost drove him out of his mind. Hands twitching to just jerk her close and kiss her hard.

"I think I'll sleep now," he said, squeezing his eyes shut in what he hoped would be a clear dismissal.

Screeeeeeech!

His lids popped up and eyes spanned wide as she scraped a chair across the wooden floor, positioning it right beside his bed, complete with that blasted needlepoint hoop she was always toting around. He forced a scowl worthy of Blaze on a bad day. Which took some doing with those plump pink lips pursed in concentration while she worked. Wisps of gold-spun curls fluttered loose from her topknot, kissing her alabaster neck like he so longed to do.

A longing that rivaled his longing to escape from her care.

But Libby had demanded Jake heal here, and Finn had ordered him to stay, least till the bullet hole in his chest was completely healed.

The one Slick Sikeston had pumped into his body.

And the one that came within a breath of stealing his life.

Just like Sheridan had stolen his heart, only she had hit dead center, a silver bullet piercing clean through.

He blasted out a noisy sigh, thinking the sound of his frustration might deter her, but he didn't hold out much hope. "Don't you have anything better to do?" he snapped, figuring it was either grouchiness or attraction, and God knows he had plenty of both to go 'round.

Those thick lashes flipped up to reveal blue eyes on a mission. "You mean besides getting you to marry me?" She went back to her needlepoint, the faintest of smiles flickering across her lips. "Nope."

"Come on, Sher," he said with a low groan, figuring he'd never heal with her wearing him down like this. "I'm too tired to argue and I really need a nap. Besides, I already told you all the reasons we can't marry, darlin', so you need to let it go because I'm just trying to do the right thing and keep you safe."

"The *right thing*, Jake Sullivan," she said with another quick glance at her watch, is for you to admit to the entire family that you love me as much as I love you. And marry me already!"

His gaze softened. "I have admitted that, Sher," he said quietly, "and I'll admit it again and again. But it's because of that very love that I refuse to put you in harm's way, so my stance on that is firm, darlin', and wild horses couldn't pull me off course"—a gentle smile tipped the edge of his mouth, hoping he could ease the blow with a touch of humor—"or in my case, a team of stubborn donkeys."

"No?" One beautiful blond brow angled high as she checked her watch once again just as a knock sounded on the door.

His sigh could have ruffled those flaxen curls skimming her beautiful neck. "Now who the devil is that?" he muttered, just wanting to be left alone.

Rising with a smirk he'd seen more than once over the last few days, she clutched that stupid hoop to her chest and marched to the door, tossing a sassy wink over her shoulder. "Why that would be your own personal team of stubborn donkeys, Mr. Sullivan, so I'll just leave you in their very capable hands."

She opened the door and Finn ambled in, lodging a deep groan in Jake's chest. "So, how's our boy doing today, Sher?"

"Cranky as ever, Uncle Finn, so I'm hoping you can sweeten him up a bit."

"Well, I'll do my level best, darlin'," Finn said, settling into her chair. He leaned back with a lazy smile and an easy cross of arms as Sheridan left. "How you doing today, Jake?"

Grateful when he heard the click of the door, Jake expelled a weary sigh while he folded his hands on his stomach, hoping to make this short and sweet. And *not* the "sweet" Sheridan wanted either. "Tired, sir. Not sleeping real well, so I was just fixing to catch a few winks."

"Me too, son, which is why I'm here."

Jake turned to look at him with a scrunch of his brows. "Sir?"

Finn offered a faint smile. "You see, we had a family meeting a few nights ago before you were shot, and it seems everybody's a mite worried about you."

A silent sigh of relief escaped Jake's lips. "Well, there's no need for worry, sir. Slick Sikeston will be locked up a good long while with the list of charges I've compiled, so things should settle down real nice and easy in town."

"Glad to hear that, Jake." Finn gave a slow nod. "But it's not the town I'm worried about."

Jake's lungs froze.

"It's here at the ranch, where me and my family are worried sick about your state of mind and heart, son, especially Sheridan."

Jake blinked, not able to breathe as Finn leaned in to rest forearms on knees spread wide, hands loosely clasped in between. But when his boss pinned him with a point-blank stare, Jake was pretty sure his pulse stopped too. "Are you in love with Sheridan?"

Jake's eyelids staggered closed, well aware fire licked at his cheeks. How had it come to this? An attraction that should have stayed buried deep, now exposed for all to see?

Including the man he admired most.

And the man to whom he'd given his word to protect his niece.

"Sheridan says you are, Jake, but I want to hear it from you. Are you in love with my niece?"

It was moments like this that Jake wished he could bald-faced lie his way out, but that had never been his way. At least since Dirk had first shown him what truth was. And *now*, Finn McShane.

Fortifying his lungs with a deep draw of air, he opened his eyes and stared right back at the man whose opinion mattered most in the world. "Yes, sir, I am, but I hope you believe me when I say I never intended for that to happen."

Finn's mouth took a twist, his dry smile loosening some of the tightness in Jake's chest. "I have no doubt about that, son, because Sheridan has come clean, and to be honest, if Libby had hankered after me like Sheridan has after you?" A slow smile eased across his lips as he stared at the floor with an awkward cuff of his neck. "Well, let's just say I'd have a whole passel of sons and daughters to go along with those nieces and nephews."

Jake smiled. "I have no doubt about that, sir, because you're a man who sets his sights and doesn't give up, something I greatly admire."

Finn peered up with a lidded gaze. "Thank you, son, but Sheridan is my blood, so I guess you could say the same about her."

Jake shook his head, gaze wandering into a faraway smile. "No doubt about that." He expelled a heavy sigh as he pinched the bridge of his nose, meeting Finn's gaze head-on once more. "But I can't let her win this time, sir, because I love her too much."

"So I hear." Finn leaned back with a fold of arms. "She didn't go into detail, mind you, but she tells me you have a medical condition that you don't want to pass on to your children."

Blood gorged his cheeks. "Yes, sir, and that's the number one reason I can't marry your niece."

"I see. So you talked to the doctor who gave you this opinion?"

Jake looked away. "No, sir, but my mother did."

"Well, no offense to your mother, son, but if it's all the same to you, I'd like you to talk to a doctor friend of mine in Carson City, who just so happens to specialize in psychiatry. I think he could give you more insight into whether your fears are well-founded or not as well as help you sort out the traumas of your past. Would you consider that, Jake?"

Mouth compressed, Jake gave a curt nod.

"Good. I'll have my secretary make the appointment and reserve a round-trip ticket for you on the V&T, all right?"

"Yes, sir."

"So, Jake," Finn began again, leaning back in his chair once more with a pensive look and arms crossed, "I assume we can establish you no longer see Sheridan as a little sister, but as a woman you're attracted to, correct?"

Heat blasted Jake's cheeks as he looked away. "Yes, sir."

"And I know for a fact that an age difference of say, eight years between a man and a woman is no deterrent to a good marriage, at least based on Pastor and Mrs. Poppy, who frankly, had the best marriage I know. Would you agree?"

Jake rubbed the back of his neck, wondering why in the devil it was so hot in here. "I guess."

"Good." Finn nodded. "Because that covers four of the problems Sheridan mentioned regarding your reluctance to pursue your feelings for her—the physical and the mental, correct?"

"I ... suppose." He glanced up. "*If* the specialist can assure me that there's no danger to Sheridan in having"—his Adam's apple hitched at the very thought—"my children."

"Agreed. But that still leaves one major problem, son, which can, in fact, negate all the others."

Jake looked up, eyes in a squint. "And what's that, sir?"

Finn's vest rose and fell in a quiet sigh as he met Jake's gaze with a frank one of his own. "The spiritual aspect to all of this," he said quietly, the question in his eyes so intense, that Jake was tempted to look away. "Now, I've always believed you to be one of the finest men I know, Jake, and I *thought* your faith ran deep like my own, so you'll forgive me, son, if I have to ask ..." He dipped his head to probe Jake with a penetrating stare. Seconds ticked by like an oil-greased fuse burning its way to one dandy of a blast as he took his sweet old time with a real slow blink.

"Do you believe in God?"

CHAPTER SEVENTY-FIVE

H EAT FLASHED FROM THE TOP of Jake's head to the soles of his feet and back, pert near scorching both his body and his temper, something few people ever triggered.

Ignoring the pain, he struggled to sit up, wincing as he pulled a tattered Bible from beneath his pillow. He all but hurled it on his bed for Finn to see. Breathing hard, he finally sagged against the wooden headboard. "Of course I believe in God, Finn. What the devil kind of question is that?"

Finn eyed him with a pensive look, gaze flicking from Jake to the Bible, upon which Jake's hand now trembled on top. "*And* His Word?"

"Yes, dad-gum-it," he bit out, remembering all too well how Sister Fred forever changed his life with the faith she'd taught from the Bible, his one life line to sanity that he'd kept under his pillow every night ever since.

"I thought so." Finn idly scratched the back of his neck. "So, I guess I can't help but wonder, son," he said slowly, his gaze needling in once again, "how your past squares with the Word of God, which says 'if any man be in Christ, he is a new creature: old things are passed away; behold, all things are become new, 2 Corinthians 5:17-18.'"

Jake shifted in the bed, not comfortable with Finn's line of questioning.

"Because," Finn continued, "Sheridan seems to think there are some 'old things' you're holding onto, Jake, that pose an even bigger threat to your soul than your past does to your mind."

"I've repented for my past, sir, if that's what you're asking."

"Oh, I have no doubt about that." Finn's smile was laced

with affection. "The caliber of man you are today speaks for itself."

He paused for several seconds, as if reflecting on something far away. "A long time ago, Pastor Poppy taught me that the word 'repentance' in the Bible is a Greek word that means 'change of mind.' Making a decision to turn around and face a new direction, to literally 'turn toward the light,' and you have certainly done that, son."

A slow, reedy thread of relief seeped through Jake's lips while Finn repositioned to face him more casually. Hunched with elbows propped on parted knees, he rested his chin on folded hands. "You already know the Bible teaches that Jesus is the Light of the World, son, a Light that illuminates our lives, helping us to see—and live—more clearly. And yet, our shadow is always behind us, Jake, looming larger than it actually is."

Finn peered up with compassion. "So, if we continually look over our shoulder, fixing our gaze more on the shadows than the light ... we can't see our life *or* the people in it clearly because not only are we not looking at them, but they're obscured by darkness."

He lifted his shoulders slightly, the action almost impassive. "Suddenly we're disconnected and alone in the dark, and you and I both know," he said quietly, his smile kind, "that God's Word says, 'it's not good for man to be alone' because He's 'called us out of darkness into his marvelous light.'"

Averting his gaze, Jake gave a slow nod. He'd felt that marvelous light himself from the first moment He'd begun living for God. His mouth compressed. *Until* he tasted the forbidden fruit and fallen in love with Finn's niece.

"What I'm trying to say, Jake," Finn said, his tone soft and low, "is that we can't grab onto the future, son, until we let go of the past."

"I thought I had, sir." Jake's voice was barely a whisper as his eyelids lumbered closed, weighted down by a past that still loomed large and lethal, inflicting death on any hope he might ever have.

"So did I, son, after Libby left the first time."

Jake glanced up, remembering Blaze talking about Finn's marriage to Libby almost twenty years ago, a marriage that had ended as quickly as it'd started with an argument that stole almost half of their lives.

The thief does not come except to steal, and to kill, and to destroy. I have come that they may have life, and that they may have it more abundantly.

The thief. Jake's heart constricted. Just like he was trying to do to Jake's life? Overshadowing the good to keep him locked in the darkness of the past?

Finn absently scratched the back of his head. "At the time, Libby and I didn't realize how young and immature we were. And speaking for myself"—he actually winced—"I thought it was all her fault, of course, because I was strong and steadfast in my faith, thanks to the Poppys."

His gaze wandered into a distant stare as the smile faded from his lips. "So, after several years of finally letting Libby go in my mind, I couldn't understand why despite having four beautiful kids I adored, a thriving silver mine, and an up-and-coming ranch, a part of me still felt like I was living in the dark."

He grunted, as if to himself. "No interest in women. No interest in a future with a wife. No interest in mending emotional fences with Libby, her family, or mine. And no earthly idea I was still living in the shadows, holding onto grievances against my sister and her husband, for abandonment that deeply hurt my nieces and nephews."

Jake peered up, eyes in a squint. "So, when did you figure it out?"

Finn laughed, the sound harsh during such a grave conversation. "I didn't. Not till the nightmares started." His gaze flicked up beneath hooded eyes, nailing Jake to the wall with a knowing look. "Sound familiar?"

Jake swallowed hard as he gave a brief nod.

"Even so, I still didn't realize what was going on until they got so bad, I sought counsel with Pastor and Mrs. Poppy, two of the wisest people I've ever known."

He paused, as if for effect. "Turns out I had a monumental grudge buried so deep, even I didn't know it was there, not only against Libby, but especially her father, for breaking us up, and it was eating me alive."

"So ... what did you do?" Jake asked with a bow of his head, eyes lagging into a vacant stare, pretty sure his monumental grudges weren't buried near as deep as Finn's. More like festering right below the surface.

"Well, it took some time, mind you," Finn said quietly, "but through prayer and counseling, I learned to forgive. And as God is my witness, His pure Light—His Son, who *is* the Way, the Truth, and the Light—chased those shadows and nightmares away once and for all."

And the light shines in darkness; and the darkness overcame it not.

Moisture immediately burned beneath Jake's lids. "And you were finally ... f-free?" His voice cracked on the last word, hardly able to believe it could ever happen for him.

"Nope. Not quite."

Jake's head lashed up.

Finn grinned, reaching out to clasp Jake's shoulder in a brief grip. "Also had to learn to forgive myself, Jake, for letting Libby go in the first place and for choosing pride over love."

He hesitated for the briefest of moments. "Sheridan didn't give us any details, Jake, but she did say you suffer from a great deal of guilt over your brutal past, whether at your hand or that of your parents, and that's simply not right, son. Galatians 5:1 says, 'It is for freedom that Christ has set us free. Stand firm, then, and do not let yourselves be burdened again by a yoke of slavery.' So that freedom is sitting right there in the light, Jake, ours for the taking. But it does no good at all if we're fixed on the shadows behind us, giving more credence to the darkness than to the marvelous Light."

A flicker of hope flared in Jake's heart as one of his favorite Scriptures burned in his mind's eye, suddenly clearer than ever before despite the tears that blurred his vision.

If the Son therefore shall make you free, ye shall be free indeed.

Free indeed.

Not temporarily.

Not partially.

Not almost.

But free.

Firmly. Fully. *Forever.*

Fingers trembling on his Bible, he closed his eyes, peace flooding his body and his mind so powerfully, he put his hand to his heart.

Until his eyes jolted open, the feel of the gauze dressing reminding him of who he was.

He was the marshal.

A marshal that Finn desperately needed.

And a marshal who owed a great debt to that very man.

Expelling a draining sigh, Jake looked up. "I thank you for your wise counsel, Finn, and I fully intend to follow through with everything you've said. Even so," he said with a cramp in his heart, "I still have my reasons for not marrying Sheridan, so I'd like to just leave it at that."

Giving a slow nod, Finn rose with a heavy sigh. "All right, son. I've done my best to convince you, but ultimately, it's your decision in the end, so I'll just let it go. You get some sleep, Jake, because we need you."

"Yes, sir."

Giving Jake a light clap on the back, Finn headed for the door.

"And, sir?"

Finn turned, hand on the knob. "Yes, son?"

Jake fought a gulp. "Thank you for everything—from the moment you first took me in at the age of twelve until this very moment. I owe you my life, sir."

Finn smiled. "I doubt that, Jake, but you've been a blessing to us too." He opened the door, then turned, brow furrowing in a squint. "Oh, almost forgot. There's just one more thing, son ..." His mouth leveled into a grim smile. "You're fired."

CHAPTER SEVENTY-SIX

"**C**AN I GET YOU ANYTHING else, Jake? More egg nog? Christmas cookies? A foot stool?" Sheridan fussed over Jake on the loveseat like he was the only one in the room. She had to! Thanksgiving literally spilled from her heart, so very grateful he was alive and able to join them for Christmas dinner along with Libby's parents Maeve and Aiden, and Angus and Gert. Adjusting the pillow behind his head, she was pretty sure she was glowing more than the candles on their eight-foot tree, its flickering radiance dancing off of Aunt Libby's painted glass ornaments.

There was no question Jake was different since Uncle Finn and he had talked, but neither would give her a clue as to why. He was no longer morose or cranky like he'd always been since she'd first kissed him that day at the shooting range, but more like the Jake she used to know. Crooked smiles and twinkling eyes and little-boy tease that always assured her she held a special place in his heart.

And, oh, how she longed to make that permanent!

But for now, the old Jake was back, and she gladly soaked it in along with the warmth of the fire in the hearth, its scent of wood smoke drifting in the air with that of gingerbread, cinnamon, and pine.

"Sheridan, sit," Jake ordered with that easy smile she so loved, patting the seat beside him with a sparkle in his eyes. "You've been running ragged waiting on me, Half-Pint, and it's wearing me out."

"Hey," Blaze said to Maggie while he held her close, the two of them sharing the sofa with Libby and Finn. "How come you don't wait on me like that?" he asked with a mock scowl, giving her waist a pinch.

"Because you're not injured, silly." Sheridan giggled as she offered Jake a snickerdoodle from the plate on the table before passing them around to everyone else.

"Although that *can* be arranged," Maggie said with a pensive tilt of her head, eliciting chuckles around the room.

"Might be worth it." Blaze dove for her neck, gobble-kissing her like he used to do with his sisters before tipping her back in a kiss that lasted so long, Shaylee wrinkled her nose.

"I say we open presents," her little sister said as she shook one of her tissue-wrapped gifts stacked under the tree, the paper crackling as much as the fire.

"Good idea." Uncle Finn rose to promptly dispense presents to one and all. One by one, each opened gifts, unearthing treasures of love. From bags of butterscotch candies and peppermint drops for Maggie and Blaze, to new decks of cards for Angus and Bert, the parlour was filled with paper and bows and laughter and love.

When it came for Jake's turn, everyone laughed when he unwrapped a tin of foot powder from Blaze and Dash, followed by a brand-new shiny marshal's badge from Finn in the shape of a star. "Since the old one is tarnished," her uncle said with a wink at Sheridan, "and you won't be needing it anymore. Figured you needed a memento, maybe to mount in a frame."

Tears stung as Sheridan blew her uncle a kiss, never believing he would actually fire Jake from the job just for her. He'd told her he'd done everything he could to sway him toward Sheridan, but in the end, the decision would be up to Jake as to what he would do.

Looking at him now as he opened his last gift, her heart swelled with affection for the man she would love forever, no matter what he would decide. Carefully pushing the tissue paper aside, he held up another sampler she'd made, and instantly she spied a sheen of moisture in his gaze.

"What's it say?" Shaylee wanted to know, and when Jake turned it around, Sheridan couldn't read it for the blur in her eyes, but she could read it in her heart all the same.

If the Son therefore shall make you free, ye shall be free indeed. – John 8:36

"It's ... beautiful, Sheridan," Jake said with a soggy smile, heart flooding with gratitude that it was finally true. After Finn had fired him three days ago, he'd been in shock, but it wasn't long before the shock gave way to the possibility that just maybe Finn was right. That it was for freedom—Jake's and everyone else's—that Christ had set men free. To stand firm forever, never again burdened by a yoke of slavery.

Yes, he knew he had miles to go before his heart and his mind were completely healed, but through the help of a doctor and the counsel of Finn and Mrs. Poppy, he believed for the very first time that it could be possible, that he could put the past behind to go forth into the Light.

But this one thing I do, forgetting those things which are behind, and reaching forth unto those things which are before, I press toward the mark for the prize of the high calling.

The high calling. Tears flooded his eyes.

Both in God.

And with Sheridan.

"It's the best gift I've ever gotten," he whispered, giving Sheridan's hand another gentle squeeze, "but there's still more to go."

She blinked as he handed her a round tissue-wrapped gift with a bow because he knew she wasn't expecting another present. He'd already given her a favorite book she'd once mentioned in a letter, so she simply stared at the gift in her palm, face in a scrunch when she finally glanced up. "But you already gave me a present, Jake, so what's this?"

He shrugged as he slid her a boyish smile that dusted her face with a pretty blush. "A little something I planned a long time ago, Sher, to give as a truce."

"A truce?" She offered a shy smile, turning the present over. "A truce for what?"

"You'll see," he said with a nod while she slowly unwrapped it.

Her smile grew into a grin when she saw a tin of lemon drops from Burdzy's Emporium, one of Jake's favorite candies, which over the years, had become one of her favorites too. "My favorite!" she said with a giggle, prying the lid open before she folded the inside papers aside with a gasp.

"What is it?" Both Maggie and Libby sat up at the shocked look on Sheridan's face.

"A necklace," she whispered with a swipe at her eyes, obviously never expecting anything as personal as jewelry from Jake. Holding it up, she grinned outright at the silver bullet hanging from a silver chain.

"In honor of that blasted shooting lesson that Blaze forced me to give," Jake said with a sheepish grin. "Figured this could be a truce to let you know I'll never balk again. And to prove it, Half-Pint ..." Pulling another tissue-wrapped present from his pocket, he handed her a flat square with a small string bow on top.

Her mouth dropped open as she fingered the tissue, more tears welling.

"Open it!" Everyone shouted in unison, and when she did, a sob actually broke from her throat.

"Sheridan Marie Donovan," Jake said as he slowly—and most precariously—slid onto his knees on the floor, taking the gift from her hand. Ignoring the gasps in the room, he held up a silver ring with a small turquoise stone on top and smiled.

The very same ring he'd made when she was small.

Because those dad-burned clover rings would never last.

The sobs kept coming as she put a trembling hand to her mouth. "Is this ...?"

"It is," he said with a wide grin. "The one I made for you

when you were four, out of the silver from your uncle's mine and that tiny piece of turquoise I found in a mountain stream when Blaze, Dash, and I were fishing." He winked. "I knew it belonged to you the moment I saw it because it matches your eyes." He turned it over with a squint. "Of course, I'll have to have the jeweler in town resize it for you and replace that pitiful stone—"

"No!" She snatched it out of his hand so fast, he almost fell over, drawing laughter from everyone in the room. "I love it just as it is!" She slipped it on her pinky finger with a loud squeal, holding it out to admire. "And we can have it sized when you're feeling better."

"Uh, Sher, hate to tell you," Blaze said with a lazy smile, "but that isn't an engagement ring until the man actually proposes ..."

Her smile faded a hair as she blinked at Jake with wide eyes. "Uh ... you are proposing, aren't y-you?"

"Ha! If he doesn't, Sher, I'd put that silver bullet in a gun and give it back," Aunt Libby said with a smirk that matched Maggie's.

Laughing, Jake's smile sobered as he took Sheridan's hands in his. "Sheridan Marie Donovan," he whispered, joy flooding his soul over the miracle God had wrought for him and the woman before him, "will you marry me for the very last time?"

With a squeal that both hurt his ears and healed his heart, she lunged into his arms. "Yes, Jacob Michael Sullivan!" she shouted, "and it's about bloomin time!"

Cheers rose as Jake bent to kiss her, the taste of tears, snickerdoodles, and Sheridan the sweetest he'd ever had. "I love you, Sheridan, and I have forever."

Her giggle was soft against his lips as she pressed a gentle palm to his jaw. "I love you, too, Jake, and I'm sure glad it didn't take a silver bullet to get you on your knees."

"Me, too," he whispered, nuzzling her lips like he'd always had in his dreams, "because truth be told, darlin'"—he kissed her again, long and slow and sweet—"there's already a hole in my heart that only you can fill."

A NOTE TO MY READERS

THANK YOU SO VERY MUCH for reading Sheridan's and Jake's story. I will admit that I struggled with the plot for this novel because in my heart of hearts, I did not feel Jake's motivation for avoiding a romantic relationship with Sheridan—his allegiance and promise to Finn and his dysfunctional background—were strong enough reasons.

So, I did what I always do when I run into a wall on my plots—I prayed, asking God to give me a rock-solid rationale for keeping these two lovebirds apart. As always, God came through with flying colors, albeit pretty 11th hour as usual—when I was just three chapters away from finishing!

What was God's answer to my prayer? Well, believe it or not, I discovered quite by accident that right about the time of this novel, "Psychopathy" (from psychopath, "psych"—soul or mind, and "pathy"—suffering or disease), was first introduced by German psychiatrists as a hereditary mental disorder. And since Jake's father was an abusive, downright mean, cruel, and deceitful person, it only made sense to have a doctor diagnose his father with a condition that Jake would *never* want to inflict on the children of the woman he loved.

As far as Jake and Sheridan being able to have children, my answer to that is when Jake sees a psychiatrist, he discovers that there are two mental disorders his father could have had, either being a psychopath (hereditary) or a sociopath (more likely the product of childhood trauma and physical, emotional abuse rather than genetic). Both mental disorders exhibit socially irresponsible behavior such as disregarding or violating the rights of others, inability to distinguish between right and wrong, difficulty with showing remorse or empathy, tendency to lie, manipulating and hurting others, recurring problems with the law, general disregard towards safety and responsibility, and reckless behavior. So, in my mind, when Jake sees the psychiatrist in Carson City, his fears are put to rest.

As far as the towns of Bannack and Hell Gate, Montana— they are real towns that existed back in the 1800s. Both of them are now ghost towns, although the town of Bannack, founded in 1862, is now a National Historic Landmark managed by the state of Montana as Bannack State Park.

Jake's biological father, Ace Conroy, is actually based on a real-life sheriff of Bannack, Montana by the name of Sheriff Henry Plummer. Henry Plummer was a hardened criminal and mastermind behind hundreds of robberies and murders across the Montana territory. His alleged gang, known as "The Innocents," were a gang of outlaw road agents who operated during the gold rush of the 1860s. They preyed on shipments and travelers carrying gold, killing many who resisted. Sheriff Henry Plummer was eventually hung by a group of Montana Vigilantes in January 1864, along with several other alleged gang members.

And now, I have a favor to ask. If you enjoyed *Love's Silver Bullet*, would you consider posting a brief review on Amazon and Goodreads? It can be as short as one or two lines stating why you liked the book. Good reviews are critical to book sales, so that's the best way to bless your favorite authors. Also, if you have read the other books in this series—*For Love of Liberty* and *Love's Silver Lining*—and have not posted a review, I would greatly appreciate even a brief generic review for all three books. If you do, *please* let me know at the Contact Julie tab of my website so I can personally thank you.

Thank you again for reading my books, and may we never forget that it was God's "Silver Bullet"—his Son, Jesus— that pierced our hearts with the Truth, the Way, and the Light!

Hugs!

Julie

ABOUT THE AUTHOR

JULIE LESSMAN IS AN AWARD-WINNING author whose tagline of "Passion with a Purpose" underscores her intense passion for both God and romance. A lover of all things Irish, she enjoys writing close-knit Irish family sagas that evolve into 3-D love stories: the hero, the heroine, and the God that brings them together.

Author of The Daughters of Boston, Winds of Change, Heart of San Francisco, Isle of Hope, and Silver Lining Ranch series, Julie was American Christian Fiction Writers 2009 Debut Author of the Year and has garnered over 21 Romance Writers of America and other awards.

Voted #1 Romance Author in *Family Fiction* magazine's 2011 and 2012 Readers Choice Awards, Julie's novels also made *Family Fiction* magazine's Best of 2015, Best of 2014, and "Essential Christian Romance Authors" 2017-20, as well as Booklist's 2010 Top 10 Inspirational Fiction and Borders Best Fiction.

Julie's first contemporary novel, *Isle of Hope,* was voted on *Family Fiction* magazine's "Top Fifteen Novels of 2015" list, and her historical novel, *Surprised by Love,* appeared on *Family Fiction* magazine's list of "Top Ten Novels of 2014." Her independent novel *A Light in the Window* is an International Digital Awards winner, a 2013 Readers' Crown Award winner, and a 2013 Book Buyers Best Award winner. Julie has also written a self-help workbook for writers entitled *Romance-ology 101: Writing Romantic Tension for the Sweet and Inspirational Markets.* You can contact Julie through her website and read excerpts from each of her books at www. julielessman.com.

OTHER BOOKS BY JULIE LESSMAN

All available in e-book & paperback except for novellas,
which are e-book only.

The Daughters of Boston Series
Book 1: *A Passion Most Pure*
Book 2: *A Passion Redeemed*
Book 3: *A Passion Denied*

The Winds of Change Series
Book 1: *A Hope Undaunted*
Book 2: *A Heart Revealed*
Book 3: *A Love Surrendered*

Prequel to The Daughters of Boston and Winds of Change Series
A Light in the Window: An Irish Love Story

O'Connor Christmas Novellas
A Whisper of Hope (formerly part of *Hope for the Holidays* anthology)
The Best Gift of All (formerly part of *Home for Christmas* anthology)
A Dream Fulfilled
A Gift Like No Other

The Heart of San Francisco Series
Book 1: *Love at Any Cost*
Book 2: *Dare to Love Again*
Book 3: *Surprised by Love*
Blake McClare Novella: *Grace Like Rain*
(formerly part of *With This Kiss* anthology)

Made in the USA
Las Vegas, NV
15 February 2021

17849917R10267